PELLEGRINO

D0380553

A Dance in Heather

Julie Beard

JOVE BOOKS, NEW YORK

A DANCE IN HEATHER

A Jove Book / published by arrangement with
the author

PRINTING HISTORY
Jove edition / June 1996

The Putnam Berkley World Wide Web site address is
http://www.berkley.com

ISBN: 0-515-11873-7

A JOVE BOOK®
Jove Books are published by The Berkley Publishing Group,
200 Madison Avenue, New York, New York 10016.
JOVE and the "J" design are trademarks
belonging to Jove Publications, Inc.

PRINTED IN THE UNITED STATES OF AMERICA

10 9 8 7 6 5 4 3 2 1

To Mom and Dad,
With all my love,
For all you have given me:
Everything.

ACKNOWLEDGMENTS

Once again I am indebted to my compatriots who supported me through this great writing adventure. Linda Wiatr, sharing her uncommon wisdom, helped me find form and shape in the nebulous beginning. Elsa Cook then helped me hone in on the characters. When the book was completed, I received invaluable criticism and praise from my friends Mary Alice Kruesi and Donna Julian. And where would I be without Chicago North RWA? Thanks especially to some of the veterans— Jimmie Morel, Sharon DeVita, and Martha Powers—for some "tough love" critiques. (They hurt so good.) A tip of the hat to Bernadette Cychner for generously sharing a plethora of research materials. Thanks to Sue Easterby for the use of her name and her indomitable cheer. I continue to be grateful to my agent, Evan Fogelman, gentleman and scholar. And finally, thanks to Martha Ambrose for reading the final version with loving care. Marty and I had lost touch for twenty years, only to discover that our dreams had guided us to the same destination.

AUTHOR'S NOTE

I've chosen a number of medieval words to add flavor and meaning to this story. There is a glossary in the back of the book for those of you who might find the words befuddling, as I sometimes do.

I did not define the term "Lollard," but its meaning should be clear in context. Though the Lollards, led by Sir John Oldcastle, were dismissed as heretics, they were really the predecessors of the Protestant Reformers. While the Protestants succeeded in creating religious change, the Lollards failed, perhaps because they tried to overthrow a king as well.

And finally, gentle readers, if the character of Sir John seems familiar to you, there is good reason. He is loosely based on one of the greatest literary figures of all time—Sir John Falstaff. Jack Falstaff is the fictional boon companion created by William Shakespeare to amuse and irritate the very real King Henry V. I trust that Shakespeare, the master, will not mind if I borrow a ray of his brilliance.

PROLOGUE

England, 1414

Flames licked up to the starry sky, and an orange glow throbbed at the center of the crowd.

The fires of hell could not burn brighter, thought Lord Richard Avery. Tugging leather reins with numb fingers, he drew in his mount at the edge of the riveted crowd near St. Giles's Field. His spirited black destrier fought the bit, whinnying in fear. The beast tossed back his mane and bared the whites of his eyes.

"Easy, Shadow," Richard murmured, scratching the horse's withers. "I don't like the smell any more than you do."

The scent of burning human flesh rose in a swirl of air so cold it stiffened Richard's nostrils, the odor so pungent he could almost taste it on his tongue, sweet and sickening.

Richard's horrified squire drew up beside him, reining in his palfrey.

"May God'a mercy on their souls," Perkins muttered.

Richard said nothing. What words could adequately express his revulsion? When the fate of mere mortals collided with the destiny of a king, lives were always expendable, like pawns on a chessboard. Who knew that better than Richard?

He screwed his gaze ever tighter on the macabre tragedy that was unfolding. The first heretic had nearly given up the ghost. He had been hung and set afire, and now twisted in the wind like a blazing torch. Six others on gallows erected beside his awaited their turn. Richard could not see their faces, could only imagine their eyes wide with terror, their lips blue with cold, too cold even to mutter a prayer.

When King Henry's executioner hung the second heretic and started a fire beneath his dangling, choking form, a hush fell over the hundreds who had come to watch—richly dressed noblemen, merchants, soldiers, peasants—all of whom shared a grotesque curiosity. Only the crackle of flames could be heard.

"Your Sovereign will meet you in Hell!" the second heretic managed to choke out as the flames danced beneath him. "Cursed by Henry of Monmouth. He's naught but the son of a usurper. His crown is stolen. His Church is a haven for sinners! You can call us heretics if you wish, but we Lollards are the only true believers!"

His anguished curses gave way to breathless screams of agony as flames consumed his body, lighting the night sky. When the heretic fell silent, too pained even to cry out anymore, a gasp swept over the crowd, as if the novelty of watching men being burned to death had finally lost its appeal.

Richard turned his frowning gaze up to the heavens, dotted with a thousand glittering stars, wondering where God dwelt on a night such as this. *God, are you there?* Certainly not anyplace where mortal man might find Him, Richard concluded with a deep shiver and a soft curse against the merciless January winds.

"Good even' now, yer lordship."

Richard heard the nasal greeting as a small hand gripped his left boot. Looking down over the white silk trappings that covered his horse, Richard found a dwarf scratching a lice-infested beard.

"Yer being the Baron of Easterby, ain't ye, milord? Seen ye on the lists, splitting one lance after another. Yer the king's champion, an't it so?"

"What of it?" Richard growled, in no mood for trifling conversations. From the corner of his eye he saw a pulse of yellow. The glow in the middle of the crowd throbbed brighter, for the fire beneath the third Lollard was now roaring.

"Well, yer being as close as a brother to the king, milord, why, I thought ye'd be a wantin' to buy a token of this night, this bein' now a victory for his Sovereign. 'Twere these Lollard heretics what led the revolt against King Henry, ain't it bein' now? An' their followers, near to eighty arrested, set for hanging. But these," the dwarf said, pointing a stubby finger at the burning men. "These suffer the burning death. They be the true Lollards. The leaders o' the revolt. 'Em with their ideas of overthrowing the Church, an' the king to boot. What despicable animals!"

Having duly condemned the heretics' perfidy, the dwarf thrust out a tiny oval portrait, his eyes glittering with greed.

"This be from a Lollard who willn't be needin' it amore. 'Tis yers for a penny, yer lordship."

Perkins dismounted and snatched the painted wooden oval from the child-sized man, handing it to his master.

"'Tis a girl," Richard said, squinting at the portrait. He blinked at her earnest beauty. She was someone's daughter, wife, sister, niece. Someone who had been blessed to gaze upon her serene beauty. Someone who was about to die a gruesome death. Richard shifted his frozen arse on his too-stiff saddle. Turning the painting over in his gloved hands, he frowned at the dwarf.

"Where did you get this?"

"One of 'em kept it close to 'is breast, outwitting the king's men. Foun' it in a cloak, ye see, after he was stripped yonder."

Richard tore his eyes from the girl's sweet face and glared down at the dwarf. "You would thieve from men who are being burned to death?" Outrage that far exceeded tonight's injustices bubbled over in the cauldron of his gut. "You vulture. Avaunt! Before I have my squire throw you into the bonfires as well."

Perkins took a threatening step toward the tattered little figure. The dwarf stepped back, offering a placating smile and sooty upturned hands. "If ye will na' pay me for the treasure, great lord, then a penny for a jest, mayhap?"

Seemingly from nowhere, a jester made several backflips in a blur of clashing colors, landing in a squatting position before Richard's horse. The entertainer was clothed in a chaotic scheme of yellow and red patches, with prongs shooting from his tri-cornered cap. He brandished a gourd rattle fashioned after a human skull.

"Death comes to visit, oh great nobleman."

The jester gave a mad cackle, which was more than the destrier could tolerate. The great black beast reared back. Richard pitched forward to keep from being thrown, wrenching his feet in his stirrups.

"Steady, Shadow," he commanded. Obeying his master, Shadow lowered his churning hooves, landing with a jolt upon the frozen earth and barely missing the dwarf, who had fallen in his mad scramble to avoid a pummeling.

"Get you gone!" Richard commanded.

"The likeness, yer great lordship." The dwarf struggled to a stand, aided by the disappointed jester. "Such a great lord wouldna' be thievin' from a thief, would ye now?"

Richard seethed as he plucked several coins from his purse. "Take your savage minstrel show elsewhere, vulture." He hurled the money to the ground and lowered the miniature through the high collar of his doublet, tucking it securely behind his shirt, against his chest. The dwarf and the jester pounced upon the coins and vanished in the crowd.

By now flames flickered beneath the fourth heretic. An agonized howl rose in dissonant harmony with the whistling wind. Richard could watch no more. Swallowing a bitter taste, he tugged on his reins, gently battling Shadow's bobbing head.

"Let us away," he whispered, sickened to the depths of his marrow by this wretched spectacle.

"My lord!" Again a voice rose from the ground.

Determined to teach the dwarf a lesson, he raised his whip. "Avaunt, I say!"

Richard spun Shadow around with a nudge to the belly. He cracked his whip downward, but pulled up short when he realized it was a woman clutching his boot, not the dwarf. More than a woman, it was the very lady whose likeness was painted in the miniature.

She sobbed with cries so primal and deep that a shiver inched up Richard's proud spine. Tears painted her reddened cheeks with a silvery sheen; her lips twisted with inarticulate groans of despair. Clutching his foot, she turned her pitiful, yet lovely face up to Richard.

"Please, save him. I beg of you. My father . . ."

Aye, of course. I'll do anything. Just name it, he thought, so compelling was her desperation. Then he remembered himself, his relationship with the king, and his face hardened.

"What do you want?"

The hood of her cloak had fallen back, exposing a lush river of auburn hair, tangled and tossed. The reddish brown strands appeared to be burnished with gold in the glow cast off from the fires. *What a wretched pity. She should not have to watch a loved one burn to death.* Richard's heart wrenched in his chest, for he knew the terror she faced—the prospect of losing a father at the whim of a king. *He knew.*

"Please," she begged him. "Do something. Help me."

Her earnest, sweet face was a quivering mass of tears and horror. She continued to clutch his foot. Her strong fingers nearly burned imprints through his leather boots, branding him, awakening his dormant conscience with their hot sting. He wanted to help her, to soothe her, oh so gently. One as lovely as she would have been a song in his soul. But as enticing a morsel as she was, evoking so much empathy, her cause was too dangerous. She had come to him too late. A lifetime too late. Long past the time when he might have considered himself a chivalrous knight. He lived for one purpose now and one purpose alone. He would not jeopardize his mission by coming to the aid of a distressed damsel, though her cause was surely a noble one. What was nobility anyway? He felt he no longer knew.

She pressed her fists to her mouth, sobbing hysterically. "You know the king. I know you do. Reason with him. If you have a heart, if you have a soul, stop this madness and save my father!" she cried, clutching his foot again.

Her father. His stomach muscles clinched, as if dealt a blow. Her plea, her loss touched too close to home. For a reckless moment, he envisioned coming to her aid. And then he imagined himself beheaded for his treachery, as would be anyone who aided the Lollards. They were not merely heretics who wanted to end the absolute power of the Church. Three days ago they were captured converging on Eltham to overthrow the king. Unlike the usual fringe heretics, these men were members of the gentry, knights and merchants, even a few noblemen, which made their sedition all the more repugnant to King Henry.

"My lord!" She tugged at his boot, jarring him from his

ruminations. As precious moments ticked by, she looked up at him as if he were her savior. "Please! What say you?"

"Maiden . . ." he began, not knowing what to say.

He wished her father had known what Richard knew beyond doubt. That King Henry V was destined to be one of the greatest monarchs England had ever known. That there was little hope of thwarting him. That a man who wanted to live long enough to see his grandchildren would learn to speak his Sovereign peace, if only to bide his time.

Richard's grim face felt as if it had turned to stone, as if it had been stung by sudden sleet, hardened by the indifference he found necessary to survive this ruthless world. Squeezing his knees, he steered Shadow in a quick sidestep, disengaging his foot from the young woman's hand.

"There is nothing to be done, maiden," he said coldly. "'Tis the king's will."

He would never forget her wrenching cry of pain. Her voice mewled like a lamb at slaughter and then deepened to a groan of savage protest when the last of the heretics began to scream in pain. She twisted around and lunged back into the crowd, racing toward the gallows, no doubt to stand as close to the flames as she could bear, calling out her farewells and desperate, agonized prayers.

Richard closed his eyes, attempting to shut out all sights and sound, shivering beneath his coat of arms. Turning his horse, he and his squire slipped into the night, into the blackness of a world gone mad.

The last thing Richard would remember of this gruesome night was the wrenching wail of a woman. A woman whose portrait had already burned a hole in his heart.

ONE

Fourteen Months Later

"Steady . . . steady," Richard whispered to himself. He licked salty perspiration from the corner of his mouth and squinted over the barrel of his hand-gunne. "Aim at the heart and hold steady."

Lord Richard Avery, the first Earl of Easterby, leaned against the crumbling, sappy bark of a fallen maple tree. He aimed his gunne at a powerful roebuck with a twelve-pointed rack. The graceful beast swung his head slowly until his dark brown eyes locked with Richard's. There was so much dignity in those distant, unblinking orbs that Richard felt a pang of regret for what he was about to do. He exhaled a slow, hissing breath. But, oh how stunning those horns would look mounted above the hearth in his great hall! More important, the buck would help feed his enormous staff.

"Now! Shoot now," his red-haired squire whispered over his shoulder.

"Not yet," Richard mouthed in return.

The buck continued to stare him down. Felling the beast would be no easy task. While gunnes had made great strides since their recent invention, they were still wildly inaccurate, suited more for warfare than hunting. But Richard had paid dearly for this latest model, with its matchlock trigger. With that improvement he could slowly lower the burning slow match to the charge of powder with a mere squeeze of the finger. The easy motion would steady his aim.

Richard felt his heart hammer with excitement in his broad chest. Gods! But how he loved a challenge. As if the buck could sense Richard's exuberance, hear his shallow breath, smell the thrill of the hunt, the beast tensed every muscle.

"Now, Earl Richard!" Perkins urgently whispered.

"Do not call me 'Earl,'" Richard growled sotto voce.

"Very well, Lord Richard, but you must shoot. He's smelled your burning match and will be off like lightning. Shoot!"

The wind shifted and billowed under the locks of golden hair that fell across Richard's wide velvet-clad shoulders. The breeze carried the scent of man and sulfur to the wide-eyed creature. In a timeless moment, Richard realized opportunity was slipping away. He was about to lose him. With a sudden, savage impulse, he pulled the trigger. Just before the slow match lowered to the priming pan, the bracken behind them rustled and someone fell through the woods into the clearing.

"The Earl of Easterby! 'Tis providence I've found you!" croaked a breathless voice from behind.

Boom! The black powder loaded in Richard's hand-gunne exploded. A shot sailed through the air and lodged horribly askew in a birch tree. The buck vanished in a rustle of budding branches.

"Hellfire and damnation!" Richard cursed, wiping black powder from beneath his eyes with a backhand. His ears rang from the explosion. He rose and placed his arms akimbo, ready to verbally blister the one who had frightened the deer. Turning, he found Friar Edmund looking up at him with an angelic expression. With his bulbous belly, he looked like a well-fed, gray-haired cherub. He twisted thick wooden rosary beads in his chubby fingers and smiled up at Richard like a child.

"Good day, my lord."

Richard opened his mouth to curse again, but settled for a rib-rattling growl, his eyes watering from the sting of sulphur pluming about them.

"Friar Edmund," he said with as much civility as he could muster, "I hope you plan to do penance for this egregious sin."

The delight painting the friar's face faded and was replaced by a look of profound confusion. "Sin, Earl Richard? Wha—"

"Do not call me 'Earl,'" he entreated, his temper flaring. "'Lord Richard' will do."

"But you *are* an earl," his squire argued, slapping his thigh impatiently. "The king made you an earl at the last Parliament. You cannot deny it forever, my lord."

"If you knew why Henry gave me the title, 'twould not seem such a great honor, Perkins. Henry is a noble king, but every gift from him has its price." He turned his tempered wrath to Edmund. "Good friar, you've just chased off the most handsome buck I've seen in a decade. He was big enough to feed my entire staff for a meal. 'Tis no small thing when merchants are hounding my steward for every last farthing."

"Saints! I did not know," the friar replied, blinking with the sad eyes of a worn-out old hound. "I ne'er imagined the great Earl of Easterby was so wanting for gold. I . . . well, then, I'll not trouble you. We've run out of flour, you see. 'Twas a hard winter. But no matter. Forgive me for the interruption, Lord Richard."

Friar Edmund bobbed his head and shuffled dejectedly toward the wooded path from whence he'd come.

"Come, Perkins, a hearty tankard of ale awaits us at the castle."

Shaking off a vague sense of guilt, Richard marched through tall meadow grass, stiff with new green shoots, toward his tethered mount. His squire did not follow.

Richard halted. He sighed. His breath condensed in the crisp morning air. Turning back, he gave Perkins a withering glare. The saintly slip of a lad had the audacity to gaze up innocently.

"Well, what is it this time, Perkins? Say what you will before I decide I've had my fill of your noble sentiments and employ a new squire. You're not my bloody conscience, you know."

Perkins shrugged. Refusing to meet Richard's furious glare, he marched forward with more than his usual air of efficiency. His freckled face was a mask of long-suffering forbearance. With great precision, his white fingers plucked the smoking weapon from his lord's hand.

"Friar Edmund and his brothers tend to the sick and dying, my lord. Unlike the Black Friars, the Friars of the Lamb have no commerce, no way to raise money save through charity. There was a pox last winter, my lord, and the goodly friars gave without asking anything in return. Without them the town would have no hospice."

"Enough," Richard groaned, marveling that his conscience still had a heartbeat. Accepting the inevitable, he started after Friar Edmund with long strides.

"Very well, Perkins. Have it your way, you smooth-faced little imp," he muttered as Perkins joyfully tagged along. "I know 'twill do no good to argue with you."

"Nay, my lord, you'll always lose an argument with me."

"I have no doubt that as soon as you earn your spurs, you'll be off chasing dragons, spouting a code of chivalry that never

existed in practice, only in romances sung by those troubadours you moon over."

"Oh, my lord, chivalry does more than exist. It thrives!"

"Not anymore. There is nothing chivalrous about a gunne,
and that is the weapon of the future. Not the sword you hope
and pray I'll use to dub you a knight."

"If gunnes mean the death of chivalry, my lord, then why
do you adore them so?"

"Power, Perkins. Power is everything. Halt, old friar,"
Richard bellowed.

They caught up with the brown-robed figure at the edge of
the woods. With a gesture that was in stark contrast to his
gruff voice, Richard gently placed his hand on the monk's
tonsure, smoothing the bald spot that crowned his mop of
gray hair. "What do you need, old man?"

Friar Edmund tucked a trembling hand into the folds of his
robe and withdrew a parchment. "See for yourself, my lord.
A list. Not too much, I pray. 'Tis no more than you gave us
last spring."

Richard felt a spurt of warmth in his chest, either from the
quick stir of a sunbaked breeze or from unwanted compassion.

"Hmmm," Richard intoned. He perused the long list with a
frown of disbelief. "I've never been this generous in my life."

"On the contrary," the friar replied. "Without you we could
not do our good works. Many other charities could say the
same. If generosity counts in our Lord's eyes, you already
have one foot in Heaven."

"And one leg in Hell," Richard muttered. He turned to his
squire, who hovered eagerly at his side. "Does Godfrey know
I spent this much on charity?"

"Aye, Lord Richard, your steward tried to convince you
otherwise, but you were not to be deterred. You said any
house of God that had given shelter to Lucy . . ."

Lucy. The Friars of the Lamb had taken her in when she was ill, when Uncle Desmond had refused to fetch a physician to the castle. *Lucretia.* Richard squeezed the bridge of his nose and rubbed away the sting of sulphur from his eyes. Even now, after all these years, he missed her. Particularly now, when he felt the king's betrayal the most.

"My lord, is something wrong?"

Richard smiled at his squire. His disarming smile, so practiced, such a perfect shield.

"'Tis nothing, Perkins." He handed the list back to Friar Edmund. "I will once again give the Friars of the Lamb whatever they need. This much and more if needed. Edmund, come to Cadmon Castle on Friday and speak with my almoner. He will give you alms aplenty."

"Oh, bless you, my lord. Bless you!"

As the elated friar scurried away, shouting his thanks, Richard scowled at the lumpy, loping figure. "You know, Perkins, I actually feel good about what I've just done."

"Excellent, my lord."

"Nay, 'tis bad. I do not want to be a man of good deeds. Life is too short for anything but reckless pleasure." The savage execution of his father had taught him that. It was a lesson he would never forget. "Besides, I do not want to be happy now, for a contented man makes a lackluster warrior."

And before King Henry set sail for France, demanding Richard's troops, Richard would raise his sword with a mighty roar. Not to claim the French crown for the Lancasters, but for his own secret ends. The time to demand justice had come, no matter the price.

"A lackluster warrior?" Perkins looked up at him with an all-too-perceptive twist of his orangish eyebrows. "You refer to the king's plans to invade Normandy?"

Richard looked down at the young man, so scrupulous, so honest and noble. How he hated to lie to Perkins.

"Aye, 'tis precisely what I mean. Now tell me, my lad," he said, putting an arm around the youth's shoulder and guiding him back to their horses, "however will I come up with the money to pay for what I've just promised the good friar?"

"Your marriage, my lord. The Earl of Haddington left behind one of the richest daughters in all of England, to whom you've been graciously betrothed by the king."

They strode side by side to their mounts, which were eagerly nibbling at a birch branch covered with breaking buds. A surprisingly cool wind gushed with a blast against their bodies, slapping their cheeks red with icy fingers.

"Of course, the marriage will one day be a boon, but revenues from Haddington's crops will not come to fruition until harvest. And I will have no right to raid her coffers until the marriage, which she could manage to delay for months."

"Nay, my lord, the lady and her gold will arrive today. Did Godfrey not tell you? Lady Tess Farnsworth sent ahead a harbinger of her imminent arrival."

Richard halted and looked down at the shorter man with a look of horrified disbelief. "Lady Tess? Arriving here today? Gods! Why am I the *last* to know the most pertinent business of this earldom?" he roared with unbridled frustration.

"At least you are admitting 'tis an earldom. That makes you the earl, as deemed by good King Henry. A much greater honor than baron." Perkins's freckles seemed to dance with glee upon his pug nose, which Richard was sorely tempted to pop with a fist.

Instead, he grunted a protest and marched on. "I will gladly accept Hal's charity, be it title or bride, but the money Lady Tess brings will do me little good, for as soon as her gold alights in my hands, Hal will snatch it for a loan. He's nearly pawned off one kingdom to conquer another. Curse the man's unbridled ambition."

Hal. Richard hadn't used his Sovereign's nickname since

the coronation two years ago, when reckless Prince Hal had transformed almost instantaneously into the pious King Henry. He had turned his back then on his oldest boon companions, including Richard. The loss of familiarity still burned in Richard's gut. He would have gladly exchanged his new title for the love Hal had once bestowed on him.

Brushing aside the memory, he hoisted himself atop his graceful stallion. His leather saddle creaked beneath his massive form. "I suppose Godfrey did not inform me of my lady's plan for fear of distressing me. He knows I've always considered marriage a loathsome matter. I wonder what Lady Tess looks like. Will she be pretty, do you suppose? And why in blazes is the damsel coming so soon? The king announced our betrothal just a month ago, and we were to be married by proxy. She didn't have to come to Cadmon Castle, unless . . . By the gods, if she's blossoming with another man's seed I'll not have her! The days of tolerance and betrayal are over, Perkins."

"I'm quite sure the lady will have many fine qualities to make you rethink your stance on marriage, my lord."

"Not the least of which is wealth," Richard replied jadedly.

Pinnnng! A small object whirled past Lady Tess, brushing through her hair. She jerked back, astonished, nearly tumbling from her pillion. The frightened horse beneath her lurched forward, and Tess tightened her grip around the waist of her beloved cousin, Roger.

"What was that?" she gasped.

"Gunnefire," Roger whispered.

His head jerked sideways, and in his profile she saw all the signs of fear—furrowed brows, pale cheeks, clenched teeth. Roger twisted around in his saddle and shouted to their escort.

"Someone is shooting at us. Gunnefire! Take cover, everyone!"

While others scrambled, Tess froze, perched behind her cousin, her mind unwilling to comprehend this impediment.

"Not thieves," she protested. "Not now. Not when we're so close! We made it through the treacherous forest without harm. How can there be danger now, when Cadmon Castle is less than a league away?"

"I don't know, but we must take cover. Men, arm yourselves!" Roger shouted.

A half dozen men-at-arms scraped their swords from their scabbards. Servants cursed as they darted behind roadside trees and into ditches. Roger's horse jolted forward again, and then reared. Tess started to fall from her pillion and cried out in distress.

"Roger! Help me."

"Whoa! Steady," he commanded his frightened palfrey. "Cousin, hold on."

Tess clawed at Roger's cloak. Breaking her nails, she pulled herself up the slick haunches of his steed, scrambling frantically to aright herself. Secure once more, she turned back breathlessly and searched for their attackers.

"Where are they?" Angry now, she wanted answers. "Why don't they show themselves? Are they cowards?"

"I don't know. Mayhap they're reloading their gunnes."

The silence that followed was ferocious. Tess's heart raced with fierce urgency, booming in her breasts. She couldn't be thwarted now. Not when she was so close. Less than a league! Less than a league from tasting the blood of revenge. Her suddenly parched mouth craved the taste of it.

Then it came. Another gunneshot. *Boom!* The sound was closer now, ear-splitting. A cry rose from the servants huddling in the dusty road.

"What ho!"

"Sir Roger, save us!"

"My lady, take care!" they shouted.

Roger's palfrey reared again. Tess had loosened her grip. She felt the weight of fate pulling her down, back over the slick, sweaty rump of the horse. She was falling. *Nay! I can't. I won't.*

"Roger! Don't let me fall. Roger!"

"Take my hand!" he shouted, twisting around on his saddle, his smooth face white with morbid fear.

She reached up. Their fingertips grazed, but he was beyond her grasp. She looked over her shoulder at the ground as it loomed closer. Closer. She was headed straight for a jagged boulder. Dear Lord, she was going to crash into it! Her head would hit first. She'd seen men die from lesser blows. *Die.* She was going to die. Here on this lonely road. And less than a league away the Earl of Easterby awaited her. Her betrothed. Her enemy. And she had come so close to making him pay.

The jagged, weather-beaten boulder loomed ever closer. At the last moment, she jerked her head away. But not far enough. *Thud!* Her skull skimmed the edge of the rock. Pain shot through her neck. *Wham!* She landed on her back, knocking the breath from her lungs. She closed her eyes and darkness called to her, so much more enticing than the sun that beamed down on her cheeks. Her thoughts began to scramble, and she saw the past flash before her in jerky, fleeting sequences.

She saw herself at the age of five, playing chess with her father in his solar. Dear, sweet Father. His wise eyes twinkling proudly when she'd cornered his king in short order. And at the age of eight, tucking a blanket around his legs when he'd dozed before the fire, reading his precious *Lantern of Light.* He'd read the tome aloud so many times Tess had nearly memorized its sermons and tracts. It was essential reading for any Lollard. The book had never touched her mind or imagination, and she knew her lack of interest in religion had disappointed her father, but what was to be done? Faith, even heretical faith, was a gift, and one that Tess apparently had been born without.

She saw herself at twelve, visiting her mother's grave, wondering what she had looked like, saying endless prayers at the grassy mound, weeping with regret, longing for a mother's arms. Her mother had died giving birth to Tess. Would she ever be able to repay the debt?

And she saw herself on a haunting moor, dancing in a patch of purple heather. But no, that was not the past, merely a foolish dream she had long ago brushed aside. Only silly girls who had naught to do but weave tapestries and daydream had time for dancing.

The years blurred by, barely visible, save for one. She saw it all in an instant, in agonizing detail. Her nineteenth year. A little more than a year ago. The year her father had been burned to death at what was now known as the Lollards' Gallows near St. Giles's Field.

She was amazed she could remember anything about that year, for it had been so painful. After her father's torturous execution, Tess had returned to Haddington Castle numb to the world, for her father had *been* her world. Thank God for Roger! She would have been lost without him. In her dazed grief, she was no longer capable of acting as chatelaine, and so he had taken over care of the estate.

And she would have starved to death, withered away to nothing, had it not been for Lady Lucretia. The strong, young, and beautiful widow of the Baron of Marcham had rushed to Tess's side in her hour of grief.

It was dear Lucy—pale, thin, but immeasurably strong— who had dashed about the castle with her trail of yellow, wavy angel's hair, giving orders and forcing Tess to eat. And it was her dear friend who had first warned Tess that an odious marriage was imminent . . .

"Since your father was condemned for heresy, as well as sedition, King Henry can strip you of all your possessions," Lucretia warned her one day as they sipped malmsey before a roaring fire in the great hall. "I'm sure the only reason he hasn't already is because he respected your father, despite his heretical views. But that won't keep you safe forever. When Henry has a mind to take your land, you will be a ward of the crown, and without land, you will make a poor match indeed. Only if you are very lucky, Tess, will the king quietly marry you to one of his favorites. The best you can hope for is a husband who will be kind."

"I would rather take my own life than marry one of Henry's. I would rather die than marry a king's man," Tess whispered in savage reply. She stared wide-eyed at the crackling flames—blue now, yellow anon. Flames just as hot as the ones that had consumed her father.

"Take your own life?" Lucy blinked in astonishment. "You do not mean that!"

"I do mean it. Any one of the king's men will be as bad as or worse than your brother. And that's saying quite a bit." Glancing up, Tess saw Lucy's eyes cloud over and felt a pang of remorse. "I'm sorry. I shouldn't have mentioned him. And I shouldn't have called him your brother when he is merely your half brother. I know you do not wish to be tied to Richard Avery any more than fate has already bound you."

Lucy shrugged. Her thin, pink lips parted in a wan smile. "I am just ashamed to know that a relation of mine turned you away so cruelly the night your father was . . . the night he passed on."

Tess nodded tersely as painful images returned unbidden. "God in Heaven, how I regret groveling before that heartless man. I pleaded with Lord Richard to save Father, clutched his boot, all in vain. He'd looked down condescendingly, as if he'd expected to find a beggar woman. He had the arrogance of one favored by the king, a certain callousness. He'd worn no bascinet or chaperon. His long golden hair billowed around his shoulders. I saw his coat of arms peaking through his cloak. An orange Sun in Splendor against azure. His emblem is a blazing sun! How ironic, when his soul is so dark. And even so, Lucy, he was *still* as beautiful a specimen of manhood as I've ever seen. And it makes me hate him all the more. That God should deign such beauty on a man with no heart!"

"My half brother is a veritable fount of ironies."

Lucy's acid reply was a reminder that she had an even greater reason to hate Richard Avery. Richard had treated his younger bastard sister callously. He had allowed their guardian uncle to send her to a cold, rat-infested nunnery when she was but eleven. The endowment given by Lucy's uncle to the strict and bitter nuns had been so paltry that she'd been forced to scrub floors, until she'd escaped and found her way into marriage with the Baron of Marcham. Marcham was a kindly, rich old man who cared more for Lucretia's stunning beauty than for her lack of a dowry. Lucy had survived, no thanks to Richard.

But all Tess's ranting and raving against Lord Richard and Henry's other unprincipled supporters had been for naught. A year after the execution of the Earl of Haddington, by which time Tess's aching sorrow had transformed into seething anger, King Henry had sent a messenger announcing Tess's betrothal, just as Lucretia had warned he would. Henry's choice for Tess was more ironic than she would have thought possible. Her only consolation was that both Roger and Lucy were present at Haddington Castle when the odious news was delivered.

After exchanging polite greetings with Tess, the Marquess

of Dolton shook off his snowy cloak, turned his considerable buttocks to toast before the great hall fire, and said: "I will be direct. The king has betrothed you to Lord Richard Avery, who has been given the title of earl."

Following a moment of stunned silence, Lucy was the first to respond. "What? Tess? Marry my brother?"

"Here now, Dolton," Roger joined in, jumping up from his high-backed chair. His youthful, clean-shaven face assumed as much authority as he could muster. "My cousin will fight this."

"Will she?" Dolton replied smugly, his doubt obvious in the curl of his fat lip. "It could be worse, Sir Roger. They will be married by proxy. Lady Tess will not even have to meet the earl until such a time as he wants an heir. The king simply wants access to her wealth. He is planning to invade Normandy and needs to buy more ships. I do not see what all the lamentations are about. Lord Richard is extremely charming and fair of face."

"And has bedded every bawd in the realm," Lucy snapped. "Nothing more than a randy cock! Furthermore, he's spent every last farthing on impractical gunnes, and on loans to the king. He's a noble pauper."

Oh, God, no! Tess thought, reeling away from the bitter diatribe. She flung herself against the embrasure, seeking support. A light snow fell outside. A refreshingly cold draft oozed between the soldered panes of glass and the thick stone wall. But try as she may, she couldn't breathe. She felt as she had as a child, standing barefoot on the beach, watching helplessly as the sand sank beneath her, washing away with each wave. *Me? Marry the Earl of Easterby?* The man had as good as lit the fire beneath her father's feet. The very idea was ludicrous!

She had never even kissed a man before. Could she disrobe and present herself to her father's enemy? Without protection, completely vulnerable and naked, as she would one day be in his bed?

Without protection. Vulnerable. Naked. That was exactly how *he* would be as well. For to sleep with her he would be without armor. He could not protect himself as he would in any other circumstance. In the moment of passion, he would be helpless against the strike of a dagger. *A dagger.* Better yet, a misericorde, a smaller blade, but equally sharp. Yes, a "dagger of mercy." They were used by soldiers to dispatch the wounded enemy in battle. It would be so simple!

Her heart began to heave excitedly, thumping madly, joyously in her chest. This was the answer. She would marry, then kill the Earl of Easterby! And the sooner the better.

TWO

"Ohhhh," Tess moaned. Still sprawled on the ground, she blinked open her eyes and saw blue sky.

Rallying all her might, she sat up, shaking her head, and memories of the past scattered like pollen on the wind. She tugged off her crumpled veil and brushed back her hair. Skimming a hand over the crown of her head, she felt moisture and found two spots of blood on her fingers. A mere scratch. She could well have cracked her head open on the boulder; she said a quick prayer of thanks.

"Christ! Tess, are you hurt?"

She blinked up at Roger's stricken face and laughed. She paid for her giddy relief instantly with a sharp stitch in her side.

"Oh, dear." She winced as she struggled for breath. "I'm fine, Cousin. Now get off your horse before the thieves *shoot* you off it."

Having survived what might have been a fatal fall, Tess was more determined than ever to reach her destination and dispose of the Earl of Easterby as planned. She had spent a month carefully planning this trip, and would not let a thief stop her now.

"For the love of Christ, Tess, take cover," Roger shouted. He jumped off his horse and helped her up.

Tess rushed toward her empty litter, ignoring the gritty road dust coating her tongue, dirtying her cloak. For most of the three-day journey to Cadmon Castle, she had disdained the gauze-covered box. But now she was grateful for the litter's protection. Halfway there, she bumped into her handmaiden.

"Oh, my lady!"

"Come along, Mellie. Climb in the litter with me." She clutched the younger woman's hands protectively in her own, tugging her along.

"Here, get in."

Tess climbed in, but before Mellisande could join her, the sound of rolling horse hooves thundered in the air, stopping everyone in their tracks.

"What ho!" a jubilant voice cried out in the distance.

Expecting a vicious marauder's cry, Tess was nonplussed to hear such a friendly greeting. She poked her head through the curtains, but was blinded by the sun. Squinting anxiously, she saw a rugged figure on a frothy-mouthed horse thunder toward them, a companion at his side. They rode the wind, carrying with them a faint waft of sulphur. Tess crinkled her nose, instantly recognizing the scent of black powder.

"Mellie, get inside!" she hissed as she drew back into the safety of the litter. But the handmaiden was frozen, a look of awe plastered on her pretty face.

Through the litter's flimsy curtain, Tess watched, holding her breath, as the riders drew up. The simple garb of the younger man told Tess he was a squire. When the second rider reigned in at a leisurely trot, Tess felt her heart plummet. It wasn't a thief after all. It was *him*.

"My God, is anyone hurt?" said the Earl of Easterby.

At lightning speed, vibrant emotions ripped through Tess from head to foot. First relief—he was not a marauder! Then anger—how dare he frighten them so? Then curiosity—she had never seen him this close in daylight. Observing him from an oddly hidden perspective, she could appreciate his beauty with some objectivity, and therefore, greater intensity.

For the briefest moment, she saw him as other women must have—a dashing blond warrior on a spirited gray, not the magnificent black destrier that had borne him the night her father was killed. Richard carried about him an air of authority so finely honed he did not have to flaunt it. His nostrils flared with arrogance, and one finely carved brow rose in amused concern as he surveyed the disarray of her entourage. Defying current fashion, which favored bobbed cuts for men, golden ringlets of hair showered around broad shoulders that offered silent testimony to hours spent wielding a sword. But on this morning, that was not his weapon of choice. In one gloved hand he held a hand-gunne. The wooden and metal device, as long as his forearm, was still smoking, the slow match still sizzling.

"Roger!" the earl bellowed in a rich, deep voice. "I haven't seen you since the joust at Virgil's Crossing. What the devil brings you here?"

"I bring you my cousin, Lady Tess Farnsworth," Roger replied. He strode to the earl's horse. "For a moment I thought you'd killed her."

"I am sorry. Truly. I saw your horse round the woodlands and thought it a roebuck I've been chasing all morning. I took aim, but luckily I missed. I realized my error, but not in time to stop my squire from taking a couple shots." The bronze-faced gallant cocked one side of his mouth in a rueful grin. "You're bloody lucky, Roger. No matter how much time I spend on these damned devices, I'm still a lousy shot. And my squire is even worse."

The more he smiled, the more Tess wanted to take his hand-gunne and shoot him here and now rather than wait until

their wedding night. He was actually jesting, apparently
unaware of her mourning. Or, if aware, uncaring.

"I relish a discussion of weapons, my lord," Roger said
coolly, "but I fear it must wait until my cousin is safely
ensconced in your castle."

"I've offended you with my lack of hospitality." A frown
forged a deep rut over the earl's perceptive eyes. "My deepest
regrets."

He leapt from his stallion, landing on sturdy legs with the
spring of a twenty-nine-year-old nobleman in his prime.

Richard spared himself no pleasures, Tess noted dourly,
and frowned disapprovingly at the extravagant gold trim that
bordered his V-necked houppelande, even as she admired its
elegance. He dressed much too richly, considering his dire
financial situation. The rich, blue velvet gown fell luxuriously
to his knees. His belt was made of spun silk, and its buckle
sprouted fat, twinkling jewels—emeralds, rubies, and am-
ethysts. With her blood approaching a rolling boil, Tess
wondered how many servants went hungry of a night so that
he would not have to part with his jewels.

But her haughty expression melted, replaced by dismay, as
he swept with lively steps to where Tess's handmaiden still
stood mutely, frozen at his approach. Mellisande was a
buxom young woman who fancied herself adept at handling
men. And yet she could do naught but stare slack-jawed as the
dashing nobleman sauntered toward her. He leveled her with
eyes so clear and blue they would fool birds for a sky. He
measured Mellie up and down, apparently considering whether
she was the lady in question and whether or not to exert the
effort to ply her with his charm. Tess saw it all and knew him
in an instant for what he was—a calculating opportunist.

"Your mistress is inside?" he said in a low voice that
crackled with charm.

Mellie nodded her head like a bell bobbing up and down,

though unlike a bell she could not muster a peep, much less
a gong, so stricken was she.

"Then step aside, maiden," he said, tucking a forefinger
under her chin, gently closing her gaping mouth, which had
fallen open in unabashed appreciation. "With any luck," he
whispered, "you'll be but a mirror of your mistress's beauty."

Tess could tell he had been thus gentle with many maidens.
Impressed, but more wary than before, she drew back farther
against the fur-lined interior of her litter, recoiling from this
awful and inevitable introduction.

"Lady Tess," he said. Flicking open the curtain, he bent
down and tucked his head inside.

Tess stiffened with a tiny gasp, shocked to be so near the
one she hated so much. He smelled of sap and heather, a
soothing combination that triggered her imagination. Had he
been climbing a tree like a lad of ten? Had he been plucking
sprigs of heather for a lover's nosegay? She willed the
curiosity from her eyes and assumed a placid countenance.
He could not know how much she wanted to punish him.

"Lady Tess?" He frowned.

"My lord?"

Did he remember her? Did he remember how she had
clung to his leg in desperation the night her father was
executed? Did he remember how he had cruelly disengaged
her by nudging his horse backward, and then turned away,
leaving her without hope?

His lips parted. Full, attractive lips. Would the words of
acknowledgment she craved flow over them? She wanted him
to remember. *Remember, damn you!* she thought wildly as her
heartbeat roared in her ears. *I want you to know I was the one
you crushed that day.*

"Lady Tess," he said. "'Tis my pleasure. Let's have a look
at one another, shall we, dearest lady?"

"Of course." So he did not remember. His lack of sensitivity was so astounding her knees nearly buckled when she stepped out of the litter. An unexpectedly cruel breeze bit its way down her back, seeping beneath her riding gown. Ready to confront him, she turned to face him fully, and then froze. Seeing him only an arm's length away in the light of day for the first time, she realized how unjust the Creator had been.

Despite his callow nature, Lord Richard Avery, the Earl of Easterby, could melt stone with his charm. Too late she realized she had come to seduce and then murder a man who embodied the meaning of seduction. When he smiled, which was often, dimples dented his handsome cheeks, and a row of healthy, white teeth flashed at her like beacons in a storm. His blue eyes snapped with life and wit. His grace and debonair gestures served only to complete the picture of perfection.

"How fortunate I am," he said. "Though my betrothed surrounds herself with lovely servants, none eclipse her own beauty."

Liar! she thought. "Sir, your words of flattery are undeserved. Grief has made me a pale portrait of my former self. I bring you my purse, but not a happy visage."

"On the contrary, my lady." He took one of her delicate hands in both of his. "The light in one's eyes reflects the soul, which is the source of all true beauty, and yours shines like the North Star."

For a moment, she believed him. He was so practiced at pretty words that she warmed to him, if ever so briefly. He had a way of speaking that made her feel as if they were alone in the world, in a private garden, surrounded by succulent roses and embracing vines; every ounce of his attention flowed from his mesmerizing eyes into hers. Refusing to be so easily taken, she snatched her hand from his, perturbed by the pleasurable warmth that had somehow seeped through his glove.

"My lord, I hope you do not take me for a fool," she said,

clinching her tingling fingers. "You speak of the soul and inner beauty. Such sentiments are noble, but only believable when one is besotted with ale or under the spell of a particularly talented minstrel. Since I am neither, a more practical approach will win the day, as well as the admiration of the Earl of Haddington's rich daughter. The *late* Earl of Haddington."

Silence. Not even the wind dared rustle. The earl's one eyebrow, the one that had slowly risen in surprise, lowered, and he grinned in appreciation.

"Well done, Tess," he murmured, and turned with a reassuring glance to her cousin. "Fear not, Roger, I've never liked insipid females. A little vinegar enlivens the broth, I say."

"She is a treasure, Easterby. Never forget it," Roger said somberly.

"I doubt it not."

This time there was no hint of a jest, and Tess felt an odd surge of pleasure. Not because she cared what he thought of her. God, no. But if not that, then why?

Lord Richard started away, but pivoted with an afterthought, his muscular calves flexing in the confines of his golden hose. She saw the constriction and thought he had fine legs. For a man.

Then with absolute certainty, and a cockiness that charmed as much as it offended, he said, "But I did speak the truth, Tess. Heed my words. True beauty lies in the soul."

He turned and crossed the distance to his impatient horse. Tucking a spurred foot into a stirrup, he pulled himself into the saddle with ease and then leveled a serious expression upon Sir Roger. "You did bring her marriage portion?"

Though he'd taken care to lower his voice, its rich timbre still carried to Tess's ears, and she bristled.

"Of course." Roger grimaced and took a step closer to the

earl. "We come on Henry's orders. Do you think I would try to cheat the king? But do let us talk about that later. In private," he added, scowling.

"Very well. Lady Tess!" Lord Richard shouted gaily, retrieving his hand-gunne from his squire. "Make yourself welcome in my home. Do as you please. You are now the mistress of Cadmon Castle."

He delivered this last pronouncement in a conspicuously monotone voice, devoid of emotion, and in its absence Tess imagined she saw a storm brewing beneath Richard's placid countenance. But then the sunshine parted the clouds in his inscrutable azure eyes. With a beaming wink, the earl dashed away, golden hair flying, leaving Tess with a gnawing wonder as to what, if anything, Lord Richard felt about taking her to wife.

THREE

Two hours later, Tess floated in a daze along the drafty stone hallways that led to Lord Richard's solar, escorted by his squire. Perkins was a cheerful fellow with carrot-colored eyebrows that rose and fell with great exaggeration as he elaborated on the magnificence of his master's holdings. Tess liked his easy manner and wondered how such an earnest and kind squire could love an unscrupulous master. But then, she reasoned, Perkins was clearly an incorrigible optimist who saw the best in everyone. He even praised her for her courage under fire.

As he led her through a twisted maze of dark corridors in the expansive castle, he seemed not in the least aware of the undercurrent of rage that rippled beneath every courtly smile and genteel gesture she conjured. He seemed not to notice the hard set of her heart-shaped lips, or the fast pulse of blood gushing nervously through an artery in her thin neck. *Good,* she thought. It boded well that she could hide her murderous intent from one so close to the earl.

When at last they reached the earl's solar, Perkins unceremoniously deposited her outside his master's door.

"Knock as you will, my lady." He gestured to the thick,

arched doorway. "I'll not interfere with your courtship. There are places that not even a squire belongs."

His eyebrows quivered suggestively. He made a short bow and launched himself with determined strides down the corridor from whence they had come.

With a pang of regret, Tess watched him go. She didn't want to face Richard alone. She stared hard at the door, wanting to flee the presence behind it as much as she was compelled to confront it. Thinking of her plot, determined to see it through despite her fear and Roger's disapproval, she forced her white knuckles against the rough wood in a loud knock. When no answer came, she entered unbidden.

She was immediately confronted with a cozy swirl of scents—dandelion wine, taper smoke, and musty parchments. Pressing a hand to her tickled nostrils, she softly exhaled a portion of the tension that gripped every muscle in her body, letting her fists unfurl. The aromas and the soft crackle of a fire reminded her of home.

Stepping fully into the chamber, she scanned the rich surroundings and found they ignited her imagination. The room was magnificent—draping silks and tapestries, a tub for the ready, and stately high-backed chairs. Directly across from her, an incredible bank of windows stretched the entire length of the semicircular chamber. Tess frowned in disbelief. What an extravagance! Then her frown melted in unabashed adoration. The light that flickered through those windows was sheer perfection. Thinking it best not to love anything of Richard's, she forced her feasting eyes to move on to other sights.

To her left, nestled near a hearth of chiseled stone, there was a large canopy bed swathed with gold tassels and purple curtains. To the far right, there was a dressing area. The earl's polished armor hung on a wooden stand next to an empty bathing tub. The earl himself sat with his back to her in the middle of the chamber at a massive table he obviously used as a desk. Seeing his form, instant hatred surged in her chest like a visceral pain.

When she crept closer for a better glimpse of the maps he pored over, her leather shoes made a soft swishing noise on the stone floor.

"Put the food there," he muttered without looking up, waving his hand to a table by the hearth, clearly mistaking her quiet entrance for that of a servant's. She chose not to enlighten him, relishing the chance to study his chamber unobserved.

On the wall behind him hung a beautiful portrait of a solemn young girl. She had cheeks the color of the palest rose, and hair a wavy wheat gold. *Lucretia*. It was a portrait of Lucy as a child. Tess's gaze fell back to Richard, combing over his long golden hair. Was it possible he kept the portrait for some sentimental reason, even when Lucy detested him so?

Wondering what other surprises she might find, her gaze roved onward. On either side of the portrait stood two rows of bookshelves that lined the entire wall. Incredibly, they were filled with books. Tess's jaw gaped open. What a treasure! She had never seen so many rare and expensive tomes in one man's possession.

Hearing her tiny gasp, Richard looked up from his document. As he peered over his shoulder and found her, his bright blue eyes deepened like the sky at dusk.

"Lady Tess, I see you found your way to my solar."

A light winked from his hooded eyes, beaming at her with supreme confidence, like a falcon that has calmly, instinctively trained on the lure. His beauty was a splash of cold water. Bracing herself, she forced a sweet smile and stepped forward, circling the table until she faced him.

"Led by your indomitable squire, there was never any doubt of my arrival."

"Indeed. Perkins will one day conquer us all with his pernicious cheer."

Tess's smile broadened. He spoke with wit and an intelligence she found attractive. That, doubtless, had helped him seduce so many women. A beautiful man with no intellect was easy to scorn. But a man with the face of Adonis and the mind of Zeus was dangerous indeed.

Tess licked her lips. "My lord, if you are busy, I will gladly retire to my chamber. My journey was long and rest will be welcome."

"Not too busy to acquaint myself with my wife-to-be," he said, flashing the easy smile she had already learned to associate with Lord Richard. Silently, he filled a chalice with wine and placed it in her hands. He pulled a chair before his desk and guided her there, then sank back into his own on the other side.

"I have not been the most hospitable lord, I fear. Roger tells me I caused you a nasty spill this morning."

"'Twas nothing, my lord. It knocked the wind from me, that is all. I suffered but a mere scratch."

"Nevertheless, I must beg your forgiveness. I requested your presence so soon upon your arrival because I think 'tis necessary to clear up a certain matter. I want to express my gratitude for your . . . consent to this marriage."

A bitter taste twisted her tongue and Tess pressed the cold chalice to her lips, swallowing the sweet liquor.

"Your marriage portion, indeed your entire estate, comes at a time of great need," he continued in a deep baritone. "Henry is calling for a full contingent of knights and foot soldiers for his attack on France. They must be fully armed. Your resources will be put to good use."

Her gaze shot up and met his in a brief, sparking standoff.

The crow's-feet at the corners of his eyes deepened as some unnamed emotion washed over his tanned face. He was testing her, prodding her, thrusting a stick into a mossy green lake and measuring the depths.

She raised her goblet to her lips again, inhaling the heady swirl of alcohol.

"Your family is an honorable one, Lady Tess. I will be proud for my sons to share your blood."

"A Lollard's blood," she said evenly.

Leaning back in his chair, Richard steepled his fingers and touched the belfry to his pursed lips. "As for your father, he was a noble man. I know you must be grief-stricken over his death. I give you my deepest sympathies."

Her mouth tightened and her cheeks hardened with skepticism. Setting the chalice on his oak desk with a thud, she rose and sauntered to the windows, unwilling to show him any genuine emotions.

"Please enjoy the view of my garden while I put away my papers," he suggested, apparently unfazed by her retreat.

As he shuffled a stack of parchments and rolled up a leather map, Tess stepped back from the windows so her eyes could encompass every piece of glittering, soldered glass. The panes seemed to magnify the sun, and she lingered in its hot rays like a cat curled up for a snug nap. From the corner of her eye, she stole a glance at Richard, hoping to gain some insight that would explain how anyone could be so indulgent as to purchase this dear glass. What she saw sent ice water coursing through her veins. His eyes were still beaming at her, now more intensely than the sun. It felt as if his eyes were boring through her gown, undressing her.

"I am older than most brides, my lord," she said breezily, pretending she had not noticed. "This match came . . . unexpectedly. In truth, I never expected to marry at all. My mother died giving birth to me. As you can imagine, her sacrifice instilled in me a sense of profound gratitude. I vowed early on to live a life of service to others, to give of myself as my mother had given of herself. My father was glad to have my help. He never remarried, and so I acted as his chatelaine. That is how I reached the age of twenty without being betrothed. But of course I am . . . happy . . . to abide by the king's wishes."

Her voice sounded flat, unconvincing, even to her own ears, and she fell silent. She brushed her hands at the lap of her dusty green silk houppelande, her fingernails tapping against the pearls embroidered in a crisscross pattern. He had stared so hard at her gown, she was certain she must have spilled some mead. Content that nothing was out of sorts, she turned back, only to find him staring still.

"I pray thee tell, what is it?" she blurted out at last.

"What is what, Lady?"

"What are you staring at?"

"Was I staring?"

"You know you were," she said, indignant at his pretense.

His narrowed eyes twinkled as his rugged cheeks cracked with a devilish grin. "Henry did not tell me I was marrying such an outspoken lass."

"Do not evade the subject, my lord. You were staring at my . . ." Her voice fell away. She wasn't sure what he was staring at.

"If you must know," he muttered, kicking his feet up on his desk, "I was looking for a swell beneath your gown."

Tess tilted her head, certain she had misheard. "Pardon, my lord?"

"I said I was looking for a swell, my lady."

"A swell?"

"A swell."

"Do you mean . . . do you mean you wondered if I were . . . if I were . . . ?"

"With child."

He rose slowly. His shoulders appeared as broad and strong as a mighty beam across the ceiling of a great hall. He towered over the room, and an implacable will exuded from every pore.

"Forgive me for being blunt so soon upon your arrival. If you are not with child, then why did you come hastily? You would not be the first lady to disguise one man's child behind the title of another. I've survived long enough in the Lancaster dynasty to know that every gesture has a hidden meaning. You were not obligated to live with me. Not yet, anyway. I wonder that you should hasten to a marriage bed you clearly do not want."

Tess swallowed hard. Her mind was racing, moving quickly beyond the outrage. His last comment was an astute observation that warned her she was not dealing with a half-wit.

"Lord Richard, what possibly could I have said in the brief time that we have known each other that would lead you to believe I do not want this marriage?"

His broad shoulders sank a little within the confines of his velvet gown. He reached for a small square object on his desk. As he leaned over, his wild hair fell down one cheek, shielding his hawkish nose and the ironic grin that had rippled across his sculpted lips. Grasping the object, he sauntered toward her, his broad shoulders looming larger with every step. Gone was his charming facade. A dark angel had alighted.

When he halted—too close—he tucked a finger under her chin, forcing her to look into eyes that were fixed and distant. She inhaled the scent of him—sun and leather—and the peppery scent of her own fear.

"Did you truly think I would forget?" he whispered harshly.

"Forget?"

In answer, he held up the miniature. Her own likeness filled her vision, and a wave of vertigo washed over her. It was the portrait of her that her father had always carried.

"Churl!" she said, grabbing it from his strong fingers as if she were snatching the very memory of her father from Satan's clutches. "Where did you get this?"

He cut a mirthless smile. "I bought it from a scavenger the night your father was executed. I did not know who it was. I merely thought to spare the treasure."

She clutched the portrait to her breasts, which heaved with every pained breath. She hugged the miniature, stifling a sob. It had been a mistake to come here. A grave mistake. Not only was the sand sinking beneath her feet, the ocean was rising around her knees, soon to swallow her.

"I did not know you were Haddington's daughter that night. If I had, I would never have allowed this match. I know you will never forget . . . our meeting . . . just as I will not."

His iron fingers wrapped around her arms. He pulled her closer, so close she could have smoothed the anguished furrow from his sun-bleached eyebrows, if she'd been so charitably inclined.

"You hate me, don't you, Tess? Because I refused to help you. You hate me."

She wrenched her arms free. "Of course I hate you. I loathe you," she rasped.

"Then why in the name of the devil did you come so quickly? Why did you not do everything in your power to avoid me?"

Because I cannot wait to destroy you.

"Because . . ." she said, choking on her own lie, "because my lord Sovereign King Henry bids me to be your wife. And I will do his bidding, or die in the attempt."

Having said the bitter-tasting lie, scalding tears drowned her vision. She felt her way to the door, swimming to her escape through murky water. She gripped a velvet chair, a wrought-iron taper stand, bumped into a chess table, gouged her thigh. The board's pawns and kings clattered to the floor like the French at Crécy. She did not feel the pain, just an overwhelming urge to get as far from Lord Richard Avery as possible.

"Did you know my father was killed by Henry's father, the Usurper?" He spoke in a sharp voice that slaughtered the distance between them.

Tess stumbled at the door, staggered by sudden and fierce doubt. She gripped the latch, longing for freedom but feeling his claws embedded in her conscience, pulling her back. Her heart pounded fiendishly in her breasts.

"I say, did you know that Henry IV executed my father?"

Still facing the door, she nodded, running a backhand beneath her reddened nose. She did know that, though she had not remembered it until now. Why hadn't she thought of that until now?

"My father backed King Richard, my namesake. 'Twas an unfortunate choice, for as soon as the Usurper stole Richard's crown, my father was drawn and quartered. Each quarter of him was carried from town to town amidst a chorus of flies. That is what happens to men of conviction. That is what happens to men who defy the man sitting on the throne. Did . . . you . . . know . . . that?"

His voice ripped the space between them, knocking the wind from her lungs for a second time that day. How dare he mention his own pain? How dare he?

She whirled around. Her gown coiled around her legs. She cast him a ruthless glare. "Am I now supposed to pity you for your loss or spurn you for your lack of principle?"

His jaw muscles flexed in the shadows of a scowl. "This is

an unfortunate way to begin our courtship," he whispered. "Go away now, Tess."

When he turned with obvious fury, she allowed a smirk. But it withered at the thought of his father. He knew what she was going through. Damn him, but he knew.

FOUR

Blind with fury, Tess crashed headlong into the sunlight. Splinters of light pricked her eyes. She blinked and winced as the door to the inner bailey crashed back on its hinges. Struggling to fasten her hooded cloak, she plunged into the chilly March air, nearly stumbling in her determined effort to distance herself from the arrogant and offensive Earl of Easterby. A swell beneath her gown! The gall of the man. Just one more reason to end his worthless life.

She flew past the earl's private garden, and dodged her way between a few knights practicing combat in the small open yard beyond. The men-at-arms used wooden swords instead of real ones, but she wouldn't have feared for her safety even if their weapons had been made of gleaming steel. Anger overrode every other emotion, giving her the strength of ten men, she was certain, and the courage of twenty. Lifting the hem of her cloak, she brushed between the warriors like a ghost, sidestepping this way and that as the men parried and thrust, aware of her presence only after she had dashed onward. She was too intent on her destination to think of going around the obstacles in her path. She had to get word to her servants to unpack immediately. She most definitely would not turn around and return to Haddington Castle, as

Roger had advised. She would stay until her mission was accomplished.

When she reached a gate that led to the outer bailey, Tess felt a bit of the weight lift from her shoulders. She craved the anonymity she knew she would find in the hustle and bustle of the outer bailey. Here the business of the castle was carried out in jostling mayhem. She breezed past the carpenter's shop, where the carpenter was setting a young man's broken leg, which she discerned by the howls of pain. She cringed to think of the pain the poor patient was enduring at the hands of the bonesetter. The thought made her own present pain a little more tolerable.

Onward she went, past the chandler's hut, where a bearded man fussed over dozens of wax tapers.

"Thirteen hundred candles we went through last night!" the chandler complained. "I can't keep pace."

"Lord Richard does love his light," an old woman allowed in reply.

Tess was aghast. More than a thousand candles had been burned last night in Cadmon Castle. What a waste! *Oh, Richard,* she thought with newly dripping venom, *I hope to teach you a thing or two about the proper way to run a castle before I put you out of my misery.*

In the distance, she saw a flutter of red and blood and flapping wings in a circle of shouting men. It was a cockfight. Was this a feast day? she wondered, thinking it entirely possible, since she had lost all track of time since her departure from Haddington Castle. Nay, she concluded, it was no feast day. These were just idle men who took after their idle master. Shutting her eyes like a martyred saint, she stalked past the unpleasant sight of the cruel cockfight and ran right into a cook loaded with an armful of live chickens.

"Beg pardon, my lady," the cook muttered as his birds flapped out of his arms. They smelled of dirt and droppings and clucked madly as they flapped their silky white wings in Tess's face. She staggered back with an astonished laugh. What else could she do but laugh and regain her balance? Feeling flustered, but much lighter than before, she was happy to know that Richard had not succeeded in vanquishing all of her humor. But why laughter now after a year of grim repose? Straightening her velvet cloak, she realized it was because she had at long last given Lord Richard a piece of her mind. How divine!

Moving onward, she reached the drawbridge just as the giant weight and pulley system lowered the wooden bridge across the moat. Moments later, a dozen hounds came barreling into the bailey from the outer world, yelping and crooning. One sniffed at Tess's hand with a cold, wet nose and yowled with an ear-piercing wail, prancing onward amongst the gathering crowd.

The falconer rode in behind the dogs with a gyrfalcon riding snowy-white and proud on his arm. A sprawling hunting party followed. Smartly dressed hunters laughed and chatted, boasting about the partridges and hares strung lifeless from their saddles. They called for their pages as their rouncies rumbled over the wooden slats of the drawbridge with shod hooves. The last horses to clatter across the bridge bore two squires carrying betwixt them a bloody wild boar, impaled with a spear.

The hunt had been a successful one, Tess noted, thinking how fond her father had been of hunting.

Once the last of a dozen hunters had entered and the porter ordered the drawbridge raised, Tess's path to the stable was clear, and yet she didn't hurry on immediately. She gaped at the hunters on their high-stepping horses and their multitude of liveried servants, realizing that the destitute Earl of Easterby would have to house and feed these lords and ladies. Her father had been wealthy beyond measure, and a goodly

liege lord beloved by his vassals. But never had such gaiety
and so many guests swelled within the walls of her father's
stone curtain, save for holidays and very special occasions.
And from what she could discern, this was just an ordinary
day at Cadmon Castle. Surely the boar would feed them for
a day or two, but noble hunting parties frequently stayed for
weeks, enjoying their host's hospitality. And if Richard had
little gold to spare, who would pay for it?

She would, Tess realized, simmering anew. She would.
Lord, how she hated him for that.

She snatched a gulp of bracing air into her lungs, her
nostrils chilling and then thawing with each strained breath.
Swallowing the bitter realization that her father's wealth
would pay for everything the earl did henceforth, she continued her angry march toward the stables. She had almost
reached her destination when yet another hurried person
breezed by, brushing against her with an ermine cloak.

Something made her reel back, as if she'd been burned: a
sixth sense, a knowing that this was the enemy. The handsome giant strode past her, his luxurious fur cloak undulating
in his wake.

"I see you have decided to stay," Richard called over his
shoulder without pausing. When she did not answer, he
stopped and pivoted, just as a cluster of children chasing a
ball dashed around his feet like a swarm of bees, buzzing past
him in a mélange of giggling sounds.

Richard smiled warmly at the children and then cocked his
head, staring down his nose at Tess with more than a little
irony twinkling in his narrowed, blue eyes. "I thought you
might be gone by now. Since you are still here, that means
you will not flee as quickly as you arrived, does it not?"

Tess reddened with the extraordinary frustration she could
barely contain. How she longed to spit in his eye!

"Do not read any victory into the move, my lord."

He sauntered toward her, plucking off first one cheverel-leather glove and next the other, then stretching and fisting his newly freed fingers.

"No victory, maiden, just a need fulfilled. I am glad to hear you plan to stay. I have just ordered another shipment of hand-gunnes. I will need your gold to pay for them. I have a garrison that must be armed."

As if on cue, a cannon exploded in a field beyond the outer curtain wall, and for the first time Tess noticed sounds she had not heard before—distant grunts, the blare of a horn, the muted thud of gunnefire.

"You're gathering an army?"

He nodded.

"Wherefore? To hunt for heretics?"

"For the king's attack on France. He means to claim it for his own. And since you live to do your Sovereign's will, as you have said, then you surely will not object if I use your gold for such a purpose. That is why Henry pressed for this marriage, so that your fortune could be used to help him reclaim Normandy. You will oblige, will you not?"

She hated the merriment in his eyes. *Oh, wretched man. Wretched world. Is there nothing on this earth that Henry has not tainted?* she thought, digging her nails into her palms.

"Your wish is my will, my lord," she replied evenly.

"Good." He tucked a fist under her chin and forced her to look up. "All I ask of you is a modicum of civility. And punctuality. I hate to be kept to waiting. Beyond that, you will find me a most tolerant lord. The question remains, can you tolerate me?"

He winked and marched away, whistling a gay tune. She took a step after him, wishing she could wipe the maddening smile from his face.

"Whyever would you crave the company of a woman who has professed to hating you?" she cried out.

He turned slowly, his blue eyes glinting like steel. "Because you won't hate me for long," he said with absolute certainty, and for a moment, as he gave her a devilishly subtle grin, she believed him.

FIVE

After an hour of hard work, tilting at the quintain with his heaviest lance, Richard burst back into his solar. He was exultant and worn out, more than ready for the bath that awaited him. He felt a peculiar tingling—partly pleasurable and partly chafing—as sweat trickled through the forest of tawny hair springing from his massive chest.

"Godfrey!" he bellowed impatiently to his absent steward. "Blast it, man, where are you?"

He paced across his solar, stripping off clothing as he went, practically peeling the garments from his skin. First his dusty aketon, then his billow-sleeved linen shirt, still drenched with sweat from his morning ride, followed by his hose and braies, all trailing on the rug behind his broad steps. He cared naught who might glimpse his tight buttocks and ample manhood through his stunning row of windows. They opened to his private garden, and anyone lingering there would have a clear view of the earl's muscular body.

The glass had been a costly extravagance. Fifteen rectangular windows stretched across a good portion of the chamber. Warm beams of sunlight filtered through the thick, bubble-pocked glass. Just outside, the budding branches of pear and apple trees waved in a brown haze, now and then tapping politely on the windows, begging entrance.

"Enter!" Richard barked distractedly, mistaking the branches for a knock. Realizing his error, he exhaled with great deliberation, rolling his eyes.

"Losing my faculties," he muttered. He had been distracted and grouchy ever since his sour discourse with Lady Tess.

Rubbing his temples wearily, he paused and frowned at a branch that continued to scrape at the window. He was mesmerized by the motion as it bobbed in front of the sun. The pane of glass turned the winking light into a rainbow prism of red, blue, and yellow. Yes, his windows were an extravagance, but well worth it to one who adored light and color.

He loved things bright and bold. He had a passion for ideas and spurned small-minded men who saw life only as a practice in conformity. He chafed at the mundane, for life could be all too short and brutal. He'd learned that at the age of twelve when his father had been executed. Soon after, his mother had passed on from grief. And then Lucy had been sent away by Uncle Desmond, their guardian, who was loyal to the Usurper. In one savage year, Richard had lost his entire family. And a year later, he had lost Marly Vale, which comprised several thousand acres of his richest land. It was stolen by the Bishop of Kirkingham, a neighboring baron. Though desperate to reclaim his land, Richard could not press his case before the Usurper, who sided with the bishop. He could only bide his time. Knowing how ruthless a king could be, especially one who had stolen his crown, Richard had learned early to smile courteously to his Sovereign. He had learned what it took to survive—half-truths, midnight meetings, loyalty to a bankrupt cause, compromise. And in the wake of his grief, he'd learned to celebrate life so frenetically, and so convincingly, that only the most astute could see the shadow of pain beneath the glint of gaiety in his eyes—eyes softly crinkled at the edges from squinting too long at savage truths, from wincing at the certainty that his existence had no ultimate meaning.

The earl stepped into a tub of hot eucalyptus-scented water. God, it felt good. Hot. Soothing. The heat caressed his calloused toes and provided a delightful contrast to the wintry spring air that seeped through the windowpanes. His flesh tingled with a chill, until he sank into the steaming water. He groaned as the warmth enveloped his aching muscles. He'd overdone his riding and shooting, as usual, and would have done even more damage if he'd not encountered Lady Tess and her entourage.

Tess. Her image loomed up in his mind's eye like an unexpected thunderstorm, stirring in him longing and anger. She was a fair-skinned, flashing-eyed beauty, with lips exquisitely molded, like a pink rosebud poised to blossom. Color dappled her cheeks, as if she'd just been told a bawdy jest and, despite a maidenly blush, lingered to hear another. Her high, noble cheeks and pert nose spoke of fine breeding and inherent dignity. Brusque and direct, unschooled in courtly femininity, she was a woman to be reckoned with. So much anguish in those tiger eyes. She tried to hide her tumultuous pain, averting her gaze when he stared too intently. But who better to recognize that sort of deceit than he? She was like a child of God who was guilty not of hiding her light under a bushel, but of hoarding it greedily from the dark souls who would bathe in her brilliance. Heathens like himself.

He sank back against the wooden tub, the water's lapping seeming a wave of regret. She had asked for his help the night her father died, and he had turned her away. He owed her something for that cruelty. Guilt slammed him between the

eyes. Gods, what a detestable way to begin a marriage—
indebted to a woman who hated him.

"My lord?"

"Ah, Godfrey, there you are," he said eagerly when his
austere steward entered, balancing an armful of parchments.
"How much is Lady Tess bringing to my coffers?"

The elderly steward, bearing as much dignity in his
pinched expression as in his finely cut golden houppelande,
dropped his load on the earl's massive oak desk. Perusing a
page or two, he sniffed with satisfaction.

"When all is said and done, my lord, you will have enough
money to buy the latest hand-gunne, as well as baubles for all
your ladies at court. There should even be sufficient largesse
to cover the expenses you'll incur when you finally beget an
heir."

"For God's sake, Godfrey, don't mention the word 'heir'
unless I have a tankard of ale in hand. I'm far too sober to
contemplate so weighty a subject. Particularly one I've
managed to avoid for so long."

"My apologies, my lord," Godfrey replied with a belea-
guered sigh.

Richard smiled secretly, always amused by his steward's
saintly patience. As Godfrey filled two tankards of ale,
Richard splashed water on the sulphur residue that blackened
his angular cheeks and contemplated his matrimonial reluctance. Godfrey had asked him once why he was so loath to
marry. He could not answer without sounding hideously full
of himself: No woman was enough for him. Nay, that wasn't
quite the problem. He'd never met a woman with the courage
to peer into his soul, to see past the illusions. He doubted
there was a woman alive who had the fortitude and cleverness
to prune the hedges he'd grown round his heart. Long ago
he'd learned that charm was a greater shield than the sharpest

sword. Gladness diffused the light of illumination. Like the sunlight that blurred through his windows.

"My lord," Godrey said.

Richard looked up with a start to find his old friend standing patiently by the tub, proffering a tankard in one hand as he sipped from another.

"Thank you, Godfrey." Richard quaffed deeply and licked the foam that tickled his upper lip. Only then did he raise his brew in a silent toast.

The steward nodded his balding head. "To your new good fortune, Richard."

"Indeed." With a long sigh, Richard stared into the sour swirl of fermented barley, a pungent brew that warmed his belly. "Do you suppose, Godfrey, that if I drink enough, I could obliterate every last pang of my guilty conscience?"

The steward raised a single eyebrow. "No need for guilt. You are giving Lady Tess a title and acceptance at Court. You may spend her gold in good conscience."

Richard sank back against the tub. His chin skimmed the water. Steam rose into his nostrils. A drop of moisture fell with a faint plunk from his nose into the placid pool. *It isn't the gold,* he thought, trying to understand his turmoil. *It's that night.* That mewling cry of hers. Her unheeded pleas for help. He had ignored her plight, just as others had ignored his when he was young. He had seen so much love and pain in her tortured expression. She was a woman of profound dignity. Gods, how ever would she put up with his . . . lusts? He could call it by no other name. He would be a kind and gentle husband, as long as she did not expect fidelity.

"I do need an heir," he said in a stilted voice.

"If I might suggest, my lord . . ."

Richard stirred. The water was cooling. The skin on his fingers and toes was shriveling. "Go on, Godfrey."

"Well, since Lady Tess is doing you the double favor of

rescuing you from poverty and, presumably, bearing your heir as well, perhaps it would be wise to court her a little. Show her the grounds, perhaps?"

"Very well, Godfrey." Trying to wash away his frustration, he held his breath and sank down until water covered his head. He wanted to drown the nagging voice that insisted Tess deserved better from this match. When he could hold his breath no longer, he burst up from under the water's surface and drew air into his powerful lungs. He shook his head, and ringlets of sodden hair danced about his shoulders.

The chapel bells rang a dozen times, a distant vibration that announced the noon hour. It was a time when the particularly holy living at Cadmon Castle gathered for a midday round of prayer.

For Richard, the noon hour was no time for holiness. It was a chance for the randy earl to spend his seed. And at the sound of twelve bells, his manhood began to rise, surging with desire, trained by habit. He'd long ago ceased to condemn his ravenous appetite for things physical. While his heart and mind dwelled on higher matters, lowlier instincts held sway over his body.

The steward ignored the obvious and familiar signs of his master's insatiable lust. He continued to nonchalantly discuss matters of estate while the earl dried off. Moments later, there was a knock on the door. It was Elsbeth, Richard's lover.

Though uninspired by their impending session, Richard's pulse quickened nonetheless, again from habit, when he spied her willowy figure in the doorway. It was simply a matter of the body, not the soul. Elsbeth was a handsome woman—a sandy-blonde beauty with a long nose and delicate freckles. And though he would never love her, he was inordinately fond of her. That was as much as Richard had ever felt about any woman.

"Good day, Elsbeth," he said, noting with satisfaction that

her taut mouth melted at the sound of his voice. "When the twelfth bell had rung, and you were nowhere in sight, I thought you'd taken up with another man."

"Nay, Richard, none could satisfy me as you do." The angular-faced woman allowed a smile as she doffed her chaplet and netting. Two plaits of hair fixed in coils at her temples fell to her shoulders. She quickly loosened them and began to disrobe. Slipping out of her gown, she said, "I was delayed because a leper outside the castle would not let me pass until I threw him a few coins."

"'Twas very generous, Beth. But you should have chased him away and called the almoner. Godfrey, make sure Elsbeth gets her share of our bounty before she leaves today."

"Aye, my lord." Dipping a quill pen into an inkpot on the earl's desk, the steward made a note of it while Elsbeth stripped off and tossed aside her last garment, a close-fitting chemise.

Richard's eyes flickered over her voluptuous, peachy breasts with distracted appreciation. His mind was elsewhere, but still he felt content with the knowledge that this woman shared herself without asking for any emotions in return. Now and then, he was shaken with the vague sense he would pay for all the goodness so freely given to him, or rather taken by him. But it was not his way to dwell on weighty matters. He would simply appreciate his lover for what she was, the rosy widow of a merchant and a woman whose appetite for a jolly good romp almost matched his own. From the beginning, Elsbeth had made it clear she wanted only his company and financial upkeep. She found it preferable to taking another husband. A husband might beat and maul her at night, smell of ale and onions, and boast of his prowess as he fell asleep atop her but ten minutes after banking the fire. Whereas a lover she could enjoy when it pleased her, and leave when it did not, though Richard knew she would never quit his company of her own accord. In fact, it was she who had first seduced Richard. And it was she who had confirmed his suspicion that he would never find fulfillment in the arms of a woman. For if he did not find satisfaction, true satisfaction, in the arms of a woman as lovely and as skilled as Elsbeth, wherever would he?

On this particular day, Richard was weary from his long morning ride. Gods, he wasn't that old, was he? The small of his back ached, his arse felt downright blistered, and his arms flinched with occasional muscle spasms. But that wouldn't stop him from taking Elsbeth. If there was one constant in his life, it was his daily pleasure-taking. His eyes shuddered at the calloused thought. Had he never wanted more?

"What is wrong, Richard?" Elsbeth entreated, running her fingers over the smooth chestnut skin of his elegant forehead.

Richard nearly shivered, for as warm as her fingers were, it felt like the touch of a stranger.

"'Tis nothing, Beth," he replied, and gave her his notorious half-smile, the one that charmed kings and courtiers with its gentle irony and lack of malice. "Whatever is plaguing my thoughts, it has done little to bridle my lust and should not interfere with your pleasure." He nodded toward his nether regions.

Her gaze lowered to the golden triangle between his legs, where his readiness was obvious. She gave him a sultry laugh.

With an arm around her waist, he pulled her nearer. She smelled of freshly cut jonquils. Richard breathed in the scent and felt his muscles relax.

"But you are distracted," she protested coyly, fingering his left earlobe.

"I am an intelligent man, Beth. I can contemplate my current predicament and still make love to you. Unless you object to me thinking about my betrothed while you and I have a . . . meeting of the minds."

He cupped a hand around one of her breasts. It was as smooth as warm butter, though the nipple was hard, a luscious purple. Blue veins fanned out from the nipple in an intricate pattern, muted beneath translucent skin.

"A wife will not change you in the least, Richard," she warned him. "But since you are distracted, I will forgo my usual demands."

She swung one leg over his chair and straddled him, her heavy breasts dangling before his nose. "I will not require the usual preparation for which the Earl of Easterby is renowned. I, too, responded to the noon bells. I am more than ready."

Proving her veracity, she sat down, letting him glide into her. She was as wet and welcoming as if they'd been making love for hours. Both groaned. Richard sighed at the heat that stirred deep inside, but the sound was muffled, caught in his throat. He was still tense. When he shut his eyes he saw *her*. Her doelike gaze. How had Tess managed to invade his thoughts so quickly? All he could remember was that savage look of hers, her golden, indignant eyes drowning in tears, the jut of her jaw, the womanly anger that made the sweet dove roar. She was like an unplucked violet in spring. No doubt a virgin. Gods! That would be tedious. But what was he doing, thinking about his wife-to-be when he was with his lover? They belonged in different worlds.

"Will that be all, my lord?" Godfrey queried when he'd finished tallying the figures jotted on his parchments. He waited patiently by the earl's side, ignoring Elsbeth's gyrations as she rode Richard's ample endowment. Up and down she moved, panting ever faster.

"Aye, Godfrey, that will be all," Richard said in a tight voice.

Just as the steward shut the door behind him, Elsbeth cried

out in ecstasy. Her hips pulsed against the earl's. She groaned and shuddered with delight. It would not be the last time she came before this noon hour was over. For Richard was still hard with a longing he found difficult to quell.

Still inside her, he lowered Elsbeth to the blood-red rug that stretched nearly the length of the massive solar. This time *his* hips did the churning and thrusting. He was determined to find the same satisfaction that so many women had found in his arms. Surely, there was a woman who could bring him the fulfillment he sought.

If only he had found her.

SIX

While everyone in the castle feasted in the great hall, Tess paced back and forth across the rush-strewn floor of her guest chamber. She refused to join the merriment, even though the feast had been planned, however hastily, in her honor.

"Oh, but you must join the others, my lady!" insisted Mellie. The petite handmaiden stood in the center of the room, watching in dismay as her mistress passed back and forth like a caged tigress.

"You should have seen the glare of anger flickering over Lord Richard's face as he waited for you at the high table, my lady. At first, he allowed no one to eat, thinking it not proper until you arrived. But as time went by, and everyone became glassy-eyed and boisterous from drink, he relented. He must have feared his alehouse would be emptied before the first course was served. Even so, the earl himself still refused to eat, until even *he* gave up hope of your arrival. Oh, mistress, you must make haste to the hall. Do not humiliate him further."

"Do not humiliate *him*? Mellisande," Tess chided, glaring at the girl, "I begin to wonder who you have been employed to serve. Lord Richard, or me? Nay, I shall not go just yet. Since Lord Richard hates to be kept waiting, I want to linger until the last possible moment. I shall arrive long after five courses of fish and fowl and frumenty have been served. Well past the time when the flowers have wilted in the wine and each petal has sunk into a burgundy abyss."

"That has already happened, my lady," Mellie said, twisting her hands in a nervous knot.

"But how long do you suppose it will take, Mellie, until Lord Richard has worked himself into a thorough lather over my tardiness?"

"I'm telling you, my lady, it has already happened!"

Barely hearing the girl, Tess pictured his handsome face mottled with anger. Oh, wonderment! It pleased her beyond telling to think she had the power to anger him.

"Perhaps I will join him sometime after the minstrels' fingers grow sore upon their lute strings. Or when a drunken stupor has descended on all."

"That happened an hour ago."

"*Then* will I make my grand entrance," she said, unhearing, pacing, trying to soften the vindictive gleam she was certain shone in her eyes. *Am I being unreasonable? Aye, I am. But it feels so glorious. And at this point, what have I to lose?*

"I do this not because I want to stoke the embers of anger glowing between Richard and me, Mellie, but because I can scarcely contain my own outrage. And that is a miserable feeling. For I am not a scold, mind you."

"Nay, my lady, you are sweet and dutiful and kindly. Except when it comes to Lord Richard."

"And if I am made miserable by my anger, Mellie, then Richard should be miserable, too."

A rap on the door rose above the soft crackle of the chamber fire. "Enter," Tess called.

The door creaked open and Roger appeared, a frown marring his smooth forehead. When he saw her, he sighed with obvious relief.

"So you are not ill. 'Twas only your handmaiden's excuse."

"Sir Roger," Mellie said indignantly. "I had to say something to assuage the earl. Did you want me to tell him that my mistress was in her chamber sticking pins into a likeness of him?"

"That will be all, Mellie," Tess said. "Go to the great hall and make whatever excuses you wish. But I will not go until I'm ready."

The handmaiden picked up the hem of her gown and departed with an audible "harrumph," as much of a commentary as she dared give her mistress.

Roger crossed his arms, containing himself like a bottle of wine stuffed so full of vinegar it would soon burst.

"Are you finally ready to go home now, Tess? Have you proven your point? I certainly hope so, for if you anger Lord Richard any further you may be cast out on your ear, and then where will you be? Perhaps stripped of everything. And without your lands and coffers, you serve no purpose to Henry, who can be a ruthless devil when he's of a mind. Come home with me, Tess, before you anger the earl any further. You can return when Lord Richard is ready to—"

"Plant his seed?" Tess offered sweetly.

"If you wish to put it that way, then aye. Until then, methinks you'd be better off at Haddington Castle."

Tess nodded and sat down on a stool at her bedside table, picking up the silver handle of a looking glass. "I'm quite certain you are right, Cousin. But I will not leave until I've accomplished what I came here for."

"You mean *killing* Lord Richard?"

She looked in the mirror and almost started in surprise, for she didn't recognize the eyes staring back at her. They were as hard and dark as chestnuts. Had all her softness been buried with her father?

"Somehow, Roger, I have to devise a way to seduce Lord

Richard," she said distractedly, placing the mirror down, "for only if he's naked will I be able to thrust a knife into his heart."

"How I wish you would abandon that dangerous notion. You know you will be executed if you succeed."

"Mellie left these perfumed oils for me," Tess continued, as if he'd merely remarked upon the weather. "She managed to buy some rouge and powder in the village. But 'twill take more than that, I fear, to lure one as experienced as Lord Richard. Oh, why have I not yet learned how to please a man? 'Twould make my task far easier."

She shakily dashed some rouge on her cheeks in uneven blotches, and then wiped most of it away trying to even them out.

Roger lovingly placed his hands on her shoulders. "You never had a mother to teach you things, Tess. And you were too devoted to your father to spend time learning them on your own. Do not judge yourself so harshly."

She sighed heavily, recognizing the truth of his words. She had tried not to dwell on how much she had missed her mother, but there were times, such as now, when she felt so wholly lacking that the loss stung her heart like a bee.

She forced a smile for her cousin's sake. "Well, never you fear. I have observed the women who flirted with you, Roger. I shall fold my hands daintily in my lap," she said, doing so as she spoke. "And when Richard speaks, I will look up with wide-eyed innocence and bat my lashes. My lips will part in awe at the wisdom of his words. And when his speech ends I shall heave my bosoms with a satisfied sigh and say, 'Oh, my dearest Richard, I have never heard anything quite so brilliant!'"

Roger threw back his head and laughed.

Tess glared at him good-naturedly. "Please, Cousin, do not tell me my flirtations will be greeted with laughter."

"Forgive me, but I cannot imagine a more unlikely conversation. You have never dealt coyly with any man. You never even gave the noblemen your father paraded before you so much as a nod of the head. You were always too busy helping the old man. And he adored you far too much to force any match. But Tess, 'tis time you began living a life for yourself and not your father. Lord Richard has his faults, but he seems to be a fair man, and certainly fair of face. Can you not learn to tolerate him? With your wealth and his status in the Court you will live a life of ease."

"Roger!" In stunned silence, she turned around to look at him fully, her silk houppelande rustling as she pivoted on the stool. "First Mellie and now you! I am here for one purpose alone, and I am at peace with that purpose."

"Well then, you'd best make your peace with Lord Richard. He is none too pleased by your tardiness."

A slow grin of satisfaction crept up her cheeks, erasing the pain from her face. "So Mellie has informed me. Now that her tale is corroborated, I believe I am finally ready to make my appearance."

Tess and Roger approached the darkened entrance to the great hall as a gale of laughter rose to the highest rafters. More than a hundred guests tittered and guffawed and slapped their knees at the antics of an enormously fat, bearded knight. The jolly graybeard held court next to Richard at the high table at the far end of the hall.

"Marry, my lord," the rotund man elaborated, "I told the bawd that I'd applaud her dance with Venus, but I'd not clap, as I've still my wits about me and would not liken to the clap of any baseborn soldier, all drooling and frothy-mouthed and daft."

"What said she to that, Sir John?" shouted out a voice from the crowd.

"She entwined her legs round mine and danced to Heaven!"

Tess smothered an embarrassed smile behind one hand and tucked the other under Roger's arm. "Hold, Cousin, I will not disturb such a performance."

"You braggart!" bellowed Richard, who sat sprawled in his high-backed chair. Giving Sir John's behind a playful kick, he said, "To hear you tell, you've been ridden by every tart from here to Glasgow."

"I have! I have!" the jolly old fellow roared, his eyes bulging with enthusiasm.

The lords and ladies sitting at trestle tables laughed again, and Sir John joined them, glancing around with supreme pleasure at his reception, his gut jiggling with mirth.

Tess blinked against the din of golden smoke. Her mouth watered at the scent of roasted hens that had been torn limb from limb by the ravenous crowd. As pleasing as it was to know she had irritated Richard, she had missed the pleasure of what appeared to have been a delicious feast. Mutton bones were thrown down in the rushes for several sleek-coated hounds who chomped contentedly beneath the trestle tables.

The long hall was as expansive and ornate as Tess would have expected of Richard's domicile. Massive tapestries, stag horns, and fluttering torches lined yellow stone walls. To her right, an enormous fireplace crackled and roared. The ceiling rose to holy heights, where the sound of merriment swirled in the shadows of wooden-beamed rafters. And from those rafters, the earl's banners hung in stately fashion.

Aside from the unusual number of ornate tapestries, it struck Tess as a great hall like any other, save for one distinguishing element. This one had more than its share of bawds. Two buxom and brazen wenches with dark and tousled mops of hair had just drawn attention to themselves by plunking down in Richard's lap. It obviously did not pain him to have the bounty of womanhood so close at hand. Tess discerned that much with a glimpse at their bosoms, which spilled over low-cut kirtles like fruit in horns-too-plenty.

Next to Richard, Sir John continued spouting his anecdotes, while another wench hung on his shoulder, laughing raucously in his ear at every joke.

"Nay," Sir John continued, swirling a pudgy hand commandingly through the air to regain his audience's attention. "I have lain with many a fair maiden in many a bawdy house, and indeed they were fair to make me pay the price of one man when I am the size of two." Sir John's fat cheeks jiggled with laughter that soon swept around the hall. He swilled from a silver tankard until the low rumble died down. "But there's none so fair as my sweet Audrey," he concluded, swinging his arm around and slapping the rump of the wench with frizzy red hair who hung on his every word.

"Aw, Sir John, ain't ye the sweetest bloody man I ever did swive!" the tart gushed in a froggy voice, her arms akimbo, swinging her hips to and fro. "And since I am no fair maiden, I'll be charging ye tonight by the pound. I'll be a rich woman then, Sir John."

"You expect me to present myself to this baseborn company?" Tess whispered to Roger in the shadows of the entrance. "'Tis unseemly that the man who will soon bed me cannot keep his hands off the nearest wench."

"The wenches did not appear until Sir John arrived, and only after Lord Richard gave up hope that you would join him. Show him your mettle, Cousin, and all will be well."

Tess squared her shoulders, brushed back some loose hair that had fallen over the front of her high-waisted blue gown, and marched down the long center of the great hall toward Richard. He leaned back in his chair with the ease of a king, his prominent nose outlining an elegant face, his sculptured lips parted in a delighted smile, his long locks of blond hair lending something ancient and mythical to him. And she thought it terribly ironic that the man she hated most—or second most after Henry—should be so excruciatingly manly and lovely to behold.

As if he could read her thoughts, his eyes flickered away from the boisterous Sir John and alighted on her, widening momentarily with a flash of remembered anger.

"Aha! At last the woman in whose honor we have feasted." His words cut the room into silence. "Lady Tess, may I introduce Mistress Alice?" he said too eagerly, nodding affectionately to the wench on his left knee. "And Mistress Maggie?"

He nodded to the woman on his right leg. "Many years ago these fair damsels hid Sir John and me in their garderobe when the king's sheriff was after us, for what crime I do not recall."

A blushing Tess took in the earthy-looking "damsels" and was startled to find on closer inspection that they were not the youthful and dainty-boned sort she would have thought Richard would take to his bed. One was old enough to be his mother, and both clung to him as would old friends, not lustful lovers.

"What did the king want to arrest us for that time, Sir John?" Richard inquired, scratching the faintest stubble of a beard on his chin.

"For corrupting the prince," Sir John said. "Little did our Sovereign know that it was Prince Hal who had devised all our wicked schemes. A father's love is always blind."

When the gluttonous old knight echoed her own sentiments, Tess warmed to him instantly. He returned her gaze with a cozy, twinkling expression.

"A father always sees the best in his offspring. Marry, 'tis true, is it not, Lady Tess?" Sir John said in a softer voice, engaging her in the way of a gentle giant.

Tess felt her lips blossom with an irrepressible smile. Sir John's cheer was obviously impossible to deflect.

"Indeed" was all she said.

But she might as well have said "Hallelujah," for Richard cast off his surly countenance and, with a clap of his hands and a dazzling smile, shouted, "Minstrels, play!"

He is relieved. She cocked her head sideways in wonder, fascinated with the realization. More than angered at her tardiness, he was relieved to see her smile, and she felt powerful and glad that she had shown her mettle, as Roger had suggested.

"Minstrels, play music!"

Murmurs of excitement swelled as the knights and ladies pushed back their benches and trestle tables, wood scraping on stone. Hounds caught in the chaos yelped and ran for dear life. Roger, who had been standing behind Tess, stepped to the sidelines to watch, leaving her conspicuously alone in the center of the hall. Tess felt a hundred—nay, two hundred— eyes beaming at her, waiting for her to have the first dance with the earl.

As the revelers clapped to the beat, they formed a semi-circle around her, halting her retreat. When Richard approached her with a low bow over one elegantly outturned foot, Tess's cheeks turned from a faint blush to a deep crimson. Sweet Mary, he was going to ask her to dance!

"My lady, a *danse à deux?*"

A dance. Lord deliver her. She wanted to faint and end her mortification. She prayed she would faint. Instead, she shook her head with a quick, tiny motion, so that only he might see. Her eyes grew wide with terror.

"What is it, Tess?"

She merely shook her head as the clapping grew louder and the men started pounding their feet on the floor.

"I can't," she whispered through clenched teeth.

"What, my lady? I can't hear you."

"I said I can't."

"You can't what?"

"I . . . can't . . . dance!"

She shouted a confession she had hoped to never even have to whisper, but the noise in the hall was so deafening that only Richard had heard, and just barely.

He frowned, contemplating her words, and when their meaning registered, his face lost all expression. He took her hands gently in his. "Why didn't you tell me? 'Tis nothing to be ashamed of."

Richard held up a commanding hand, and after a few moments the crowd reluctantly stilled. "Randolf!" he barked.

"My lord?" An enormous man of powerful strength, who sported a wiry, raven beard, stepped forward.

"Start a farandole, will you?"

"Aye, my lord." The giant hulking man began to dance with surprising agility. He led the others in a chain, weaving through the hall in set patterns, skipping and turning beneath one another's arms.

Tess watched with envy the very dance she had seen so oft in her father's hall, but in which she had never indulged. She'd thought it necessary to maintain decorum, to act the dignified hostess of her father's castle. And now she wanted nothing more than to join the merrymaking, but she could not, for she would make a fool of herself.

When the dancers were focused on their own feet, or flirting with their partners, or both if they were skilled, Richard grabbed her by the hand.

"Come with me."

He pulled her through the crowd under the cover of chaos.

They bumped into one dancing body after another, Tess heedless of where he was dragging her, until they reached a cool, open antechamber amongst the grand columns of the entrance. She struggled to catch her breath, taking in the sight of him warily.

He wore long red hose and a short black velvet doublet with a high white scalloped collar that neatly framed his prominent chin. Humor curled his lips, irony dimpled his cheeks, and a sensual haze shadowed his smoky eyes. He was much too attractive. And yet, it was more than attraction she felt.

"Thank you," she said reluctantly. "Though I chafe to admit it, you spared me great embarrassment. I am grateful for your consideration of my position."

"I have done little else but consider your position since you've arrived. Though I admit my actions do not always show it."

She nodded, more in resignation than agreement, and then nearly started out of her tingling skin when he smoothed a strong hand around the S-curve of her waist and pulled her close. She pressed her hands against the soft velvet that covered his granite chest.

"What are you about, my lord? What? What is this? Let go!" She pushed him away and skittered back into the shadows, leaving him empty-handed and thoroughly bemused, by the look of his corrugated brow. "Are you taking advantage of my vulnerability?"

"I am trying to teach you to dance."

"By touching my waist?"

"What part would you rather I touch?"

"No part at all, my lord. I do not want to learn."

"Oh, yes you do," he huskily replied, closing the distance and snatching her hand. "You're dying to dance."

His hand burned on hers, and his face took on a mask of

such certainty that she thought she was looking at a mirror reflecting her soul. God, what sort of man was she tangling with? Perceptive to boot? Weren't beauty and charm enough weapons in his arsenal?

"I may be dying to dance, my lord," she said pointedly, wringing her hand from his grip, "but not here. And most certainly not with you."

She quit his company with a toss of her head and marched indignantly back into the great hall.

Oh, how bold she felt! Just like one of the women who flirted with Roger. Or like one of Sir John's bawds, demanding a price, setting her terms. She pushed her way through the crowd, until it began to part before her as if she were Moses. A tingle of warning crept up her back, and she turned just in time to see Richard stalking toward her. He, of course, was the real reason the dancers had stilled and scattered before her. The golden, beloved god of Cadmon Castle. He loomed ever closer until he towered over her, his solemn expression downright eerie in the shadows of his long hair.

Her gaze climbed past the embroidered yellow sun that adorned his black doublet, and up over his broad shoulders. Craning her neck, she searched his eyes for compassion, but they smoldered with something altogether ungentle. She had refused him once too often. Oh, why hadn't she agreed to dance? She suspected dancing would have been easier to get through than what she now faced. Now he was all hardened muscle and mean intent and intemperate masculinity. She felt it the instant he tucked an arm around her waist and smashed her against his chest, bending down—nay, swooping down like a falcon—and devouring her lips.

"Ooooohhhh!" the crowd murmured in unison, expressing just a portion of the shock she would have expressed if he hadn't stolen her breath away.

His lips covered hers with heated insistence, until she could no longer resist and allowed her lips to mold to his. It was the most curious sensation she had ever felt. His mouth was warm, almost hot, and made her own tingle and throb. His lips barely moved, and yet infused her with some kind of elixir, for she was suddenly aware of nothing else but his lips. She inhaled the sun burnished on his tanned cheeks. It was like the arrival of spring: One day you awaken after a long winter to hear birds singing outside your window, and suddenly there is hope again, magic, and infinite power. All this she felt in his arms.

When Richard pulled away at last, Sir John put his hands together in slow applause. Soon others joined in, all riveted by the spontaneous display of affection.

"Here, here!" someone shouted, and those who had not been dancing raised their tankards in a toast. "To the new lady of the castle!"

"To love," another shouted.

"To love," Richard intoned, raising a tankard someone had thrust in his hand. His eyes smoldered with fire meant only for her.

"To love!" Tess nearly shouted in dizzy wonder, but bit her tongue into silence, and would have bitten it off completely before she'd make a toast to love in this man's presence.

"A song, my lord?" the lead minstrel inquired as all three musicians surrounded Tess and Richard. The long-fingered, bony lute player struck a vibrant chord that made goose bumps rise on Tess's arms. Then, much to her surprise, it was Richard who began to sing:

"The sweetest maiden's love to know,
Is like a rose at dawn.
Each petal will unfold so slow
Revealing the sweetest song."

His honey-smooth voice filled the hall with such beauty that Tess could do naught but wonder what other talents he possessed. As he sang two more verses, he shut his eyes in deep concentration. The words tripped lightly off his moist lips; his cheeks drew in with each breath. The soft rise of his Adam's apple quavered with a rich vibrato.

When the song ended, the ladies in the hall initiated a long applause, nodding approvingly. Veils dangled and bobbed from the wired-up headdresses and the pointed templers of the married women.

Stirring from his poetic trance, Richard opened his eyes and humbly bowed his head. He then led Tess—stupefied and thoroughly enchanted—back to the dais, where Sir John and Audrey were dabbing their eyes.

"Oh, that was sweet, young wag," Sir John said, blowing his nose as loudly as a clarion into a snot-encrusted rag. "You're cruel to make an old man weep."

"You'd weep for want of a piss-pot, you old sot," Richard returned affectionately as he and Tess took their chairs on the dais.

Sir John snorted a laugh as he sopped his tears. "Right you are, my lad. Right you are."

The minstrels broke into a melancholy ballad, a tale of love lost, and a bittersweet contentment fell over the crowd as a cold wind howled outside the hall. Tess settled in her chair between Richard and Sir John with a curious sense of familiarity. When the singer ended his second verse and began to pluck a musical interlude, Sir John leaned over the arm of his chair and whispered to Richard. His breath reeked of ale.

"Do you remember, sweet wag, when love's potion fell so heavy upon our eyes? You and Hal and I would go from tavern to tavern, falling in love with every maiden. What a scallywag our sweet prince was then," Sir John said, drops of perspiration beading on his brow. He blinked earnestly. "Hal said, 'I'll ne'er forget you, John. Not even when they crown me king.' He said that, Richard. You were there. Do you remember?"

Richard's cheeks hollowed as he drew in a long breath. "I remember."

Curious about the melancholy tone of Richard's voice, Tess listened intently.

"Ah, life's mysteries. 'Twas a bitter turnabout, eh, Richard? Can a man change so quickly? Overnight? As soon as the golden wreath has touched his head? I miss him, Richard. I miss him dearly."

For a moment, the briefest moment possible, Richard's expression of ease turned bleak, but then he smiled and held out a hand, which Sir John clasped as if for life. "King Henry is not so very changed. Perhaps he would give you audience again, John."

"Do you think so, Richard? Surely not after he threw me in prison. Do not say 'aye' to salve the wounds, wag. Speak the truth."

"'Tis possible."

"Mayhap 'tis so." Sir John sank back in his chair and kneaded his pudgy hands together. "I have two barrels of ale from the Boar's Head Inn in Eastcheap. Best damned ale in Christendom, Hal would always say. I thought I might bring a barrel to him, for old times' sake. May I come with you and give it to him when next you see him?"

"If you wish, John."

"We shall laugh and drink until the wee hours and wench to our hearts' delight, you and me and Hal," Sir John said, his eyes brightening with a distant light. "I will make jokes and Hal shall laugh again, casting off his heavy mantle. And if we like, we shall jump into the Thames and be washed nearly to sea. Do you remember that time, Richard?"

Sir John started to giggle, which for him was a basso profundo affair. His voice pounced from his thick jowls and burst out into the hall.

Richard did not laugh, but watched his old friend with a melancholy grin. His blue eyes glittered with love and concern, Tess thought, watching this emotional turn with fascination.

"And we shall dance!" Sir John said, jumping to his feet. "Minstrel, play a merry tune, one that you played for us when sweet Harry was in our midst."

The minstrels, who followed Sir John from castle to castle and tavern to tavern, knowing that a celebration and, therefore, a few coins of payment would ensue wherever the jolly knight caused merriment, strummed a lively jig. The enraptured crowd in the hall began to clap to the rhythm. Sir John held out a thick hand to Audrey.

"Sweet Audrey, dance with a moon-eyed reprobate, won't you, lass?"

"Oh, aye, Sir John," Audrey replied, fairly pulling him into the center of the festivities. With their arms entwined, they madly jigged around the hall, nearly overturning a bench. When at last the music reached its crescendoed peak, the crowd roared with applause and whistles. Excitement slithered down Tess's spine, and she began to clap as well. *What freedom to dance thus!* she thought enviously, long-forgotten joy racing through her veins.

"By God, let sweet Harry see me dance about like this and he'll remember the way it was!" Sir John shouted with glee.

But his glee was cut short. His eyes widened. His cheeks grew pale. The sweat beading on his forehead seemed suddenly to pour down his temples. He clutched his heart and tried to cry out in pain, but no breath would come, and the sound gurgled in his throat.

"Perkins, fetch the physician," Richard ordered as he rose from his chair.

Tess leapt up automatically. He was dying! She was sure of it. She'd seen a man fall just so in a tournament, and his face had looked exactly like Sir John's—as pale as the underbelly of a bloated fish, eyes filled with dark terror, the shadow of the Reaper's scythe. Sir John clutched his chest with one hand and fell back in a swoon into the arms of several squires who had dashed forward.

"Oh, me God, 'tis his heart!" Audrey cried, clapping her hands to her cheeks, tears bursting on her red eyelashes. "He's been feeble ever since the king spurned him two years ago. Broke his bleedin' heart, King Henry done."

Tess slowly crept around the table until she was at Sir John's feet. Audrey fanned his head while Sir John's silent and much-abused page devotedly brushed a cool rag on the knight's forehead. Richard stalked to his side, fury sharpening his fine features.

"Do not die, blast it," he ordered Sir John, kneeling at his side, pulling the old knight into his arms as best he could. "I command you! I am an earl now, you bloody scoundrel, and you will follow my orders."

Richard grunted as he tried to enfold John more thoroughly in his arms. It was the first time Tess had seen any loss of composure in Richard, and she felt distinctly uneasy. His temples gleamed with sweat. Hollow fear flashed across his face like the unkind beat of crows' wings, making him flinch and brace himself for the worst.

Richard loves this man, Tess realized. Or was it more? Could this lowly boon companion be like a father to Richard? After all, he had long been without one.

Richard was as beautiful in grief as he was in joy, and a part of herself she hardly knew felt a well of compassion overflow in her heart. Incredibly, she longed to wrap her arms around him. Nay, she felt nearly compelled to. To tell him all would be well. To assure him that even if he had lost a father, he would be loved. Lord, yes, a man like this would be loved. *She* could love a man like this. The priests had always said as long as there was God there would be love and . . . *forgiveness*?

No, not that. Tess bolted upright, so quickly she lost her balance and staggered back, just as a physician rushed forward and the crowd scattered. She receded farther from the circle gathered around Sir John, eager to reclaim distance between herself and Richard. She backed farther and farther away, hugging herself, heart-stopping fear pounding in her head. She had learned something tonight that she did not want to know: Richard was a loving man. He had a heart and a soul. The kind of soul she could dance with in the darkness. Dance as she had never even conceived of. Until now.

SEVEN

Sir John did not die. The physician, with his leeches in tow, sent the jolly knight to bed for a week and confirmed what Audrey had surmised: The old sot was suffering from a broken heart. However, it was much more than a broken heart that nearly sent Sir John's soul winging its way to Heaven. He ate and drank to excess, and suffered from gout and a host of other maladies associated with overindulgence.

But as Sir John had learned long ago, illness has its rewards. He adored the attention that accompanied his poor health—particularly the sympathy and daily visits from Lady Tess, whom he considered one of the most virtuous and kind women he had ever met. He relished their conversations.

Their visits were healing for Tess as well. The feast given in her honor had left her feeling strangely off-kilter. She had always viewed people as good or evil, black or white, but never both. Now she had glimpsed the portrait of a man painted in endless shades of gray. As much as she longed to, she could not define Richard and then dismiss him. He had somehow managed to touch in her a well of tenderness so achingly sweet she scarcely knew what to do, save pray for mercy and then, conversely, give thanks for an ability to feel anything so intense. She was still committed to his demise, she reassured herself, but hoped it would not come too quickly. At least not before she figured out why his kiss had felt so utterly divine, and just what caused the darkness in his eyes that only she seemed to see. He was a conundrum, and one she wanted to understand thoroughly before she put an end to his wicked life.

After her cousin Roger said his farewells, she had concluded that the only way to continue under the same roof as Richard was to immerse herself in the role of bride-to-be. Like one of the great traveling actors, she would assume a character. A character who was in love with the Earl of Easterby and longed to welcome him into her bed. With this logical reason for temporarily setting aside her seething hatred, she was able to relax and observe her new home—at least by day.

Her nights, filled with thoughts of her father, were hard to bear. She had recurring nightmares about his execution, dreams made all the worse by a terrible screeching she heard in the wee hours. The sound was almost inhuman in its misery and never failed to send chills cascading down her spine. Tess assumed the cries came from a mad relative locked away for his own good. That was common enough, but Tess had never heard a madman whose cries were quite so forlorn.

Her days were much more pleasant, in great part because of Sir John's entertaining company. In the days following his collapse, Audrey kept vigil by his side until she grew weary. Then Tess took her place, stitching her embroidery and humming softly as the aging knight slept. When he roused and regaled her with stories, she listened intently, recalling the hours her father had expounded on religion and the philosophies of Hus and Wycliffe, the men whose ideas had led to his execution.

"Did I tell you about the time Richard and I rode naked

through Petersbury and ran into a procession of townspeople departing for their yearly pilgrimage to Canterbury?"

Without looking up from her stitching, Tess arched her brows in gentle reproach. "Nay, you did not, though I'm sure you're about to. However, before you launch into another risqué anecdote, I wonder if you've noticed that all the stories you've told me regarding Lord Richard revolve around mischief, debauchery, or lechery."

"What? Well, I never . . ." Sir John sank back into a pile of pillows. He scratched his bushy beard. "Saints, now that you mention it . . . But surely you don't believe those who say that Lord Richard is naught but a randy cock who crows his victories o'er the hens in his roost, a selfish boy who plays when he should work, and who spends money he does not have. There are many more sides to Lord Richard. Ah, what a noble young man he is! Do you not see it, Lady?"

I do see it, though I do not want to, she thought as her hands grew still. She gazed into the torch that fluttered and hissed on the wall by Sir John's bedside, studying the orange flames as she considered her thoughts carefully.

She saw Richard's nobility not in his outward actions, but in the glimmer of kindness, the instant compassion, the inexhaustible humor, the joie de vivre.

"I see his charm, Sir John, but true nobility can only be proven with courageous action. And courage is never more tested than when we are forced to choose between our principles and our friends. And while Richard is charming and handsome, he is highly irresponsible. He entertains far too lavishly for a man who has debtors clamoring at his gatehouse."

Sir John strummed his fingers on his belly, buried under a pile of covers. "Marry, I cannot argue. Especially since I have enjoyed his hospitality more than most. But he has so many other good qualities, my lady. He is brave beyond any tale ever told, braver than the heroes Taliesin sang about. Why, I recall . . . what year was it? 1409 or 1410? 'Twould have been . . . why yes, I remember now. 'Twas 1410 when the prince's forces finally defeated Owain. Lord Richard led the charge, knowing what was at stake for his dear Prince Hal if he did not defeat the Welsh. An arrow lodged betwixt Richard's armor, nearly piercing his heart. He plucked the weapon off as if 'twere a fly and proceeded until the day was won."

"Bravery is commonplace and all too often motivated by base desires," Tess countered archly, resuming her stitching. "He knew he would be rewarded for his heroism, and so he has been. Henry made him an earl."

"But in title only. Unlike the grand dukes of France, the honor does not necessarily come with lands here in England. And before he came of age, the vast farmland he once owned was stolen by the Bishop of Kirkingham, that thieving cleric so beloved by the Archbishop of Canterbury. Richard was hoping that once Henry ascended the throne, he would force the bishop's hand. But the king refused."

After sitting up in his fervent telling, Sir John sank back onto his pillow, exhausted. Softly, he added, "In that way he turned his back on Richard just as surely as he turned his back on me. The title of earl is little appeasement when the heart has been betrayed. Oh, Henry did give him new land indirectly, by arranging your marriage. Richard's marriage to you will give him more acreage than he could hope for, and acreage far richer than the fertile Marly Vale. But the vale was his father's legacy. He will not rest easy until 'tis his again."

Tess pictured herself in Richard's place and felt anger over the injustice. Perhaps they had something in common after all: mistreatment by the king.

"If they are friends, why did Henry turn his back on Richard?"

"If I knew that, dearest lady, I could die at peace with myself. All I can tell you is this." He motioned for her to lean closer, and she obliged. "The night he was coronated, Prince Hal secluded himself with his confessor and spent the night in prayer and God knows what other state of spiritual turmoil. When dawn broke, he was not only King Henry, but a man his friends of old hardly recognized." Sir John licked his dry lips. "He turned into a monarch so pious as to be mistaken for a saint, save for on the battlefield, where he has shown himself to be as ruthless as ever. He listens to his confessor and to the Archbishop of Canterbury as he once listened to Richard and other boon companions. That is why he will not force Kirkingham to relinquish Marly Vale, for Kirkingham is a bishop, albeit a thieving, dishonest one." His rancorous words hovered momentarily between them. "And Henry's heart now belongs to the Church. So you see, Richard's title is not everything 'twould appear. I worry for him, Lady Tess. How long can a man wait for justice? And until then, how much injustice can he endure?"

"I do not know." Tess pictured Richard, that dazzling smile of his, and at last understood the darkness behind it. And understanding it, she heard the first faint strum of a cord that bound them together. *No!* a voice suddenly screamed in her head. *I do not want to understand. I will be avenged!*

Or would she? She had assumed Richard was like Henry in every way, that their wills were one. And that assumption was the basis for every action she had taken since the Marquess of Dolton had announced she must marry the Earl of Easterby. Was it possible she had misjudged Richard utterly? A more reasonable person would have wondered sooner, but she did not want to be reasonable. She did not want to understand Richard's predicament. Understanding and reason were the enemies of vengeance. Someone had to pay for the crime against her father. And what chance would she have to exact her revenge upon the monarch of England?

"Are you ill, Lady Tess?" Sir John asked, propping himself up on one elbow. "Your rosy cheeks have turned as pale as a lily, and your chestnut eyes are filled with bewilderment."

"Nay, Sir John, do not worry about me. I . . . I was just wondering when you were going to finish your story about your naked ride through Petersbury."

"Ah, Petersbury," he said, grinning and clapping his hands together. "Richard and I had been swimming with two ladies in a lush stream just south of the city. He and I lingered in the water while the ladies dried themselves off on the stream's bank. Then suddenly, the mischievous tarts thought 'twould be a clever jest to steal our clothes and leave us in the lurch. And so we had no choice but to ride into town searching for a tailor. Unfortunately, we were riding down the main street, like Lord Godivas, when the parish priest began a procession with the burghers for their annual pilgrimage to Canterbury. Why, for a moment, the holy pilgrims thought we were two of the four horsemen come to announce the Apocalypse!" He ended his tale with a laugh that turned into a wrenching cough.

Tess patted his hand indulgently, smothering a smile. "You see, Sir John, yet another tale of Lord Richard ends in mischief."

"Alas, I cannot argue," he sighed after regaining his composure. "But . . ."

He poised a hand in midair, as if to snatch a memory from the distant past. Grasping it in his mind, he jabbed the air in recognition. "Now I remember what I wanted to tell you. 'Twas the same day Lord Richard found a crippled orphan child on the road between Winchester and Cadmon Castle. He lifted the boy up on his saddle and brought him home. He's now the earl's master gunner. Richard has such heart, Lady Tess. You just have to accept his weaknesses."

"I see." Her voice was a wisp of air.

Satisfied that he had made an impression on Lady Tess, Sir John nestled into his pillow and moments later was fast asleep.

Tess sank back into her chair with a confounded sigh. *Richard, who are you?*

Just as he filled her thoughts, the door creaked open and there he was. His broad shoulders strained against a billowy white shirt tucked into tight beige breeches that hugged his lean hips. He scanned the room, and when his searching eyes found her, like two smooth beads of blue glass, Tess's heart lurched into high rhythm.

"Tess," he whispered in a weary voice, his lips parting in a lopsided grin. "I am glad to find you by his side. You have been good to my friend, and I'm grateful."

"My lord, Sir John has told me all about you. I learned every detail of your youth, short of the time you walked on water. He thinks most highly of you."

Richard nodded, his golden features turning solemn. He sauntered to the end of the bed, an arm's length from Tess. *He has just bathed,* she thought. His skin smelled like soap and the underside of his long locks were wet.

"When my father died," Richard began, and then smiled ruefully. "When he was *executed,* I determined that I would trust no man. That every person, be he friend or foe, would be dealt with politely as an enemy."

He sat at the end of the bed. "It was not until I met Sir John that I allowed myself to trust again. I do not do so lightly, Tess. Aside from Sir John, my confessor is the only other person who knows my thoughts and hopes. I have seen too much ruthlessness to trust just anyone."

She wanted him to move closer. Staring at the smooth,

burgundy curves of his lips, she wanted him to sit at her side. Lord, was that possible? *Wanting* him next to her?

"Ruthlessness, my lord?"

"You know how my father died. I did not tell you how I first learned of his death. I had come to visit him in the Tower. But he was not inside as I'd expected. His head, thrust on a pike, greeted me at the gate, drained of life. I'd call that ruthlessness." These last words he whispered.

She felt a stab of his pain as if it were her own, and she knew he was a dangerous man. She was feeling sympathy for a smooth-talking devil. She took a deep breath of the cool chamber air to clear her head, then willed her heart to harden against his sad tale. How could she exact revenge on a man she wanted to console?

She resumed her stitching, as if his words had had no impact. And yet she felt the intimacy that comes with confessions. Her skin prickled with excitement that he, who trusted few, would share his innermost thoughts with her. Like a fine and rare wine, the taste of which she could not abide but which she hoarded greedily in her cellar nonetheless, she seemed to crave knowledge of Richard because of its scarcity. Impatiently casting aside the needlework, she heaved a frustrated sigh.

"But if a king has caused you so much pain, my lord, would you not set your course to prevent others such sorrow? Having suffered from the loss of your own father, couldn't you have done something to spare my father?"

Guilt shimmered across his face like the ripple in a pond that follows after a stone falls deep. "I regret that I turned you away that night, in your time of greatest need."

"I have enough regret to last me a lifetime. Yours will do me no good." She turned her head away, a slowly closing door.

He slid from the foot of the bed to the edge next to her

chair. She felt his nearness like a surge of the sun, warming her cheeks, making her woozy for a cursed reason she could not fathom.

He leaned forward, rested his forearms on his thighs, and took one of her hands in his. Tingling, she started and pulled away, but his grip tightened, catching her fingers in his snare. His hand was hot and strong around hers. A pulse of pleasure throbbed up her arm, infecting her with unreasonable desire with every beat of her heart. She scowled accusingly at his hands—nicks, and calluses, and blue veins bulging beneath tanned skin.

What magic did his hands possess to make her feel want for a man she had sworn to kill? She was aware of nothing but his touch—she heard no clarions when they blared from the parapets, smelled no sap sizzling on a log in the fire, felt no chill nipping down her back. Just the gentle stroke of his fingers on the underside of her wrist, where blue veins wove the tapestry of her life.

"Is there nothing I can do to earn your forgiveness?"

"Jump in the Thames and drown?" she offered tartly.

He edged closer, stroking her temple with the back of his fingers. "Is that humor?"

"Not if you must ask."

His nostrils flared and his eyes glittered, the only acknowledgment of a jest that might have been worth a laugh in another time and place. His face was close now. She saw old scars as thin white lines on his smooth, bronzed cheeks. His nose nearly touched hers.

Oh, God, he's going to kiss me again, she thought, licking her lips. *Yes, please, yes.* Their noses touched first, softly, intimately. A sweet touch. A tingling touch. His lips brushed hers, taunting her, promising more, denying more.

Kiss me! she wanted to scream. *Just bloody well kiss me!*

And he did. With one fell swoop he rose and pulled her into

his arms, engulfing her in warmth. The fire ignited immediately. Unlike their first kiss, this time his lips were no strangers. She knew how to greet them, how to purse her mouth, how to let the heat in her face rush through that portal of their pleasure, how to loosen her lips at the right moment and consume his tenderness. And she was hungry. She had never known how hungry until now. It wasn't supposed to go like this. She was supposed to be above him, removed, in control.

"Nay," she muttered, and pulled away, pushing at him when he would not release her.

He paused, frowned, studied her expression, and smiled all too smugly. "Aye," he countered, and dove for another kiss.

She wrenched her mouth free. "You arrogant beast! Let me go." With a good shove, she broke away and slapped him hard on the cheek. The sound cracked in the air. Her fingers stung. Their imprint rose pink on his cheek. *Oh, Lord, what have I done?* His face hardened, and she drew back, expecting a blow in return.

"You're shuddering." Sparks flew from his eyes as he scowled at her. "Do you think I'll strike you?"

"Aye."

"Is your opinion of me truly so low?"

"Why wouldn't you? Don't brutish men strike their chattel at will?"

"Stop it." He gripped her by both arms, pulling her roughly to him. "I'll never strike you. Never."

As if he'd just noticed his less than gentle grip, he released her and stepped back. He smoothed a hand over his face and surveyed her again, this time with a hint of amusement playing about his handsome face. "I won't strike you, Tess, but I'll not turn the other cheek either. I think 'tis time you learned something about obedience."

Tess's jaw dropped and her spine stiffened. "Obedience, my lord?"

"Aye. Obedience to public opinion. I cannot command you to respect me, Tess, but you can bloody well learn to pretend. Or is that too difficult for one to whom fate has been so unutterably cruel?"

At the sound of his mocking voice, fury flamed in her eyes, burned in her throat. "From anyone other than you, Easterby, I'd consider that insensitive comment worth a challenge."

He sauntered forward, azure eyes glittering mischievously. "Good. We're making progress. At least you've admitted that I, too, have endured my share of tragedy. But I do not go about beating my breast. I have fun. I highly recommend it."

"Fun?" she said, as if the word were a drop of poison upon her tongue.

"Aye, fun. You've heard of it, I'm sure."

Tess felt the first traitorous tug of a smile at the corners of her mouth. "Aye, I've heard tell."

"Do you know how to have fun? Doubtless not."

He was but inches away from her, taunting her, breathing down her neck, tempting her, daring her.

"Let me show you how 'tis done."

"You arrogant rogue," Tess returned, arms akimbo. "Did it ever occur to you that I am just as capable of having fun as you, but that I have more important things to do and choose to do them because I am responsible and you are not?"

"Prove it," he said, arching one brow above playful blue eyes.

Tess felt a slow, wicked smile creep up her cheeks. "You want a merry lass? Merry, indeed."

She stiffened her spine. By God, she would prove she could have fun, even if it killed him.

EIGHT

"How shall we begin?" Richard gallantly queried.

"With ordinary circumstances," Tess replied. "No ale, nor traveling minstrel shows, nor spontaneous feasts. The greatest pleasures are the simplest ones, are they not?"

"The greatest pleasures were invented in the Garden of Eden. But that is beside the point. Let us survey the castle. I have never given you the grand tour. That should be simple enough, methinks."

With the adventuresome spirit of a boy, Richard grasped her hand and tugged her along. Tess had little choice but to follow, and a little under an hour later—after touring the ale and bread houses, the garrisons, the beehives and dovecote, and the chapel—she had a greater understanding of the workings of his magnificent castle. She couldn't help but notice an extraordinary amount of waste and inefficiency, but she resisted pointing it out, since that was contrary to her mission—to have fun. She resisted, that is, until they came upon his mother's solar, which no one had slept in since her death fifteen years ago.

"My lord," Tess said, pointing to the far corner of the solar. "Who are those women stitching that enormous tapestry?"

"Those are my mother's ladies-in-waiting," he whispered,

regarding three matronly women with obvious affection. "Margaret is the plump one, Edith is the stern one, and Rose is the sweet one."

Hearing their names, the women looked up from their work. "Good morrow, Richard. Richard! Hello, dear boy," they muttered nearly in unison.

"Good morrow, ladies," Richard replied, and continued onward, gripping Tess's elbow, guiding her.

"You've kept them on all these years?" Tess persisted. "They are ladies-in-waiting with no lady."

"Until now," he amended.

"Richard!" she burst out at last, halting next to a fluttering torch in a narrow hallway. "Thus far I have been good-natured, as you requested, but I must tell that this is a lamentable waste of money. No wonder you are destitute."

"They've been stitching the greatest tapestry ever created, in honor of my parents," he said. "Greater even than the Bayeux Tapestry. How could I turn them out? You cannot put a price on loyalty and honor, Tess."

"*You* can't," she persisted logically, "but the merchants you owe money to can. And look at that page."

She gaped accusingly at a boy who jostled by carrying a suit of armor. He bore a short tunic covered with an open-sided tabard trimmed in fur. His white stockings were embroidered with gold thread.

"He dresses as finely as a page who waits on the king. Is there not a simpler tunic he can wear to save you the cost of his fine livery?"

"How can I myself dress in the finest if I am too miserly to properly outfit my pages and squires? Tess, Tess, Tess," Richard said, placing his hands on her arms. His fingers branded her skin like hot coals. She wanted him to pull her into an embrace, but he was apparently intent on a reprimand.

"You are failing miserably at the task at hand. You are not having fun. You cannot judge and complain at every turn."

"I have not judged and complained at every turn," she answered indignantly.

"I've got it," he said, snapping his fingers. "We will practice lighthearted conversation."

He tucked her arm in his and continued their stroll through the corridors. "I will begin. Now I want you to respond appropriately and courteously to whatever I say. Do you think you can manage?"

"I'll try."

"Very well. Hmmm. Now how shall I begin?" He cleared his throat. "Tess, this morning my falcon caught two hares and a quail. Now what do you say?"

"*My* falcon snagged three hares and four quail," she answered petulantly.

"Nay, nay. That won't do at all. Try again."

Tess swallowed, determined to quell her stubborn nature. "I say, Oh, my lord, how impressive!"

"Good! Very good!" he nearly shouted, patting her hand, which was tucked in the crook of his arm.

Tess flushed with pleasure. She had pleased him. And yet her conscience still nagged.

"Richard," she argued, staring up at his handsome profile, "if I say things I do not mean, then you cannot believe me. Not even when I truly mean to flatter you."

"Hmmmmm." He pursed his lips, considering this, and looked down at her with genuine affection. "You're right, Tess. I think 'tis your willingness to be honest I like most about you. Well, I suppose that means you should continue to insult me. Do you think you can manage?"

Her eyes locked with his, and she felt like she was gazing at an old and dear friend. He was a good man. Richard Avery had done wrong, but he was a good man.

"I think I can manage," she answered. *Resisting you,* she added inwardly, *will be another matter altogether.*

When they finally ended their tour in the bailey, dusk was beginning to fall like an old gray soldier in the twilight of his career, and with it fell the sun's promise of spring. A bittersweet and wintry melancholy scattered about them, a thoughtful appreciation of the cold that's possible only when one knows beyond doubt that a crackling fire awaits inside.

Tess felt so comfortable with Richard that she said, almost as an afterthought, "Who is the madman who shrieks every night?"

"The madman?" Richard inquired.

"Aye, the one who keeps me awake at night. His screeches are unbearable. I can only assume he is a mad relative you do not wish others to see."

A light of recognition brightened his countenance, and a slow grin spread across Richard's cheeks. "Lady Tess, what you heard was not a madman at all. 'Twas nothing more than the lamentations of Baron Philmore. We're not related, though some say there is a striking resemblance between us."

Tess crossed her arms. "Well, if he is not insane, the poor fellow must be miserable."

"Oh, he's quite sane," Richard replied. "Most definitely sane. But he's a veritable beast in the presence of ladies. My steward begs me continually to throw Philmore out. But I feel responsible for him. I saved him from an unknown fate when traveling home from a pilgrimage years ago. Come, I'll introduce you. He has a soft spot for the ladies. Perhaps under your influence he won't carry on so through all hours of the night."

Since the proposal was presented as an act of charity, Tess could not refuse, even though his answer aroused vague suspicion. She followed Richard to the second story of the castle's private quarters.

"Philmore!" Richard called out when they reached a chamber door at the end of the corridor. Standing tall in the narrow, dark hallway, he banged on the door and swung it open.

Tess entered first, stepping into a faint haze of incense. She blinked against the heady cloud, and found a man in a turban sitting on a pillow. His legs were crossed. She could tell by his smooth olive skin that he was a Persian. He wore a beige silk gown that hung in loose folds around his slight figure. Clearly, he had been praying, or meditating as it would be called in his country. He looked up slowly and pierced her with intense obsidian eyes. There wasn't a wrinkle on his face, though the depth in his eyes bespoke a wisdom that comes with age, and perhaps some wile as well. Though he smiled, there was no genuine warmth in the gesture. Tess had the uncanny sense that with a look he had discerned everything about her, including her purpose here at Cadmon Castle. Swallowing thickly, she refused to avert her eyes. He couldn't possibly know what was in her heart. She had no need to hide.

"Lady Tess Farnsworth," he said in a clipped accent.

"Baron Philmore?" she replied.

"Nay." He jumped up gracefully from his collection of silk pillows. Stopping a few steps away from her, he bowed briskly. "My name is Tarjaman. Baron Philmore is at the window, taking his evening meal."

Tess turned toward the light. There, in the embrasure, sat a monkey. She recognized it instantly, for she'd seen one with a wandering minstrel as a child.

"Baron Philmore?" she said incredulously to no one in particular, but the monkey answered nevertheless. He cocked his little head, bared his teeth, and screeched in the same voice that had kept her awake half the night for the last week.

"Your lunatic," Richard said, mirth ringing in his voice. He shook with silent laughter until the sound burst forth like a cannon. Booming laughter. It took up the whole room, just like his presence. And soon Tess was laughing out loud as well, nearly hysterically, as the tension from the past week gushed forth in welcome relief. Remembering her somber concern over the "madman," Tess doubled over with laughter and clutched Richard's arm for support.

When at last they regained control, Richard wiped tears from his eyes and scooped the monkey from the hands of Tarjaman, who had been petting the tame creature. The monkey scrambled to Richard's shoulder, then touched his cheek to the earl's.

"What say you? Do you think we resemble each other, as some have suggested?"

"Nay, except perhaps in your shared sense of mischief," she replied. "Oh, Richard, he's wonderful!"

"So you're not as practical and serious as you would like me to think."

"I do appreciate a sense of the absurd now and then. And owning a monkey is absurd."

"Is it?" he mused, crossing his muscular forearms. "Well, then, Lady Tess, I have something else to show you. Come along."

Richard grabbed her hand. "If you think Baron Philmore is exotic, wait until you see Belle."

She surrendered to his infectious grin and found herself being tugged down the hallway, then up a winding tower stairwell. Richard bounded along enthusiastically, shouting orders to a string of servitors who fluttered in his wake. He either did not notice or did not care that Tess's legs were restricted by her long gown. He expected her to keep pace with his wide, manly strides, and she desperately wanted to. Saints, did she really care what he thought of her? Though it was wrong and bad and faithless of her, she wanted to share this moment with him. It was a moment completely unique to her. She felt lighter than she ever had before. A stone lighter—skipping, breathless. Freedom blew through her soul like a shrieking, rebellious falcon, and she began to laugh.

Catching her sudden glee, Richard bellowed a laugh as he threw open the door to the battlements. "I am lord of my domain, and let no one doubt it!" he roared into the whipping wind, helping her from the dark stairwell into the golden light of the waning sun.

"I pray you, my lord, let me catch my breath. I am not as sturdy as you. I spend my days at the loom and ledgers, not at the quintain. Go slowly."

"Never slowly, Tess. Life is too brief an affair for that." He cupped one of her cheeks in his hand. "But until you catch your wind, I'll carry you."

Gently pulling his hand away, she chuckled softly at his jest, but then realized he was serious. Shaking her head, terror flitting across her flushed face, she backed away. "Forsooth, my lord, you cannot. 'Tis unseemly."

He scooped her into his arms. "'Tis only unseemly if we're seen. There is no one here on the battlements but a few sentinels, and they're busy looking for enemies on the horizon. Now quit squirming, lest I drop you over the curtain's edge."

They stood forty feet above the ground on the eight-foot-wide wall-walk, a path that topped the curtain wall encircling the entire castle. The only barrier to keep them from blowing over the edge of the battlements was a jagged, waist-high parapet.

Imprisoned in Richard's arms, Tess managed a glimpse over the edge, and her stomach rocked at the thought of plummeting from this dizzying height. She clutched his back and neck, clinging for safety, or so she told herself. Truth to tell, she enjoyed being in his arms and sank a little farther into them with a sigh. Allowing her cheek to mold against his shoulder, her chest ached, for she realized how long she'd been without comfort. It was a pleasure that brought sadness she could neither explain nor expel, and her lack of understanding made the pain that much more acute.

Richard paced to the far edge of the wall-walk in silence. "Here you will get the best view," he said, halting before a breathtaking stretch of farmland and heather.

She self-consciously pulled away from his shoulder. Lord, couldn't she at least pretend to resist his allure?

"Let me down," she managed to sputter, ashamed to realize how wanton her successful attempt to have fun had made her. She pushed against his chest until he lowered her feet to the stone pathway. Tess's legs buckled, and she reached out to steady herself, gripping his granite forearms. Oh, how she longed to collapse into that strength, to bury herself in it, to wrap his grace and raw power around her like a dazzling cloak.

"Look down there." He pointed to a field beyond the moat.

She followed his line of vision and gasped. "An elephant!"

"By the gods, you knew instantly. Good girl! The elephant's name is Belle. And if I had asked anyone else what Belle was when she first arrived, they would have said she was a dragon."

Tess pulled her incredulous gaze from the elephant and frowned at Richard in disbelief. "Who would mistake an elephant for a mythical creature?"

"Elsbeth, for one," he answered dryly.

"Elsbeth?"

"Hmmm. Never mind. You have enough names to remember already."

"Perhaps Elsbeth did not have the advantage of an education. I recognized the creature because I've seen drawings in books at a convent near Haddington Castle. But I never imagined elephants were so big. And see how she collects the hay into her mouth with her trunk. 'Tis a marvel."

Yearning to reach out and pet the enormous creature, Tess clutched the rough edges of the stone crenellation and watched with the wide eyes of a child as Tarjaman led the gray elephant around an earthen path that encircled the huge barn.

"Belle arrived a month ago. She's the latest addition to my menagerie. Tarjaman is teaching her to fight on the battlefield. Nothing struck more fear into the hearts of the Crusaders in Persia than their first encounters with charging elephants wielding spears with their trunks. If we can somehow manage to train this one and ship her to France, she might be of use to the king."

"How intriguing. What other animals do you have?"

"A camel, a leopard, and of course Baron Philmore."

"May I see them? Not now, of course. But sometime. When you have time."

"Aye, that would be fun, wouldn't it?"

She dashed a sly grin his way. "I'll never admit it."

The elephant let out a bellowing snort that seemed to shake the very stones of the battlements. "Where did they come from?"

"Belle was a gift to the king brought over from India when she was young. When Henry realized how much it cost to feed a grown elephant, he gave her to me. He must have assumed I could afford such an extravagance now that we are to be married. Baron Philmore and the leopard I found three years ago, half starved at Calais, abandoned by a French nobleman who had lured Tarjaman to France with promises of incredible wealth. When I met him, Tarjaman had sold everything but the clothes on his back to feed his animals. I couldn't let these magnificent creatures die in a dirty port stall in a foreign land, now could I?"

When Tess turned to him with a gaze of reluctant admiration, he waved her off, scowling good-naturedly down below. "Tarjaman is like a minstrel, always turning a wise phrase when you least expect it. Now if I could just figure him out . . ."

Tess envisioned the Persian's unsettling black eyes. "My lord, if you do not trust him . . ."

"'Tis not so much a lack of trust. He's an enigma. I suppose that's why I keep him around. When you're as brilliant at figuring out the essence of human nature as I am, Tess, life can be a frightful bore." He gave her a wry smile. An I-know-you-know-I'm-frightfully-arrogant grin.

Clarions pierced the sky suddenly and the men-at-arms dotting the battlements jumped to attention. Richard squinted into the distance and tensed, for in the lingering orange glow of the setting sun, the silhouette of a traveling party had appeared.

A sentinel came running up. Moments later, Perkins, out of breath, his face stricken, dashed to their sides as well.

"My lord," the sentinel said after making a deep bow. "The porter bids me ask you should he lower the drawbridge. 'Tis Bishop George Throwly of Kirkingham."

Richard nodded tersely. "Let him in." The sentinel dashed off. "Perkins, escort Lady Tess to her chamber."

Without so much as a "Godspeed," Richard strode toward the tower stairs.

"My lord," Tess called out, more in disbelief over his sudden change of humor than in anger. "Where are you going?"

Without looking back, he shouted grimly over his shoulder. "To greet my enemy."

His flapping cloak billowed around his broad shoulders as he descended the tower stairs and disappeared, taking with him her gleeful mood. Her fun. Leaving her feeling oddly vulnerable.

NINE

Tess dashed into the bailey. When she saw the pained figure dangling from the gallows, she came to a skittering stop. The taste of bile prickled on her tongue. Her gaze slowly rose upward. The body circled around and around, twisting in the wind. She did not know the Lollard, but felt sick for him nevertheless. Nay, it was not a man. It was a woman! Her long hair fluttered in the breeze. Then Tess heard a crackling sound. In terror, her gaze fell to the kindling. Flames licked the dry wood, fluttering in the cold breeze, but not succumbing to it. Rather, the wind fanned the flames. The Lollard started to scream in pain. Two men stood before the fire. One wore a turban. He turned to Tess and grinned maliciously. It was Tarjaman! The other man wore a black hooded cloak, his face swallowed in darkness. He poured a bucket of resin on the fire, and the flames roared out of control. Tess squinted against the blistering heat. She pulled a gunne from the folds of her cloak and took aim at the executioner's back, trying to still her shaking hand. Her finger went to the trigger. But then the cloaked figure turned. Demonic eyes flared at her. Handsome cheeks rose with cruel glee. RICHARD! She screamed. A long inhuman screech of madness.

* * *

"Richard!" Tess bolted upright in her feather bed. Her heart clanged riotously against her ribs. When the blanket fell away from her naked breasts, the sweat drenching her body curdled on her skin with a chill. She shivered and looked around the chamber in confusion. Where was she? she wondered, until she heard the familiar screech again.

Baron Philmore. She was at Cadmon Castle. Her hand-maiden was sleeping on a pallet on the floor by her bed.

"Mellie, Mellie, wake up."

"Hmmmmm?" the handmaiden moaned. She turned over on her mattress of stuffed straw, but her eyes did not open.

"Mellie, I think I'm going to strangle that precocious monkey if he does not keep quiet. I . . . I dreamt he was a Lollard heretic, enchained somewhere in Lord Richard's castle."

"Hmmm . . . oh," the sleeping maid replied, a dreamer's smile alighting on her placid face.

"I can't shake this dreadful, gnawing feeling, Mellie. What did the nightmare portend? Was it a warning? I felt uneasy about Tarjaman when I met him. Now I wonder about him all the more. I must ask Richard more about him, for I do not trust him a whit!"

Tess sank back into bed and pulled the covers to her chin, content in the feeling that more knowledge about the sinister Tarjaman would allay her fears. But when she forced her eyes closed, it was Richard's face, so demonic in her dream, that flooded her vision, not Tarjaman's.

"Oh, Mellie, I am disturbed to the core that Richard was so . . . so evil," she whispered into the darkness. "I suppose 'twas just the reminder I needed after having such a delightful day with him. After having *fun*."

Wide awake now, she propped herself up on one elbow and

fought against the shadows creeping along the floor to see her handmaiden's face. "Mellie! Mellie, are you asleep?"

"Hmmmm."

"Mellie, I've been thinking. This idea of revenge seems so absolute. If Lord Richard has broken ranks with King Henry, even if only in spirit, then I need not hate him for my father's death. Don't you think? Perhaps he is just a victim of circumstance, guilty only by association with the ruthless monarch, but himself noble in heart. Mellie, how else can you explain a man with so much perception and grace and compassion in his position? When he held me in his arms atop the battlements, I felt . . . I felt a sense of peace and comfort like never before. 'Twas as if he knew me better than I knew myself."

Goose bumps rippled on her arms and legs, and she began to shake in earnest. "Oh, Mellie, Mellie, I do not want to kill him. I . . . I want to make love to him."

She waited for a reproach, but none came, neither from Mellie nor from her relentless conscience. "I say that and expect the world to crumble about me, but it didn't. I swear, Mellie, I've never thought of a man in such an intimate way before. I swear it. But I want *him*. I want to feel our skin melt together. I want . . . Oh, I don't even know what I want. I have no imagination." How could she want that which she had never even imagined before? "But does he want me in return? I mean truly *want* me?"

The question burned inside of her, igniting a sense of wild excitement. Throbbing at the very core of her being, she rocked back and forth, hugging herself, sore with regret, but powerless to stop her feelings.

"Oh, Richard," she whispered. "You are the devil in an angel's disguise."

She looked down at the still form stretched out on the pallet. "I still hate him, Mellie. Just because I desire him doesn't mean I don't hate him as well. He is a devil, tempting me. But before I spurn him as such, I'll enjoy just one more day in his company. After all, there are no Lollards burning in his bailey. That was just a nightmare. And he did not light the fire beneath Father. Just one day of pleasure. Is that too much to ask?"

Silence was her answer.

"Good night, Mellie," she said, laying back down in her now cold bed.

At daybreak, the castle yards were busier than usual as servants ran to and fro preparing for a feast in honor of Bishop George. His bevy of canons floated in a cluster through the bailey and hallways, tutting over this detail and that, looking collectively like a low-lying cloud in their billowing robes of white. They made it clear to all that the bishop's presence was a great honor, and that perfection in everything, from service at meals to the consistency of the venison en frumenty, was of utmost importance.

Tess, feeling a little irritable for lack of sleep, watched the entourage in wonder. The bishop's presence gave her an eerie feeling. Why had he come? Why had Richard allowed the entrance of his mortal enemy? Did he not have the courage to make his enmity known to the man who had stolen his precious land?

She knew she would get no answers directly, so she observed the guests from a distance, avoiding close contact. When Perkins announced that the earl wanted to ride alone with her, she welcomed the chance to flee the tension hovering over the castle, though she knew riding with Richard would be far more dangerous. Dangerous because she could not guess where her fancies of desire would end. Dangerous because the haunting images from her nightmare still clung to the sticky cobwebs of her mind.

Still, she readily followed Perkins through a back corridor that led to the stable.

Perkins threw open the door of the dark passageway to the brilliance of the clear morning sky. Tess blinked and shielded her eyes from a sun that seemed as relentlessly cheerful as she knew Richard would be. Throwing the hood of her cloak over her head, she braced herself against the nip of the air and strode toward him as he tightened a leather strap around the girth of a chestnut palfrey. When he looked up, she slowed her approach, stunned anew by his beauty. And when he smiled without guile—in fact, seemingly with pure affection—his bright teeth flashing, his dimples deepening, her traitorous legs wobbled beneath her and she halted. Lord, he was beautiful. She could see naught but that. No wickedness, no sinfulness, just beauty, and for the first time since her arrival, she considered running away as fast as she could. But it was beyond her power. In truth, there was nothing she wanted more than to simply be in his presence.

"Come, maiden, do not play coy with me," he said teasingly, holding out a hand. When she stubbornly resisted, he thrust forward his open hand a second time in gentle encouragement. "Come hither, Tess. I dreamt of you last night."

She forced her gaze from the safe anchor of his boots to the infinitely more dangerous territory of his eyes, searching them suspiciously. "You dreamt of me? Why, I dreamt of you as well."

"Was yours a good dream, Tess?"

"Nay, 'twas not."

He drew his brows together. "I'm crestfallen. 'Tis a pity. I had such a sweet dream about you. We were dancing."

He tugged on a stirrup, making the final adjustments with the easy confidence with which he handled every other minute detail of life.

"Dancing, my lord? That is odd, as how I would dread to take even a step."

"Seemed perfectly natural in my dream. You were utterly enchanting and as docile as a lamb."

"Then it *had* to be a dream."

His gaze shot to hers, and he smiled gently at her sardonic humor. "You were the picture of grace."

"How could you possibly dream something so contrary to the truth?"

It must be that inner vision of his, she thought, strolling closer, feeling the magic of his spell, his illusions. "Where were we dancing? In the great hall?"

"Nay, on the moors somewhere. In a field of heather."

Tess gave a tiny gasp.

Richard looked up. "What is it, Tess? What is wrong?"

"Where . . . who told you that? About the heather?"

He shrugged. "'Twas just a dream. Why? What is it?"

She licked her lips and shook her head distractedly, casting aside visions of purple heather. She was losing her sanity. How could he have known? She had told no one. "Nay, 'tis nothing. I do not know why I . . . it just reminded me of something."

He gave her a long glinting stare, his arms akimbo. "When are you going to let down your guard and trust me enough to speak the truth? I've upset you and I want to know why."

"You are the last person who should lecture me about trusting others, my lord, and do not flatter yourself to think you have the power to upset me at every turn."

When a stable hand trotted toward her with a foot-mantle bundled in his arms, she accepted it with a nod of thanks and breezed past Richard, but he stopped her, not ungently, with a tug on her sleeve.

"I'll find out, you know," he whispered seductively, his breath tickling her ear. "I'll find out what upset you. And I'll find out about your secrets. I'll uncover your hidden desires. I'll learn how to caress you just so, until you quiver in my hands like a butterfly. I'll do whatever it takes to make you call my name deep in your throat, panting the word like some jungle beast. I will do these things, because I can."

The horse nickered, his lips quivering with a snort.

"My lord," she said, clearing the astonishment that had congealed in a large lump in her throat. "Your horse grows impatient. Shall we mount?"

God, how stupid! she railed inwardly. *"Shall we mount!" Did I actually say that?* She dared not look into his eyes to see his reaction. "Rather, shall we begin our ride?"

"Did you hear me?"

"I shall pretend that I didn't."

"As you please. But these things shall come to pass. This I promise you."

He hoisted himself into his saddle, and with an incredible show of strength, pulled her up onto a pillion behind his saddle. She had no choice but to clutch his muscular back to steady herself. It felt wonderful. And terrifying. *What have you done to me, Richard Avery?* she thought, lost and confused and thrilled. *What have you done to me?*

"Will I return from this ride with my maidenhood intact?" she queried in a high-pitched voice, trying to sound calm.

Richard barked out a laugh. "Oh, how I love your frankness, Tess. Do you know that?" He beamed a delighted smile over his shoulder as he nudged his horse into a rocking walk. "If you want to put me off, then act coy and wilting like so many other women who aim to please. I've had my fill of them. But you! I can't seem to get enough of your vitriol and condemnations and rancor. 'Tis the sweetest elixir."

"Fortune smiles upon you, then, for I've plenty of rancor in store."

He chuckled again. "I see my lesson on polite banter was wasted. Ah, well, 'tis for the best."

Tess said nothing, but wondered again at how comfortable she felt in Richard's presence. She knew she could talk to him about anything. That in itself seemed like the most precious gift anyone had ever given to her.

"I had a terrible nightmare about you and Tarjaman," she ventured, and frowned as the black and terrible images from her dream blotted out the beauty of the passing hillsides. "He seemed so . . . blithely malicious. What do you know of this man? I do not trust him at all."

"What do you mean?"

"Where is he from? What do you know of his family?"

"He is a direct descendant of Rukn ad-Din Khurshah of Persia. One of the grand masters of the *Hashshashin*."

"The *Hashshashin*?" Tess replied, more alarmed than ever.

"You know of their history?"

"You forget that my father spent a lifetime studying different religions and philosophies, which he would expound upon in my presence."

"Then you likely know more than I."

"Well, according to Father, the *Hashshashins,* or the Assassins as they became known in English, were a sect of the Shiite Muslims. They claimed the right to murder anyone whom they considered an enemy of Allah."

Tess scoured her memory. And the more she remembered, the more reason she found to mistrust Tarjaman.

"Father said according to legend the leader of the Assassins sect had a private garden in the city of Alamut. In the middle of the desert, this garden was filled with water fountains and lush flowers and some of the most beautiful young women in the land. Young members of the sect were given so much hashish that they would pass out and awaken in this garden, where the women would fulfill their every desire. When the young men returned to the outside world, recovered from their hashish euphoria, they were told that they had glimpsed the rewards given to martyrs in Heaven who die for their faith. And so the young men, bent on killing the enemies of Allah, eagerly sought out suicide missions, willing to lose their lives in order to return to the garden."

"Your father was very knowledgeable," Richard said when she fell silent.

"He knew enough not to house an Assassin."

"You needn't fear Tarjaman. The Assassin sect was wiped out more than a hundred fifty years ago by the son of Genghis Khan. Tarjaman is a Suni Muslim."

"Richard, the Assassins pretended to be many things they were not in order to gain the trust of others."

"What is it, Tess?" he said, looking over his shoulder. His long locks flew softly across her face. "Why are you so concerned?"

She shook her head. "I do not know. 'Tis just a feeling. Has Tarjaman . . . has he said anything to you about me?"

"Nay. What would he say?"

That I've come to murder you, she almost whispered. But did Tarjaman really know this? Or had guilt just induced her to imagine it?

"Nothing. He would say nothing, I'm sure."

"I cannot argue with your history, Tess. But there comes a time when a man must judge another on instinct. I have always believed that Tarjaman was trustworthy, mayhap because he is kind to animals. Time may prove me wrong, but until then, I still cling to my assessment: Tarjaman is to be trusted. But enough of weighty topics. Let us enjoy our ride, for when we return, we must deal with the bishop. For once, we will forget the woes of the world and enjoy what nature has given us. *N'est-ce pas?* We shall have fun."

"Oh, joy," she rejoined.

He laughed and spurred his horse into a canter, forcing Tess to wrap her arms more tightly around his waist, and soon she was having fun, in spite of herself.

They continued at an exhilarating pace through farmlands owned for hundreds of years by Richard's forebears, and then past the stone fence that bordered Marly Vale. Beyond the vale, they rode to the top of a sloping hill, where high mist and low clouds joined in a mystical union. Richard reined in with a tug, fighting their mount's impulse to fly, for a horse could fall lame stumbling on the stones that dotted the empty hillcrest. The rocks were all that remained of a hill-fort dating back to the Saxons. Richard pointed out to Tess a circle of darkened soil where a wooden palisade had once protected a simple donjon, later replaced by a stone keep, both of which had crumbled under the ravages of time and nature. Now all that remained was a misty hilltop, where wind whistled in the tongues of ancients, divulging mysteries no longer understood by civilized man.

The site never failed to transport Richard into another time. Thoughts of the haunting past raised goose bumps on his muscular arms. He inhaled the moisture that hung in gray wisps of air. He held the horse steady, feeling his heart lunge in a steady rhythm, feeling the burning embrace of his beautiful lady, and soon a profound quiet descended, marred only when he cocked his head to catch the distant cry of a peregrine. The motion wrung a groan from his leather saddle.

Suddenly, he felt an ache in his cheeks from smiling too much. He did not have to feign joy with Tess; he felt it in his heart. Perhaps he could at last let down his guard.

"Tess, if a man lowers his shield during a joust *à outrance*, 'tis often a fatal mistake. Is it not so with love?"

A monumental silence followed.

"I would not know," she replied at last.

"But you could know if you wanted to. So could I."

Again, silence. Wanting to hear something, anything, he nudged their mount into an easy walk and soon heard the *swish-swish* of hooves through heath bramble. Tess leaned her head against his back. The gesture electrified him, filled him with longing and gratitude. He wanted so badly to turn around and embrace her. But he wouldn't. Not yet.

He wondered what it was about Tess that affected him so profoundly. He was grateful that she seemed at peace with him in this place of nature. They needed no words to share this moment. The truest affection, he mused, required no proclamations. Just the setting down of armor.

In companionable silence, they traveled on at a gentle pace until they reached a vast moor. The heath stretched as far as the eye could see. It was lonely and haunting, a pastel spray of purple, green, and brown. Such beauty! Richard took in the sight of undulating heath rushes, brambles, and heather with a contented sigh.

"There have been many times I've walked alone on this moor with no company save that of a falcon. I never thought I'd want to walk with anyone here. Until now. I sensed you might love it as much as I."

Proffering his arm, he helped her slide over the horse's haunches, then jumped to the cushiony earth himself with the clink of his rowel spurs. Tugging her with one hand and his horse's reins with the other, he strode enthusiastically into the endless heath, as if into a future unknown, bravely, his hawkish nose flaring in the face of a sharp wind. He spoke not a word, for it seemed a sacrilege to disturb the perfection of nature's chorus. Wild peregrines soared above, emitting shrill caws that echoed hauntingly across the sky. Moorfowl chimed in. A herd of wild ponies rambled across the moor in the distance, hooves rumbling over the earth. The wind whispered, beating their cheeks, whirling and moaning, laughing even.

When they stepped onto a patch of barren earth amidst a circular cluster of pink heather, he turned to her, exhilarated.

"Dance with me, Tess. Then my dream will have come true." He dropped her hand and the reins and held out his arms. "Humor a romantic rogue. 'Tis in your power."

The corners of her mouth curled up sweetly, but then she shook her head, casting off a million unspoken thoughts.

"Nay, I cannot."

"Why not?"

She hugged herself and tilted her head sideways, her hazel eyes turning to a liquid gold of churning emotions. "Did you know about my dreams?"

He shook his head.

"I have always dreamt of dancing in heather." Her sad, sweet smile was unutterably beautiful. "Why someone who cannot dance at all would want to dance in heather is beyond my reckoning, but I have dreamt of that all my life."

Richard frowned in amazement. How could he have known? How could he have dreamt her dream? But he had. And suddenly he felt as if he had been here before. As if he had had this conversation in some distant past of his. As if he and Tess had met before.

"So you have dreamt of dancing with a man in heather?" She nodded.

He looked down at the clusters of pinkish red flowers sitting so heartily against their dark green leaves. They were excruciatingly lovely. It was as if being in Tess's presence stripped the veil of cynicism from his eyes. "I can understand completely. What else blooms year-round? What else has the tenacity to brave frost and snow and sleet?"

His assessment won a smile from her, and it seemed a payment vastly superior to any other he could have contrived. He suddenly wanted her to feel like the most beautiful and extraordinary woman in the world.

"Who was it? Who did you dance with?" He put his hands on her shoulders, but she tugged free, turning away with a petulant pucker of her lips.

"Not you, Richard. Do not flatter yourself that I would dream of spending even a moment in your arms." Her words were harsh, but her voice was breathy, unconvincing. "'Twas just a fantasy, you see. A simple way to touch another human being without succumbing to passion and . . . and risking all in a birthing bed. A silly dream. Dreaming is for those who live to have fun. That has never been what my life was about."

"That is *all* my life has ever been about. What sad creatures we are. You've not had enough pleasure, and I too much."

"We are different. Too different."

"Nay, do not say that," he urged her, feeling the sun melting on his shoulders as his bright, secret dreams turned to darkness. "Do not condemn us so."

"Richard, there is no hope—"

"Shhh. Do not say it. Do you want to be loved?" He gripped her arms, inhaled the lemon wafting from her skin, watched her pink nostrils flare as she bit her lip and shook her head, battling private demons. And then she surprised him.

"Aye. Yes, damn it. I do want to be loved. Always have. Is that what you want to hear?"

"Is it the truth?"

Two huge teardrops poured from the ducts in her eyes, coursing a wet path down her flushed cheeks. She nodded, all pretense gone. "Aye, 'tis the truth."

Oh, blessed, blessed lady, Richard thought. *Oh, blessed God. To give me such a wife! I am not deserving.*

She wiped the tears and frowned at him, curiously, accusingly. "What is it about you that makes me confess that which I would not even admit to my confessor?"

He smiled, for they had begun: the secrets that he had

promised to pry from her. But he would not remind her of his gloating prediction. Some women bandied about their secrets and hopes like jewels to be admired and traded and stolen. But not Tess. He was struck with the profound responsibility knowing her—truly knowing her—would be.

She shivered and hugged herself. "I am growing cold. Let us return to the castle. There is so much to be done. I should check your ledgers to make sure your steward has been spending wisely. I must have seen a torch every ten paces in your corridors. I heard the chandler say you've burned thirteen hundred tapers in a night. That's nearly a hundred-weight of wax and tallow. What an excess! A little darkness will hurt no one going from one chamber to—"

"Hush," he said, pulling her close, fairly lifting her off her toes. The wind surged and blew his long locks across his face, blinding him.

She reached up and brushed back the strands, her fingers trailing his sculpted cheeks like hot honey on his skin. Gods, he wanted to possess this woman. To fill her. To feel her. He brushed his lips across her forehead, and when skin met skin, he heard an exquisite chord, as if troubadours had appeared suddenly from nowhere. Surely it was his imagination. But the sound had been so clear. Was it the song of his soul? he wondered. And did Tess hear music as well? Or was his mind simply addled beyond repair?

"Do you hear it?" he whispered.

"Do I hear what?"

"A song. Voices. When I kissed you."

"I heard nothing," she hoarsely replied.

He opened his eyes and studied her mask of confusion. He did not believe her. She had to have heard it. Was he alone in his madness? Would he be alone evermore? Was that his awful fate? To be given an extraordinary wife who could not understand his peculiarities?

"Listen!" he ordered her, and brushed his lips against her forehead again.

"To what?"

"Music. On the wind. In the mind. Somewhere. Just listen."

"I hear nothing, for I have little imagination."

"I do not believe that," he argued, shaking her, cutting through her doubt with the force of his conviction. "I will not hear you say that."

"'Tis true!" she returned angrily. "I barely have enough imagination to believe in God, let alone a heretic's God. Why do you think I did not follow in my father's footsteps? Not because I didn't have the courage to be a heretic, but because I didn't have the faith, and faith is nothing more than imagination with conviction."

"I will not allow you to underestimate your own magic, Tess. Gods, how I weary of those who do not realize their own goodness."

He was not a good man. Knowing the choices he faced, knowing the choice he would make—a choice that would hurt Tess more than he already had—he knew he was not a good man.

But she was good. She was the test of mankind. If a woman as good as Tess did not see her worth, what hope was there for heathens like him?

"I am not like you, Richard. I don't imagine I hear music. I don't imagine anything. I cannot go about dancing and laughing my life away. I am not . . . I don't deserve that."

Her words were fast and furious, her lovely face contorted with anguish he had not even begun to imagine she suffered. He stroked her cheek gently.

"Tess, you deserve nothing but joy and love and happiness. How can you think otherwise?"

"Because I killed someone. Don't you see? I killed my

mother. I am alive because she died for me. And what have I done to justify that? Nothing. So do not waste my time talking about music and dancing. I am who I am, Richard. You cannot change me. You can force me to marry you. You can use my father's money as you please. But you can't change me. I am who I am."

"Nay, you are not. You are not yet who you were meant to be. Neither am I."

He clutched her head between the palms of his hands, wanting to shake some sense into her, but careful not to cover her ears. His lips were inches from hers, and he inhaled her sweet breath. The simple warmth of her breath filled him more completely than the moist depths of any other woman ever had.

He kissed her, and the music came again. His lips lingered while he listened. She did not struggle. She returned the kiss sweetly. And at last the mystery was solved. He withdrew and smiled.

"I am not going mad after all," he said, brushing a thumb over her moist lips. "The song I heard was from my memory. From my childhood. Somehow being with you reminded me of that gentle time."

He began to hum. Dum, da, da, da dum. Her eyes crinkled with recognition and delight. And then her voice joined his.

"You know it!" he shouted with delight.

"My father used to sing that melody to me when I was young," she replied.

"Sing some more," he demanded.

She tossed her head back and her voice swelled on the wind, lovely and clear as a bird's. Tenderness sprang furtively from her eyes like daffodils in the leafy, hidden bed of a forest.

"Dance with me," he demanded.

Her sweet humming ceased. She frowned. "I do not know how. I told you that."

"You do not have to know how. Not with this music. Come, just follow me."

Letting the horse shy away in dumb amazement, he took her in his arms and skipped about the field. He sang their childhood song in a wild and boisterous tempo, and the melancholy of the tune faded, giving way to a celebration of life.

Submitting utterly to a sweet madness, Tess followed his lead as best she could, trying not to trip. Their free-form steps soon took on an exaggerated chaos until they were spinning in circles, holding each other's hands, laughing madly, the years falling away with abandon. When Tess finally stumbled back and landed with a thud on the ground, Richard fell on top of her, halting his weight at the last moment so as not to crush her. Out of breath and still laughing, they embraced.

She was warm and soft. Her essence oozed tenderly from every pore. She was like a delicate flower he wanted to cradle and protect. She could not have revealed herself more completely if she'd stripped before him. He'd never held such tenderness before. It was like coming home.

He kissed her hot forehead, her eyes, her gleeful mouth, her high cheeks, her reddened ears. She smelled of spring flowers and sunshine.

"Gods, how I want to make love to you, Tess."

She stiffened in his arms as if she'd turned to stone. Wariness throbbed in her hazel eyes and she shook her head. "Nay, for me 'twould be a death sentence."

"Nay . . ."

"I would get quick with your child and then die giving birth. I know I would. That is how my mother died. You do not understand what you ask. You do not understand."

She tried to twist out of his arms and he tightened his hold, nestling his nose in her silken hair, inhaling her freshness.

"Shhh," he murmured. Her anxiety tingled between them. He had thought little of the consequence of the lovemaking he so desired. But she was right. She could die as a result. He tried to imagine his arms empty of her. The thought of losing Tess made him want to steel his heart. But there was no going back. Not now. No way to erase the knowledge she possessed of him, and he of her.

He kissed her forehead again. "'Twould be callow of me to argue, Tess, since I am not the one who would have to risk my life. But more women survive that fate than not."

She twisted out from under him, and he let her go, the loss of her stripping away his extraordinary happiness. She sat up, brushing her lips with a backhand.

"Women who bear a dozen children give birth to children who have a dozen children in turn. My mother died. Therefore . . ."

"Your logic does not follow. If all women of one family were to die in childbirth, that family line would soon die out."

She hugged her knees to her chest in sullen silence.

He longed to console her, but did not have the words. What could he say? "I will protect you from death"? "I have the power of God"? Of course not. He did not even have the power to protect her from the pain that he knew lay ahead. He had wanted to make love to her now, for he knew she would soon hate him anew.

Casting aside his dark thoughts, he gently pulled her to a stand. "Come, maiden, I will settle for a dance in heather. At least for now."

Despite the somber change in Tess's mood, during the ride back to Cadmon Castle, Richard felt lighter than he had in years. *Why?* he wondered. Why, when their exchange had raised as many questions in his mind as it had answered?

Then he realized they'd left heavy burdens behind in that field of heather. Both of them. Shields.

When Tess and Richard returned to Cadmon Castle and drew up to the stable, Sir John's gusty laughter boomed out of the great hall and ricocheted against the curtain wall.

"That scallywag! He should be abed," Richard grumbled as he dismounted and helped Tess to the ground. "I shall see to it myself."

Tess stayed him with a hand on his elbow. "Sir John says he is feeling much better, my lord. Perhaps you should let him make merry. Celebrating is as much a part of him as your sword arm is a part of you."

"You're much too kind, Lady Tess," he said, touching her cheek fondly. "But fear not, I will be gentle with the old sot."

Just as Richard strode off toward the great hall, Perkins bounded to her side. "My lady, your handmaiden is quite distressed. You've left her all day with naught to do but stitch at the great tapestry. She says the old women are frightfully dull. I offered to take her on a visit to the village, but she says she needed your permission since you might want her to attend you upon your return."

Tess headed toward the inner bailey, with Perkins at her side. "Poor Mellie. Of course you may take her into the village. I will not need her services . . ."

Her words fell away when she spied three people being herded out of the prison tower. She could not see their faces clearly, but one was a woman who looked vaguely familiar. And the dark midnight blues of Tess's nightmare swam before her eyes. The people blinked up at the sunlight as if it were a miracle, and Tess knew instantly they were prisoners.

"What is it, my lady?" Perkins queried when she came to an abrupt stop and pressed a fist to her mouth.

"Who are they?" she whispered, anxiety quickening her heart.

"Prisoners, my lady."

"Aye, but what kind of prisoners?"

"Why, Lollards, my lady."

Tess shook her head against the tide of dread that washed over her. "Lollards. Are you certain? You are not mistaken?"

"Aye, my lady. I am quite certain. Peter Chapman, the tailor, recognized them a week ago at the village fair. Lord Richard had no choice but to have them arrested. They'd managed to escape the night the Lollards attacked Eltham and have been wanted ever since."

Tess shut her eyes and immediately saw the malicious grin of the Richard who'd haunted her nightmare. All the while she'd been dancing with him, these prisoners were suffering in his prison. She felt ill-used, and a pain stabbed at her heart. Her eyes fluttered open again, half lidded, heavy with bitter irony.

"Aye, why *wouldn't* Richard imprison my father's friends? There is political gain in it for him."

"'Tis the law, my lady. All Lollards must be brought to justice, by order of Parliament. And as Lord Richard is a Peer of the Realm—"

"As well as a king's man," she interjected acidly.

"—he can hardly ignore the law."

"Of course not," Tess said, her words seething through her constricted throat. "How long will they be here?"

"Not long. By law he has ten days to hand them over."

Tess quickly calculated. If they were captured a week ago, Richard had to relinquish them in three days. She had three days to set them free.

"I want to meet them," she said.

Perkins shook his head. "Nay, I cannot take you to the

prison tower. The gossips in the castle will be calling you a heretic."

"Aren't they already?" Tess challenged him. "Go tell the earl I wish to visit with the Lollards. Tell him they may have known my father and can tell me something about his last hours. Tell Lord Richard that and he will give his permission."

Or would he? Perhaps he was not as gentle a man as she had concluded. Clearly he wasn't. Anyone who kept Lollards in prison . . .

She would not think about Richard now. She would think of nothing else except meeting with the Lollards.

TEN

Perkins led Tess up winding stairs to the top floor of the prison tower, where the Lollards were kept in comfortable chambers. In years past, the tower had been temporary home to many a nobleman awaiting ransom, Richard's squire explained. And since Lord Richard was known for his hospitality, each prison room was comfortably furnished with a bed, a table, and chairs.

By the time Tess mounted the last stair, she was winded and anxious, knotting her hands together in dreaded anticipation. She almost wished Richard hadn't given her permission to come here. Who would she find behind these doors? If they were friends of her father's, her heart would break yet again over the king's savage injustice. Better that they were strangers.

"Who goes here?" a burly guard said. He folded hairy arms across his massive chest, blocking their way at the top of the stairs.

"Leave him to me, my lady," Perkins said sotto voce, and puffing out his chest, he turned to the guard. "On command of Lord Richard himself, my lord and sponsor, we have come to see your wards. There is a woman here. What chamber?"

The guard nodded toward the end of a short hall and

stepped aside. Perkins led the way, and when he lifted the latch on the door the guard had indicated, the clinking sound echoed in the rafters above.

"Perkins, let me go in alone," Tess said in a breathy voice. Who would she find inside? She knew many of the women who were Lollards. Often her father had entertained them along with their husbands at Haddington Castle.

Perkins swung open the door. "I will wait for you at the guard's station, my lady."

Tess thanked him and entered the prison chamber, but didn't immediately see the prisoner. Though a taper burned in a wall sconce, darkness still hovered in clusters, casting long shadows on a small square table and a high-backed chair padded with an embroidered lavender cushion.

Tess blinked against the darkness, and in a narrow shaft of light spilling from a high window, she at last found the woman she'd seen in the bailey. Her rounded shoulders were slumped in a simple but elegant forest-green gown. Her coarse gray hair fell in a tumble to the middle of her back. Her face was as worn as a map of Britain. Though weary, the woman was obviously proud. She reminded Tess of . . .

"Lady Gertrude?" Tess whispered.

The elderly woman looked up. Her thin lips parted and her gray eyes fluttered with recognition, then doubt. "Tess? Is that you?"

"Oh, Gertie!" Tess cried, and dashed across the room. The regal Baroness of Wakefield rose and pulled her into her arms. She was tall and big-boned and easily cushioned Tess against her ample, soft breasts.

Tess squeezed her father's confidante as if she were life itself. As if Lady Gertrude's presence would somehow bring Tess's father back to life. It was like embracing home again. And for the first time in a long while, memories of home came rushing back—long hours of carding wool as her father read from his books; leisurely walks in the herb garden with Roger; her cozy chamber where she mixed her flower waters, placing vials of lilacs, violets, and roses in the embrasure to stew in the sun. What sweet memories!

"Gertie, I did not know you were imprisoned. You are alive! Thank the saints above, you survived. You feel so good and strong. Oh, Gertie, I should have known they would never vanquish you."

Lady Gertrude had been a crucial member of the Lollard movement. Along with Sir John Oldcastle, Baron of Cobham, she had introduced many people to the heresy's tenets. She boldly and unapologetically led masses for other heretics, taking the place of a priest, fiercely clinging to the Lollard principles that women shared equally with men in their understanding of God and that priests were unnecessary to commune with the Creator. She also held the heretical notion that the bread and wine offered during Holy Communion did not turn into the body of Christ at the moment that the words of consecration were spoken by the priest. For that reason, Tess had thought, Gertie might have suffered the burning death as well.

When at last Tess withdrew from her embrace, compassion softened the baroness's wrinkled cheeks, but determination glinted unequivocally in her slate-colored eyes. Though imprisoned, she was clearly not broken.

"Oh, Gertrude, just looking at you brings me comfort. So much has happened since last we visited together."

Tess launched into the agonizing details of her father's death and her subsequent betrothal to the Earl of Easterby, whom Tess cursed bitterly for Gertrude's imprisonment.

"You cannot judge the earl too harshly for locking us up. Lord Richard is only obeying the law," Gertrude reasoned. She sat on the lavender chair while Tess plunked down next to her on a clothing trunk. "Lord Richard has treated us well. Better than we would be treated elsewhere, I daresay. He lets us dine in his hall when there are no guests, and he only parades us in chains to assure all gossips and spies that we Lollards are dutifully treated as prisoners and not as honored guests. And thus far he has not turned us over to the diocesan authorities."

"But he will," Tess said glumly. When she pictured his laughing visage, she felt a wave of betrayal and anger. He had lulled her into seeing a false kindness in him, and it angered her to realize how gullible she had been. "Though he did not light the fire beneath my father, Richard watched him burn. Just as he will watch you burn if I do not do something to save you, Gertie."

"There is nothing you can do for me, Tess. I am too old to run and hide. Nay, do not worry for me, child. I am ready to die. Henry has crushed our cause, but the seeds of our thoughts will take root in generations to come."

"Will they?"

"Aye. There will be reform in the Church. That it will not be in my lifetime is of little importance."

The old woman's lips parted, exposing pale yellow teeth clenched in determination. "But you must tell your children what your father and I died for. If you do, then our lives will not have been wasted."

Tess looked away, unwilling to tell Gertrude that she never wanted to have children, even though she knew that Gertie, of all people, would understand why: She had been there at Haddington Castle when Tess was born.

Suddenly, with a swift and profound wave of melancholy, Tess realized this might be her last chance to talk to Gertrude about that fateful night. She knew, too, that it was important she do so. The prospect of bearing Richard's child had made her think about her own mother's plight, and she'd realized it was difficult imagining herself as a mother when she'd never had one herself.

"Tell me, Gertie, about the night I was born. Tell me all that you can remember of my mother. Tell me in case . . ."

"In case we do not meet again?" Gertrude's morose smile acknowledged the direness of her predicament. She patted Tess's hand. "Very well. I've told you much about your mother, but never about the night she died. Your mother was so like you, Tess. So determined and bright. I will never forget that night, twenty years ago. 'Twas a haunting October eve when the leaves swirled around the castle yards in their violent final dance, churned in a wind that whispered winter's onslaught. We stoked the fire the night through, beating back the chill, and all the while your dear mother was sopping wet, perspiring in her battle for life. Your father was in London, engaged in the king's business.

"After hours and hours of excruciating labor, the midwife told your mother—sweet Alice—that you were not going to make it out alive. Alice's face twisted into a fierce mask of rage, and lifting herself on her elbows, she glared down at her enormous belly and started to shout.

" 'Live!' she cried over and over to you as you fought your way out of her womb. 'You must live!'

"She had been in labor for seven days. Four days of light pain followed by three long days of pushing. She was sallow-cheeked and weak from her loss of blood. I thought she would die before you were born, taking you with her, but she was so determined. She loved your father so dearly that she wanted to leave him some legacy, some reminder of the love they shared. And she wanted her own life to have meaning. She was so practical that way, even though she was only nineteen. And by then I think she knew she was going to die. So sad.

It was so sad for all of us who witnessed her enormous courage. . . ."

While Lady Gertrude moistened her lips, Tess awaited her next poignant words.

"Finally, you pushed your little head to freedom, gulping your first breath of air with a wail that liked to bring down the stone walls of Haddington Castle." She chuckled deep in her bosom at the memory. "It was clear to all that the best of your mother's spirit, already leaving her body, had transported itself into you. Her kindness and loving soul was evident in your soft and tender little face. But there was something more. Your fierce cries spoke of a raw strength and determination that would carry you through much greater hardships than your mother had ever known. She gave her best with a loving heart, but life felled her too early, as oft it does the tenderest beings. I knew you were destined to survive, Tess. Have you ever wondered why? For what purpose?"

Tess nodded, feeling as if her mother were in the chamber with them, breathing hard, clinging to life.

"Well, in truth, only God knows the answer, child. But I will tell you what your mother wanted for you. Do you know what her last words were?"

"If . . . if I could guess," Tess whispered, "I think she would have wanted me to look after Father, to be practical, to make her sacrifice worth something."

"I should have known you would come to that noble conclusion. But you are wrong. Her last wish was this: 'I hope my girl will find love as true and sweet as I have known. Above all, let her be loved. And if her love be disagreeable to king or country, let her be an outcast in the eyes of man. But let her be loved.' And then on her very last breath, she said, 'Tell Haddington that I loved him more than life itself.'"

Tess hung her head and sobbed, wringing the tears from her soul. "Oh, Mother . . ."

She cried for the longest time, profoundly deep-felt and healing tears.

"Why?" Tess said at last, withdrawing a hand-coverchief from her pocket and wiping her nose. "Why did you never tell me this before?"

"Because you never asked. And even if you had, you were not ready to hear it until now." Gertrude sighed contentedly. "I dreamt of you last night, Tess. Even without knowing you were here in my midst, I dreamt that you came to visit. Isn't that remarkable? When you truly love someone as I love you, then you can dream about what will soon come to pass. You can even dream the same dreams as that person."

"I will not let you go without a fight, Gertie. I now know I was born to survive."

"And to love."

Tess brushed aside Lady Gertrude's amending sentiment as easily as she brushed aside a strand of hair that had tucked itself into the corner of her mouth. "I will come back soon, Gertie."

Tess bade farewell to Lady Gertrude with a fervent kiss and a promise to bring her some sweets from the kitchen. When Tess shut the door and turned, she came face-to-face with the man she most distrusted.

"Tarjaman!" she gasped, jumping back a step. "Tarjaman, I did not expect to see you here."

"Ah, but I expected you." His lips smiled, but his eyes were cold as hoarfrost. "Have you told Lord Richard yet why you have come to Cadmon Castle?"

"Explain your meaning," Tess replied, assuming her haughtiest expression.

"Outwardly, you've come to marry him. But inwardly, you are driven by another purpose, my lady, if I may be so bold."

"You may not. The more pertinent question is why are you

here, Tarjaman? What do you want with these Lollards?" She did not try to hide her antipathy, which was evident in her blunt questions.

"Before I left my country, I was imprisoned by Mongol invaders. I know the tedium of a long prison stay. I thought I would entertain Lord Richard's guests with some anecdotes from my homeland. Do you object?"

She did object, but could not justify her distrust of the man. Not yet, anyway. "Do as you please."

"Though you are a great lady and I am but a humble servant to the earl, we have much in common," Tarjaman said.

"Oh?"

"We share the same sentiment toward Lord Richard."

"What sentiment is that?"

He smiled again. "Why, love, of course."

When she did not answer, he nodded respectfully and entered Lady Gertrude's chamber. As he brushed past Tess, she glimpsed a book tucked under his right arm. She could not read the title, but determined that she would find out what it was.

Perkins was waiting for Tess at the top of the stairs. She ordered him to stay in the prison tower until Tarjaman had left, fearing for Gertie's safety.

Descending the winding tower stairwell alone, she pondered her curious conversation with the animal trainer. He said they shared the same sentiment. And yet she was certain he knew of her quest for revenge. He was the kind of man who could look past a person's facade to detect true motives. But did he, too, bear ill will toward the earl? For some reason, Tess felt that he did, and she found herself worried for Richard's safety. But not for long. Her concern was overwhelmed by her fury over Gertrude's imprisonment. If

Richard thought Tess would sit by meekly while her friend languished away, she would disabuse him of the notion immediately, in the most uncompromising fashion.

She had much work to do. It was no longer enough to avenge the past—she now had to avert tragedy lurking in the future.

ELEVEN

"But you cannot afford to build a chapel in town, my lord," Godfrey said matter-of-factly.

The steward peered over the earl's shoulder. Both surveyed a master building plan spread out on Richard's desk.

"If you spend all of Lady Tess's marriage portion building a chapel," Godfrey continued, "before King Henry has a chance to borrow the gold for his military expeditions, there will be hell to pay indeed. The king has sent several queries wondering when your loans and troops will arrive, not to mention the status of the Lollards in your prison. You must respond soon."

Richard ignored the admonition. Leaning over the parchments with intense fascination, his eyes scanned a stately church design rendered by Master Armand. The master builder stood confidently with crossed arms at Richard's side, awaiting the earl's verdict. Armand was a lean and bright-eyed young man, who had already gained repute as one of the greatest master builders in Britain. He dressed the part, with a floppy yellow sugar-bag hat and a luxurious silk houppe-lande with enormous bagpipe sleeves.

"This is perfect," Richard said, pointing to the lofty arches at the chapel's entrance. "I want the name 'Haddington Chapel' prominently engraved over the door."

"Certainly, my lord. The name can be put anywhere you like. On the cornerstone as well, an' please you."

"Shouldn't the chapel be named after a saint, my lord?" Godfrey interjected, his arched gray brows giving him the air of an owl. "You do not want to incur the wrath of God."

"God will not mind, Godfrey, if I name a chapel in honor of Lady Tess's father."

"God may not, but King Henry will."

Richard looked up and was reminded by the stern set of Godfrey's pursed lips that there was a price to be paid for every act of good conscience.

"I will deal with Henry when the time comes. Until then, not even a pack of stampeding elephants would keep me from giving Tess this honor. Do I make myself clear?"

Godfrey sighed and bowed his head in deference to his lord's will.

Richard turned to Master Armand. "When can you begin construction?"

"We can mark the territory presently, my lord, and will start to dig as soon as the ground thaws completely."

"Good. I want you to work as quickly as you can."

Richard's heart swelled at the thought of the joy this would give Tess. But he wanted it to be a surprise. He would take her to the site in town at the first opportunity. He just hoped that in some small way this would help ease her grief. Somehow, somewhere along their rocky journey together, it had become his personal mission to make her happy.

By the time Tess arrived at Richard's solar, she had worked herself into a neat fit of anger, ranting under her breath in an imaginary conversation with the earl. She felt a keen sense of betrayal. She had been deluded by Sir John's stories into believing Lord Richard was a compassionate man. Now she knew the truth: He was the worst sort of political animal. One who would not only stand by and watch her father's execution, but who would doubtless send her father's friends to such a fate as well, charming her all the while. The rage seethed in her chest, making her heart ache, making her long for some sort of reprieve.

When she reached the door to his chamber, she did not knock. And when the door had the audacity to jam, she didn't hesitate to throw her weight against it. She heaved her shoulder against the oak, stumbling in on the wave of her momentum when the door flew open with unexpected ease.

The door banged against the wall. Tess flew into the center of the chamber. Richard and his companions looked up with a start as she staggered to a halt.

"Tess, I did not expect you. Is everything all right?"

"Aye."

"May I introduce you to Master Armand?"

"Nay." She could not force a false smile to her quivering lips.

Richard's warm expression turned to one of dismay. "Tess, what is it?"

"Do you plan to kill them, too?"

"Do I plan to kill whom?"

She gritted her teeth. "The Lollards in your prison tower."

In the silence that followed, Master Armand rolled up his last drawing with a rustling sound. Richard glanced irritably at the renderings that only moments ago had given him such pleasure.

"Leave us," he muttered.

The men obliged. When they were gone, Richard paced to his windows. Locking his hands behind his back, he strolled through the filter of dappled light. His yellow hair fell down his back like an angel's. A fallen angel's.

"If I thought you would react so violently, I would not have given you my permission to visit my prisoners."

"Richard, *please*!" she begged him. "Please let them go."

When he did not answer, she ran forward, her feet dragging over his rug as if she were running through a mucky bog, oozing with peat, sucking her down. She felt so heavy, the reality of her sorrow pressing down on her shoulders, crushing her, it seemed.

"My lord, was it another man who danced with me so tenderly in heather? Was it another man who spoke so compellingly of his father's execution?" When she reached him, she tugged on his V-shaped doublet, searching his hardened face for the compassion she had seen so often since her arrival. "Were you not moved at all by my loss?"

"Of course I was," he said harshly. "More than you will ever know."

"Then grant me this one wish. Let the Lollards go."

His cheeks reddened and veins bulged at his temple. He looked as if he would explode.

"Nay, I will not. You know not what you ask. Do not ask it again."

His voice was hollow and as cold as a frozen dagger plunging into her heart. What a fool she had been to open up to him. "Oh, heartless, heartless man."

He spun on her, eyes afire. "Do you expect me to throw everything away for three idiots who are fool enough to defy the Church openly?"

"Should they have done so in secret?" she returned. "Would that have been better?"

"'Twould have been safer."

"Safer! Is that always your highest concern—safety? How ignoble you are." She shook her head disapprovingly. "And to think your father died for his conscience. You would not recognize your conscience if it bowed before you in your own livery." She spat the words at his feet.

His nostrils flared and his lips turned as white as seething embers. "What do you know of my father?"

"Only what you have told me—that he was a man much like my own. A man who was willing to die rather than part with his beliefs. Just like your prisoners. Unlike you, who would sell your own soul if it would profit you in Court. Does your soul come so cheaply, my lord?"

"Silence!" he roared. "You know nothing of my plans or my reasons. Damn you, woman, I will still that tongue of yours one way or another."

In three quick paces, he was at her side. Gripping her arms, he pulled her close. There was so much anguish in his twisted brow—smooth, blond velvet gnarled in rage—that she regretted her harsh assessments. Who was she to judge? Had she been any truer to her beliefs? Did she even have any beliefs for which she could sacrifice all that she was asking Richard to sacrifice? Would she even care about the Lollards if it weren't Gertrude's life at stake?

"A woman so superior and self-righteous should not be so irresistible," he complained bitterly.

Like a falcon swooping down to fell a dove, his mouth attacked hers. She did not resist; she kissed him back, wanting and bold. It was a forbidden thing, this desire between them. She hated herself for giving into it, but she could not pull away. She could not pull away. He felt too good. He smelled too real, like wind and summer rain. And be he the devil himself, he was someone to touch, someone to reassure her she was alive and desirous, despite her lifelong devotion to duty. *And he is so beautiful,* she thought, running her hands over his fine, chiseled cheeks, through his flaxen hair, seeing him with her fingers.

The kiss ended of itself, leaving them panting in unison,

foreheads touching in mutual defeat, arms flung carelessly about each other. With her eyes still closed, Tess licked the lingering taste of him from her faintly swollen lips. Stepping back, she smelled stale wine in a warm goblet on his desk, a welcome reprieve from Richard's intoxicatingly masculine scent.

With some distance, she dared to open her eyes. And for the briefest moment, she knew that he knew her. She saw it in the familiarity lingering in his murky blue eyes, thinly veiled with long blond lashes, eyes that had seen too much, that had lost their innocence. She longed to take him in her arms, stroke his anguished brow, and tell him about his goodness.

And then the moment passed. She would not be so naive. She dragged a backhand across her mouth, as if filth had lingered from his kiss.

"Do not think that because I can't resist the lure so many other women have fallen for before me that I am blind to your faults."

His somber face broke with laughter. "I had no delusions on that score, Tess."

"You can laugh at anything, can't you, my lord?" she said contemptuously. "The merry Earl of Easterby. Well, you may have my fortune, and do with it what you will, but until you set the Lollards free, you will also have my undying contempt."

She indignantly jerked the hem of her gown from a tangle of rushes gathered at her feet, and pivoted. With her chin leading the way, she strode for the door, cutting through the dense air. But as much as she longed for it, she would not have the last word.

"You will join me at the head table tonight," Richard said, calmly and absolutely. His voice was a slap on her back, and she paused. "You will play the gracious hostess to a feast given in honor of the Bishop of Kirkingham. And though you loathe the Church as much as I, albeit for different reasons, you will hide your contempt as well as I do. The bishop suspects foul play on my part, and I wish to give him no cause for concern."

Tess turned. Seeking his face in the shadows of the far corner, attracted to the mystery of the man, she said, "Does the bishop have reason to fear you?"

"I do not want him to suspect there is any discord between us, Tess, so you will treat me with all the respect due your lord," he answered without answering. "You will obey me in this?"

"Oh, aye, my lord. I am a most obedient woman. And for my obedience, you are my reward."

And on that rancorous note, she finally departed.

TWELVE

Thud! Richard's lance struck the quintain with a muted sound. The earl galloped past the wooden manikin warrior before it could swing around on its horizontal pole and knock him from his horse.

The crowd cheered its approval at the ease with which he accomplished both tasks. Reining in his spirited destrier at the end of the tilting yard, Richard pivoted to watch the dummy swing round and round in a comical, wobbling motion. Then, with typical immodesty, roaring with victorious laughter, he galloped past the stands of spectators, golden hair flying. He stretched out one arm and embraced the crowd's applause.

This unusual nighttime spectacle, thrown together for the bishop's sake, was illuminated by a multitude of torches—as many, it seemed to Tess, as there were stars above. No wonder the earl was destitute, she mused dourly. Lighting the night as if it were day! The resin torches lining the stands fluttered in his wake, spewing acrid smoke and casting fiery light that made Richard's shoulder-length hair, waving over his broad shoulders as he loped past the crowd, look like spun gold.

Tess observed the festivities in a special section cordoned off behind a waist-high barrier. She sat in an ornate chair on a dais under a burgundy canopy next to the portly bishop, a puffy-cheeked, beady-eyed man who watched the display with faintly masked enmity. He snorted in disapproval now and then. But, Tess noted, that didn't keep him from enjoying the presence of a pretty young girl. His hand never left her thigh. Behind them sat the bishop's bevy of canons. The rest of the knights and lords dwelling in the castle were waiting for a chance to joust. They had each taken a turn at the quintain before Lord Richard, and had then donned their gleaming jousting armor.

The canopy blocked the worst of the billowy March wind. It was a pleasant enough evening, Tess concluded with a tortured sigh, if one did not think about Gertie in the prison tower, or the strained countenance of the bishop, who watched Richard's display of arms with unease, or Tarjaman, who seemed never to stray far from Tess, always watching her with his illegible onyx eyes.

But amazingly and frustratingly, Tess forgot all those concerns whenever she focused on Richard. Despite her nearly overwhelming urge to strangle him, he was the most maddeningly charming man she had ever met. The more reasons he gave her to be angry, the more she seemed to see his pleasing attributes. It was a unique twist of fate. Probably God's way of making murder difficult. Richard was simply a likable man. A devil-may-care sort.

Take the torches, for example. They represented a lamentable waste of fuel. But he didn't care how much gold he spent on resin. He obviously had faith there would always be more, and he didn't care what others thought of him. Though he didn't possess any of the self-sacrificing qualities that endeared subjects to a saintly liege lord, at least he had the audacity to be fully and utterly human. And by the vibrant smiles on the faces of his vassals, and the wild applause in the stands, she could tell they loved him for it. He made no excuses for lusting after things of the flesh—be they weapons of war or women.

Richard turned his horse around at the far end of the yard and frowned at the boisterous crowd before him. When his searching eyes trained on her, Tess felt a flame inside flicker to life. He tossed his lance to Perkins and touched his spurs to the belly of his mount. The destrier's hooves rumbled over packed earth, spewing straw.

All eyes turned to Tess, for it was obvious to whom he eagerly galloped. To any stranger, he wore the mask of a determined suitor. But Tess knew that beneath that mask there was a wicked glint of the conqueror. Richard was about to teach her a lesson, and the hair on her nape rose to attention.

Richard reined in before the canopy and looked down at Tess over his hawkish nose with the air of a king. He gracefully dipped his broad shoulders this way and that, balancing as his black destrier pranced forward and back with high, impatient steps. He had yet to don his jousting armor and wore a simple mail hauberk covered with his coat of arms.

"Lady Tess, I would have your favor!" he bellowed for all to hear, and held out an open hand, awaiting a scarf or garter to drape upon his lance. With the other hand he skillfully tugged and manipulated the leather reins barely restraining his mount. The beast whickered and snapped his tail with a swish.

"Your favor, madam."

He wasn't asking for it—he was demanding it. Tess felt the bishop's gaze rove to her and the world closing in on her. He was waiting to hear her response, and she remembered Richard's admonition: The bishop mustn't know of their discord. She tried to swallow, but her throat had suddenly turned into a desert. Surely there was some way to abide by their agreement without giving Richard the satisfaction of her complete submission.

Dutifully, she rose and stepped to the short wooden barrier. She curtsied and looked up with a sweet expression. "My Lord Richard, you hardly need a favor from a damsel to win your match. Your enemy is but a wooden dummy, a lifeless knight hanging from a *board*, who most certainly will not claim my affections and goodwill, unless, in your company, I become *bored* as well."

Tess's play on words garnered a low rumble of appreciative laughter, especially from the women. Emboldened, she continued, her eyes twinkling with subdued anger and mischief.

"It should be obvious for whom I cheer. While your opponent is woody, you are witty, and I do so appreciate a sense of humor in a man who would be my lord."

By now even the bishop and his canons, sitting in their furs and silks, were chuckling with amusement.

Tess rushed on with a confident sweep of the hand, gesturing to the manikin hanging from the quintain.

"While he is hard, you are soft. And a pliant husband is much the better, methinks."

Richard's exquisite mouth turned up with an ironic smile. "I can assure you, maiden, I will not be soft when I come to your wedding bed."

The crowd burst into uproarious laughter. Outwitted, Tess fairly simmered.

"Come then, Countess-to-be," he commanded loudly. "Give up your wit and rhyme. You're no match for me. You do not belong behind a minstrel's harp, weaving words into puns. You belong in my saddle. There you will feel for yourself what is hard and what is soft."

Before she could argue or retreat, Richard grabbed her by

the arm and yanked her up into his lap. He held her back secure against his chest—a rock-solid mass of muscles.

"How dare you treat me like one of your bawds!" she seethed, tugging at his vicelike grip on her waist. "I am not a prize falcon to dress your arm. Put me down immediately."

Richard ignored her and nudged his mount into an easy canter, then made a wide circle around the tilting yard, so that everyone in the cheering crowd might glimpse the spectacle.

"Must you humiliate me so?" she railed through clenched teeth.

"'Tis no humiliation to submit to the greater wisdom of your lord and master," he answered. "At least in public. Now smile, damn it."

"I hate you, Richard Avery," she cried out. "Do you hear me? I loathe you. I hate all that you stand for."

"That has been obvious from the start," he said, drawing up his horse at the end of the tilting yard.

Two knights began the first joust, thundering on their horses along the lists with lances pointed at one another, drawing the crowd's focus. Richard lowered Tess to the ground, where Perkins awaited with a steadying hand. When Richard leapt from Shadow's back, the squire led the destrier away, leaving his ill-fated lovers to their tumultuous solitude.

Richard pulled her close, gripping both wrists. In the flickering torchlight, he blinked hard, his eyelids wings, his eyes two birds scanning the horizon for shelter, weary on the wing, hovering, ever hovering.

"Your hatred is obvious. What is less telling is your reason for coming sooner than needed. Why, Tess? Why did you not resist this match?"

"Because I've come to kill you. And the sooner the deed is done the better," she rasped with so much venom her throat hurt. The words quivered between them and then dissolved in

the crisp breeze. She had blurted the truth because she wanted
to hurt him. And because it was the truth. Even Richard—
perhaps especially Richard—deserved that much.

"How appropriate," he said, his rich voice betraying no
emotion. "The woman I am to marry is waiting for a chance
to stab me in the back. Somehow I find that comforting. I
have lived all my life with danger and betrayal and have
always found the thought of marrying for love anathema."

He started away, his broad shoulders hunched over in a rare
display of exhaustion. Tess nearly called out to him, but he
saved her the pains by turning back with a bemused expression.

"How do you plan to fulfill your mission?"

"My lord?" she whispered.

"With poison? A broadsword? Nay, you could not lift one.
A poleaxe? One clean stroke with that might work."

"Richard . . ."

"Well, what is it to be? How will you kill me?"

Tess gritted her teeth. "With a misericorde."

"Ah, yes." His eyes flamed with appreciation. "'Twould fit
neatly in your hand. The hilt of such a dagger would be no
longer than your fist. But you'll need to make a clean slice
across my throat. Else, might harm me but little. I've had
more than one misericorde plunged into my shoulder and
chest, and the wounds healed well enough. Let me give it
some thought. There might be a better way. Something more
efficient. Meanwhile, I expect you to join me in the old hall
after the jousts. I want you at my side when I meet with the
bishop." Shadows etched his drawn cheeks. "Do not disappoint me, Tess."

When he marched away, she knew that she already had.
And she felt sorry for it. When she returned to the dais to
view the jousts, her handmaiden rushed forward, making a

great show of straightening the train of Tess's houppelande. She knew that Mellie's attentiveness was just an excuse to study her reaction to Lord Richard.

"Oh, Lady Tess! How exciting. Isn't he the most romantic nobleman you have ever seen?" Mellie gushed.

Tess watched Richard as he gave orders to his squire, who helped his master don his jousting armor.

"Romantic?" Tess scoffed. "Is this romance? Then minstrels should be drawn and quartered for misleading maidens with their tales of love."

An hour and a half later, Tess sat awkwardly in the oldest part of the castle with her hands folded neatly in her lap. The old great hall was all that remained of the castle built by Richard's great-grandfather. Though the square structure had high ceilings, it was shorter and cozier than the new great hall, and more private.

A row of hissing torches lined the wall in between hanging tapestries. Tess sat by a crackling fire, every muscle in her body rigid. She berated herself over and over again for being too honest. Oh, why had she told Richard the truth? Her honesty would one day be the death of her. Perhaps sooner than later. What was to keep Lord Richard from putting her in prison? Perhaps she would be shoved into a tiny oubliette in the dungeon where she would be forgotten, until all that remained of her were bones cloaked in a tattered gown. If Richard understood the seriousness of her intent, he would consider her a threat. Why had she told him anything?

The double arched doors opened, sucking a whirl of air. The fire faltered, then leapt with new life. A long beam of golden light from the hallway fell at Tess's feet, and a figure appeared.

"Tess! There you are."

It was Richard. His voice was the sound of breaking glass, shattering her nerves. "Aye, my lord?"

He looked like a giant in the distance, and all the more so as he headed her way. He was sweaty and winded and keenly alive, as one could be only after a victorious joust.

She forced her eyes to meet his, for she refused to cower before him, at least outwardly. He was a dashing devil, she concluded defeatedly. How dare he look so handsome under present circumstances? Even with mud smudged on one high cheek and hair matted to his forehead with perspiration. He had cast off his plated armor and his arming doublet, and had changed into a clean, billowy white shirt tucked into breeches. The linen hung over his massive frame, draped over the honey-gold mat of hair glistening on his chest.

Her eyes followed the crisp front of the shirt until it disappeared at his hips, which loomed closer and closer until finally he halted before her. She raised her eyes with trepidation, dreading what fierce emotion she would see in his dashing face. His massive chest strained against his shirt as he breathed deeply, drawing a breath with which to rage at her, she was sure.

She braced herself, hardening her cheeks, staring him down as if he were the devil himself.

And then came her reprieve.

"Easterby," growled the bishop from the doorway, like an intemperate overfed dog denied a second bone. "Just what is the meaning of this?"

Kirkingham waddled in, waving away members of his fluttering entourage, who closed the door behind him. He stopped at the end of a long, sleek wooden table that dominated the hall. He wore no miter or vestments, just a simple alb. His breasts protruded like a woman's against the pliable white gown. His humped gut bespoke his life of leisure, and a half dozen twinkling rings bespoke his penchant for treasures.

"What is the meaning of what?" Richard returned.

It was as uncivil a voice as Tess had ever heard from him. When he turned his focus from her to the bishop, it was as if the singeing rays of the sun had been defused by a cloud. The absence of Richard's attention was a relief and a loss. She loved his anger. This was the real Richard, she realized with a spark of excitement, observing him furtively through dense, brown lashes, seeing him with new eyes. This angry man was Richard, not the politic man the world always saw.

"I refer to this . . . this ugly display of might," Kirkingham answered, snapping his jaws. "Do not act as if you do not take my meaning."

"My Lord Bishop, I am most aggrieved. I do my best to entertain you on short notice, and you find the fare wanting."

The older man's puffy lips puckered with displeasure. "You were not entertaining me, Easterby, you were trying to intimidate me with a show of force. You've wasted your time. I already know you've amassed a veritable army. Beyond the thirty knights who owe you fealty, you've hired mercenaries. You've bought up every cannon and hand-gunne before they're even cast in London or Bristol. You mean to attack my lands. Admit it, Easterby."

"I gather my army for the king's cause, my Lord Bishop. Have you not heard? Henry means to attack France. Troops are already gathering at Southampton."

The bishop gave him a blank, disbelieving look. "Of course I know of the king's plans. What sort of idiot do you think I am? The question is, what is to keep you from making an excursion before you set out for the Continent? An excursion into Marly Vale."

"Kirkingham, I have just welcomed my wife-to-be to

Cadmon Castle. We will have but a few short months at most together before Henry goes to battle. I plan to spend every possible moment begetting an heir, not risking my life in battle."

He took Tess's hand and kissed it, regarding her with shimmering sarcasm.

Never one for silence, particularly when silence would be appreciated most, Tess batted her lashes at Richard with sugary sweetness. "I pray you, my lord, do not leave to fight in battle. I cannot live without you."

His eyes flared with alarm, and she smiled all the more sweetly.

"*Please,* my lord."

"Why, dearest, I wouldn't dream of it."

The bishop scowled at their affectionate display. "I am touched to see such a chivalrous sense of duty to your lady, Easterby, but from what I have heard, you could bed a different lady morning, noon, and night and still have the strength and wile to defeat and capture a few nobles for ransom. I see I shall get nowhere with you under diplomatic circumstances. Nevertheless, this visit has answered many questions for me."

The bishop started for the door in his uneven gait, but paused before swinging open the arched doors. "As for the Lollards—"

"We will discuss the Lollards later," Richard interrupted, and his implacable tone left no room for argument. He stared hard at the bishop until the old man nodded in acquiescence. Then Richard's tense gaze glided over Tess, pausing only a moment to assess her reaction. Or was he merely studying a mote of dust as he lingered on a stray thought?

The bishop gathered himself into one last imperious stance. "If you test Henry's love for you against his passion for the

Church, you will confront your own mortality quicker than you might have thought. Remember that, Easterby."

Richard said nothing, but as he turned away from the bishop, putting an end to the tense conversation, just before he shuttered his soul Tess saw liquid rage in his eyes. Seething, bubbling rage.

THIRTEEN

Richard squared off against his squire just before midnight. Just as the night sentry blew his trumpet from the distant parapets.

Alone in the great hall, they were warriors battling the shadows of night. Each held a sword, Richard confidently, Perkins anxiously. The squire's eyes glowed like hot embers in the light of the dying fire.

Adjusting his firm grip upon his sword, Richard felt a tug at his heart, a tenderness that surprised him. He loved Perkins. He loved his vigor and his eternal optimism. They were opposites. Richard was darkness cloaked in light. How he hated that darkness.

"Pour le coeur de guerre," he whispered. "For the heart of war," his family motto. The words felt ironic and bitter on his twisted lips.

"Pour le coeur de guerre," Perkins echoed, raising his sword with two hands. The blade was almost too heavy for the lad. It quavered over his head.

Richard raised Taliesin high. A flicker of awe and terror flitted across the young man's untarnished face. Perkins had seen the mighty bejeweled sword many times before. As Richard's squire, the youth had polished the steel blade and had buffed the emeralds on the mother-of-pearl hilt. But never had the magnificent Taliesin been raised against him.

"Are you ready, Perkins?" Richard whispered.

"Aye, my lord." He padded his feet, searching for a sturdier position.

It felt as if Taliesin were a hundredweight. The muscles in Richard's arms burned. Not just because he'd spent himself in jousting, but because of the weight of history this sword represented. The responsibility. His father had borne Taliesin in the battle of Crécy. Save for his land, nothing was more important to Richard than this sword. This was his legacy. This blade he would raise at long last in rage, in revenge.

"Come forward," Richard ordered.

The squire licked his hips and hesitated.

"Well, come forward, I say," Richard groused irritably. "What is wrong? Are you afraid?"

"Nay, my lord."

"You want to earn your spurs, don't you? You don't want to be a squire for the rest of your life, do you?"

Perkins blinked his wide eyes. "'Twouldn't be such a bad fate, my lord, if I were to continue serving you."

Richard's eyes shuttered at this pitiful display of affection—pitiful because it came from one he loved, and he knew that all those he loved would one day betray him.

"One day, Perkins, you will be a knight in your own right. You will have your own squire and pages. You will earn honor in battle. One day you may even raise a sword against me."

Perkins lowered his blade in dismay. "Never! Never, my lord. Since I was seven, you've been like a father to me."

"Do you think the bonds of family and friendship are enough to keep a dagger from my back?" Richard threw back his head and howled with laughter. Laughter tainted with unshed tears. His giddy voice ricocheted off the high, dark beams, sifting through the red and gold banners. When the laughter died, he wiped a too-broad smile from his face.

"My lord, what has gotten into you?"

"Nothing. Actually, I've never felt better. First there was Uncle Desmond, then Hal, and now Tess. Betrayal has become an old friend of mine. Are you ready?"

After a moment of doubtful silence, Perkins raised his sword. "Ready."

"Pour le coeur de guerre!" Richard roared, and launched himself at Perkins like a wild boar.

He brought Taliesin down with a savage swing, but his squire was indeed prepared. He tilted his blade at a side angle and deflected the blow, forcing Richard to lunge past him and circle for a second try.

"Good boy!" Richard bellowed with a grim smile. "Save yourself, Perkins, or I'll kill you. I swear it."

"Nay," the boy gamely replied, assuming a determined frown. "I'll not let you."

Richard swung again. And again. And again. Each time he advanced a wide stride, pushing the boy back. Each time Perkins masterfully parried. He had learned his lessons well. In the back of his mind, Richard felt proud of his squire. But that was not by any means the foremost emotion he felt. An even stronger one was eating away at Richard's spleen.

He felt as if a red-hot poker had been plunged into his entrails, burning, seething. This Tess had done to him. For he had seen such grace in her. The chance of salvation. She had held that chance in her arms, but had cast it aside for a bloody misericorde.

Richard did not know how long his mock battle with Perkins continued. He only knew when their war-play ended: when Perkins, having gained much confidence, sent Taliesin clattering to the floor with one mighty blow. Richard gasped, shocked back to reality. His palms stung from the absence of the powerful sword. It was a life-form of its own, an entity, and Richard felt naked without it. He paused, breathing hard, breath scraping into his burning lungs. Gods, how he longed for war. War was certain. War was savage, but it was certain. Unlike battles of the heart.

"Thank you, Perkins," he rasped between breaths.

Perkins's face was ablaze, beet-red with victory. "Thanks for what, my lord?"

"For reminding me that victory is never certain." *And I should thank Tess,* he added silently, wiping his drenched brow with a forearm. He should thank her and the bishop, for they had both led him to a new beginning. The beginning of war. A war in which no prisoners would be spared.

"Bless me father, for I have sinned. . . ."

Richard began the litany even before the old priest had settled on the other side of the partition that separated them. It was well past midnight. Past matins. Richard could not sleep. His bout with Perkins had ruined any chance of sweet slumber.

"Ah, Richard, I thought I might see you tonight."

Richard felt a rush of peace hearing that familiar voice. He blinked in the darkness of his confessional.

"You usually know my thoughts before I speak them, Father. Perhaps I needn't waste my words here in confession. You can divine my restless thoughts and determine my penance that way."

The old man chuckled, a hissing expulsion of air. "Perhaps I can. You have always been my favorite and most ardent sinner."

Richard always tried to imagine the expressions that matched the words of the man who had heard his confessions ever since childhood. But he did not need to see Father James to picture exactly how he looked. The old man's legs would be crossed at the ankles beneath his robe, which hung in loose folds over his gaunt frame. The only padding on the aging figure came from his hair shirt, nagging his skin beneath the robe. His gnarled hands, polished by age like the smoothest marble, were gently folded in his lap. Blue veins protruded at his temples in a maze, barely covered by skin. His pinkish lids blinked slow and often over milky, nearly sightless eyes. And just as often his tongue skimmed over wide, dry lips. Tufts of gray hair sprouted from his ears. His gums had receded so far his teeth looked like those possessed by a skeleton, long and useless.

Everything about the man was shrinking, except for his heart and his wisdom. Father James had been the confessor not only to Richard, but to his father. Richard could think of no man he trusted more, and no other priest who would be willing to hear a confession after midnight matins. The old man slept little in his doddering years and welcomed company at any hour.

"What troubles you, my son?" he said in a high, hollow voice, for there was little air in his feeble lungs.

"I am about to betray King Harry. And already the weight of guilt sits on my shoulders like the yoke borne by an ox."

"So the time has come to reclaim Marly Vale."

"I will attack Bishop George in a matter of days, against Henry's wishes. I have come to ask forgiveness again, for I know breaking my vow of allegiance to Harry is a sin, and yet I will do it anyway."

He would break his vow even to the man who had once saved his life. He remembered it as if it had happened yesterday, that fierce battle against the Welsh in the march-lands. . . .

"God almighty, Easterby! Get up, man."

"Hal! I cannot rise," Richard had sputtered through a mouthful of salty blood.

The bold silhouette of England's future king was all shadows and sunlight as Richard squinted up at him from his fixed bed of muck and sod. Knocked from his destrier with a powerful blow of a Welshman's sword, Richard had landed on his back. Every inch of him, including his fingers, encumbered in heavy armor and leather. The more he churned and lurched, like a silver, overturned beetle, the farther he seemed to sink into the sucking mud.

"Take my hand," Henry insisted, steadying his angry destrier. The beast stomped his massive hooves next to Richard's head. Each step made a popping noise as the horse pulled his shod hooves from the gooey clay.

"Take hold, Richard. Take hold."

Richard strained to reach the gleaming gauntlet extended toward him. That precious hand had dubbed Richard a knight on the eve of this battle. *Knighted yesterday, and bound to die today,* Richard thought ruefully, appreciating the irony despite his desperate circumstances.

"Grab my hand, Easterby. Quickly!"

"I can't. Hal, go on. Leave. You should not be alone here."

The English cavalry had chased the mad Welshmen toward the woods, leaving the prince and Richard virtually alone on the field. But by the swell of animal-like voices that came unexpectedly from the rear, Richard knew Hal's livery had been spotted and that a few Welsh stragglers who had escaped the force of English soldiers had turned back to capture the greatest prize of all.

Lifting his head from the muck, Richard could see the approach of a half dozen feet of Owain's soldiers, clamoring after the heir to the English throne. "Go, Hal. You should not be alone on the field."

"Grab my foot," the prince persisted.

With a grunt, twisting his stomach muscles to the breaking point, Richard managed to lurch forward far enough to grab

Hal's foot with his gauntlet-covered hands. Hal nudged his horse back a few paces, pulling Richard along with him. He staggered to a stand.

"Up with you, Easterby." The prince's fair face glinted with the fierce determination that even at so young an age made him such a feared military leader. They were each one but six and ten years of age.

Richard had gratefully clutched the proffered arm and hoisted himself up onto Hal's destrier just as the Welsh soldiers closed in for the kill. Richard's life had been spared by the man who would one day rule England. He could not think of a more profound debt.

Richard blinked away the memories and sucked in a breath of incense-choked air.

"I owe Henry my life. But how am I to honor my vows to a liege lord who embraces the Church more soundly than he does the spirit of God? What Kirkingham did was wrong, and I must right that wrong, no matter that he wears the robes of the Church. No matter that Henry will feel betrayed. 'Tis a matter of honor. Is that not so, Father?"

"You have changed, Richard."

It was neither praise nor condemnation, but a neutral observation designed to lead Richard's thoughts down a certain path. But which path? Richard wondered, letting out a ragged sigh.

"Two years ago, when Harry assumed the throne and did not right Kirkingham's injustice, I knew the time to strike had come," Richard continued. "And I have been preparing for it ever since. A shipment of hand-gunnes should be on the road from London as we speak. And I've just ordered another shipment with the bounty that Lady Tess has brought to Cadmon Castle. I have known all along that these actions would lead ultimately to a confrontation with Henry. As soon as I strike, Henry will intercede."

And that is where the Lollards enter. Uneasy thoughts of the Lollards faded and Tess filled his vision. He could not think of the heretics without thinking of Tess.

"I wonder, Father, what my life would have been like if I had cared more for what is right than I cared for surviving."

"You would be dead by now," the old man said flatly.

Richard smiled ruefully. "Tess holds the idea of chivalry so dear. And for that reason I will never find love in her arms. I am too tainted."

"If I forgive you through God's grace, then you will be cleansed."

Richard wanted it to be true. And if Father James said it was true, it had to be. But Richard did not believe it. There lay the limits of his faith, embedded in self-condemnation.

His arse had fallen asleep against the hard wooden chair. It was time to go. "What is my penance, Father?"

"You have not committed the sin yet, my son. Come to me when the deed is done."

"So I must face death in battle without the comfort of your absolution? You selfish old man," he said, feeling his composure and habitual facade of elegant wit return.

"Very well. If 'twould ease your mind. Go to your chamber now and say the rosary a dozen times."

"Perhaps I should borrow one your hair shirts," Richard concluded sardonically, and the priest choked out a rasp of air that signified laughter.

Richard did not count his rosary beads with prayers that night. He was drawn irresistibly to his maps of Marly Vale and the surrounding territory, sprawled on his desk, edges tattered from the fervent grip of his fingers over the years.

"My course is set, Perkins." Deadly resolve sat like a rock where his heart had been. It did not beat. It merely oozed cold determination.

"Aye, my lord." The carrot-topped squire barely glanced up from his meticulous work at Richard's armor stand. He had polished Richard's armor, ensuring that no perspiration remained to incite rust, and he had carefully put Taliesin back in its ornate scabbard, yawning all the while.

"The attack on the bishop will be simple," Richard continued, giving his squire little attention, for Richard's mind—nay, his whole being—was turning inward now. "'Twill not be easy, but 'twill be simple. I am willing to die in battle. That is all my men can ask of me. The willingness to die, too."

"True, my lord."

"Perkins? How old are you now?"

"Six and ten, my lord, near to seven and ten."

"The same age as I when Hal gave me my spurs." Richard sauntered to the fireside, feeling his chest swell with gratitude for Perkins's many years of service. "You gave me quite a fight tonight. You should be proud. And you've been a good squire, Perkins. You've earned your spurs. I'll dub you before Henry invades Normandy. You're young for the honor, yet deserving. Does that suit you well?"

Perkins's face grew still, his eyes filling with realization, joy, and a sense of manhood that always comes with such news. He looked up at last with a deeper intensity than Richard had ever seen in the easygoing lad.

"'Twould please me greatly, my lord."

"Too bad. I shall miss you and will have to break in another squire once they're calling you Sir Perkins."

"You'll survive, my lord," the youth cracked.

Richard nodded and left Perkins to his duties, then wandered over to the portrait of Lucy. Her image was frozen in time, eyes the color of raindrops, hair golden and burnished. Would she at last be proud of her older brother for doing what was right, regardless of the political consequences? In truth, he had no notion at all. She was a stranger now. He could not rebel for her sake any more than he could rebel for Tess's.

He turned back to the desk and grasped the miniature portrait of his reluctant betrothed. She would sooner see him hang than aid his quest. Or would she see him in a different light after his attack on Kirkingham? Would she give him a portion of the profound respect she had given her father?

Never. Not in a hundred years. As if she were a ghost, her face came to mind—lovely, indignant, self-righteous. Untouched. He felt her tongue on his again, slick and flickering. He tasted her honeysuckle lips. He remembered the nectar he'd sipped from her mouth, and it made him want to tear her down from her marble pedestal and crush the stone to pieces. He wanted to possess her, to make her feel carnal and as passionate as a woman could feel in his arms. He wanted her to pant and writhe beneath him, to beg for more. He wanted her to surrender. Then, just mayhap, she would know his worth and his power.

The door creaked open behind him and a slender shadow stretched across his desk. "Richard? Are you awake?"

Turning in wild hope, he recognized Elsbeth's familiar form and his eager anticipation slipped away, his shoulders slackening beneath his brown velvet doublet. "Oh, 'tis you, Elsbeth. Come in."

Sensing her hesitation, regretting his own disappointment, he stretched out a hand, grasping hers, and kissed her affectionately on the forehead.

"Forgive me for being so absent, sweetling. I have been preoccupied ever since Tess arrived."

As Perkins gracefully excused himself, Elsbeth studied Richard solemnly, her thin, even brows quirking ever so slightly. Coming to some private conclusion, she nodded and pulled back the hood of her cloak, shaking free her loose hair.

"You needn't apologize for giving your wife-to-be the

attention due her. I did not know whether to expect our . . . interludes to continue. I was certain they would, that marriage would not change you one bit. But as the days stretched into weeks, I began to wonder."

"Take off your cloak, Beth," he said as he poured two goblets of malmsey.

"Nay, not just yet. I would warm myself a moment first."

He motioned to two stools before the hearth, and they both sat and sipped in silence.

"'Tis good to see you again," he said, longing for the comfort he had always found in her arms. "I've missed you. I did not mean for so much time to pass. And fear not, my marriage will change nothing between you and me. Tess hates me already. Doubtless she will be relieved to find out I have a lover to keep me away from her bed."

Though he tried to sound casual, he could not keep the scratchy bitterness from his throat. "Fortunately, our marriage is not starting as a love match, and as it goes from bad to worse I will be spared the quiet agony of watching affection wither. Believe me, Beth, my marriage will not interfere with our lovemaking."

He leaned forward and kissed her thin lips in the flickering firelight. She responded with a hungry groan, and her hand slid along his thigh until she gripped his manhood within the soft folds of his braies and hose.

Richard waited, but nothing happened. Elsbeth abruptly ended the kiss and frowned quizzically, still caressing between his legs.

"Why, Richard, I have never seen you so . . . inattentive. You are not even remotely hard tonight. Have I lost all my appeal?" she whispered.

He did not smile at her coy entreaty, for he was heartily dismayed at his inability to respond to that which had never failed to arouse him before. He grasped her wrist, eased her hand away, and leveled her with what he knew would be a devastatingly sexy grin.

"'Tis midnight, Beth. You usually come to me at noon, when the church bells are ringing. Go ask the priest to ring them now and then watch me rise to the occasion. In my old age, I've become a creature of habit."

"Good," she murmured, "for I intend to be a habit that is hard to break."

Elsbeth rose and unfastened the tie at her neck; her cloak slid over her shoulders, crumbling to the floor, exposing her naked body in the firelight. Her nipples immediately hardened.

"You have nothing on," he said like a half-wit seeing a naked lady for the first time.

"Very observant." She placed his right hand on one pear-shaped breast. "This will work much better than church bells."

He stood and tucked an arm around her waist, kneading a breast with his other hand, kissing her thin lips. She did not taste like Tess. The moisture from Tess's mouth was like dewdrops on a pink rose in the morning, quivering with life. When he kissed Tess, his lips hummed with an energy of their own. Kissing Tess felt right. This felt wrong. He withdrew, chafing under the weight of his conscience, which sat draped upon his shoulders like a heavy shirt of mail.

But Elsbeth did not notice. She knelt before him and unfastened the points tying his hose to his doublet. Then she tugged the hose down and pulled off his braies. With her help, he stepped out of the crumpled remains of his undergarments and tugged off his doublet. She pulled him to the bed and slithered into it, spreading her legs seductively.

"Come, Richard, lay down with me."

"You are a lovely sight," he said. The compliment sounded more like an apology, for though she was beautiful, he did not want her. Unwilling to accept that fact, he lowered himself into her arms as he had a hundred times before, but still he was flaccid, and no amount of writhing and moaning on her part could change that.

At length, she ceased her eager squirming beneath him and looked into his eyes with the intensity of one scalded with embarrassment. He propped himself up on his elbows and smoothed his hands over her forehead, kneading away the tension there.

Softly, they breathed in and out with the familiarity of two old lovers.

"'Tis over, isn't it?" she whispered. A surge of emotion flooded her eyes and her lids fluttered like the faltering wings of an injured bird. "You do not want me anymore."

"Nay, Beth . . ."

"'Tis because of her, isn't it?"

"Aye . . ."

"You want her now. Only her."

"Nay . . ."

"Well, is it aye or nay?"

"Both."

She turned her head into the pillow and pressed the back of her fingers across her eyes, spurting out little cheeping sounds of sorrow as she fought the rain of her emotion.

Compassion surged in his heart like thick, sweet honey. "Elsbeth, please do not weep. I am not worth the tears. I do not know why I cannot do this now. . . ." He growled softly. "Mayhap 'tis because I will soon be married to her. Mayhap somewhere inside of me there is a chivalrous knight with virtue untarnished. Mayhap, after all the years of intrigue and half-truths and halfhearted promises, I can no longer do falsely. If so, 'tis as much a surprise to me as to you. I cannot explain this sudden inability. But it has nothing to do with you, Beth."

She had stopped crying and now only sniffled softly. He whispered in her ear, "Do you remember the night we first made love?"

She nodded.

"You told me that you had long wanted to bed a cock of such renown. You made me swear that if we became lovers I would never fall in love with you. Do you remember?"

She nodded and turned to him, her eyes twinkling with the shared memory. "Of course I remember, and I see where this is leading, but I am not in love with you, Richard Avery, Earl of Easterby."

He smiled. He didn't believe her, but he was grateful for the lie. "Good. You know that I can arrange a match for you with any man you wish."

"Nay. Let me live my life in peace."

He nodded, thinking that he should wish for such a fate. "I do love you, Beth."

"But not in *that* way."

"Nay," he said ruefully, never knowing until now what *that* way was. Wishing to God a woman named Tess, a self-proclaimed enemy, was not sleeping several chambers away from his, distracting him beyond endurance. Wishing to high Heaven he could make her pay for this. If Tess truly hated him, he would make her hate him doubly so. Then she might know the agony he felt now.

FOURTEEN

The door to Tess's chamber flew open and crashed back on its hinges with a bang.

"Good morrow, Lady!" a male voice thundered.

Tess bolted upright in bed and blinked determinedly, trying to focus her sandy vision on the figure looming like a bear in the doorway.

"Who goes there?"

By his arrogant stance she would have thought him a Viking, or a marauder. But she knew it could be none other than the damnable Earl of Easterby.

"My lord?"

"Aye, my lady, your beloved and devoted husband-to-be has arrived." His voice dripped with sarcasm. He strutted forward, casting her a disparaging look. "What is this? Still abed? Why, the sun has been up an hour."

"My handmaiden was supposed to rouse me. Mellie? Mellie, wake up!"

"Hmmmm," Mellie moaned, and rolled over on her pallet, raising not so much as an eyelid as she snuggled under her covers.

Giving up on the girl, Tess turned reluctantly to her marauder. Devilish intent burned in his eyes like blue flames in the hottest forge, searing her to her crumpled sheets. Filled with foreboding, she pulled a blanket up to her chin.

"What, pray you, do you want?"

"Get up."

"My lord, I will not leave my bed until you quit this chamber."

"Get up," he repeated, and yanked the covers away from her body. She was utterly naked.

She gasped. He paused. But only for a moment, when she shrank back in surprise, covering her bare breasts with one arm and drawing her knees into herself like a startled fawn stripped of the cover of foliage. And in that moment, seeing the soft pink clusters at the tips of her breasts, he stiffened in the way that Elsbeth had wanted him to. It was just as he had feared: It was this lovely, aloof, self-righteous madonna who quickened his blood, and no one else.

"God's Wounds!" he cursed, enraged that Tess held such power over him. "Get dressed."

Gripping a silken, narrow wrist, he pulled her out of bed, gently but firmly. Then, leaving her shivering in the dawning light of morning, he went to her trunk and rustled around for something appropriate to wear.

"You must dress, for there is not much time."

"There is not much time for what?" she shot back, hands akimbo. "Civility?"

"There is not much time to kill me." He kept his back to her as he searched the trunk. "I will be leaving for the Continent as soon as my soldiers are trained and armed for Henry's attack on France." *But only after I attack Kirkingham,* he added silently. "That gives you little time to murder me. And it will take weeks for you to learn to shoot. After much thought, I've concluded that shooting me will be the best way to do the deed."

When he finally found a pale blue kirtle, simple and

utilitarian, he turned to find her standing erect and proud, as if she were fully clothed. *Well done, Tess,* he thought. She wasn't about to let an immodest bully strip her of her dignity. With a swift glance downward, his admiration for her mettle transformed to appreciation of her other attributes—high, round breasts; a nicely narrowed waist; smooth, curvaceous hips; and a lovely, dark triangle at the apex of her thighs. She was positively luscious.

"And why must I learn to shoot?" she inquired.

"So that you can murder me without the necessity of brute force, which is lacking in women." He forced his gaze to flicker back to her defiant eyes, but fearing his eyes would rove southward again, he thrust the gown into her hands and turned his back. "Please, my lady, do not make me dress you myself. I cannot promise any civility at all if that were to happen."

"What hurry is there to put on my gown?" she said icily. "What difference does it make if you see me now or after we exchange vows at the church door? I have been stripped of far worse than my clothing, to be sure."

Richard waited patiently while she dressed. He could see her lithe motions in the reflection of a looking glass propped on her small table. She bobbed enticingly in and out of view as she slipped into her chemise and pulled on her kirtle, fastening its narrow sleeves at her wrists. She bit her lower lip, pink as a flower, with pearly white teeth as her earthy eyes studied each button. She fondled the small blue orbs in her strong, yet utterly feminine, fingers.

"I am . . . decent," she said at last. "Until our wedding night, that is."

He turned from the mirror to find her looking ever so regal as she brushed the lacy edge of her high collar.

"Tess, has it occurred to you that I may not see you on our wedding night at all if you learn to shoot quickly enough?"

"Please, my lord, do not humor me as if I were a child," she scoffed as she fastened the last of the buttons inching up her delicate throat. "You have no intention of letting me kill you. Don't pretend otherwise."

"I think you underestimate the power of explosives. If you learn to use a hand-gunne properly, you could fell me from a distance and there would be nothing I could do about it. It will not be a matter of *allowing* you to do it. You will be able to kill me of your own free will."

Tess paused to consider this, looking at him with the solemn eyes of a doe. "Truly?"

A glimmer of trust softened the hard set of her lips, demanding honesty from him. Cursed, blasted honesty.

He cleared a frog from his throat and concentrated on twisting an insignia ring around the middle finger of his left hand. "If there is any gift I would give you, 'twould be the gift of power. The kind of power to decide your own fate. Hand-gunnes can give you that power."

She frowned at him earnestly, a brilliant flush of life coloring her cheeks. *Gods, but she is lovely,* he thought.

"Do you really mean that? Aye, you do mean it. I can see it in your discomfort. Why, of course, you are right. I had not considered that a woman might operate a gunne as easily as a man. After all, gunnes have broken all the rules of warfare. Why not to a woman's advantage? For once you've said something that makes sense, Richard."

"Thank you." His lips curled in gentle irony. "That was a compliment, was it not?"

It was hard to maintain his angry stance in Tess's presence. He loved the outward signs of her bright, churning thoughts— her knitted, white forehead and her pursed, rosebud lips.

"I suppose that might be interpreted as a compliment," she replied. She stepped toward him, smoothing her collar, looking up prettily with earnest curiosity twinkling in her chestnut eyes. She smelled of crushed mint and rose petals. Her long, full gown brushed the top of his boots. The intimate rustle of leather and silk hardened him further.

"But why?" she whispered, an angry hint in her little-girl's voice, distrust flaring with a shiny glint in her narrowed eyes. "Why would you do this for me? Knowing what you know. Knowing that I want to . . ."

"Kill me?"

He longed to kiss her, to plunge his tongue into the moist depths of her honeycomb mouth. Her waist was narrow and near; his hand would fit neatly around it. Her breasts were high and lovely, perfect for his gruff hands to snatch and hold.

"I do not know why I want to give you power, Tess. But you deserve it. A woman like you deserves power, and so much more."

He was aware of nothing but those lips, moist and pink. They were so close.

Without moving a twitch, her face flushed with understanding and gratitude, then hardened with her perpetual and prim doubt.

"Is that the only reason?"

"Nay," he said, suddenly tired of words. "I can't wait to bait and badger and berate you at the shooting range."

"So I thought."

She seemed relieved. She dabbed violet water behind her ears and prattled on lightly. "Do you know, Richard, I'll take every insult you can offer if it gives me the chance . . . just the chance to defend myself. I do not even have to succeed. Just to hope is more than I have ever dreamed. A woman's lot in life is not all the minstrels who sing romances would have one believe."

She smiled with sad wisdom, and he thought her as fine as a rose in full bloom at the height of summer. Did she know she was blossoming? Had blossomed? Did she know adversity had made her fully a woman?

"Teach me," she whispered. Her lips barely moved, but the intensity of her thoughts was evident in the sudden burst of color on her cheeks, in the unexpected grip of her thin fingers on his forearm. "Teach me to kill you."

"Then let us get to it," he answered impatiently. "You needn't dust your cheeks with powder. They'll only turn black once you've fired your first shot."

"But my hair," she protested, plunging her fingers into her thatch of uncombed locks. "'Twill singe if it gets near a burning slow match. I would have Mellie plait it, but the indolent girl wouldn't rise if I screamed 'Fire!'"

"Come hither," he ordered. He placed his hands on her firm, proud shoulders and guided her to the chair at the small table where she kept combs and flower waters. "Sit in the chair. Here, take the looking glass and watch. I will plait your hair myself. If you fear you'll end with naught but a rat's nest, watch and instruct me."

She looked at his reflection in the mirror, which in turn reflected back to Richard an intimate view of her reactions. First bewilderment and then amusement played across her features, as in a subtle musical interlude when dark and ominous minor chords transform into lighthearted majors.

"Very well," she said. "Do as you please with those fumbling, big man's hands of yours. Just remember that however it turns out you will be seen with me upon your arm, and my disarray will speak poorly of you."

"Nay," he said in husky tones, running his fingers through the long sheet of her hair, "I will say you were just bedded and were so drunk with love you had no wits to hide the telltale signs of lovemaking."

Her cheeks pinkened, as if already rubbed raw by the shadow of a man's whiskers.

"My lord, you are absolutely horrid."

"You shall start with a hand-gunne," he said, almost under his breath, lost in the future. Already he had separated her silken hair into three thick hemps and intently entwined them in a steady rhythm, just as he had braided his mother's hair when he was a child.

"Though I recommend you kill me with a hand-gunne, you should also know how to handle even the heaviest weapons. I will teach you to fire a cannon as well. There's been more than one chatelaine who held her lord's castle under siege. You may be in the same position, and knowledge of all the weapons here at Cadmon Castle can only help you."

"I do not plan to remain here after your demise," she said with a distinct note of sarcasm, primly arching her brows, "so I doubt I will be defending the castle against a siege."

"What if we were attacked tomorrow, and I, much to your everlasting horror and sorrow, were slain in the first hour? Would you not do your best to defend the castle? If not, you could be taken prisoner."

"If you were mortally wounded, I would call the priest for last rites and proceed without pause or tears to the prison tower to free Lady Gertrude and the other Lollards. And then I would return to my father's castle. Or to Lucy's home, since my father's castle is no longer my own."

"Do you have a ribbon?"

"Did you hear what I just said?"

"Of course. You said, in essence, that you'll dance on my grave. Now where do you keep your ribbons? I am at a critical stage here, having perfected the art of plaiting."

She pulled a green ribbon from a small ivory jewelry box that was carved with a scene depicting Tristan and Iseult. "This will do."

He wrapped the thin material around the end of her thick braid and proceeded to tie a bow. "There you are."

"'Tis a shame I won't defend your castle, for I would have made a good chatelaine. It would have been quite a challenge to put Cadmon Castle in order."

"'Tis a shame for more reasons than that."

He dropped the braid and smoothed it down the middle of her back, his damnable groin lurching pitifully at the meager pleasure, and she tilted her comely face up to his.

"Why is that, my lord? How is it a shame in your eyes?"

"Because I could have loved you." The words, half whispered, ached sweetly in his throat. The truth had never hurt so good.

Her eyes widened, and he heard the sudden absence of her breathing. He had disarmed her with love. Or the pale, ghostly, misspent chance of love. And though the victory was his, the spoils of this war were too melancholy to bear. He pivoted like a stiff soldier who has smelled the blood of defeat on the wind, and then he marched to the door. "Come along. Time is wasting."

She followed obediently, unable to mutter a word of protest, though he could tell by the luscious swell of her breasts that she had restored her ability to breathe.

"Oh, my lady!" Mellie exclaimed, rising from her pallet on the floor and rubbing the sleep from her squinting eyes. "I thought I heard voices. Can I help you dress for the day? I am at your service."

Tess glared at the disheveled girl. "Oh, you are both impossible!"

She snatched a light cloak from a chair in one hand and a handful of her pleated gown in the other. Lifting her hem from the scattered twigs amongst the rushes, she sailed from the room.

Richard looked from the too-efficient lady to her slothful handmaiden and barked out a laugh of delight at the irony.

* * *

After three days, Tess knew as much about explosives as any of Richard's soldiers. She learned to load her own cartouches, packing each hand-sized vessel with one charge of bullet and black powder before hanging them from a belt she slung around her waist. She learned to load a shot and ramrod it into the barrel, and then to crumble a cake of corned powder and sprinkle it into the priming pan. And if she should ever wish to mix her own explosives, she learned the proper mixture: equal amounts of charcoal and sulphur in addition to forty-one percent saltpeter.

She also learned to squeeze the trigger as if it were the breast of a woman, as Richard had crudely, but accurately, instructed her. Gently but firmly, so that the Z-shaped serpentine would lower the burning slow match to the charge without jerking movements. And finally she learned to squint her burning eyes against the sizzle of the slow match and to brace herself just before the butt of her weapon slammed back against her bruised shoulder for the umpteenth time.

Having learned all this, though, is not to say she could shoot straight enough to hit a target, and she quickly discerned that a good deal of practice would be required of her.

She had two excellent coaches. One was Sir Oswald, the crippled orphan whom Richard had taken in many years ago, as Sir John had recounted. Ten years younger than the earl, Oswald was just eighteen years old. But he had a commanding presence born of skill and knowledge, and with his hair parted neatly down the center of his squarish head, a certain earnestness about him. He had lost his left leg below the knee as a child and used a peg leg. Since he could not hold his own in a sword fight, he had become a master gunner.

Tess trusted that he would not accidentally blow apart the artillery quarters before she had a chance to fulfill her mission. And yet she was aware that many a gunne backfired, often causing fatal damage. That was a risk she was willing to take, and a risk that seemed palatable in the presence of her second coach, the incomparable Lord Richard.

Inured to the grit of black powder that coated her cheeks and her tongue, she shoved aside the physical torments borne at the range for the chance to practice at Richard's side. Even though he was belligerent, condescending, and suffocatingly arrogant, she felt she was learning just by watching his passionate precision. When taking aim, his brow was ever whittled into furrows, like carved marble. He stared unflinchingly after each shot to see if he'd hit his mark, softly cursing when he did not, grinning with profound satisfaction that deepened his cheeks into dimples when he did. Tess was as mesmerized by his love for the sport as she was by its potency and destructive force.

"What does it feel like to kill someone?" she queried idly on their third day of practice. She frowned in concentration as she jammed her ramrod down the barrel of her gunne. A waft of sulphur billowed from the dark hole, an odor she no longer hated, but associated with her growing passion for shooting. Her cheeks were flushed with perspiration, and she was breathing hard from the intense labor of lifting one heavy weapon after another.

"I mean, is it pleasurable? Does it make one feel powerful?"

"You will just have to wait and see, won't you?" Richard answered.

She looked up and found him leaning on the fence that surrounded the shooting range. That meanness of spirit she'd seen in him of late sparkled viciously in his blue eyes. He'd taken great pleasure in tormenting her the last three days, and she'd been patient, knowing it was her penance for her regrettable honesty. But on this day, exhausted from her physical labors, she was in no mood for sarcasm.

"If I wait until I kill you, Richard, then I won't be able to discuss with you the joys of the experience, now will I?"

"Well, then let us discuss it now. What will you be most pleased to be rid of when I pass from this earthly vale?" His whimsical half-grin vanished as he focused on her preparations. "You're putting in too much powder, Tess. How many times do I have to warn you about that? You'll blow us from here to kingdom come."

He loomed over her and impatiently plucked the weapon from her hands. Tess spun around, ready to blast him, but bit her tongue. Patience. She must be patient, she knew. She needed this knowledge.

"I think I shall be most eager to rid the world of your stubborn insistence that you know more about everything than anybody else," she said, forcing her weary cheeks into a broad, too-sweet smile.

"'Tis not stubbornness," he countered, matching her smile with a cocky one of his own as he fiddled with the gunne. "'Tis an acceptance of fact."

Why did the twist of playful arrogance on his lips make her want to kiss them? She still did not understand why she longed to embrace him, now more than ever. Watching his long lean fingers caress the weapon, seeing the gleam of manly sweat on his brow, smelling the powder and leather that permeated his houppelande, feeling the power of his muscles when he brushed up against her—all made her long to tackle him and squirm in his arms. She would miss that desire if he were gone.

"Here." He gave her back the weapon, his fingers wrapping around hers for a moment longer than necessary. The air about them stilled. She looked up and realized with agony that his lips were only inches away. She could steal a kiss if she wanted to, except that she did not want to give him the victory in their ongoing battle of wills.

"You are ready to shoot," he said somberly, his eyes stroking her face until she tingled.

"We've run out of targets," she protested. "Look at that poor mock soldier yonder. He's been demolished, straw scattered everywhere."

"Nay, you haven't run out of targets."

With a graveness she did not at first comprehend, he turned and walked thirty paces. Then he faced her and opened his arms wide. "Here is your target. The one you've been waiting for."

"What . . . what do you mean?"

"Shoot me. I am your target."

Tess's bemused expression turned to one of terrible sadness. She moistened her lips, licking tangy salt and bitter black powder, then tried and failed to laugh off his suggestion. The laughter stuck in her throat. He was trying to please her by offering himself as a sacrifice. What kind of woman had she become if this was the gift others perceived her as most wanting? What kind of savage, revengeful crone had she turned into since her father's death?

Her silent questions surged with long-overdue perspective, then a rush of shame. Her ears prickled with heat. But habitual bitterness roared to life, overcoming any qualms of conscience, and she boldly raised the barrel, aiming at Richard's heart.

"Thata girl," he said calmly. "You've wanted to do this for a long time. Now you have the knowledge and the power."

"Do you want to die?" she asked as she focused over the barrel, squinting an eye at his lithe form. The slow match sizzled softly in her line of vision.

"Nay, I am glad and somewhat surprised to say that I do not want to die."

"Nor did my father," she seethed, strangling the gunne until her knuckles turned white, her fingertips an angry red.

"I am sorry for that, Tess," he said.

Genuine sadness softened further the deep timbre of his voice, but he did not appear frightened, and she wanted him to be. She wanted him to be so frightened he would piss in his braies.

"You're not sorry enough, you bloody bastard."

"Then shoot me."

"I will!"

She put her forefinger on the trigger. But as she began to squeeze it, a voice deep inside screamed, *"No!"*

She hesitated, perspiration springing through every pore, blood booming in her temples. She was suddenly light-headed. She lowered the gunne. Black dots skipped before her eyes. She blinked as her blurry vision turned one Richard into two, and then two into four. She *should* kill him, she told herself. If she had any courage. If she were true to her word she would kill him now.

"You bastard!" She spewed the epithet over her numb lips and raised the gunne again. It weighed a hundred stones, burned the muscles in her arms. She took deadly aim.

"No!" the voice screamed again. She heard it. It was real. She looked behind her. A few soldiers were laughing, unaware of her. She blinked. Slowly. Who was it? She knew the voice.

"No, Tess!" Father. It was her father's voice, or at least the memory of it.

"Come on, Tess," Richard goaded her. With his arms stretched out, he looked like one of those beautiful portraits of Christ hanging on the cross, his eyes martyred, his hair flowing.

"My father—" she started to say, but ran out of steam. Her father would not want her to kill Richard. The Lollards were pacifists. *Nay, damn it, I do not want to be reasonable. I don't care what Father would have done.*

"I am not my father!" she shouted. "I am less noble than him."

"That I can understand," Richard answered patiently. "Now do it, Tess. You know you want to."

Her weary arms began to shake. She wanted nothing more than to lower the gunne. It was so heavy. *Put the gunne down,* the voice of reason argued. *Richard is not the enemy.*

Now bathed in a sleek coat of sweat, she lowered the barrel. "I can't," she muttered, tortured with frustration. "I can't."

A wind picked up, blowing her hair, twisting it around her face. She wanted to sink into the earth, to lose herself, to forget who she was, to run and hide from the truth just revealed to her. She had hoped she was strong enough for revenge. She was certain she wasn't strong enough to forgive.

But this wasn't really about forgiveness. This was something much more terrifying. This was . . .

No, I won't consider it.

She whipped the hair out of her eyes and stared him down. "You bloody bastard, you knew I wouldn't."

She threw the gunne down as if it were a writhing serpent and stalked toward him. She hated him suddenly. Hated him for a whole new reason. "You knew I wouldn't do it."

"I did not know that."

"Bastard!" she cried. Closing the distance between them, she flung herself at him, shoving him with all her might, and still he didn't budge. "You knew I wouldn't do it. You knew!"

She saw nothing but compassion in his eyes. No! She wanted him as an enemy. Not as a . . .

Run away! If you look in his eyes any longer he will know.

She turned and ran, her feet brushing through clumps of new spring grass and little mushrooms of earth. She raced through the grassy field toward the castle, urgency spurring her on, stumbling when her foot sank into a rut. Pain shot up her leg. She landed with a grunt, dewy grass pricking her face, then she rose, hurtling onward.

"Tess! Tess!"

His voice grew louder. She couldn't face him. Not now. One look in her eyes and he would know. She loved him. But how could she, with the Lollards still imprisoned? As her sides began to ache, as her lungs burned in their thirst for air, she had the most profound and terrifying realization of her life: Love was illogical and infinite. Love could behold evil and goodness at once and embrace them both. Staggered in the presence of such infinity, her feet began to slow.

"Tess!"

Having finally overtaken her, Richard gripped her arm and swung her around. She fell against his chest and gripped his strong shoulders, and then she melted. Their lips met halfway, as if they'd waited a lifetime for this joining.

"Richard," she muttered. Had a single utterance ever said so much? *I am alive. I want you. I love you, Richard, my enemy.*

Her tongue was thrusting into the sweetness of his mouth. When had she become so bold? She wanted more, but he ended the kiss abruptly, separating them by an arm's length.

"No," she protested. Hearing herself, she bit her tongue and studied his infinite, cerulean eyes.

He was as astonished as she. He licked his lower lip and eyed her speculatively. But he didn't know. He hadn't guessed. And she would not tell him. She could never tell him. For him it was just physical. Crude desire. He must think it was so with her as well.

"Tess?"

"Aye?"

His gaze flitted between hers, so much unspoken. *Don't say it,* she pleaded inwardly. *Don't say anything.*

"I will meet you tomorrow," he said calmly, his eyes alive with hope and tenderness. "Same time. Same place."

"Yes. I mean, what for?"

"To shoot."

"To shoot," she repeated, still dazed. "Oh, yes. Another lesson in shooting. I'll . . . I'll be here."

And that was it. She forced herself to turn and walk away. Or did she float away? That was how such scenes ended, wasn't it? One always departed nobly. The one with the upper hand. Upper, lower, sideways—she no longer knew which hand was which. But she'd be back. Oh, yes, she'd be back. She wouldn't resist. Just as she had never resisted peeking under her bed as a child when she was certain a monster lurked beneath. A horrifying and irresistible monster.

FIFTEEN

During their lessons in the days to come, there was little need for them to talk, neither in affirmation nor in rancor. Tess felt Richard's approval every time he gently smudged his thumbs over her stinging, blackened eyes to remove the grit of black powder. Or when he pulled her up from the ground whenever a blast knocked her on her rear.

Tess had never felt more at one with herself, nor had she ever enjoyed the company of another as much as she enjoyed Richard's presence. She did not consciously think about love, or that her happiness was due to her realization that she loved Richard. That would have been much too overwhelming. She had decided, instead, to tiptoe into the future, seeing how far fate would compel her to go, enjoying the journey as it unfolded.

She practiced with Richard every day. But eventually exhaustion set in, overcoming her determination and her newfound passion for gunnes. It happened on her fifth day at practice. That morning Richard and Sir Oswald were called from the field to the castle on urgent business. Tess elected to stay out-of-doors, practicing with the encouragement of Perkins. Near the end of the day, when the sun bent to touch the earth, leaving a trail of vibrant orange, she dropped a hand-gunne from her blistered fingers, wiped a forearm across her drenched brow, and said to Perkins, "Enough! I shall die if I take another shot."

"But Lady Tess, your aim is lamentable. You must learn to hold the weapon steady."

"I couldn't hold a horn of ale steady." She held out her hand, and her shaking fingers proved her point. "I am exhausted. The more I practice, the worse I become. And I am nearly deaf from the noise. My ears are ringing."

"You should soak your muscles in hot water. May I order a bath for you, Lady Tess?"

"Aye, and enough servants to carry me to it, for I do not think I can hold myself upright much longer."

"Very well, my lady," Perkins replied with an impish glint in his eyes.

In the earl's solar, Richard's commanders argued vociferously. Richard sat perfectly still behind his desk, but his placid countenance hid mottled anger. With his chin propped on a fist, his eyes followed the conversation as it bounced between the seven other men. There was Gaveston, commander of the cavalry; Jack Hughes, who trained the archers; Richard's steward, Godfrey, and castellan, Sir Randolf; as well as Oswald and two of his gunners. When their voices rose to a fevered pitch of accusations, Richard cut in with a simple, coolly delivered command.

"Enough."

The men fell silent. Some stared sullenly at the maps stretched out before them on the earl's desk; others awaited Richard's decision about the disturbing new development that had spawned the argument. It was a development that had retaught Richard an old lesson: The most carefully thought-out plans were always vulnerable, and victory was always far from assured, no matter how righteous the cause.

"How could anyone have stolen nearly an entire shipment of hand-gunnes?" Richard said at last.

"Quite simply," Godfrey offered, "the thieves attacked your men-at-arms on their way back from London, fresh from the gunner's shop. Perhaps the proprietor who sold you the shipment wagged his tongue about their destination."

"I paid him dearly to keep silent," Richard said, his voice strained and flat. "Methinks there must be a traitor in our midst."

Several nodded and grunted their assent.

"The question is, who?"

"I'd lay my purse on that damned infidel from Persia," said Sir Randolf. The giant of a man—raven-bearded and gruff— sneered as if Tarjaman's name were too filthy to be uttered.

"Do not be too quick to point a condemning finger at Tarjaman, Randolf. I do not think he would betray me."

Randolf's thick beard rippled as he ground his teeth. "Richard, how many years did you fight the Welsh with Prince Hal? Certainly long enough to know that you cannot trust the word of a man whose blood runs a different color."

Richard waved him off. He did not want to think that Tarjaman was the one, but he silently girded himself for the worst.

"Leave Tarjaman be. If he is the traitor, we will find out soon enough and can exact justice when we do. Until then, do not lay a finger upon him, Randolf."

The castellan grunted in reluctant acquiescence.

"My lord," Oswald said, taking a lurching step forward. "The traitor could easily have been a spy planted by Bishop George."

"But who, Oswald?" Richard countered. "Only a handful of people knew about the shipment, and only those closest to me. You have not told your men that I plan to attack the bishop before we join the king's forces, have you?"

"Nay, my lord." Randolf spoke for all the commanders. "But did you tell Tarjaman?"

Richard glowered at his persistent and able castellan. "Aye, Tarjaman knew."

Randolf smirked and turned away.

"The financial loss is great indeed," Godfrey said, breaking his observant silence. "But your men are otherwise well armed and trained. If you lay siege to Kirkingham's castle, your cannons will be sufficient. And after all, hand-gunnes are still unproven in battle."

Godfrey was right. Richard's insistence on ordering hand-gunnes had been more an indulgence in his obsession than a sound military decision.

"The loss of weaponry is devastating not so much in terms of function, or even in terms of money lost. The true loss, my friends, is trust. Someone close to me tipped off the thieves, and I want to know who."

"What about Lady Tess?" Sir Randolf nonchalantly queried as he gazed out of Richard's stretch of windows, his back to the small audience.

The room grew very still. The hair on Richard's nape stiffened like hogs' bristles. "What about her?"

"She hates the king. She would have motive enough to insure that those weapons were never used to fight Henry's cause in France. She doesn't know you planned to use them to attack the bishop. 'Tis clear to all you have not won her over to your side yet, my lord."

So his private battles with Tess were common knowledge. Richard's jaw muscles flexed with the sudden flare of his temper.

"You will not inpugn my lady's honor, Randolf, be advised," Richard said, rising to his full height. "I'll have the head of any man who tries to defile her character. She is not the traitor."

His glaring eyes met those of his chief commander. Richard felt the fool for defending a lady who would gladly dance on his grave, but it did not matter. Her integrity was above reproach, and he'd die defending it if need be.

Just then the door burst open and Perkins marched in as if he owned the castle.

"Oh, my lord, I did not know you were in. I thought you were inspecting the garrisons. Did I hear you mention Lady Tess? How providential. I've ordered a bath for her."

The squire bustled toward the far corner of the solar, pushing aside Richard's suit of armor and pulling the wooden tub out before the fire. A string of servants followed moments later. They carried pail after pail of recently boiled water.

"My lords, we will continue this discussion at another time," Richard said quietly.

He could tell by Sir Randolf's frown that he disapproved of Perkins's seeming impertinence. But Richard was grateful for the quick end to what had become an increasingly difficult discussion. And if he knew Perkins, the lad had probably been listening outside the door and had entered at precisely that moment to relieve his master.

Tess appeared in the doorway, disheveled and unbalanced on her teetering legs.

"Why, Lady Tess, you are just in time!" Perkins exclaimed, rushing to greet her.

Tess paused in the doorway, shocked to see a crowd.

"Perkins," she whispered. "You did not tell me I would be bathing in the earl's solar. In front of an audience, no less."

"Never fear, my lady," he whispered in return. "The audience shall soon depart. Put yourself at ease while I attend to the bath."

"By Beelzebub, what have we here?" said Jack Hughes.

Raising bushy gray brows, he took one look at Tess's blackened cheeks and began to laugh.

"You looked no better when you were learning to shoot, Hughes," Sir Oswald countered, jumping to her defense.

"Here, here," Godfrey agreed.

Tess did not care what anyone thought of her current condition. She was too sore to care. Every muscle in her body screamed in protest after lifting so many heavy weapons, and she was aware of little more than her overwhelming desire to sink into a hot tub. If only it wasn't at the other end of the chamber! As Richard shooed everyone from the room, she made her way to the nearest respite—his bed. Unable to hold herself erect a moment longer, she collapsed on the down mattress just as he shut the door. She knew he would not misjudge her reason for throwing herself before him, for not only had he witnessed her herculean efforts at the shooting range, he had gamely encouraged them.

He tested the water in silence and then sat down on the bed at her side. She cracked open one weary eyelid and found him studying her, his piercing blue eyes roving over her analytically.

"Aye, you bear all the signs of a novice—exhaustion, exhaustion, and exhaustion. Do you hate me—"

"Aye."

"—for making you learn how to shoot?"

"Oh. Nay, I do not hate you for *that*." She heaved a sigh and smiled up at him. "I am happy to learn. If I'd had a hand-gunne a year ago, I might have saved my father's life."

He leaned forward and placed on her dirty forehead the gentlest kiss she'd ever received.

"Mayhap you could have saved him, sweet lady. More than likely, 'twould not have helped that night. No weapon can quash the absolute will of Henry. Oh, do not frown. We will not talk of the king now. Here, give me your arm. I know all too well how the muscles burn there."

His giant hands wrapped around and began to knead her upper arm, which was encased in a tight-fitting linen sleeve.

"Ahhh," Tess groaned. "That feels delightful."

He continued in silence a moment, and then cleared his throat. "Tess, I've been contemplating a matter of great importance. I want us to be married in jointure."

"What? Why on earth . . . ?"

"That way you will share equal possession of my estate—and your own—and Henry will be hard-pressed to force you into another match should I die."

"Well, of course, I know the implications. But in jointure? My lord, you are too generous. I have no bargaining power in this match. Such a gift is not necessary. Even without it I am entitled to at least a third of your holdings upon your death."

"Which may come sooner than you think."

He must mean Henry's war in France. A wave of melancholy washed over Tess. Thinking of Richard's death filled her with an illogical sense of loss. Perhaps it was because he was so close and his touch felt so good.

"My lord . . ." She lifted a hand to affectionately stroke his even brow, but her arm was too weak. Her trembling fingers fell to her side.

Richard seemed to know what she was about. He leaned forward and kissed her lips. The kiss felt perfect on her mouth—hot, hungry, tender, artful. There weren't enough adjectives to describe how good it felt. She groaned her acceptance and felt a slowly kindling fire building inside her. It was as if her weariness had shuttered all resistance.

He pulled away, breathing raggedly. His hand roved across her shoulder to the top button of her kirtle; he popped it free with a flick of his fingers. Her nipples tingled and rose to stiff attention.

Terrified, Tess clinched his wrist. "What are you doing?"

"Unbuttoning your kirtle."

"Yes, I know. But why?"

"To undress you."

A long pause. *"Why?"*

"So that you might bathe. The boiled water will be cool enough by now. Have you forgotten how filthy you are?"

She felt sweat trickle between her thighs, and a new moisture prickling in those private depths.

As he spoke, she loosened her grip and he continued. *Pop* went another button, and then another, inviting the cool air to seep further into the valley between her breasts. Panicked again, she tightened her grip, halting his progress.

"Please, Richard, my handmaiden can help me undress."

He held very still, breathing deeply. "I want to see you," he whispered.

Goose bumps rippled along her arms. *Oh, Lord,* she thought, *he wants to see me, and I want to be seen!* She wanted to be utterly naked in his presence. She longed to curl up sleek and bare beside his long, hard body.

Blushing, she nodded her submission. He continued his slow descent, unfastening one button after another. *Pop. Pop.*

She flung an arm over her eyes, seeking darkness, a shadowed place. "Is it not a sin to be so wanton before marriage?" she whispered.

"Nay," he said reassuringly, "tomorrow the priest will post the wedding banns. 'Tis common for those betrothed to take pleasure as they will."

When his hand reached the last button at her navel, with her arm still covering her eyes, she whispered, "What . . . pleasure? Do you plan to . . . ? I mean . . . will we . . . ?"

Using both hands, he gently nudged aside the folds of her kirtle, exposing her breasts beneath the sheer and dainty chemise. Her rose-colored nipples pushed against the samite material like tiny mountains. He put his mouth to one, suckling gently through the silky weave. She shuddered with unheard-of passion, for no minstrel had ever put passion in these terms. Ending his sweet torture, he knelt on the bed and lifted the arm still flung over her eyes. He was so close the tips of his long hair caressed her shoulders. His warm, sweet breath fanned her face.

"I only want to look at you. Nay, that is a lie—I want to make you scream with delight. But not tonight. I will soon, though, you know."

"Will you?" It was a breathless question, like one whispered to a wisewoman hunched over scattered runes. Oh, he was merciless, going in for the kill with his cornered game. He knew she wanted him. He knew she would not resist.

"Oh, yes," he murmured confidently, running a hand over her breasts, squeezing the nipples, smoothing his fingers lower over her concave belly, over the mounds of her hips, touching the edge of her thatched fur. "'Tis just a matter of time. Would you like that?"

She was aware of nothing but his hand, wishing it would lower farther, to the dark, moist place where fireworks were igniting.

"Would you like that?" he repeated.

She couldn't say nay. Tears welled in her eyes as she submitted to the truth. "I *would* like to . . . join with a man. At least once."

"You would like to join with just any man?"

God, how weary she was. Her eyes were growing heavy, sultry with passion, groggy from the physical release. "With you," she said, too tired to lie. "Just with you."

His lips curved up in cool triumph. "Now you will know the bittersweet I have tasted, sleeping with the enemy."

But he wasn't the enemy. Not anymore. She wished he were. She wished she still wanted to kill him. That was far safer than wanting to make love to him, for how could she feel desire and protect herself at the same time?

He tugged gently at her shoulders, pulling her kirtle over them and down her arms, undressing her as her nursemaid had done when she was a child.

"I know a lot about you, Richard," she said in a groggy voice, surrendering to his ministering.

"Like what?"

"I know what you fear. I know about your hopes. I know your goodness."

He had just pulled her up into a sitting position, and when she said the word "goodness" he slipped his arms around her for a hug, kissing her nape. "I thought you might. I hoped you might."

"And I know your faults," she said as solemnly as a child, groaning at his sensuous kiss, wrapping her arms around him.

He laughed, ecstatic to hear such honesty. It was so rare. "My faults would be hard to miss."

"You can ravage me as you will, but—"

"Thank you."

"—but I will still hate you. Always will."

"Of course," he murmured. He kissed the smooth skin at the base of her throat, and she shivered. By now her gown hung limply around her waist. She was bare save for her flimsy chemise. He pulled her up from the bed by both hands.

As she nearly collapsed, her wobbly knees buckling, he scooped a muscle-corded arm around her waist and pulled her close, smashing her breasts against his chest.

Impulsively, he threw her over his shoulder, her rump in the air, and tugged on her gown as he headed for the tub. He pulled the green silk over her hips, then dropped the gown to the floor.

Tess hung limply, not even attempting to protest the intimacy. He deposited her by the tub, appreciating her raw beauty through the chemise, which he promptly tugged over her head. He gently pulled her naked form close and gave her a drugging kiss. His tongue dipped into the dark depths of her mouth as his hands crawled over her bottom, scooping two handfuls of softness.

Tess arched against the hardness at his groin, her womanhood burning.

"Get in," he ordered, assisting her into the tub.

She did as instructed and moaned with ecstasy as the soothing water engulfed her aching body. As he lathered soap on a washcloth, she closed her eyes.

"My, my, I have my work cut out for me," he said. Kneeling next to her, he began to scrub her face.

"I'm not a child," she protested, sniffing at the stinging soap.

"Nay, but you look like one, with dirt and black powder smeared everywhere. Now do not fuss."

Her father used to bathe her as a child with the same gentle strokes. Tess felt protected and cared for, the very emotions she had tried to provide for everyone at Haddington Castle. It was good to have someone caring for her for a change. He would spoil her doing this. And she would enjoy every minute of it.

"Richard?"

"Aye?"

"I could have loved you, too."

She peeked open her eyes, thinking she would find a glimmer of satisfaction upon his face, or at least a look of smug triumph. Instead she saw a flicker of doubt, and something else altogether more ominous.

SIXTEEN

The young priest posted the wedding banns on a morning that blew in the certainty of spring. The radiant sun glinted on the parchment nailed to the church door, illuminating the announcement of Richard and Tess's impending nuptials for all to see.

The very act instilled an air of excitement in the castle, for everyone knew the wedding feast would be grand. Invitations were sent posthaste by the earl's messengers to neighboring nobles and merchants. The elderly ladies-in-waiting began to stitch a wedding gown, clucking over Tess at every fitting. Hunters combed the earl's forest for pheasants and wild boar. And Sir John, nearly apoplectic with joy, ordered his minstrels to Tess and Richard's side at every turn to sing romantic ballads of love everlasting.

Tess was mortified by the songs. It seemed every verse was about freshly plucked roses and thorns. It was not hard to read between the lines to interpret the lusty implication. The minstrels sang pointedly to her about an act that both excited and terrified her—the act of making love.

To make matters worse, the gushing songs reminded her of the lamentable confession she'd made while bathing. It wasn't enough that she had foolishly blurted out her plan to kill Richard; she had to be honest about her tenderest feelings as well. *Oh, why must I always be so damned honest?* Her admission that she *could* have loved him was tantamount to saying that she *did* love him. When she recalled his response, she wanted to wither and die. The blank stare in his eyes, the frown of warning. He obviously pitied her foolish confession.

And so on the second day of nonstop accompaniment, when a sappy-eyed troubadour began to strum his lute, smiling at her knowingly as if it were an accepted fact that she was hopelessly in love, she gripped the frets of his instrument, stilling his vibrating chords.

"Enough," she hissed, and marched off in pursuit of her unwanted benefactor.

Tess cornered Sir John in the outer bailey, where he relented, promising to call off his musicians. She thanked him profusely, and when she bid him adieu, she found Richard waiting for her not twenty paces away, leaning casually against the door to the carpenter's shop, arms crossed, muscles rippling beneath the tawny gold hair that brushed his forearm.

"Looks like you gave our friend a good tongue-lashing," he said when she strolled to his side.

He smelled faintly of horse hair and leather, and she assumed he had been riding.

"Good day, Richard."

She felt strangely at ease, contrary to her expectations. His eyes held none of the darkness that had embarrassed her so after her bath. Had she imagined it? Presently, his gaze glinted keenly at her, or through her, making her blush, making her feel special. There was no ominous darkness. There was, however, a new intensity. A restive quality. And she had the distinct feeling that she was its cause. She liked thinking she had at least that much power over him.

"What were you admonishing Sir John for?"

She shrugged. "Oh, 'twas nothing."

"I see. Actually, I do not see, but no matter. Will you shoot with me?"

"Of course."

He reached out and Tess gravitated to his side, feeling a sense of peace when she slipped her hand into his. Perhaps everything would be all right after all. Perhaps her admission had not been such a horrible mistake. Perhaps she had misinterpreted his blank reaction. Or perhaps she was so foolishly besotted that nothing mattered as long as she could hold his hand.

As they strolled together, Tess seized a breath of fresh spring air, feeling alive, feeling that she was at one with nature, that nothing separated her from the air, the grass, the sun. Not even her skin.

When their silent stroll led them to the new grass sprouting on the practice field, cushioning their leisurely steps, Richard greeted a half dozen gunners who were practicing at the range and then immediately fetched a gunne.

"Let me see you shoot," he said. He gave her a lopsided grin that held a challenge as he placed the long weapon in her hands. "Perkins thinks you're getting pretty good."

Her arms lagged under the weight. "Oh, Richard, I am still so weary."

"You do not think I will let you off so easily, do you?"

When he crossed his arms and smiled even more broadly, her heart pitter-pattered. She smiled back, no longer able to hide her attraction to the man.

"Nay, I suppose not. I can manage," she said with genuine sweetness. Had she ever been sweet before? Practical, yes, but sweet?

Wanting to show her strength and eager to engage again in her new hobby, she raised the weapon, but her traitorous shoulders, overwrought, began to shake from the strain.

"You were right. You're suffering, poor lamb."

His voice was soft and gentle, as gentle as the spring breeze that soothed the goose bumps rising on her arms.

"Here, give the gunne to me. I will start things off and let you work yourself up to the occasion." He took the gunne and prepared it for a shot.

Though Richard belittled his own skills as a gunner, affecting a modesty that no one took seriously, he was, in fact, a master. It was evident in the way he wrapped his arms gracefully around the gunne, caressing the wooden and metal weapon almost as if it were a lover. His broad shoulders embraced each explosion, barely registering a jolt. His blue eyes coalesced in meditative concentration as he refilled the priming pan with black powder, crumbling a cake of corned powder with long, fluid fingers. His flashing white teeth clamped down on his lower lip as he took aim. He tossed his hair back over his shoulder as he centered his gaze down the barrel, scowling at his target. And when he fired and hit his mark, as he did presently, oh, what joy to behold! A riot of enjoyment washed over his face, blazing in his eyes, curling his lips with supreme pleasure, lodging in every muscle, so that even his stance was lively. Tess could watch him for hours.

"Now 'tis your turn," Richard said, and after reloading the weapon, he placed it in her hands. "I will help you."

He stepped up behind her. Placing his hands over hers, he raised the weapon for her. She noticed for the first time how snugly their bodies seemed to fit. His chin just touched the top of her head. His groin nestled against the small of her back. Heat radiated from his chest, washing over her with a tingling sensation. She knew his fantastically sculpted lips were near her ear, for she felt the heat of his breath, smelled its sweetness. She moistened her mouth, swallowing desire. It was as if his lips were shooting out flames of heat, drawing her like a moth to a fire on a sultry summer night. Lord, how she longed to turn and kiss him.

"I did not mean to overwork you, Tess," he murmured, low and sexy. His words slipped inside of her, sending a tickling curl of desire down her spine. Each syllable permeated her skin. She shivered and tilted her head to one side, exposing her bare neck, daring him to kiss her, craving it.

"Perhaps I should have remembered how painful it is to build your strength."

"I do not blame you for the pain, my lord."

"Good," he replied. Like a fish biting the lure, he stole a kiss that branded her neck in the small valley above her collarbone.

Tess shivered, and knew then what he was about. She understood the distraction she'd seen in his tanned face when he'd found her in the bailey. He wanted to make love to her. He was seducing her. A fissure of fear ripped through her body with a chilling, jagged motion. She shivered again. They could not make love. She was afraid. But fear would make her a virgin the rest of her life. Fear would deny her her passion.

"Now take aim," he whispered.

She obliged, too aware of the warmth of his body molded to hers to be bothered by the acrid wick that sizzled inches away from her flaring pink nostrils. Aiming at the straw soldier, pretending it was her fear, she pulled the trigger. The blast knocked her more fully into Richard's arms. Instead of retreating, he leaned into the motion and let out a whoop of joy.

"Good shot!" he yelled, and wrapped his arms around her, hugging her soundly.

Delighting from head to toe, she knew that she had to act before all was lost. She plunged through his interlocking arms like a shot from a cannon. Spinning around, she stared at him half accusingly and half gratefully.

"Are you trying to seduce me?"

His eyes narrowed with a devilish glint. He thrust out his lower lip. "What if I am?"

When she did not answer, he swept forward. The force of his magnetism, instead of drawing her to him, nearly bowled her over. She took a step back, but he tucked both his hands beneath her hair, encasing her neck with hot fingers. He rubbed them with exquisite skill over a taut tendon.

"You are so soft and white," he whispered, trailing his fingers down the tendon to the base of her neck. "Tess, I have resisted this. I have truly resisted this. You may not believe it, but I have."

Hearing the anguish that screwed his voice into an angry growl, she looked up at his perfect face and saw a storm churning in his eyes.

"I want you. I need you. You will not deny me," he said, and his mouth descended with incredible force. His lips seethed against hers. She groaned, a gasp of awe, a whimper of excruciating desire. Then his kiss deepened, and she melted into it.

Nay, I will not deny you, she thought, her head spinning, drunk with his intoxicating taste: salt and ale.

Suddenly, thunder cracked in the sky. She lunged farther into his arms, without breaking free of his devouring mouth, thinking it was her heart that had cracked open.

In the darkness of her closed eyes, she saw a muted flash of light. Then another rattling crash of thunder ripped through the sky, rumbling off into the distance.

Richard ended the kiss, concluding with three small pecks to her swollen lips. He looked up at the darkening sky with a mischievous grin.

"That's very good, Tess. Next thing I know the earth will be moving beneath us. And we are still fully clothed. Just think what 'twill be like when we are as Adam and Eve."

She chuckled, not nearly as embarrassed as she thought she

would be. She was still too woozy with desire and pleasure. She sniffed in the distinct odor of rain, that metallic, ineffable smell that always preceded a whopping good storm.

"I saw nothing but sunshine until this moment. You must have distracted me," she said, her brow twisting with irony.

"We'll be drenched soon."

As soon as he had said it, a powerful wind whipped through the air and bent the trees on the horizon to its will. The soldiers practicing nearby started to pack up their equipment. They worked urgently as the leaden gray sky turned to midnight blue.

Richard frowned at the sky and then at Tess, running his hands through his hair. He shook his head, arguing with himself.

"I should get you back to the safety of the castle. You'd truly curse me unto eternity if I allowed you to be struck and killed by lightning."

Tess smiled at his dark humor, casting her gaze on the distant trees, which quavered, seemingly in fear. She inhaled the warning scent of rain and felt goose bumps of anticipation rise at the electricity that crackled unheard and unseen in the air.

"Aye, we should go," she said unenthusiastically.

"Do you want to?"

"In truth?" She grinned wickedly. "Nay, I do not. I want to be a bad girl and let my clothes become drenched, to skip about in puddles and muddy my shoes."

"Then we shall do that very thing."

"I love storms."

"So do I." They grinned at each other, delighting in their common likes.

"The air is fantastically cool." She lifted up her hair and bent her head so the wind could swirl around the moisture gathering at the back of her neck. Sweat was as common to her these days as fragrant oils had been before she began her shooting lessons.

Richard placed a warm hand beneath her hairline, a highly charged bolt of lightning, and she had to fight her body to keep from arching with a jerk. He massaged the tight muscles that corded along her spine. How much anger had lodged in her body she could not guess, but her neck was thoroughly knotted with past venom.

"You are a gentle man, Richard."

"Shhhh. You'll ruin my reputation."

The rain began to fall. Slowly at first. A big fat drop here. Another there. The soldiers jogged off the field, dashing back to the castle, shouting to Tess and Richard to seek shelter. A zigzag of white light throbbed across the sky. A moment later a bone-splintering crack pierced their ears, followed by a fading rumble of thunder.

Tess jumped at the sound. Richard pulled her into a comforting embrace. "Fear not. I will protect you."

Defying his mortal vanity, the heavens opened and a deluge of water fell about them, pelting the grass at their feet with a steady drumming sound. In an instant they were thoroughly drenched.

Richard laughed. "So much for my knightly power to protect."

Tess tilted her head back, leaning against the support of his arm. The water made their bodies rub together in a slick and sensual way. She welcomed the onslaught as she hadn't since she was a child. Cool drops pelted her face, moistened her thirsty tongue. Laughing freely, she blinked and sluiced the water from her face.

"I love this!" she shouted.

"Come, I have a secret place to wait out the storm," Richard said. "But we will take our time so the little girl can trounce in the puddles as we go."

She laughed deep in her throat, loving him at this moment. Loving life.

He led her slowly back toward the castle. She jumped from puddle to puddle, swinging her arms, giggling madly. He stopped her when they reached the animals' barn. "Would you like to see the elephant and the leopard?"

Her eyes widened with excitement. "Is it safe?"

"Of course."

She bobbed her head up and down, still the child.

Richard pulled open the wooden door to the giant structure. Tess walked into a wall of warm air, fetid with the smell of animals, hay, and lingering incense. She blinked at the powerful odor, and then relaxed when her nose and lungs became acclimated. She was starting to feel the beginning of a chill. Her nipples hardened beneath her wet gown, and the cozy warmth of the barn was a welcome change.

Richard dismissed a boy who tended the animals in Tarjaman's absence, instructing the lad to run back to the castle and inform the animal trainer that his creatures would be safe for the duration of the storm. The boy fled, eager to please the earl, leaving them utterly alone.

The solitude seemed as palpable as a third person, looming over them, warning Tess of danger. Her eyes flickered to Richard's. She saw the danger there, but it was mixed with an erotic blend of another emotion she could not tag. Her gaze dropped to her feet.

"I should not be here," she said softly.

"Nay, you should not." His voice was a husky rasp.

She had expected an argument, but he was too honest, at least in this moment. And with that, she brushed all logic aside. She no longer cared about what she should do, about what was safe, or right, or proper. Her skin oozed with feeling beaten into her by the rain. She craved the heat of his skin. She was chilled and thrilled and dying to dance. She looked back into the swirling heat of his hungry gaze and swallowed thickly. Oh, yes, he wanted her. Just as much as she wanted him. But not yet. Not just yet. She could not yet entirely brush aside the fear that she had lived with all her life.

She sidestepped him and entered the barn more fully, and then halted just as abruptly, for her gaze alighted on an exotic yellow creature with black spots sprawled leisurely in a pile of hay in the far corner.

"Saints! Is that . . . ?"

"A leopard. We call her Bathsheba."

Responding to her name, the sleek beast raised her head and cut loose with a spine-tingling growl. Tess stiffened, and then pressed her hands to her gaping mouth. "Oh, she is incredible."

The cat's white whiskers undulated with a grimace. She proceeded to clean one of her hefty paws, lathering over her black pads with a long, pink tongue, not unlike the cleansing ritual of Tess's cat at Haddington Castle. Except that this cat was tethered to a long chain attacked to a thick leather collar.

"Come and see," Richard coaxed Tess. "She'll not hurt you. She's as tame as a kitten. Besides, she barely has any teeth left. She's very old. Tarjaman feeds her minced meat every day."

Richard took Tess's hands and led her to Bathsheba's side, where they both knelt. The leopard twisted and flipped her body, rolling on her back. She was obviously waiting for a good belly-scratching, which Richard readily provided. Tess stroked the short fur on her forehead and ran her fingers through the soft furry folds of skin beneath Bathsheba's neck. The big cat's mouth opened, her tongue fell out with a pant of contentment, and she exhaled a musty gust of air.

"What a pussycat," Tess said, utterly charmed.

"But not nearly as sweet as Belle," Richard said. "Come and see for yourself."

Tugging Tess's hand, he pulled her past a short wooden divider to the open area of the barn, and once again Tess's mouth dropped in wonder.

"Oh, my," she whispered, letting her gaze crawl up the length and breadth of the enormous elephant she had heretofore seen only at a distance.

"She's a sweet thing, is she not?" Richard inquired. Stepping up behind Tess, he placed his hands on her waist. His fingers were firm and possessive, tightening around the bones protruding at her hips, softly kneading her narrow waist. A twist of longing awakened in the most secret part of her.

"This enormous creature? Sweet?" she managed to mutter.

"Aye," he replied. "Look at her eyes, gazing down on us with affection. See, she's offering you a gift."

Tess started back with a gasp and a sputter of delight when the elephant raised a trunkful of hay, waving it at her like a peace offering.

"I see what you mean." Tess reached out and embraced the gift of dry stalks. Belle extended her trunk in acknowledgment of the exchange, widening the lips of the proboscis with a spew of moist breath.

"Oh, she is wonderful," Tess responded, feeling as if she'd been kissed by the gray beast. Suddenly, life was so vibrant, and it was because of Richard, she knew, feeling the sting of moisture in her eyes that always came with gratitude.

"Belle, I want you to meet the woman who will soon be the Countess of Easterby. Lady Tess, this is Belle. Would you like to touch her?"

Tess nodded. Richard took her hand in his and gently pulled her forward until they were a foot away from the elephant's leg. Richard uttered soft murmurs of encouragement.

"That's it. Do not be afraid. Easy. Easy."

When Richard pressed his cheek to Tess's, cozying up behind her, she reached back and drug her fingers across the sharp plains of his face, stroking his leathern skin, his whiskery chin, his silken lips. She was aware of nothing but him, even as he pressed her other hand to the elephant's tough, wrinkled hide. The elephant gave a blustering snort of approval.

"She seems so incredibly gentle," Tess said, letting both hands drop to her sides. "How ironic, when she could easily crush me."

"I've had the same thoughts about you," Richard noted dryly, tucking an arm around her waist, forcing her back closer to his hard, lean figure.

"Whatever do you mean?"

"Your nature is far softer than you would have anyone believe," he whispered in her ear. "And yet you've the power to crush my heart."

The rain beat steadily outside the barn. The hypnotic thud-thud-thudding on the thatched roof entranced Tess, yet she was jarred from any possible reverie by Richard's daring revelation.

"I have the power to crush you?" She pivoted in his arms until she could see his face.

"Aye."

She had wanted the power to crush him. At first to make him pay. But now simply because she wanted to know he was as vulnerable as she.

"Richard," she whispered—a plaintive plea, a dangerous beginning, and a cowardly retreat all in one. "Do you mean that? If you are lying . . ."

"I cannot lie to you." He pulled her even closer. His powerful charm seeped through all resistance. "Believe me."

She did not believe him. Not until she pressed her hands to his chest and felt his wildly beating heart through his sodden doublet. If the pulse thumping against her palm was any indication, he was just as excited and fearful as she was. Nay, not as fearful. That was not possible. He had nothing to lose by doing what she openly feared, and secretly hoped, would come to pass between them. But she had everything to lose—her self-control, her soul, her heart, even her life. She felt as if she were being peeled alive. There was nowhere to hide, neither from her fear nor her desire.

"I cannot. Do not ask me to do this. Not ever."

His cheeks hollowed as he swallowed the grim realities of life. "But I cannot let you go. Not ever."

His torrid eyes raked over her exposed flesh, landing squarely at the crest of her bosom. His gaze quavered there and then shot upward darkly to meet her wide eyes.

"I must make love to you, Tess. You will feed my soul, my lost and wayward soul. I feel it. I want to be with you, in you. I want to feel my heart again. God, I don't know if I can still feel, Tess. I mean really feel. Don't you see? This you can give to me. That which no one else has given."

He tangled his fingers in her wet hair, gripping the satin threads in his roughened hands. His feverish lips pounced on her neck, kissing her with aching sweetness and the erotic swirl of his tongue, drinking raindrops.

Tess shivered in his tight embrace and threw back her head.

She writhed against the torment of his mouth, flabbergasted at the cavern of desire that was yawning suddenly to life. Scrunching her eyes together, she saw blood and sky and a burning yellow sun, every color on earth, but more intense than ever before, so that her eyes ached. She throbbed in the deepest part of her, and flexed the muscles of her inner thighs. Her breath came in shallow pants, as if she'd been running hard. The blood whooshed in her ears. She felt his words vibrate through the soft skin of her neck, his moans, his demands, his incoherent mumblings. What was he saying? She couldn't hear. She could only hear the demands of her body as she arched and squirmed with desire, as her womanhood burst to life like a gushing new spring that flows after a quake has ripped the earth in twain. And suddenly, after all these years, she understood one of the reasons why women risked death giving birth. Because the source of the seed gave so much pleasure. Blinding pleasure. Drugging pleasure that made her forget what was at stake.

"You want to be inside of me, but you will leave behind a remembrance," she groaned, reason wrestling with passion. She groped for his face and slid her hands along his temples, gripping him forcefully, not allowing him to lunge for another kiss on her nape. She stared hard into his hungry eyes.

"Nine months from now that remembrance will rip its way from my body. Will you be there then? Will you hold my hand when I scream in agony? Will you beat back the Grim Reaper should he come to call? And if I die, will you remember me evermore? Will your memories of me be enough to have made my life worthwhile? Will they be enough to justify the ultimate price I'll have paid? Will it be enough?"

She gripped his head in her small hands with angry passion, the words sputtering in a desperate rush. He blinked against their onslaught. Her words were tiny daggers piercing his heart. She saw that in his many small winces and knew in an instant that he would never willingly hurt her. He had too much heart.

"I don't know, Tess. I have no answers." He shook his head as sweetness and sadness painted his tanned features a paler hue.

He bent his legs and wrapped his arms around her waist, lifting her in a bear hug. Their hearts beat against each other's, more soundly and rousingly than any minstrel on his drum. With her head buried against his shoulder, she breathed him in, his masculinity, his cozy tenderness. She sensed a oneness of heart and mind, which she would never have known if she had not spent so many hours shooting at his side. Wrapping her arms more completely around his neck, she hugged him with a trueness of spirit that was as rich and potent as the finest claret, and equally as intoxicating.

"You're cold," he said.

She paused at this observation and heard the chatter of her teeth. "The chill is from the rain," she murmured, nestling farther into his protective embrace. "I'm soaked down to my chemise."

"You must change into something warmer."

"Yes, I'd like that." As soon as the words were spoken, she cringed. She drew back. Danger, that third person, had risen from repose, casting a long, dark shadow. Tess shook her head. "I'll be fine. Truly. Mayhap we should get back to the castle."

"Nay, 'tis still raining," he answered authoritatively. Richard marched to the far end of the barn and walked into a stall. Moments later he reappeared with a garment in hand.

"I will change into a pair of Tarjaman's breeches. I've laid out one of his robes for you. He converted this stall to a sleeping chamber. You can dress in privacy."

"My lord, I hardly think it proper . . ."

"Is it proper to let you catch your death of a cold? Fear not, maiden, I'll not accost you."

She gave him a sassy smile. "You already have. Or is lovemaking so commonplace that you had not noticed your own actions?"

He narrowed his eyes with mocking threat, tossing his breeches over his shoulder. "You are asking for a good blistering spank, young lady. How dare you insult the lord of the castle? The affection I bestowed on you," he said, interlocking his long, graceful fingers with hers, "was just a foreshadowing of things to come."

She tilted her head up, listening, but also hoping he might kiss her again.

"But until that time, you will not accost me either." He wagged a finger at her in admonishment.

She licked her telltale lips and grasped her hands behind her back like a chagrined child. "Very well."

"When you are dressed and ready to rejoin me, give me fair warning. I would hate for you to catch me in a state of dishabille."

"Very well, my lord, I will do as you wish, since I see you are so frail of body and fearful of mind." She cocked her fine brows and pivoted with a twist, swishing her way playfully to Tarjaman's sleeping stall, then throwing Richard a taunting slash of a smile just before she disappeared behind the wooden structure.

Once inside Tarjaman's simple little chamber, she quickly pulled off her clinging gown and slipped into a woolen robe, hugging herself to dispel the chills that rattled her teeth. She pulled her hair back and slipped her fingers through the frizzy tangles, then remembered Richard's request for a warning and decided to ignore it. Feeling like a reckless child intent on an impish plot, she peeked her head through the doorway and saw exactly what he had warned her about. He was naked, murmuring something to Bathsheba, Tarjaman's breeches poised in one hand. His skin was a soft chestnut hue in the rainy gray sunlight beaming down from a high window. His long, lean legs were a mass of corded, steel-tight muscles. This she could tell from a distance, but she wanted a closer look.

With her heart thumping nearly out of her chest, Tess slid noiselessly toward him, her bare feet rustling softly over hay.

"You are insatiable," she heard him say to Bathsheba, then

watched breathlessly as he knelt to stroke the leopard, unaware of the presence of his interloper. "I could pet you a fortnight without pause and still 'twould not be enough to satisfy you."

In the pale stormy light seeping through shutters high above, the ridges of his spine rose beneath his skin as if out of a mist. His finely honed body was like a rendering in a book on anatomy, she concluded, drawing a slow breath through her suddenly watering mouth. A brushstroke of tendons here, an inky blot of muscle mass there, taut and virile—all thinly veiled beneath bronze skin. With his haunches resting on his heels, his paler buttocks stood out in contrast.

"I have never seen a more beautiful sight." The words came hoarsely and unbidden from Tess's throat.

He twisted around, his face registering surprise.

"I have had a lifelong habit of speaking the truth," she explained, brushing aside a tendril of hair that was blocking her view and driving her to distraction. "Say it: I am too bold. I know it but cannot help myself. And I will not change my ways now."

He stood and spanned the distance between them with two strides of his graceful, lean legs. His clear blue eyes were murky in the shadows cast down from his forehead. Incapable of feigning reluctance, she allowed herself to drink of his beauty.

"I wouldn't want you to change a thing." His voice vibrated sensually in the thick muscles spanning his fleecy chest.

As he had once assessed her, her gaze slid from his handsome face down over his mountainous collarbone, past the bronze mounds of his chest, crested with small, brown nipples. Daring all, she allowed her gaze to wander farther— along the narrow line of hair that trailed from his chest down his flat belly to the thatch of gold that ensconced his manhood. Before her eyes his long member took on new shape. It was incredible. A perfect monster. She stared in wonder and then looked up with all the innocence of a child.

"Are all men this beautiful?"

With this groin-wrenching question, Richard went rigid. How could he answer? To his way of thinking, he was an ugly man beyond his surface beauty. Politics had made him dirty. But in her presence, he was clean and new. The blood of longing surged through his veins, pulsed through his temples, sent raging desire shooting through his broad hands. Hands he now slowly fisted in frustration. For as much as he longed to, he would not reach out to touch her, since he knew their next contact would seal their fate. He had to make love to this woman. She had insinuated herself into his consciousness. She was air he needed to survive. Lilac-scented air that permeated his lungs, filling him with her essence. He had smelled her being, and now he wanted to taste it.

Not knowing the contract she was about to sign, or perhaps knowing and fearlessly scrawling her signature with a touch, she reached out and curled her tantalizing fingers through the mat of hair on his chest. His face felt leathern, too world-weary and worn to express his sheer gratitude and joy. She had reached out to him. He would take her now. Gently. But completely.

His fingers besieged her narrow wrists. "Tess, 'tis time."

Her head lashed to one side, as if his words had dealt a physical blow. Her long, raven lashes fluttered against her cheeks. Flicking her tongue over her lips, she looked up at him with excitement and terror shimmering in her eyes. "Is it, Richard? Is this the time?"

"If not now, when?"

She nodded, then pulled the sash at her waist. The robe slackened, exposing her nakedness—hard rosebud nipples on high and firm breasts, ribs pushing delicately through creamy skin, a thatch of dark hair at the apex of her thighs. She slipped the woolen weave over her shoulders and tossed the robe aside. For a second time, she stood naked before him. This time, however, her eyes would not meet his.

"Are you ashamed?"

She looked at him then, pride forcing her chin up. "Nay."

"Afraid?"

After a pause, she nodded.

"Afraid that I will hurt you?"

She shook her head.

"Afraid of begetting my child?"

"Afraid of dying giving birth to your child."

He nodded, considering her plight, loving her for her courage in light of these fears. "There are ways to avoid that."

She gave him a puzzled look.

"Leave that to me. Now, my love, I cannot resist you any longer." Retrieving Tarjaman's robe, he cast it down on a puff of hay next to Bathsheba.

There are ways to avoid that. The words echoed in her mind as he pulled her down. Down. Down. Down into his arms. Down against the satin bristles on his chest. Down onto the muscled ridges of his flat belly. Down onto the stiffness that lay between them. *What ways?* she thought, her reasonableness fighting for survival as he rolled her onto her back and cupped her womanhood with a hot, probing hand. As she spread her legs with a groan, seeping with longing, she wondered what ways he would have to spare her life. How would she avoid her mother's fate? By a magic potion? Alchemy? A divine miracle from God? She'd not visited a wisewoman for special herbs. She'd never thought she would need them. She'd thought she would kill him before he could plant the seed that would end her life.

"Richard, Richard." Her voice was pleading and praising.

She placed her small hand on the monumental tendons of his warrior's neck and pulled him closer. She coiled against him. He responded with a heady kiss; his lips rotated over hers, his tongue dipped in for a taste of her, flickered away tauntingly, then delved in again. He kissed her with the same charging rhythm with which he explored her depths. A crazy, mad, seething charge of ecstasy bolted through her body, shaking her, as if a giant had shaken her like a rag doll.

"Oh, my darling Richard."

"Tess, my sweet Tess. I knew you would respond this way. I knew it. I will make you do more than quiver." His words were hot licks in her ear. She pressed against him, scraped her nails over his back, skimmed his buttocks, pulling him closer, craving him, demanding him.

She inhaled their combined scents—raw, primal, earthy—and exhaled every last bit of pretense. This man knew her. No one else ever had. No one. But this man did. She wanted him to know more. Everything. She sat up, nudged him down on his back, and fell upon his chest. Her hand roved over his side and slipped downward until she clutched his perfect monster. Richard jerked in response. She smiled. Pleased. Powerful.

"I shall make *you* quiver," she taunted him, stroking him.

He surrendered to her ministering until he thought he would burst. He gripped her wrist, stilling her. "You have the power to make me do far more than quiver. I am going to make love to you now. Do not be afraid."

The voice screaming "No!" was far away now. Almost too far to hear, and certainly not very convincing. Desire, she realized, was far more powerful than fear. *Yes, I want you now. I'll have you. Damn the consequences to hell.*

She did not resist when he rolled over her. She sank back until she fell upon an unexpected wall of hot fur. There was a panting sound other than her own. Tess realized she was leveraged between her lover and a leopard.

"Bathsheba," she said with a woozy laugh. She caught Richard's delighted, lusty gaze. "I don't know who feels better," she said to him. "You or the beast."

"I *am* the beast," Richard growled, and consumed her neck, nipping and swirling his tongue over her tasty flesh. As his kisses progressively descended, he took her free hand and entwined her fingers with his own. He reached over her and rubbed their joined hands against the leopard's spotted fur. Tess gripped a loose fold of fur and wriggled her fingers against the silky texture. Responding, Bathsheba stretched out her legs, pressing her back more soundly against Tess's. The fur was slick. Like Richard's skin. Like his manhood pressing between her thighs. Like his tongue that flickered erotically over her taut nipples.

"Oh, Richard, you please me so."

Tess's head began to spin. She was a jumble of sensations. She panted with need. Sweat trickled down her neck, cool and tickling. Rain beat in a soothing rhythm overhead. Her heart surged over and over. Her womanhood pulsed, needing, needing. Then she felt a coolness on her back. She realized Bathsheba had risen, apparently bored with the thrashing of human lovers. Tess sank into the warm spot the animal had left in the hay.

Then Richard swept over her body, warming skin that had chilled for lack of contact. His manhood pressed at her opening. And she was open to him, or at least her body was. The slick passage had been prepared. With one swift lunge he would be in the depths of her and she would arch to meet him.

"I want nothing more than for you to be inside of me," she whispered in the flower of his ear. His hands embraced her head. His lips were inches from hers. His breath heated her cheeks. She inhaled, for it was sweet. It was him. Her lover. Her man. "But I am so afraid. Richard, Richard, do not let me die."

"Nay, never."

"Please, do not let me die." Tears boiled from her eyes and burned down her cheeks. Tears of love and anguish. Wonderful tears of feeling and compassion and passion.

"Do not let me die," she sobbed, her chest heaving against his. Anguish, fear, hate, love all poured from her eyes, cleansing her, freeing her.

"I will never let you die. You will live forever," he promised, kissing her cheeks, over and over. "I will never let you die. You are too great to die. Your spirit is from God. God will not let you die. Not when you have so much to give. Oh, Tess. Give to me. Give to me."

In that moment of intimacy, she believed him. Risking all, she wrapped her legs around his waist and opened herself completely. At once, he entered her. She gasped. He held still. She felt him throb inside her. They looked at each other. She saw wonder in his eyes.

"This was what I was missing," he whispered hoarsely. "All these years. This was it. This was it." This last sentence was choked with emotion. A frightening fire ignited in the depths of his eyes and he began to lunge into her.

Again. And again. Again. She met him lunge for lunge, thinking he would cut her in twain, thinking she would like that. Each thrust wound her tighter and tighter until at last she exploded with pleasure she had never even imagined before. She growled like a leopard, clawed his back, left bloody streaks. She jolted like an untamed mare, bucking beneath him, whickering with pleasure that verged on pain.

"You will live forever!" he shouted as she rode the peak. "Forever," he bellowed, lunging into her.

When she had collapsed beneath him, he kissed her tenderly and then spiraled to his own fierce conclusion. He let himself go with a kind of strangling noise. But not before pulling out of her, then spilling his seed on her abdomen.

Utterly spent, he fell over and collapsed beside her, panting desperately for air. She stared at the sticky pool gathered at her navel, while listening to the steady drumming on the roof.

It seemed like forever before Richard's breathing returned to normal. Then the hay rustled beneath him as he propped his head on an elbow. Tess felt his eyes following her gaze to her belly.

"As long as my seed is not in you, it cannot hurt you," he explained.

She turned on her side and stared into his soulful eyes. "Do you not want sons?"

"Aye, but not as much as I want you. If you think there is danger, I'll not risk it. I want *you*, Tess. Do you understand? I'll not let you die. I meant what I said."

"Aye." She nodded. She kissed him with love-swollen lips. And as she lovingly kissed him, she knew it was a different woman who now kneaded his lips with her own. She understood so much more than she had ever thought possible. She knew the way between a man and a woman. She knew the few moments of immortality that joining could bring. She knew they were bound together forever by a knowing and a wanting and a compassion that needed no words. And most of all, she knew love.

At long last the rain stopped. He heard the last muted drops fall haphazardly from the thatched roof to puddles in the rutted ground below. Belle gave a mellow snort, as if she, too, had noticed. The storm had broken. A brighter sun shone through the high window. The inky clouds had parted. It was a clear day. But how long would it last? How long would the sun shine?

He hugged Tess closer in his arms, careful not to wake her. Her passion had exhausted her completely. Poor baby. She slept heavily in his embrace, her sweet pink lips blustering softly with each deep breath. He kissed her forehead. It was satin. He kissed her brow. It was velvet. Rich brown velvet. He couldn't stop kissing her. Even as she slept. He wanted to memorize everything about her. He wanted to remember her roar of ecstasy, remember how it had shattered his eardrums. He wanted, long after the scars had healed, to recall the pain of her nails carving his flesh. He prayed he would never forget how, for one brief moment, their bodies had fallen away and their souls had touched, creating an intimacy he'd thought reserved for angels and cherubs and demigods. He had known her. He had known love. He would never be the same.

He would not forget. Even if the days ahead ripped them apart. Even if his plans, so long in the making, so irrevocable at this point, made her run from him in horror, in hatred. He could not go back now. He could not set a new course. Would she spurn him? Would she loathe him? Maybe. Probably.

But he would never forget that once, on a rainy afternoon, she had loved him.

SEVENTEEN

On the appointed wedding day, Tess rose early and dressed in silence. Fluttering servants dashed in and out of the chamber at Mellie's command. Tess was in a heavenly daze. Everything in her sight seemed like a precious gift—especially the loving ladies-in-waiting, who clucked and oohed and aahed over her, dabbing Tess with violet water and pinching her cheeks. Even Mellie seemed like a gift.

The handmaiden nimbly combed Tess's hair, letting it fall loosely down her back in lustrous waves, and then entwined a string of pearls in a circle of flowers crowned atop Tess's head. The pearls had been a wedding gift to Tess from Roger. He had arrived yesterday, traveling from his new barony for the nuptials. King Henry had been so pleased with Tess's ready acceptance of this marriage that he'd given her cousin, a simple knight, his own small manor. Doubtless, Tess mused, the king assumed that no maiden would ever make any move were it not for the advice or force of her nearest male relative. In any event, she was happy for Roger. He had always been a loyal supporter, never jealous that fate had given her so much and him so little.

"Hold steady, my lady," Mellie ordered her.

"Very well, Mellie, you are the chatelaine today."

Tess smiled warmly then, while Mellie pinned flowers in her hair, took these relatively still moments to study her reflection in the mirror. How much her face had changed! There were faint lines of contentment, the beginnings of laugh lines on her otherwise smooth cheeks. Her eyelids were hooded with greater wisdom, and a new vibrancy pinkened her high cheeks. All this love had done to her.

"My lady," Mellie said. "'Tis time to don your wedding dress."

Tess caught the glimmer of her own brilliant smile as she set aside the mirror and looked up into the expectant eyes of the breathless girl. "I am ready, Mellie."

The handmaiden and the three ladies-in-waiting raised the magenta-colored gown over Tess's head. She slipped her arms into the cool satin and waited while helping hands fastened several dozen buttons lining each sleeve.

"You look stunning!" exhaled Margaret when all the busywork was complete. Tess smiled delightedly at the gray-haired lump of sugar.

"I only hope I please Richard," Tess said. "Thank you for being here, Margaret. Thanks to you, Edith, and Rose, too. You have all made me feel so welcome."

All three ladies encircled her with their arms in a spontaneous hug. Sniffles abounded, and Tess was glad to realize she wasn't the only sentimental bucket of tears in the chamber. She withdrew from their cushiony arms and dabbed her eyes.

"Now look what you've done," she said, smiling through blurry tears at the sniffling women. "Now I have no hope of getting through the ceremony in one piece. I'd best spend a moment alone to collect my thoughts."

"Why, of course, child," Edith said, arching an imperious brow at the others. "Hurry along. We must let Tess have a moment alone."

Tess watched them go with a swell of affection in her heart. She had never thought she would feel love again, the kind of love she felt for her father and Roger. But the heart does mend, she realized with a sense of exceeding hope.

There could be no further delaying, she knew; she had to hurry on to the church. Roger was waiting to escort her through the bailey. She started for the door, but paused, remembering something. Her smile faded. She trod softly to her clothing trunk. Placing a hand on the cold silver latch, she hesitated a moment before lifting the lid. She dug through her neatly folded gowns and grasped her leather purse. Pulling wide the drawstring, she withdrew her misericorde and swung the small blade from its sheathe. The cold metal gleamed in the sunlight beaming from the embrasure. She had brought this dagger to kill Richard. It would serve a purpose still. Sheathing the blade, she fastened the small scabbard at her waist under the many layers of her wedding gown.

"Come," Roger said, "I will take you to your husband. By the rood, Tess, I've never seen a more beautiful bride."

He held out his hand as she exited the private chambers and greeted the brilliant spring morning. Tess blinked at the yellow haze and smiled lovingly at her cousin, hugging him.

"I still can't believe you're here. How proud of you I was, Roger, when you arrived yesterday and the porter announced the arrival of Sir Roger of Parnbridge. Just think! Lord of your own manor now."

"You could have been no more proud than I am of you. You have changed, Tess. My, how you have changed. I didn't think you could become any lovelier, but you have. There is a softness in you I've never seen so clearly before. A softness methinks you've been hiding until now."

She nodded, smiling sweetly in the shadow of his adoration. Her dear cousin would always be on her side.

"Come," he said, "the crowd at the church awaits the bride."

Tess took his arm and followed his lead. When they reached the church steps, the crowd parted, making way for her. She could feel the excitement, the eyes drinking her in. The anticipation setting her nerves on edge gave her a vibrant sheen, an air of aliveness that turned the moment into an extraordinary event, one that would be long remembered in the minds of the witnesses.

When Tess mounted the last step, coming to Richard's side, she looked up to find him more resplendent than ever in a formal houppelande that flowed to the ground in swaths of dazzling gold and white velvet. His hands peeked out from wide, fur-lined, funnel-shaped sleeves that hung to the ground. He was positively regal. The sight was almost too alluring. She cast her eyes downward, shy in the face of love.

"You are beautiful," he whispered before turning to face the priest.

"So are you," she whispered back.

His cheeks dimpled at her impertinence. "Why, thank you."

The solemn proceeding began. They exchanged their vows at the church door, as was the custom, so that all might witness the permanence of their union. But Tess was not as teary-eyed as she had thought she would be. She kept picturing Richard naked, as he would be that night. She could hardly wait.

"To the best friend a reprobate carouser could have!" Sir John bellowed through the crowded great hall. "To Lord Richard!"

"Here, here!" rose a baritone chorus of voices. Knights and lords stood beside their ladies at the trestle tables and raised their tankards high into the smoky air.

"And to the fairest maiden in all of Christendom!" Sir John added, raising a tankard filled with a portion of his precious ale from Eastcheap, the ale he planned to share with the king. "To Lady Tess, the Countess of Easterby!"

Tess blushed and rose from her thronelike chair on the dais at the end of the hall. Raising her chalice, she nodded demurely to Sir John, then to the crowd.

"And to your good health, Sir John," she said, and then swilled with gusto. The crowd roared its approval. Richard bellowed an approving laugh and swilled at her side.

It was a raucous and merry wedding feast. Many of the village merchants were in attendance, dressed in their finest, honored to be invited to such a grand affair. Two earls were guests at the high table, as were a number of barons and a few men of lesser rank whom Richard had befriended in rowdier days. There were at least a half dozen minstrels. One sat at the entrance to the hall, strumming delicate ballads for those who entered. Four near the high table played in unison, either bouncing dance songs or romantic ballads, depending on the mood of the moment. There was a dancing bear, jugglers, and jesters. Tess enjoyed them all as she sat cozily in her chair, leaning ever closer to Richard as the night and her mood wore on.

Now and then he leaned over and swirled his lips upon hers. When he did, all sound faded for her—the clinking of tankards, the belches of contented guests, the titters of laughter at a bawdy minstrel's verse. All smells disappeared—the mouth-watering aroma of roasted capons and marrow fritters, the burning torches, the spring flowers scattered in the rushes. She smelled only Richard: musky, masculine, full of the promise of ecstasy.

Ending one particularly mind-shattering kiss, he touched her chin and whispered, "Do not drink too much, my love, for I want you to feel everything tonight with the utmost clarity."

"Hmmmm, I can feel it already."

"You wanton girl."

"You rogue."

Their repartee was shattered with the loud bang of two cooking pans. At the opposite end of the hall, a page led a procession, banging a drum.

"What is this?" she queried.

"The pièce de résistance," Richard said, a smile brightening his already vibrant eyes.

Following the drummer, trumpeters blared their horns in a harmonious fanfare. Behind the hornsmen followed a half dozen cooks who held up a giant swan on a large oval platter. The swan had been cooked with its feathers in place, so that it looked as it had in life. Baked apples and pears framed the magnificent white bird. When the cortege passed before the high table, the proud cooks lowered the platter for Tess's benefit and parted the back of the roasted swan. From the empty cavern, a host of starlings frantically flew to freedom, dashing about the rafters. Then the pages and a few game guests flitted around the hall with nets, trying to capture the small birds, laughing madly as they flung their nets hither and thither. The crowd burst into applause, thoroughly amused.

"Oh, delightful!" Tess exclaimed, clapping enthusiastically.

Richard turned to her and smiled. He raised her soft hand to his lips. "I am glad it pleases you, my lady. My wife."

The horns sounded again and four more cooks entered, carrying a three-foot-long ship sculpted in sugar. The hard sugar had been molded into a cog with red and yellow sails. A collective gasp of awe and anticipation rose in the hall as the cooks paraded their masterpiece before the ogling guests.

The evening proceeded in a raucous and free way. For a spell Sir John quoted love poems, and then he gave everyone a start when he danced with Audrey.

"No!" Tess cried out, gripping Richard's arm. "Do something to stop him."

"That's like telling a volcano not to erupt," Richard grumbled, but rose nevertheless to still the old sot. Sir John, however, ignored all graceful attempts to remove him from the center of activity. Instead, everyone pushed aside the trestle tables and joined in.

"We cannot fight the forces of cheer, I fear," Richard said resignedly, returning to the dais and holding out a hand. "Dance with me?"

"I would dance with you to the ends of the earth."

Richard firmly led Tess to the center of the hall and then pulled her close, scooping a strong arm around her waist.

"Do not be afraid," he said with majestic grace. "Pretend that we dance in heather."

Somewhere, sometime in all the tumult past, she had learned to trust him. She followed his steps without a thought to her dignity, or lack thereof, and her absence of fear lent a coordination to her steps. They danced in a wild jig, trying to outdo Sir John and Audrey. The room was festivity itself—bystanders stomping their feet, whistling and hooting encouragement. Tess began to giggle, her face moist with perspiration from the heat of the room and the heat of Richard, which radiated out in sensual waves. His face glistened with sweat, evoking in her delighted mind a memory of their mingled scents after making love, musky and slick.

The dance ended with a rousing cheer from the crowd. Immediately, a slow drumbeat stilled the lords and ladies, who turned this way and that, looking for the source of the commanding sound.

"The mummers," Richard said excitedly. "Step back. Everyone make way!"

Out from an alcove at the end of the hall came a string of mummers, and the guests fell back into a circle, eager to see them perform. A dozen men bearing masks hopped from one foot to the other in their ritualized procession. Some were dressed in the garb of the Crusaders, wearing white robes with red crosses. Others wore the billowing pantaloons and turbans of infidels. Engaging in a mock battle to the beat of the drum, the mummers reenacted the brutal fight over the Holy Land between the Crusaders and the Arab infidels.

Tess stood next to Richard along the sidelines in rapt attention, until a familiar voice whispered in her ear.

"I am quite sure," the man said, "that if my Persian brethren had fought as cowardly as these mummers fight tonight the Christians would not have lost so many soldiers in their quest to make the Holy Land safe for Christian pilgrims."

"Tarjaman." She knew him without turning and felt a newfound softness toward him, no doubt inspired by the happy occasion. "I've heard tell the infidels were most fierce and brave," she whispered back, meeting his inky black eyes with a warm look.

The animal trainer drew up beside her, nodding to Richard, who tore his fascinated gaze away from the spectacle only long enough to nod in return.

"I am glad to see that you have finally grown to appreciate my master's attributes," Tarjaman added quietly.

Tess smiled. Then, remembering Tarjaman's ability to see beyond the obvious, she blushed. To which attributes did he refer? Did he know they had made love in his barn that rainy afternoon?

"Indeed, Tarjaman, I misjudged Lord Richard in many ways. Perhaps I misjudged you as well."

A rare smile parted his bluish brown lips. "In that case, may I have a moment with you?"

Tess surveyed him with an assessing glance, and seeing none of the veiled hostility she had seen—or imagined—

before, she nodded and slipped away unnoticed, following Tarjaman to an arched recess where a torch fluttered on the wall. They sat on a bench and watched the mummers' spectacle from a distance that allowed their thoughts to wander to objective observations.

"Lord Richard is enjoying the mummery so," she mused. "I enjoy watching him almost as much as I do the performers."

"And he watches you, Lady Tess, with even more fascination."

She turned from her turban-topped companion to see that Richard was, in fact, looking back at her over his shoulder. He seemed to approve of her tête-à-tête with Tarjaman, for he cast her a glowing smile and turned his attention back to the mummery.

"He cares for you deeply," Tarjaman said. "Therefore, I think the fate of Lady Gertrude and her companions is sealed with this marriage."

Tarjaman sipped from the goblet and stared out at the hall. "If Lord Richard listens to anyone regarding the fate of his prisoners, 'twill be you, Lady Tess. And I trust you will intercede on their behalf."

He tossed her a gaze that discerned as it pleaded. Tess turned her focus to Lady Gertrude and the other Lollards. They mingled in the crowd like any of the other welcomed guests. Richard had known Tess would want Gertrude here. But there was still no doubt that she was a prisoner. By law, he should have given the Lollards over to the Church days ago. Tess's fear for her friend was a thorn still wedged between husband and wife.

"Of course I will do all that I can," she answered Tarjaman. "But what can I do to spare her?"

"You must tell Lord Richard how important it is to you that she be freed. No matter what happens, you must argue forcefully."

Tess's eyes darted to Tarjaman's, and her stomach plunged when she saw uncharacteristic distress furrowing his brow.

"What could happen, Tarjaman? What are you talking about?"

He blinked slowly, thoughtfully, and sipped from his goblet again. Licking his lips, he leaned back against the stone wall. "I cannot say for sure, but I think I understand Lord Richard better than most. And the Lollards will yet play into his plan to reclaim Marly Vale."

"Marly Vale? He plans to reclaim Marly Vale?"

"Lord Richard plans to attack the Bishop of Kirkingham."

Tess shot Tarjaman a skeptical look. "How do you know this?"

"It does not matter, Lady, how I know. What I know is of far more importance to you."

"When will he attack?"

Tarjaman shrugged. "Soon, methinks. That is why you must plead for the Lollards' freedom. Attacking a bishop so powerful as Kirkingham cannot be ignored. If Lord Richard fails miserably, 'twill be just as easy for the king to execute him as to withstand the anger of the Archbishop of Canterbury. To our pious King Henry, in the wake of the Lollard uprising, heresy and sedition are one and the same. He will not be able to ignore this transgression. And if Richard fails, Henry will scoop up the Lollards without pause."

Tess closed her eyes, feeling new urgency and fear. Richard's life was in danger. And more than ever, so was Gertrude's. And Gertrude's fate, according to Tarjaman, now rested in Tess's hands. She felt a sickening lack of confidence in her ability to carry that burden.

"Why would Lord Richard abide by my wishes?"

"Because he loves you. Do you not know that?"

Tess blanched. "Will love be enough?" she whispered.

Tarjaman gave an ironic twist of a smile. "If not, then we are all lost."

"Why are you telling me this now?" she snapped irritably, not wanting the heavy mantle he offered her, still distrusting him somewhat. Did he really care for Gertrude, and if so, why? "Why are you burdening me with this knowledge tonight, on my wedding day, when I should know naught but joy?"

"Because," he said in his clipped Persian accent, "I do not want to see the misericorde hanging beneath the folds of your gown unsheathed."

Tess's shocked expression bore into his timeless eyes. He was so chillingly confident of his knowledge that she wondered if he were a warlock. How could he have known?

"How do you know there is a dagger beneath my gown?"

"There are many things I know without being told, Lady Tess."

"And many things you don't know," she returned, cocking her brows in a gesture of superiority. "At last I have caught you in an error, Tarjaman. I *do* have a dagger beneath my gown. But I do not plan to kill Richard with it, and you mistakenly thought that I did."

His onyx eyes deepened to a blacker hue as he digested this new information. "I am glad to hear you bear him no harm. I do not mind being wrong about that. I do not try to look into people's hearts. It just happens. Oft I am wrong. I am not a magician, or an Assassin."

She blinked in embarrassment over having her suspicions so baldly revealed. "I am sorry if I have misjudged you."

"But you still do not trust me."

She gave him a wan smile. "Not yet. Not entirely."

"'Tis no matter," he said, rising. "My work here is finished." He bowed and started away.

"Wait!"

He paused and turned to her expectantly.

"You once said that we both loved Lord Richard. Was that true?"

"The light of morning will reveal all the answers you need, Lady Tess. Meanwhile, I bid you peace." He gave a curt bow and disappeared in the crowd.

Tess surged forward, wanting to stop him, but she forced herself to hold, placing her hand on the cold stone archway. She sighed as a tumult of new emotions flooded her body. Biting her lower lip, she pondered the best way to approach Richard over the Lollards. And then, remembering what Tarjaman had said about the impending attack on the bishop, joy erupted, and she sought Richard out in the crowd again. He was applauding the mummers vehemently, laughing, tossing back his golden hair. She loved a man who not only made her feel incredible passion, but who planned to attack the Church. Maybe her father's death would be avenged yet, in a roundabout way. Maybe the Church would pay after all. Her joy was shadowed only by one simple thought. Tarjaman had spoken ominously about the part the Lollards would play in that attack. What could it be? She brushed the thought aside. Tonight was a time to celebrate.

EIGHTEEN

Much later, Tess slipped away from the merrymaking, exhausted, her heart heavy. Tarjaman's warning about the Lollards nagged at her conscience. And for the first time in a long while, she thought of Lucretia. She had never really asked Richard why he had so cruelly turned his half sister away. Tess began to wonder if she had been blinded by love. Who was this man to whom she'd given her body, her soul? Did she really know him? She had the chilling feeling she'd seen just one small part of the man. What revelations lay in store for her?

As if it were made of the thickest quarry stone, she slowly pushed open the door to Richard's solar. Much to her surprise, she was greeted by the ladies-in-waiting, who stood in a row by the bed like three merry blackbirds.

"Hello, dear," said Margaret, her eyes glittering with love.

"You were lovely tonight," Edith added.

"Transcendent," said Rose.

Tess let out a burst of relieved laughter. "My conceit shall be great indeed if I spend much more time with you ladies. But oh, I shall enjoy my vain downfall!" She embraced each one. "I am exhausted and drenched in a most unladylike fashion."

"We have a bath waiting," Edith said, and supervised her undressing. Tess slipped into the tub, and when she was thoroughly refreshed, she allowed the women to dry her and slip a robe over her shoulders.

"You must be terrified of what will soon come to pass in this room," Margaret said with a note of glee.

"Now, do not frighten her, Margaret," Edith chided.

"I do not frighten so easily, my dears," Tess reassured them, dabbing beads of water behind her neck with a towel. She would not scandalize the women by informing them that this would not be her first lovemaking with Richard and that, moreover, she was eager to lie with him again. "Where is Mellisande, by the by?"

"We sent Mellie along her way," Margaret said. "She's a dear girl, but much too young. We have done this before, you see."

Tess was intrigued by the plump matron's satisfied and proud smile. "You have done what before, Margaret?"

"Why, prepared the wedding bed! We did so for Richard's mother. My, my, 'twas so long ago." Margaret let out a sentimental sigh and her eyes twinkled with distant memories.

Edith handed Tess a silver chalice. The metal was cool and moist, the liquid aromatic.

"Here, my dear, drink this. 'Tis malmsey. 'Twill soothe your nerves."

Tess sipped the sweet liqueur as she strolled past the bank of windows, some of which were open, allowing a refreshing breeze to swirl through the chamber. The malmsey trailed a hot path down to her belly, where butterflies flew with excitement. She took in the sight of the ladies-in-waiting, all watching her eagerly, and wondered if they were at all envious. Had they ever longed for marriage? Did they consider their peaceful lives of servitude well spent?

"Tell me, why did you stay on at Cadmon Castle after the

death of Richard's mother? Why did you not make matches of your own?"

"Richard's uncle was a cruel man," Edith said flatly. "We did not trust that he would care properly for the young lord. Especially after he broke our hearts by sending Lucy away."

"Oh, such a sad day that was!" Margaret said, tears bubbling in her soft eyes.

Tess stopped her aimless stroll around the room, realizing her ladies had unwittingly opened a door she was eager to step through.

"Why did Lucretia have to go? And why did Richard allow it?"

"He had no choice," Margaret replied. She raised her eyebrows as if the answer should have been obvious to anyone with half a brain. "He was but a child of twelve himself. Though he was lord of the castle, 'twas his wicked uncle who held all the power. There was nothing he could have done to protect Lucy. He begged his uncle not to send her away, but to no avail."

"Lucy blames Richard," Tess said.

"Well, then she is looking at the past through the eyes of a child. As a child she undoubtedly thought her older brother could protect her. If she would but reconsider the circumstances as an adult, she would find it in her heart to forgive, methinks, for she would see that he could have done nothing."

Tess felt a surge of relief. So Lucy's misery wasn't Richard's fault after all. "Go on. Tell me more."

"After Lucy was sent away," Edith continued, "'twas impossible for us to leave Richard alone here with his malfeasant uncle. Richard was like a son to us. And when he was grown he gave us the freedom to live as we please in comfort here at Cadmon Castle. That's rare freedom for a woman. Who knows what sort of matches we would have made? Perhaps dreadful ones. And Richard's mother was such a noble woman. We truly wanted to honor her with a tapestry."

"It seems that one day turned into the next until these fifteen years have passed," Margaret concluded, putting her arms around Edith and Rose.

"How lucky Richard was," Tess said and cast them all a loving gaze. "I had no mother, but he had four. His own and you three who love him just as dearly."

"That we do," Margaret said. "Now come and see what we have done for this special night." The gray-haired woman tucked her soft, wrinkled hand into Tess's and pulled her gently to the bedside. "Look!"

Margaret pulled back the ermine covers and Tess found a bedful of rose petals. The floral scent eased soothingly into her lungs. How lovely it would be to lie with a man in a bed of roses.

"Lean closer and breathe deeply."

Tess obeyed and was pleased to smell lavender.

"The sheets were washed in lavender water."

"A thoughtful touch," Tess said approvingly.

Margaret patted her smooth palm on Tess's warm cheek. "Such a lovely maiden as you deserves no less, my lady."

"Do you know what to expect when Richard comes to your bed?" Edith said delicately.

Tess's cheeks heated. "I have heard tell," she replied as nonchalantly as possible.

"Richard will take good care of you, to be sure," Margaret said in a singsong voice. "He is experienced, and by the number of women who have sought his attention, one can only assume he will be gentle."

"But not too gentle," Edith said with a knowing wink.

Tess shot her a look of surprise. "Perhaps you three have not missed so very much, despite your lack of marriage."

Margaret chuckled.

"Are you ladies making fun of me?" Richard said, appearing suddenly and radiantly in the doorway. He held a rectangular wooden box in one hand and a scroll of parchments in the other.

"Ah, Richard!" Edith replied. "I expected a parade of rowdy young men to carry you to your bride."

"They've all passed out under the trestle tables."

His eyes twinkled with more than their usual charm, Tess noted, as he patiently accepted hugs, kisses, and pats on the back from all the women. "Isn't it past your bedtime, ladies? Or do you plan to spend the night with me and my new bride?"

"Oh, Richard!" Edith chided, her wan face turning red. "We were just set to leave."

Tess followed them to the door and waved. She was aware of Richard's silent presence behind her, feeling his eyes caress her back as surely as if his strong hands had stroked her spine. She turned, knowing what would come to pass between them. Aching for it. She found him frowning at her, as if he were trying to figure something out.

"Are you looking for a swell beneath my robe?" she queried, thinking they had come a long way from their first exchange in this solar.

"Nay, I was just wondering . . . what is it about you?"

"My lord?" She meandered toward him, drawn like an animal in heat.

"When you are in a room, I see no one but you. I want to touch no one but you. And I am quite sure I will never make love to any woman but you for the rest of my life."

She smiled with the glow of uncommon and mischievous wisdom. "Do not make promises you may not be able to keep, my lord."

"You doubt that? Well, then, let us discuss this thirty years from now and you will see that I was right."

Thirty years with this man. It seemed too great a gift. God had been good to her after all.

"What are you holding, and why? Put them down so you can hold me instead."

He cocked an enticing brow. "Wait until you see. Come. Sit."

He lowered his gifts to the bed, then sat, tugging her down beside him.

"My first gift," he said, unscrolling the parchment, "is a master plan for a chapel."

She coolly surveyed the lines of the elegant structure.

"Haddington Chapel," he said proudly, tapping the parchment.

She blinked and frowned, absorbing the name. "Haddington Chapel? You mean . . . ?"

"Named after your father. I am building a chapel in his name. A testimony to his goodness that will pass the test of time."

His softly spoken words walloped her heart, and she caught a choked breath. Tears stung her eyes. She blinked them back determinedly, realizing that an old wound could still bleed.

"Richard, this is not necessary. I . . . I know we have our differences . . . I . . ."

" 'Tis necessary," he whispered, and scooped her right hand into both of his, then kissed her fingers.

She shut her eyes and ran her other hand over the cradle of his head, over his flaxen hair. "Oh, Richard . . ."

He tucked a hand around her neck and pulled her close, then kissed the corner of her mouth chastely. Yet the kiss was more intimate than another more carnal one might have been, for the walls between them had truly fallen now. This man was her friend. Had she ever thought otherwise? This man was her love.

"And my next gift." He proffered the wooden box. "Open it."

She obliged, and found a dull steel hand-gunne sitting in velvet casings. "A gunne. I suppose I deserved this," she said ruefully.

"Nay, 'tis not a thing of sadness. It represents the power I would give to you. The freedom to decide your fate."

She saw the innocent, loving light reflected in his blue, blue eyes, and she shook her head wonderingly. "However did I misjudge you so, Richard? It seems incredible to me now that I wanted to kill you. Which reminds me . . ."

She skimmed across the room to her wedding gown, which Rose had draped over a chair, and fumbling in the folds of material, she withdrew her misericorde. Returning to the bed, she sat cross-legged and placed the cold dagger in his hand.

"I had every intention of plunging this misericorde into your heart. How absurd that seems now. 'Twould be like killing myself. Besides, my father would never have wanted that."

His long fingers wrapped around the hilt. He nodded as a frown of pain flickered over his features. "Do you know, Tess, that part of me *wants* you to want to kill me? I just may deserve death. And I am so used to betrayal it seems . . . natural." His defenses fell as clearly as a castle wall heaving down at the mercy of a battering ram. He bore no expression, just the essence of himself, fine and tender. "I do not know if I want love, Tess. There is something . . . wholly dangerous about giving one's heart."

Tess sprang forward and put her arms around him, holding him tight, consoling him, stroking his hair, feeling the heat of his skin, loving it. "Oh, Richard, Richard, I am so sorry that anyone ever betrayed you. I am sorry for misjudging you."

He found her lips immediately, and muttered against them. "I need you, Tess. I need to feel you. To drown in you. To drink from you."

His mouth covered hers and the hunger in her roared to life. They fell to the bed in a heated fit. She helped him rip off his houppelande, furious that anything dare impede her pleasure. Then they made love with fierce intensity. The first time came swiftly. He tore off his braies and dashed aside her robe, sliding into her moist depths like a man lost in the desert, drinking from a mirage.

A lioness this night, she wrapped her legs around his waist, imprisoning him, taking all of him as deeply as she could. And when it came time to withdraw, when he tried to spare her the danger of his seed, she would not let go. It was madness. She knew it. But she was mad with a sense of immortality, with a desire for all the dangers and pleasures of being human.

"God, no, Tess. Let loose. I can't hold back," he cried out, his powerful buttocks straining against her viselike legs. But she merely gripped him all the harder, determination glinting from her flushed, moist features.

"Nay," she shouted. Seconds later he stiffened and bellowed, filling her, arching, thrusting, freezing, and then collapsing in surrender.

He weighed a million pounds, but he did not crush her. He melted into her. Their skin fused. After a long time of slow, rhythmic breathing, Richard raised his head and studied her with a touch of joy and a dollop of bemusement.

"Why?" He stroked her face in the darkness, searching for a reason. "Why risk it?"

"Because . . ." was all she answered, her loving embrace explaining more than words ever could. She was a goddess of wisdom this night. A seer of human greatness. In his arms, she was greater than a human—she was a queen of passion.

She would not die. Nay, surely not one so great, not one who could love so intensely.

"Just because," she whispered.

Because she loved him. Because the desire to mate finally and profoundly, to bring forth issue from their passion, had overcome her fear of death. Because she realized as her body had exploded in pleasure that a life that does not give more than it takes is no life at all. Because she loved him so much she wanted their souls to join in the creation of another. And that was worth any risk. *He* was worth any risk.

NINETEEN

When Tess woke the next morning, the brilliance of spring consumed the planet, leaving no doubt that Mother Nature ruled in all her glory. An exhilarating breeze burst through an open window, carrying the breath of sweet heather and lilacs. Spring had most definitely arrived. Tess could almost hear the millions of furry gray buds in nearby forests cracking open their nubby casings, erupting with green shoots.

She sat up in bed with an extraordinary sense of contentment. Her body was lax and satisfied; her skin enveloped a new sense of fullness as a human being.

"I absolutely adore spring," she said, distractedly running a hand down Richard's muscular right arm, over the golden coils of hair.

"Hmmm?" he replied, barely awake.

"'Tis a time of infinite promise. Spring, I mean. A time to seek out a warm spot in the sun on a grassy knoll and count one's freckles."

"Or a time to find a warm nook in someone's arms." He tugged her back into an embrace and entwined his legs through hers.

"I could not possibly make love again," she demurred.

"With a little practice you'll toughen up." His blue eyes twinkled with the utmost confidence.

Loving that pure light, that freshness of spirit, she giggled deep in her throat and nestled closer, finding his lips with her own, which were mightily swollen. She kissed him and was thrilled to realize the act came as naturally as breathing.

Drawing back, she traced a finger over his blond brows, down his perfectly sculpted cheeks and through the faint stubble of a beard to his prominent chin. "I am told that in most noble marriages lovemaking is infrequent, dictated only by the needs of procreation."

"That is true for some," Richard allowed, sensuously smoothing one hand up and down the valley between her ribs and hips. "But since I want to have many, many children, we must do our best to make that possible."

Tess felt him stiffen against her thigh as his hips gently pulsated.

"You are incredible!" she cried in disbelief, pushing his chest and propping herself on one elbow. Tucking some wayward strands of hair behind an ear, she stared at him aghast. "You really *do* want to make love again! How many times is possible?"

"How much time do you have?"

"How much time do *you* have? You are the lord of the castle. Don't you have business to attend to?"

"I have trained my staff well. They know never to disturb me in my solar without very good reason. There are few emergencies my steward and castellan cannot handle without me. That is the prerogative of being the lord of the castle: I can delegate as I please."

"I should have lived by your code when I was chatelaine of Haddington Castle. I thought I had to do everything myself. The more work there was to do, the more I welcomed it, because it made me feel productive. I look back on it now and wonder why I never thought to live more for pleasure. But then I had no inkling of what pleasures I was denying myself."

She cupped a hand around his groin and smoothed her fingers up the exquisitely slick skin of his taut manhood. Richard merely smiled devilishly as her fingers roamed up to the fur matting his chest.

"Lucy would be happy to know I am taking pleasure at last," she said, her thoughts suddenly taking a serious turn. Her gaze roved to Lucretia's childhood portrait, hanging over Richard's desk. "I wonder what she would think of my willingly marrying you."

"Not much, I avow." Richard blinked against the onslaught of ancient pain, dulled by time. "Lucy will never forgive me for what happened to her. She was sent to a god-awful convent when she was but nine, a little flower about to blossom, stolen from the sunlight and thrust into a dark cave. 'Twould have killed the spirit of a lesser woman." He exhaled his sadness. "Fortunately, she had the pluck to escape and managed to find a rich old man who wanted no marriage portion, merely a comely girl to keep his feet warm at night."

"Perhaps Lucy will soften after I persuade her of your noble character."

His wan face begrudgingly flushed with color. "When you figure out why I can look only at you in any given chamber, let me also know why I see the world with hope in your presence."

Pleasure surged in her heart.

"If you could explain my actions to my sister, I would owe you not only my devotion and fidelity, but my gratitude as well."

He kissed her forehead.

Nestling against his shoulder, she knew the time had come to speak of the one issue still standing between them.

"Richard, there is something you could do for me as well."

"Name it, love, and 'tis yours."

Biting her lower lip, she tried to still the nervous beat of her heart. "I hope you mean that. For what I'm about to ask will anger, I fear. But nothing I ask could have more importance."

"Speak it, love. Do not be afraid."

"Free the Lollards."

Silence fell, save for the doves that cooed in the orchard.

"Let them go. I cannot let Lady Gertrude meet my father's fate. Tell me . . . please tell me you will not send her and the others to their deaths."

She could feel the tension settling in his heretofore loose muscles. Then came a heartfelt sigh, air breezing through his teeth. She sensed a moroseness darkening his countenance, like the shadows that fall almost unnoticed when a cloud darts in front of the sun.

"I will consider your wishes, Tess, and do my best to abide by them."

Consider my wishes? What did that mean? Was it reason to hope? She inched closer, studying the tiny creases in his lips, the wedge beneath his nose, the pink hue of his earlobe. "Does that mean you will spare her?"

"It means I will try my damnedest not to disappoint you."

He touched her cheek, his hard eyes softening, and she felt relief. She trusted him. He would do his best. Wouldn't he? She grasped his hand and pressed the palm to her lips, kissing him. "Thank you. Thank you," she said. *Please, please,* she thought.

"Nay don't, don't thank me yet." He stroked her cheek, and then tweaked a nipple. "Wait until I've made love to you again."

He pounced on her with a playful growl, and then slipped into her as quietly as a thief in the night. Except it was daylight, and they made love casually, watching each other with rare joy, concluding their heated interlude just as the noon bells began to ring.

"I am spent, my lady," Richard protested, flinging himself back on the bed. "Nothing in the world could make me rise again. Not even the noon bells."

"The noon bells?"

"'Twas a jest from the past."

Just as he thought he might have to explain, a pounding on the door grabbed their attention.

"My lord, I must speak with you," Godfrey said, a strain in his normally composed voice. "I would not disturb you were it not urgent."

Tess drew a sheet to her chin. "Let him in."

"Enter, Godfrey."

Tess's heart skipped a beat when she saw that his owlish face had gone pale. What had happened to so disquiet the normally impervious steward?

"What is it, Godfrey? What has happened?"

"'Tis Oswald, my lord."

Richard stiffened. "What about him?"

"He's been abducted, my lord."

"Abducted! When? Where?"

"On his way to Bristol to pick up your latest shipment of hand-gunnes."

"Gods!" Richard cursed, flinging away the sheet and jumping out of bed. "What about the weapons?"

"They have disappeared, just as Oswald has."

Richard stalked to his clothing trunk and snatched up a doublet. He cursed as he dressed. "If anyone harms that boy, Godfrey, I will personally see the knave has a long and painful death. Do you know who has abducted him? Is anyone asking for ransom?"

Godfrey shook his head. "We do not know who has done

the deed. The Bishop of Kirkingham is an obvious candidate. But there's also . . ."

"Who? Damn you, speak up!"

Godfrey pursed his lips consideringly and then arched his gray brows. "Well, my lord, Tarjaman left Cadmon Castle last night and has taken all his possessions. No one knows where he's gone or why he left. But he might have something to do with this."

"By God, Randolf, I want him found and I want him found now!" Richard pounded his desk with a fist, unheedful of the pain it would cause him. His solemn commanders surrounded him with glum expressions. Godfrey sat in a chair on Richard's left side and Tess sat to his right.

"My lord," Sir Randolf replied, crossing his bearish arms, "we have sent a spy to learn what he can from Kirkingham's men. Oswald headed a party of a half dozen well-trained knights. Since the men returning from London a week before had been robbed of their gunnes, we had heavily armed Oswald and his men, fearing the same fate. Even so, they were overpowered by a dozen who wore no livery. The marauders were dressed in tattered clothes like thieves, but my men say they were too skilled and well organized to fit the part. Very likely they were men-at-arms playing the part of vultures."

"I have no doubt they were Kirkingham's men," Richard growled. "But again we are left to wonder who told them about the timing of Oswald's journey."

Sir Randolf's broad, confident face curled with disgust. "Can there be any wonder? That bleeding infidel, Tarjaman."

"Do you know that for certain? Do you have proof?"

"Tarjaman is gone, my lord," Godfrey reminded Richard. "He even left behind his animals. He will not be back, I fear."

Richard didn't like any of this. It made no sense. "What

would it profit Tarjaman to betray me? I saved him from starvation."

"Do you think an infidel feels any sense of loyalty?" Randolf countered.

"Not only an infidel, but an Assassin," Tess said quietly. All the men turned to her. She cleared her throat. "Last night Tarjaman approached me. Apparently knowing my sympathies for my father's friends, he seemed to imply that he cared about the fate of your imprisoned Lollards. Perhaps that was designed to elicit my sympathies in the case of some future treachery on his part. And perhaps the future is now. Historically, the Assassins were known for going to great lengths to establish trusting relationships with their intended victims."

"I've known Tarjaman for years. If you're implying that he established our relationship simply to betray or kill me, why would he have taken so long to do so?" Richard argued. "He could have killed me at any time."

"If Bishop George is victorious, then Tarjaman won't have to kill you himself—'twill be done for him," Sir Randolf countered. "A wise approach for a Persian who does not want to be drawn and quartered in a hostile land for murdering an earl. And what better way to insure the bishop's victory than to steal your master gunner?"

Richard sank back against his chair and steepled his fingers. He did not want to believe them. Their arguments smacked of a very ignoble prejudice. He had always assumed Tarjaman stayed in his service out of loyalty, for it would have taken some strong motive for the animal trainer to endure the antipathy most Englishmen harbor against Persians. But if it hadn't been Tarjaman, who else had betrayed him?

"Though I still do not know why Tarjaman would do this to me, you may be right. Since I can think of no one else who might have done the deed, you can send out a party to search for him. Take him, but do not harm him until he and I have spoken. That is, if you find him. And if Tarjaman does not want to be found, 'twill be a difficult task indeed."

Sir Randolf gave a quick nod and a seldom-seen smile. "'Twill be done."

His sense of betrayal dealt with for the moment, Richard turned his focus to Oswald. He shut his eyes as a jab of pain seared his heart. Dear Oswald. So much unfairness had befallen the lad—losing his parents so young, then losing a leg. The thought that anyone would take advantage of a man who was so obviously at a disadvantage filled Richard with rage. He pinched the bridge of his nose and rubbed his eyes.

"Dear God, I pray that Oswald is alive."

"My men say he was alive when the marauders took him, flailing and hooded," said Gaveston, the commander of the cavalry. He wore a thin mustache as neatly trimmed as the square bangs lining his short forehead. "The thieves took three cases of weapons, apparently unaware that there were two more following in a cart a half-mile back. So we still have something to show for the journey. Except the most important prize of all—Sir Oswald, our master gunner."

"Gaveston, I want you to send a garrison of men to comb the land looking for him," Richard ordered. "Godfrey, send a messenger to Kirkingham asking him directly if Oswald is taken and how much ransom he desires. Sir Randolf, let me know as soon as you hear from your spy. I want a full report when I return."

He sensed the shift in the room as everyone sat up a little more attentively.

"When you return? Where will you go?"

It was Tess who had spoken. Her voice wafted over his shoulder like a gentle wind.

He felt a severe pang of guilt and squeezed her soft hand.

She loved him. It was so obvious. Turning to her, he could see how rich with love she'd grown. Her cheeks were still flushed from their marathon lovemaking. Her lips were swollen and inviting. But most of all, she trusted him. His promise to regard her wishes in deciding the fate of the Lollards left him with a sickening feeling. If he did not fulfill that promise, he would have betrayed her in the worst possible way. That was why he had to go now, to talk with the king, to find a better plan to reclaim Marly Vale than the one he'd formulated thus far.

"Tess, I am going away for a sennight or so. I have some unfinished business that must be settled. But whether 'tis settled or not, when I return we will begin our attack on the bishop. 'Tis about time justice ruled, is it not?"

She smiled, obviously proud of him.

"But what about Oswald, my lord?" Godfrey asked. "Are you not worried that he will suffer if you attack the bishop?"

"If we have not received a request for ransom in two weeks, then Oswald is a dead man. Besides, I do not think the bishop abducted my master gunner to prevent war. He did it to insure his own victory. He would welcome this overt attack. For then, if he is victorious, he can rightfully ask the king for my head."

"But who are you going to see?" Tess asked.

Love is persistent, he thought, and turned to her with all the gentleness in his soul. "The king, my love. I'm going to see the king."

TWENTY

So the day of reckoning has come, Richard thought as he stepped around his mount to adjust the length of his left stirrup. Working in darkness, he tugged on the leather strap, relying on his sense of touch to measure the distance from his saddle. Golden sunlight was just beginning to shatter the clean blue shadows of morning. The bailey was still quiet and serene.

One of the most profound moments of Richard's life was slipping into place as if this were the dawning of any ordinary day. With no fanfare, no warning, he would at last confront Henry. He would give his old friend one final chance to make good on a promise, with no strings attached to strangle the new love that Richard shared with Tess.

When all the knights were in attendance and their squires had mounted, Richard heaved himself into his saddle. After Perkins followed suit, the earl raised his voice like a clarion.

"Let us away! God speed us all, noble knights."

Leading the way toward the gatehouse, trotting lightly on his horse, Richard knew that Tess was waiting there to bid him one last farewell. Anticipating her kiss, he thought, *No matter how far I travel, half of me—the better half—will remain here with her.*

"Richard! You rogue! Halt! For God's sake, lad. 'Ave mercy on an old round-gut! Richard!"

The inimitable hue and cry of Sir John somehow managed to rise above the clatter of clinking armor, creaking saddles, and clopping hooves. After giving a thought to ignoring the old sot, Richard recalled John's years, nigh on seventy, and forced himself to give the veteran carouser his due. Chafing with irritation, Richard drew his horse short, waiting impatiently as the mass of a man loped toward him.

"Richard, you'll not be leaving without me, will you, gallant?" Sir John gasped for air, his cheeks glistening like polished apples in the light of the torch he clutched.

Caught in the act, Richard growled softly to himself. "John, go inside. You'll catch a cold. This morning feigns a mean-spiritedness."

"Nay, I'll not go. You may call me fat-witted, or a misleader of youth, as our sweet Hal oft referred to me, but I'll not be bludgeoned away. Oh, sweet saints . . ."

He gripped his heart like a mummer in the climax of a tragic tale, but Richard knew he was not acting. The pain in John's body was real. When it had subsided and he could finally stand erect again, desperation and indignation glittered like an inferno in his eyes.

"I'll not be put off so easily, young wag! You promised me I could come. Will you put me off like a coward's dog? I who have drunk with princes and dukes! I who taught Venus herself how long the night is, putting younger men to shame. You said that when next you went to see the king I could go with you and give him a barrel of ale from Eastcheap."

"John, 'twas before you fell ill. . . ."

"A plague upon you! Give me a cup of ale and a horse and you'll see my keen state of health. Why, I'm as fit as a lizard's spleen. As forthright as a lion!"

"The king banished you, John. He sent you to prison and

then mercifully winked at your escape. Do not test his patience. He's done with the past. Do not pain yourself with another rejection."

John's fat lips parted and he licked them with great effort. Gripping Richard's knee, he whispered placatingly, "I've not long to travel this earth, princeling. Soon I'll be vulture's pudding. Is there no mercy, anon? No redemption for a soul burning on earth? Must I wait till my soul sizzles in the devil's bosom for all my thievery and drink to see if God will forgive me my slithering weaknesses? Just a word of forgiveness, a syllable of love from Hal is all I ask. Mercy! Is there no mercy yet, my earl?"

"Mercy on earth?" Richard's eyes shuttered involuntarily, and in that glimpse of darkness he was in Tess's arms again. "Mayhap there is mercy yet. Oh, very well! Come along. But I'll not wait on you, you slave-of-ale. Keep pace or you'll be left behind. My purpose is direct. 'Tis no social visit I'm making to our liege."

"Oh! I will keep pace, Richard. I promise you." John turned at the sound of a soft *clip-clop*. "Here! Here is my mount now. My page has packed my pouches. The ale is loaded behind my saddle. If I fare poorly, I'll stop at an inn along the way and you may proceed without me."

Staring at John's scurvy, bowlegged nag, Richard groaned inwardly. He could not bear to see Sir John's heart broken again, for it would surely sunder in twain if Henry turned him out a second and final time. But a grain of hope sprouted in Richard's cynic's heart. He would let the old man have his way, and if there was a merciful God, then the beefy knight would meet the peaceful end he so craved.

"Mount up, John. You can catch up the rear," Richard said, starting again for the drawbridge.

"I cannot wait to see Henry's expression when he sees us riding up together. The ale! Is it secure, boy?" John groused at his squire, a patient young man who merely nodded and did not even grunt when heaving his master into his saddle, though his knees sagged beneath the burden.

"Let us away!" Richard commanded, and kicked his palfrey into a fast trot. Then he pulled aside at the gatehouse, letting the others pass over the drawbridge, and quickly picked Tess out of the small band of women who had come to bid the men farewell.

Seeing her distress, he was reminded of the first time he'd seen her in a crowd, the night her father had been executed. But this time, pride was visibly etched at the corners of her mouth, where a tremulous smile formed two tender grooves.

"My lord," she said, reaching up and grasping his outstretched hand with small, tender fingers. "God speed you to the king and safely back again."

"My beautiful Tess," he murmured.

Now that she was married she covered her hair, as was the custom. With her hair caught up in small templers above her ears, crowned with an elaborate fillet, she looked the part of a countess. But she was ever more earnest and soulful than any noblewoman he'd seen before. Love shone in her eyes, glinting up like two sparks of sunlight, warming his soul. Leaning over, he kissed her soundly, remembering his new reason to live. "God be with the villain who would waylay my return. I'd cut down an army singled-handedly to return to your arms. Trust in me, Tess."

She nodded, her eyes glistening with moisture.

"Farewell!" He gave her a stout wave and bolted away.

Tess watched him disappear into the blazing sunrise, his incandescent hair afire, thinking with pride that it was her husband, her beloved who rode to his spectacular destiny. How much had changed so quickly! They had resolved the discord between them. And yet not all the pieces were in place. Thinking to set them aright, Tess headed to the prison tower for a visit with the only person whose blessing she still craved, her link with the past.

"Good morrow, Lady Gertrude," Tess said, shutting the creaking prison door behind her.

Gertrude held her in a studious gaze for a long time. She had been combing her hair as part of her morning ablutions. Lowering the comb now to her lap, her hawklike eyes softened. "Good morrow, Countess of Easterby."

"So I am." Tess gazed down at the black and gold embroidered trim lining the edges of her rustling flame-colored taffeta gown. If Gertrude had not been at the wedding, or seen the flush of passion in Tess's visage, she might have guessed her change in status by the luxury of her gown. Under Richard's tutelage, Tess had succumbed to every vice—beautiful clothes as well as frequent lovemaking.

"I . . . I am the countess now," she said, feeling a little rueful as she looked at herself through the eyes of the past, mirrored back to her in Lady Gertrude's implacable gaze. "'Tis hard to fathom that not a month ago I had never even been to Cadmon Castle, and never met the earl. I had only heard wicked tales about him from his sister."

"Do you rail against your change in position?"

Tess looked up. "Nay, I do not. I have come to view Richard differently."

"Ah . . . Do I see the blush of love in your cheeks?"

Tess turned away, idly running her fingers along the dust clinging to a groove in the stone wall. Not a quarter of an hour ago, she would have shouted yes to anyone who asked. Now she hesitated, feeling guilty.

"Richard is . . . an extraordinary man. I hope my father will forgive me for saying that."

"I think your father would have wanted you to find love, Tess. I know your mother wanted that."

Reminded of her mother's compassionate nature, Tess felt at ease again with her new love. Eager to share that affection, she went to Gertrude and began to comb her long, gray hair. It was as coarse as a horse's mane.

"I have good news, Gertie. Richard says he will consider my wishes as to your fate."

"'Consider your wishes'?"

Tess pivoted and surveyed the old woman's skeptical expression. "I thought you would be happy to hear it. Is this not outstanding news? I was overwhelmed with relief. This means you will not be executed, Gertie. Aren't you happy about that?"

"If 'tis true, then I am happy. More for my companions down the hall than for me, since I am old and ready to die."

"And yet . . . ?" Tess offered, sensing there was something Gertrude wasn't saying.

"And yet I wonder where Richard went this morning. I saw a mighty entourage heading up the west road."

"To visit the king."

"Ah. So I imagined." Gertrude shrugged. "Then he may have changed his mind regarding our fate by the time he returns."

Anger flamed to life, burning in Tess's abdomen. "You were the one who praised him before when I had naught but harsh words for him. Why do you now distrust him so?"

"Why do you defend him so?"

"Because he is my husband. Not chosen, but accepted. Do you not know by now that I am loyal above all?"

"Aye, I do know that. I also know you have fallen in love with your husband and your judgment cannot be trusted. Richard will not hesitate to use us to bargain with the king, for whatever purpose. And Henry can be very persuasive."

Indignation stiffened Tess's spine. Full of Richard, still smelling his musky scent, which seemed to have soaked into her permanent memory, thrilling in the deepest part of her just at the thought of his lovemaking, she thought him infinitely more powerful than any mere monarch. Who could possibly dissuade Richard once his mind was set? In her mind, he was like a god who graced the earth, visiting from Olympus. Could anyone who made love so passionately not have the power of a god? Certainly she had never felt more powerful. Together they could conquer the world.

"I do not think you should underestimate Richard's willingness to do right," Tess said in a cool voice. "I have misjudged him until now. I think he is our last, best hope. That is what Tarjaman said. Richard is on his way to see the king now. I cannot tell you what he plans for the near future, but I think if you knew you would approve."

"Have you ever met the king, Tess?"

"Aye, I have."

"Then you know his charm and his intense will."

"The king will not charm Richard into breaking his promise to me."

"What promise?"

"Well, the promise to . . . to . . ."

"Did he promise to set us free?"

"Well, nay, not exactly. But he will try."

"He will *try*?"

"Really, Gertie, you are acting as if I brought you bad news. I thought you would be happy to hear this."

"I am, my dear, but I am old enough to know that nothing is certain in this world."

"Well, I am certain that Richard will do right. I have seen his goodness in the most astoundingly intimate way possible. He will do right by you, Gertrude. You can count on that. I do."

Tess began to weave Gertrude's thick hair into a braid. She forced her mind to a different topic, and her thoughts landed at the feet of another conundrum. "Tarjaman has disappeared."

"Has he?"

"You do not sound surprised. Did you know that he is suspected of betraying Richard? Sir Randolf believes 'tis Tarjaman who abducted Sir Oswald and several cases of weapons."

"Tarjaman did not do it."

Tess's hands stilled at the certainty in Gertrude's voice. "How can you be so sure?"

"I am a keen judge of character. I know he would not betray Richard."

"Then why did he leave so suddenly?"

"Even if I knew I could not tell you."

Tess fastened a ribbon around the bottom of Gertrude's braid, pondering how best to explore this further. Her elderly friend obviously felt some affinity for Tarjaman and would not say anything to incriminate him.

"Lady Gertrude, one day when I was visiting you, I passed by Tarjaman in the hall. He held a book in his hand. When he saw me, he tucked it under his arm so that I might not see the title. What was it? What did he bring to you?"

Gertrude went to her bed and reached under the feather mattress. She pulled out a book and handed it to Tess.

Tess's eyes widened. "An English version of the Bible! Gertrude, you must not be found with this in your possession. 'Twill be proof of your heresy."

The Church did not want its followers to read and interpret the Bible for themselves, without the intercession of a priest, fearing it would make the faithful too independent. Therefore, the Church condemned English translations of the Holy Gospel.

"Tarjaman has compassion for those who are persecuted for their beliefs. He wanted to make us more comfortable. If he was willing to take the risk of bringing the Bible to me, I was willing to risk being found with it."

"Perhaps he wants you to be found with incriminating evidence. Are you certain of his motives? Gertie, Tarjaman's ancestors murdered in the name of Allah. He could do the same."

"He could. But he won't. I wish I could tell you more. Perhaps one day. Meanwhile, I will just say to you, Tess, that I hope you do not condemn a man because of your lack of understanding of his beliefs. If you do, then you are no better than the people who stood by and cheered while your father burned to death."

Tess laid the Bible on Gertrude's table, feeling the sting of her rebuke. "How complicated 'tis to live a noble life, Gertie. If only the world were black and white."

"Then you would never marvel at a sunrise, nor swim in the blue of your lover's eyes. You are doing well, Tess. Trust your heart."

Tess kissed her cheek. "I will come again as soon as I can."

Lady Gertrude watched her go, calling out just before she closed the door. "Tess?"

"Hmmm?" she replied, tucking her head back into the chamber.

"Did you conceive a child on your wedding night?"

Tess frowned as blood rushed to her already heated cheeks. "I can hardly know that, Lady Gertrude, until the next moon."

"Sometimes there is a way of knowing without knowing."

Tess frowned, wondering what that way was. She shrugged. "We shall see."

"Indeed."

Leaving the tower, Tess pressed her hands against her abdomen, trying to feel in the magical way that Lady Gertrude had implied she might know of such things. Dear God, had she conceived a child so soon? In the heat of passion, she had yearned for it dearly, but now, in the light of day, the prospect seemed so ominous.

Suddenly, she wished Richard had not gone. Already she missed him dearly, and she would not feel at peace until he returned. Even if she were with child, he would make it all right. He would keep her safe. Surely he had that power.

TWENTY-ONE

At noon on their second day of travel, Richard and his entourage entered London via Bishopsgate Street. He inhaled London—the wretched stench of horse manure, human piss, and pig's blood trickling over cobblestones. A moment later, with a slight shift of the wind, he breathed in the glorious aroma of foreign spices, freshly baked bread, and cut flowers. The call of good-natured neighbors, the curse of a disappointed beggar, a trill of laughter—all rose in a skin-prickling blare.

London! Gods, how he loved this city. He'd caroused here thinking himself immortal, bedding in the arms of any woman who would have him. Wistfully, he traveled on to Westcheap and then to Paternoster Row. Along the way, Richard absorbed the glorious bustle. Stocky butchers slammed their knives into the marbled meat of newly slaughtered calves. Fishmongers spilled buckets of oysters in their street stalls, the shells clattering softly, the nose-tingling scent of saltwater rising briefly. The stalls, about ten feet square, lined the wending roads. Above each stall loomed a two-story, whitewashed timber and plaster building. The deeper they rode into the city, the denser the streets became; everywhere were unwashed bodies, hungry dogs, and poor, dirty children. The thickness of humanity choked off any wind. Richard felt stifled. And vibrant.

He led his men at a meandering pace until they hit Fleet Street, then he picked up speed, anxious to reach Thorny Island on the other side of London. He saw the great spires of Westminster shooting up long before he reached the city's marshy outskirts. Seeing that vast compound, a virtual city in itself, Richard's spine went as rigid as the towering walls of St. Stephen's Chapel.

A half hour later, he was kneeling in the chapel's front pew, saying a prayer before heading to Westminster Hall.

"Easterby. They told me you had come."

Richard recognized the voice of the powerful Bishop of Winchester, Henry Beaufort, and felt Beaufort's certain, long fingers grip his shoulder.

"Greetings, my lord." Richard rose from the wooden pew, new alarm squirreling in his gut. He was being welcomed by the most powerful man in the country, aside from the king. Henry Beaufort was not only a bishop, but the lord chancellor of England, as well as the king's half uncle and most trusted advisor. "Good to see you, Beaufort. I must be moving up in the world to be greeted by you."

"I am always available to my nephew's friends, Richard, you know that."

Richard embraced the bishop, feeling the familiarity and comfort of old ties, along with the strain of new alliances and higher stakes.

"I've come for Henry," Richard said, the first to withdraw from the embrace.

"Then you've just missed him." Beaufort's graying brows forged together. "He's heading to the Tower, where he will stop briefly before riding to the coast."

"S'blood!" Richard cursed, pinching the bridge of his nose. "I must speak with him. 'Tis urgent."

Beaufort's frown deepened. "Why? You have had many opportunities to come to London before now, Richard. Henry has sent you several missives and you have not responded to a single one."

"I will now. Send a messenger to the Tower, Beaufort, and tell the king to wait. I must speak with him."

The tall, regal prelate, who bore a distinct resemblance to his royal nephew, smiled, his lips parting like the beak of a hawk. "Ah, Richard, I cannot halt Henry's progress. His army is gathering at Southampton. He wants to insure that his host will be ready to depart soon. The Earl of Dorset is organizing the fleet. Harry had hoped you would oversee the departure as well, but he tells me you have not responded to his summonses. It seems you have been scarce here at Court since your investiture at the last Parliament. Are your new responsibilities as earl so weighty that you cannot aid the king who gave you the honor?"

A chorus of rich male voices chanting in Latin rose from the silence, seemingly from the walls, for no monks could be seen in the stained-glass reflections of the chapel.

"Come, you have ridden hard and need refreshment." The bishop's long, elegant fingers, with nails groomed as artfully as any nobleman's, curled around Richard's elbow.

Richard dug his heels in place. "I must see Henry. If he has gone, I will ride after him."

The facade of warm welcome cooled, revealing the sharp intelligence of the king's uncle. "He will not see you, Easterby. Not until you make your commitment to his cause known, not in words but in deeds. Go back to your castle and gather your lances. The Earl of Salisbury has mustered forty men-at-arms and eighty horsed archers; you would be expected to provide no less. Bring them to Southampton without pause. Then you will have Henry's ear. And not a moment sooner."

"Did Henry tell you this?"

The bishop nodded. "He is also waiting for your steward to visit the Earl of Arundel. You have a rich wife now, Easterby. Make your gratitude known. Seventeen thousand pounds would be a gesture much appreciated by the king. As a loan, of course."

"Of course." New fury simmered through Richard's veins, permeating every part of his being. He cocked his head, musing. "It saddens me, Beaufort, to see what friendship has wrought. Henry loved me once."

"Don't be naive," Beaufort answered with an impatient sneer. "Friendship is a luxury that comes last to any king. If you are a friend, then you will help Harry solidify his reign. And war is the best way to do that. Help Harry, Easterby, and he will help you. Love or no."

Richard thought briefly of Sir John, his pitiful love for Henry, his inconsequence in the scheme of it all, and he shuddered.

Shake it off, he thought. After all these years, he still felt too much, and even more so now that Tess had opened his heart. He pushed past Beaufort. "Will you see a missive gotten to the king?"

"If it bears good news," the bishop intoned.

"'Twill bear the best news of all." *For myself*, Richard added silently. "If you will excuse me, my Lord Chancellor. I will fetch a scribe, and then I will depart for Cadmon Castle . . . to do the king's bidding."

"What of the Lollards?" Beaufort called after him.

Dread stopped Richard in his tracks. He twisted around. "What *of* the Lollards?"

"Word comes to Westminster that you have three Lollards in your prison—one of them Sir Andrew Warton, who helped plan the attack on Eltham. We've been searching for Warton for months."

"Aye, I have Warton. I will turn the Lollards over in due time."

Beaufort nodded, suspicion glimmering in his eyes. "See that you do. Will you not rest and sup with me before you depart?"

The bishop received no answer, for already Richard was lost in a swarm of chanting monks filing through the chapel doors. He was compelled by a sudden and overwhelming concern for Sir John to seek him out, and could not wait for polite farewells.

Sir John did not need the sharp eye of a falcon to find his way to Eastcheap. He knew the city so well he could shut his eyes and steer his mount blindly, gently veering this way and that. His horse lumbered along Westcheap, past the goldsmiths and the spice markets. John inhaled into his rattling lungs the pungent scent of saffron. His stomach grumbled, and he wondered what Mistress Nell would be cooking at the Boar's Head Inn this evening.

"Come along, sweetling," he urged his mount, who sagged beneath her burden, clanking her shod hooves against the ancient cobblestones with each lethargic step.

"Forgive me, Richard," John muttered. He was fond of talking to himself these days, for he could find no companion of quicker wit, nor any with as much compassion as he might give unto himself. "I could not lollygag at Westminster, Richard, waiting for you like a manservant. If the king is not there, why stay? You'll find me at the Boarshead when you're ready to leave, young wag. I know you'll find me."

The Boar's Head Inn. He had not been carousing there since the king had thrown him in prison. John had thought it prudent to avoid London. Until now. Seeing the city crowds, he realized this was his only home—no single dwelling, but tavern after tavern, the multitude of which comprised his residence. Here he had lived larger than life. Here he had laughed with the bawds and drunk the hardiest knights under the table. Here Prince Hal had laughed at Sir John's jests until his gut ached. Here he and Hal had often shared a strange bed, too drunk to find their own.

"Whoa! Halt," he commanded his scurvy mount. "I will walk."

Dismounted, he was closer to the piss-filled gutters and kitchen windows billowing the fumes of boiled cabbage and frumenty. Now his feet and knees ached under the weight of his barrel of a belly, leaving him to rail against age, to long for youth, to know his time was not long for this world. Where did an old drunk go to die? In a vat of ale? he wondered with a pleased chuckle. He'd heard of naval commanders pickled at sea in casks of wine, for preservation, of course. It seemed to John a delightful way to go.

"Before I die," he told his nag, whispering in her ear, which she cocked forward, "I must see Henry. I must see him. I must."

His horse whinnied, understanding.

"'Forgive me, my prince, for whatever I have done to wrong you,' I will say," John mumbled as he wandered, tugging on the reins. "'Do not deny me your embrace, for I am old and weary. I would have my shoulders sag in your strong arms, young prince. For you are the golden one. You are the hope of mankind. You have been my family. You have been my cause. Say good night, princeling, and I will fade into the dusk. Quietly. Not like the old fool I have been all my life.'"

His horse whickered. *Tell me more,* John heard the beast urge him.

"'John,' Hal will say to me, 'gods, how I've missed you. I grow weary of these ministers and diplomats and councils and canons. All I need, John, is a good cup of ale and a joke.

Do you know any jokes anymore?' And do you know what I shall say? I shall say, 'Your Grace, I have a barrel of ale mounted on my horse at this very moment. Will you drink with me?'"

"'Do you remember any jokes, John?' the king will say. 'I am surrounded by fools. A king gets naught but fools to laugh at—those with bells on their hats and those with bells between their ears. Stuffy lot, these politicians, John. Tell me a joke as you used to.' And I shall reply, 'Oh, aye, Prince Hal.'"

He looked into the dubious eyes of the slow-blinking steed, and when the animal whickered and blew a snort of air, John scowled at her. "'What, you say, Your Grace? You do not think I still have it in me? Why, just the other day I brought the walls down with a jape. A merry ditty about a traveling minstrel who . . . who . . . Well, I cannot remember now, but 'twas hilarious, my liege. It was about a minstrel who . . .'"

Damn it, but he could not remember. He could not remember when it mattered the most. No wonder the king had turned him out. *Fool!* he railed inwardly. *Fool! Old, forgetful fool!*

Beads of perspiration sprouted suddenly on his forehead. The air came slow into his lungs. He couldn't get enough air and thought he would pass out. And just then, he saw him. *Him.* The king! Not in the reflection of a horse's eye, but in the flesh, in all his glory, approaching from a distance behind a dozen men-at-arms. Clarions blared with glorious fanfare.

"My king!" John shouted, scraping his voice raw with desperate vehemence. "Hal! 'Tis I, Sir John!"

John lunged into the crowd that was quickly gathering in the street.

"The king! The king is coming!" children cried, and their

parents scooped them up upon their shoulders to see the royal entourage.

John pushed through them all, lunging forward willy-nilly. "Step away. I am a friend of the king's. Step back."

He squinted against the beating sun that glared off the brilliant silver armor of Henry's escort. A dozen mighty men-at-arms bearing the king's regal livery approached in formation on their high-stepping steeds. They trotted smartly through the street, the crowd spilling aside to make way.

In the crowd's wake, John spotted the coat of arms he would have recognized had it been a mile in the distance, the blue and red arms of King Henry, quartered with English leopards and French fleurs-de-lis. John froze in place, unable to move, even as the white horses clopping closer threatened to trample him. His heart began to pound in his chest. *Boom. Boom. Boom.* Could he say what he wanted to say to Henry? Would he remember the words? Bystanders fell to their knees as the shadow of Henry's fine gray palfrey fell over them. *Clip-clop, clip-clop* went the hooves of the sleek, white-eyed beast upon the cobblestones.

John thought the shadow would pass. He thought the gray would trot onward with the magnificent and fearful Presence upon its back, but the shadow of the king lingered. It fell over John and hovered. He looked up, searching for Henry's piercing, sharp eyes, but the shadow was too great, too overwhelming.

John, who had had the audacity to remain standing before the Presence, fell to his knees.

"My liege," he tried to eloquently say, but his voice caught in his throat, leaving his pillowy lips to work the words soundlessly, ineffectively. "Ale! I have ale from our tavern," he mouthed, nearly crying in frustration when the words would not come.

"Hail to the king!" someone shouted from behind him.

"Hail to the king! Hail to the king!" a chorus rose in answer, drowning any further futile mutterings John might have managed. The shadow, and the giant of a man who had made it, passed onward then. When the last man-at-arms followed up the rear and trotted away, the crowd fell in behind, cheering on the king and laughing at their good fortune to have seen their magnificent monarch so close at hand.

"But my liege! Henry! 'Tis I," John sputtered, staggering to his feet, finally having found his voice, though it did no good, since Henry was long out of earshot.

Defeated, John fell back against his horse, his head banging against the cask of ale. He turned and clutched it like a lover, and fumbling with the straps that bound it to his saddle, he pulled the wooden container into his arms. His arm muscles strained as splinters slipped into his once-callused fingers.

"Hal!" he shouted. "I have a gift for you. Hold, sweet wag, do not leave me now."

He ran in the crowd's wake, clutching the cask to his great girth, holding it as dearly as he did the memory of his days with the prince, nearly laughing one minute at the thought of their antics and weeping the next when he thought of all that had come and gone. He had thought he would be young forever; he had thought Hal would love him for an eternity. For when they had laughed together, when the prince had bestowed his bonny smile on him, John had known a kind of immortality. But all things pass, he now realized, watching the king's entourage round a corner and disappear. The whinnies of horses faded. The street sounds resumed: a child kicking a ball; the splash of a piss-pot from a second-story window.

All things pass, he thought, slowing his gate, feeling the heaviness in his lungs again. *Boom. Boom. Boom.* A sudden, fierce pain gripped his chest and shot down his arm. So fierce that John could do naught but clutch it.

"Ahhh," he groaned.

The barrel of ale fell to the ground. It landed with a thudding crack on the pavement and split open. The amber liquor leaked out onto the filthy cobblestones, mingling with the feces of chickens and horses.

"My ale," John wheezed, clutching his chest. He could stand no more and fell to his knees. Landing on a sharp stone, he groaned with yet another pain. The ale soaked his sagging hose. He laid one hand into the fast-running liquid, cool and dark. "Oh, Hal, I am so sorry."

He fell on top of the barrel's remains, which splintered completely beneath his weight. It seemed he lay there unnoticed for the longest time, his chest aching. Finally, he mustered the strength to roll on his back. His frayed houppelande was soaked utterly with ale, and he thought it an ignoble way to depart the earth, looking for all the world to see as if he'd let loose with the greatest piss a drunkard could let. He blinked open his eyes, and much to his surprise, he found a towering figure shadowing him from the sun as only the Presence could.

"My liege? Is that you?" He shadowed his eyes against the sun that haloed the figure, but still all was darkness and light and he could not make out the features. "Hal? Harry, is it you?"

The figure nodded.

"Oh, God, Hal. I'm dying." The tears of a child burned his eyes, but he was not ashamed to weep. He did not want to part this world. He held up his hand and the Presence gripped it with his own.

"I loved you, my liege. A man never served his king with more devotion. Did you love me, sire?"

The figure knelt and stroked his cheek. "You were the best friend a king could have, Sir John."

John blinked hard, doubting his ears. "Do you mean it, Hal? Is it really you?"

The figure nodded again.

John allowed a smile then, knowing he could face the darkness. The Presence scooped John into his arms, and in their strength and warmth all thoughts did indeed give way to that fearful lack of light. But he was not afraid. Not anymore.

The next day, leaving his men-at-arms to tend John's cold and lifeless body, Richard departed London with only Perkins at his side. The streets were stifling and smelly. He couldn't wait to reach the grassy fields beyond the city's borders.

It was a long and painful ride home for Richard. Hunched over his reins, in sunshine and pelting rain, he drove his steed hard through meadows and dales, forests and moors to reach Cadmon Castle, to reach his love. She was his only consolation now. Her arms encompassed his new world, for the old was shattered beyond repair. That much was clear from his discussion with the king's uncle. To proceed with his attack on Kirkingham now would be an act so contrary to the will of Henry, so perpendicular in nature to the direction Henry was leading the nation by the sheer force of his considerable will, that Richard would be scorned as a madman or a fool. Either way, the mission would be one of suicide, politically speaking. He might as well be an Assassin from Persia.

Shortly before noon the following day, when Cadmon Castle appeared like a crown jewel in the distance rising from the mists, Richard slowed his pace. He was a new man approaching an old and familiar sight, and he wanted to look at every leaf, every twist in the road, every gnarled tree with his new eyes. Perkins reined in at his side, clearly as happy to be home as Richard.

"Sir John is the lucky one," he said, eyeing the tousle-haired youth. "Do you know that, Perkins? He died in a state of delusion, with the hope of a child beating in his faulty but passionate heart."

"Aye, my lord, he did not live to see the slaughter that will take place in France. 'Tis a blessing."

Richard tossed back his locks of hair, offering his bronzed face to the sun, daring the wind to kiss his stony cheeks. He wanted the spring breeze to beat against his face, to vanquish the last painful memories, to make him forget the glassy gaze of John's eyes when his limbs had finally ceased his struggle to live. Most of all Richard wanted nature to make him feel alive, for he felt so hollow inside.

"The body crumbles, Perkins. The soul flies. Survivors remain behind, making merry, making sense of their mortality, until another goes—a friend, a lover, an acquaintance, a wrinkled and lifelong mate. Even an enemy seems a loss when time has ravaged the illusions of immortality. And in the end, whether your questions have been answered or not, 'tis your time to go. Alone. Into the night.

"How valiantly and tenaciously that old sot fought off the Reaper," Richard added softly when they stopped by a roadside stream to let their mounts drink. "I adored him for that. He never took life for granted. He was intemperate, a braggart, and sometimes even a thief, but I cherished him."

"I know, my lord. 'Tis a great loss."

Richard nodded. The loss was so great it impelled him to the only person who could prove to Richard that he was alive. Tess. All he could think about was how incredible it would feel to hold her again.

He would dock in her arms like a ghost ship that had found a harbor at last. A creaking, weather-beaten vessel, a cog that had ridden the last wave to safety, just in time.

Remembering the raw sweetness of her embrace, her

guileless kisses that seemed to spark from her very essence, he cursed himself for all the years he'd wasted on women for whom he cared but little.

"You know, Perkins," he said, tugging on the reins and forcing his mount back on the road, "when I was young, I thought life would go on forever and bedded one damsel after another. It seems so foolish. I see now that all our days are numbered. And I cannot even remember the names of all the ladies with whom I've lain. I can't even remember how many there were."

To this Perkins said nothing. He merely blushed.

I must get home to Tess, thundered a voice in Richard's head, whether it was God or conscience or common sense.

"Keep pace!" he shouted to Perkins, and launched into a gallop. He had to make love to Tess. *Not for pleasure's sake, but so that she knows she is loved. To share a moment of eternity with her before it slips by, laughing at man's vanity, for it is a vain man who does not see that time is precious. Curse the gods, rail at the darkness, but the end will come in the blink of an eye. Will you have loved a woman well?* he asked himself sternly. *Will you have left a legacy of truth and justice? Will your seed spawn another or will it have been cast aside?*

I will conquer life with savage joy. I will live it so fully the earth will not easily forget my name or the roar of my victorious voice.

"My lord, what ho! Draw back!" Perkins called from behind.

Richard reined in abruptly at his drawbridge. His ruminations had led him blindly but instinctively to his destination. He was home.

"Whoa!" Richard called to his steed. The thundering beast reared back, angry to end his rabid ride just short of shelter. Tugging at the reins, Richard gave terse orders. "Perkins, go to Lady Tess. Tell her I have arrived. I will join her shortly. But there is something I want to do first."

"Aye, my lord."

Richard galloped off to the moor where he and Tess had danced together. He was weary from the exhausting ride, and it took great effort to swing his leg over his saddle to dismount. But when his feet landed in a crush of heather, the sweet smell encompassing him, soothing him, creaking open his heart, he felt whole and excited again, and more urgent than ever to see his lady.

He bent and plucked a few sprigs in his callused hands. The pinkish heather blossoms filled his eyes with wonder. Even amidst life's great tragedies, flowers blossomed everywhere, lush and lovely to behold. Life was beautiful, at least to those who had the wits to see it. He saw it, he realized with relief. John had seen it, too. And Tess. A triumvirate of hopelessly idealistic hearts.

"God!" he cried out with an excruciating pang of gratitude, slapping his thigh with awkward wonder. "Thank you for this life!"

The words spurted through his tangled lips, the first utterance of a prolonged moan of agonizing joy. Bitter and sweet, sorrowful and elated, his emotions swirled in an overwhelming eddy as he clutched his pitiful bouquet. He wept, each tear laden with gall and honey. And when the tears dried, leaving faint tracks on his dusty cheeks, he remounted stoically.

On the ride back to the castle, he saw only her face—shell-pink cheeks, a sultry little heart-shaped mouth that blossomed more beautifully than heather, and chestnut-colored eyes as earnest and soulful as the earth. *Tess. Tess. Tess.* Her name was a drumbeat, pounding to the rhythm of his horse's hooves.

When those hooves clamored over the wooden slats of the

drawbridge, he heard one "Hail, my lord!" after another and realized he was home. Truly home. Perhaps for the first time. All because of Tess.

As soon as he entered the great hall, Godfrey and Sir Randolf greeted him. As he clearly had no intention of stopping for anything, they fell in, one on either side, briefing him on recent events as they traversed the long, high-ceilinged hall. Their voices echoed in the emptiness.

"My lord, there is a request for ransom for Sir Oswald," Godfrey said fretfully.

"From the bishop?"

"Aye, Richard. Kirkingham is holding Oswald. He is alive and well."

"How much does he want in exchange for our master gunner?"

"Twice what you were paid for the safe return of Prince Owain's steward."

Richard whistled long and low. "Kirkingham is a greedy whelp."

"But he is willing to give you Oswald back freely, without payment," Sir Randolf piped in with his gruff voice.

"Nothing is ever truly freely given away, Randolf."

"You do not have to pay a farthing," the castellan clarified, "if you are willing to sign a document saying that you legally deed Marly Vale over to the dear bishop."

Richard would have laughed at the preposterous notion, but he knew the time to waste his precious energy was long past. "The battle begins at dawn two days hence, my friends. Tell the men to prepare."

"What of Oswald?" Godfrey asked.

"He'll have to endure a bleak prison chamber for a few more days. The bishop will not harm him. He'd rather be paid ransom, which I will do if I must. But first let us try to win his freedom in battle."

Sir Randolf's perpetual scowl softened with a gleam of warmth. "We've been waiting a long time for this moment, haven't we, Richard?"

"Too long, my friend. Far too long."

If I'd had half of Tess's moral outrage and courage, the battle set for tomorrow would have been played out long ago.

"Good night, friends." Richard's brief dismissal told them that they would not see him for the evening meal. He would spend the night alone with Tess.

When he swung open the door to his solar, she was sitting on the rim of the wooden tub, dipping a hand into steaming water, swirling the surface.

"Tess . . ."

Her golden eyes darted through the shadows, gleaming like blinking twin stars. This was his universe.

"Richard . . ."

Still treasuring the bouquet of heather dangling from one hand, he keenly took in his surroundings, voraciously consuming every nuance of light and color. Tess's rich brown hair fell loose and full about her shoulders, a delicate eggshell white. Her lips were full and as red as the blood that pulsed in her generous heart.

"You've been waiting for me."

"I've scarcely breathed since your departure."

He noticed that the covers on the bed were turned down and a trencher of fruit and cheese awaited the taking on his desk. Appreciating every sign of her caring, his hand tightened around the clump of heather. Mutely, he held it aloft, not knowing what to say, except "I love you," and that was far too simple, despite the fact that he had returned in haste to say those very words.

"I brought you a gift," he said instead.

"Really?" She stood like a child who had been enticed with

a sugared treat, and yet there was a womanly serenity that beamed from her perfect face.

"Some heather from the moor where we danced," he said.

She glided forward and took the unlikely bouquet into her hands, cradling it as if it were a precious jewel. She sniffed the rustic fragrance and her face lit up with love. He was sure of it.

"This is a precious gift." She smiled up at him.

"Tess . . ."

"Aye, my lord?"

He was in the harbor now, the ghost ship docked. He heard the creaking sigh of the weary hull. He was home. *Tell her. Tell her how you ache. She can take it. She is strong. So strong.*

"Tess, Sir John . . . is dead."

"Ohhhh . . ."

No greeting, no exchange of formalities, no protestations of love. Just the brutal truth.

"How? When?" Tess stood transfixed, her face stricken with sorrow.

Richard explained everything—their arrival in London, John's venture on his own, his collapse in the street. And as Richard spoke he tugged her by the hand to their bed, where they sat side by side.

When his tale came to a whispered halt, Tess cleared the emotion from her throat and blinked back pools of tears. "You let John die thinking it was the king, and not you, who had held him?"

Richard smiled tenderly, sadly. "Aye. I lied so that he might at last find the forgiveness and love he so craved."

He looked in her eyes and found understanding. She did not judge him for that small sin. Sighing, he continued. "His squire and I dragged the old sot into the Boar's Head Inn, which was a stone's throw away. 'Twas the very place he and

I and Prince Hal would carouse until the wee morning. Nell, the innkeeper, put him to bed and soothed his forehead with cool rags. She was happy to see him after so long an absence."

"He was still breathing then?"

"Oh, yes. His body may have been half dead, but his mind would not succumb. Nell brought him a cluster of spring flowers and he played with them on the ends of his fingers, muttering to himself the Twenty-third Psalm. 'The Lord is my shepherd . . . he maketh me to lie down in green pastures.' "

Tess expelled a breath of wonder. "I would not have thought Sir John to quote the Bible, debaucher that he was."

"It seems the greatest celebrant of life the world has known feared death more than any. Though I'm not certain 'twas fear, really. He was loath to leave his sagging body for that other world. 'God, God, God!' he called out shortly before he passed on, whether in prayer or condemnation I know not. And in the last moments of his life, he managed to scramble out of bed and seize my sword, waving it at an unseen specter. His eyes, wide like two ominous orange moons, glared at the shadows of the chamber, his mouth working in indignation, his arms flailing the sword. Nell and I stepped back to give him berth.

"He cried out, 'I'll not go, Reaper! You vulture! Off! Off with you, now! I have supped with princes and dukes! I'll not go, I say.' Then just as abruptly he dropped my sword, which clattered to the floor, and he fell back in bed. Clutching his flowers again, jutting out his lip, he said, 'I am no coward, Richard. Tell the others I was brave to the end. Only those who dare not live and laugh and scoff at men's rules are cowards. I fear death because I have braved life and know how sweet 'tis and how bitter to part with.'

"'Farewell you well, John,' I said, and bent to kiss his

mouth. He smiled up at that, his eyes brilliant, glittering jewels. 'I saw the king, Richard. He has forgiven me, whatever my sins were that grieved him so. Did you hear?'

" 'Aye, John, I heard it.' Then the old man pressed his head back into the pillow, his face going white, the look in his eyes distancing like the tide receding from the shore. 'We are all forgiven, then,' John said. 'In the end . . . forgiveness . . .' They were his last words. His eyes lowered to half-mast and froze, forever glimpsing the afterlife."

Richard halted. He couldn't go on. *Forgiveness.* Was there truly forgiveness in the end? he wondered, feeling as if the very word had cleaved his heart in two. Forgiveness for everyone? Was it possible? Was God so great? Forgiveness even for Richard's failings?

Tess burst into tears, covering her face with her hands. Her soft whimpers of sorrow and love pricked his heart with tenderness. He pulled her close, inhaled her womanliness, until her sobs grew quiet. Her tears cleansed them both and reassured him that life goes on, even in the presence of death. For feelings, he knew, whether joy or sorrow, were the only true signs of life.

He kissed her forehead, and then his thoughts turned from yesterday's crises to tomorrow's. "Tess, the battle to reclaim Marly Vale will begin in two days," he whispered gently, but urgently.

She pulled away and searched his face with concern and a flicker of excitement. Then she pressed her lips to his and gave him a long, possessive kiss. It was an official seal, her stamp of acceptance. And in that exchange of loving energy, it seemed all was healed and life was reaffirmed.

She ended the kiss as directly as she had begun it, then rose and began to tug him along to the tub. "I want you to bathe now."

Once he had undressed and settled in the soothing water,

she lathered soap on her hands and smoothed them over the tendons in his neck, gently massaging away the grit from his arduous journey.

"Next," she continued, "we must hasten to bed and make love the night through."

"So that you might weaken me and the bishop can finish me off for you?"

She smiled coyly, slapping his bare chest with a wet washrag. "Nay, surly boy. So that I might bear a son called Richard whose name will live on into eternity."

Knowing how frightened she was of childbirth, he thought her words the sweetest he had ever heard. Love was a greater aphrodisiac than desire, or passion, or lust. After swiftly drying off, he carried her to bed, where they made love for hours in every position known to man or woman. For both knew that depending on the outcome of the battle, this night together might be their last.

TWENTY-TWO

At midnight, Richard's eyes slammed open. Sweat gathered on his chest, trickled through the coils of hair, and itched his skin. He'd dreamt of mangled bodies, the steam of blood rising from a scorched battlefield, and fatherless children. That was what war wrought. Fatherless children.

These images—wide, tear-filled eyes of snotty-nosed, dirty little children, begging for a crust of bread—had the effect of a vice squeezing his chest, leaving no room for air. Tess's slow, even breath was his only comfort, and he longed to embrace her. But he didn't deserve comfort now. Not until his conscience came clean. He sat up as a chill sent goose bumps cascading down his arms. This night offered not only his last chance to make love to Tess, but the last opportunity for absolution.

He stole away from bed. Pulling on his braies, hose, boots, and a doublet, he slipped out of the castle and into the church, seeking the forgiveness Sir John had thought he had found in the end.

"I go to war and seek your blessing," Richard said once inside the confessional.

It seemed an eternity before Father James replied. As the seconds ticked by, blood pounded in Richard's ears. A mind-shattering montage of images galloped through his head—fixing a sparrow's wings, braiding his mother's soft, red hair, kissing his first maiden, killing his first enemy. Tess. Beautiful Tess. Thighs spread. Watery flower. Drinking its dew, his due. Filling her. Sleeping. Loving her. Leaving her. Dying. Blood spilling. Swallowed by the earth. Darkness.

"Nay, I will not give you my blessing." The rasp of a voice finally seeped through the wooden partition separating them, ending Richard's flight of fancy. "Do not fight against the bishop. If you lose the cost will be too dear."

Richard was so startled by this absolute position it took a moment to recover. He squinted at the vague image of Father James through the slats of the partition.

Richard cleared his throat. "Lend unto Caesar that which is Caesar's, and lend unto the Lord that which is the Lord's. Need I quote Christ's words to you, old man? The price of earthly goods, even my life, is not too dear if it means reclaiming my conscience by fighting for what is right."

"Oh, Richard! How many good men have I seen fallen in my time? Too many. I cannot watch you fall, too. I loved your father as much as a man can love another. We shared our hopes—he for greatness in his world of kings and noblemen, and I to rise in the Church and in the eyes of God. Our hopes were dashed when the Usurper came to power. I was there when your father was killed. Richard, Richard, do not meet that same end. I promised your father . . . I *promised* . . ."

"What? What did you promise him?"

James exhaled a hoarse sigh. "Nay, nothing, I . . ."

"What? Tell me."

"I promised to advise you as I advised him. But better than I counseled him, for something went terribly wrong. He died too young. Much too young. If I'd only . . ."

"Father James, our bodies are not your concern. Merely our souls." *What has come over him?*

Chastised, the old priest made a sniffling noise Richard recognized as weeping. It unnerved him, for he did not like to think he knew more than his confessor, that he had become the advisor.

"Very well," the priest muttered after recovering himself. "I bless you in the name of the Father, and the Son, and the Holy Ghost. Amen."

"Amen."

Richard rose and departed, feeling ill at ease. The blessing had been halfhearted. Too many laden thoughts remained unspoken. For the first time, a visit to his confessor had left him angry and anxious.

Outside, the drone of bees from the hives seemed acute in the stillness of the bailey. The stars twinkled with rare brilliance overhead, but the signs of nature did nothing to bring him peace. He'd gotten what he wanted: the priest's blessing. But it was little comfort, having come so reluctantly. And a reluctant blessing on the verge of a battle seemed like an ill omen. What in hell had come over Father James? Instead of his having gained spiritual wisdom in his doddering years, it seemed his judgment had become clouded with earthly emotions.

Shrugging off his discomfort, Richard went to the garrison to check on his men, who he knew would undoubtedly be as sleepless as he.

The next night, under cover of darkness, Richard's garrison made a hasty trek to the east side of Hawk's Mound. The sky was blessedly overcast, dulling the moon's bright rays, and created a perfect cover for the haul. Their equipment included cannons, shots and powder, longbows, maces, pikes, tents, and mongonels. After pitching tents, some made a halfhearted attempt to sleep before their early-morning attack.

Scouts went ahead to assess the enemy's territory. They returned quickly with sobering news.

Gaveston entered Richard's tent with a frown. Fidgeting, he looked from Richard to Sir Randolf and back again. "My lords, the bishop is utterly prepared. His troops are armed to the teeth and waiting for us a half-mile beyond Hawk's Mound in Avondale Grove."

Sir Randolf smacked his fist against his palm, and his bronzed cheeks puffed out against his bushy beard. "S'blood!" he shouted.

Richard merely crossed his arms, his lips puckering with displeasure. "So our spy has done his work well."

"God curse him and may he burn in hell," Randolf growled. "I'll wager we'll see Tarjaman's body trampled on the other side when the battle is over and naught but smoke and the stench of blood rises from the field. And if not, I'll seek him out and throttle him myself, the traitorous dog, the bloody, cunning scoundrel."

"Tarjaman has been missing for a week, Randolf," Richard said quietly, perusing a map of the region spread out on a small table. Avondale Grove was marked by a cluster of Xs. "I didn't give the final marching orders until two days ago. He could not have known."

"He has his spies in the castle, Richard, doubt it not."

"I do not doubt 'tis possible." But he still didn't want to believe it. "It matters little now. We have no choice but to attack head-on with the first light—a pitched battle, unfortunately. I had hoped for a siege of the castle. But this last betrayal forces us to make a much more dangerous frontal attack."

"Aye, my lord," Gaveston said. "I will tell the men to prepare accordingly."

The cavalry commander bowed and departed.

"By God, when we do find our traitor," Richard whispered

savagely, "I will have him drawn and quartered. Even if it is Tarjaman."

Tess imagined the worst as she watched the battle from the parapets. She strained on the tips of her toes, peeking through the crenels atop the battlements. All she could see was smoke rising from a grove of trees in the distance. But her fears contrived a pale imagining compared with the scarlet and rueful reality of war. She had never known how red blood was in copious amounts until she saw the first wounded soldiers. They were hauled back to the castle in a horse-drawn cart. She dashed down the tower stairs and pushed her way through the gathering crowd at the gatehouse, but when she reached the cart, she stopped and gasped, flinging her hands to her gaping mouth. Blood bathed the weather-bleached floorboards of the cart. By each body there were puddles of sticky, thick, apple-red blood.

"Dear God, get them to the garrison chamber," she ordered, her sense of duty overcoming her ghastly shock. "Alert the barber-surgeon. Hurry!"

As horrified servants rushed forward to do the countess's bidding, it became apparent that one of the soldiers was already dead. His eyes were wide and glazed, his mouth twisted in a permanent pose of pain. Tess's knees nearly buckled. Death was so near. And nearer still to Richard. She made the sign of the cross. *Dear God, be with him.*

"Hurry!" she ordered the servants. "And get the others to bed."

In the garrison chamber, where a dozen cots stretched from one wall to the other, the barber-surgeon was waiting with boiling oil to pour into the wounds. Margaret, Rose, and Edith were also standing by, their sleeves rolled up. Tess joined them, undressing the soldiers and cleansing their wounds.

After handing one soldier over to the barber's care, Tess turned to another who, for some reason, evoked a powerful blast of empathy in her. His thigh was badly torn apart, obviously by a gunneshot. He was a young soldier, with tousled and sweaty black hair, a quick smile, and big teeth.

"Are ye . . . are ye Lord Richard's wife?" He blinked against the stinging perspiration that dripped into his eyes.

"I am. And who are you?" she asked as she cut away his breeches with a knife. The blood had been stanched, giving her a clear view of the largest gaping hole she had ever seen in a man. *So this is the work of gunnes,* she thought with a shudder.

"I am Bartholomew Miller. My family has worked yer husband's land fer nigh on three generations now."

His words confirmed what his simple garb had suggested: He was a foot soldier—a crossbowman, she guessed by the thick trunks of his arms.

"Ye should have seen the earl fight, milady."

Concerned about Bartholomew's snowy-white cheeks and his giddy speech, she touched the back of her hand to his forehead. His skin was on fire.

"You should be still, Bartholomew—you have a fever. The barber-surgeon will tend to your wound soon."

He gripped one of her wrists, squeezing so hard his callused fingers pinched her skin. "He led the charge. He himself! Lord Richard! As like I'd never seen. And by all that's holy, milady, I felt a pride swell within me chest as like I've never felt before. He galloped to the fore, leading the way. That he did."

"He put himself before all others?" Tess asked in hushed amazement.

"Aye. We ran behind him down the hill, all misty and gray and what, and fell on the enemy like attacking bears, that we did. Yer husband, he swung out o' the way, and the first row of longbowmen cut loose with a bloody rain of arrows, that they did. A *whoosh* from it all near to deafened me. The sky, 'twere black with arrows, an' we felled the first row o' the cruel knaves defending the bishop who stole Lord Richard's land. The knaves, they charged us back, milady, but we had right on our side, ye see.

"Lord Richard, he was the bloomin' god of Mars, he was. The earl, he was so noble with white trappings on his black warhorse, he himself cutting such a fine figure. *'Pour le coeur de guerre!'* Lord Richard cried out his motto fer all to hear. 'For the heart of war! Long live the Easterbys!' His voice boomed like a roaring cannon, so that every bleedin' man 'eard him. I swear a snake slithered down me spine at the force o' it. And then the battle madness took hold, just like wid me father in his battles against the Welsh. After we charged the cavalry came, that they did. And ne'er once did the Earl of Easterby shy away from the enemy."

Tess's scalp tingled with pride. Richard's herald would have fodder for tales that would enthrall generations to come. When Bartholomew began to shake with chills, she tucked a blanket around his shoulders.

"Was Lord Richard injured?" she asked urgently.

"Oh, nay, milady," the young man replied through chattering teeth. "Nothing could vanquish a lord so brave. Nay, never. He raised Taliesin a thousand times if he raised it once. Shots whistled past 'is ears, spitted out o' hand-gunnes stolen from the earl 'imself, but he was struck nary once. He moved too fast, that he did. Too fast."

Tess had shut her eyes, and saw every second of what had transpired. As Bartholomew described Richard's brave actions, she experienced them. She *was* Richard as he strained to raise the heavy sword. She swallowed the rawness in her throat from his savage battle cries. She knew the fury and fear of his battle madness, and her heart thundered in her chest. If

Richard died on the battlefield, she would feel the wound, too. She would bleed. She would mourn, and keen, and defy God. She would die, too. A part of her would. The most important part.

"Thank you for telling me, Bartholomew." She squeezed his hand, blinking open her eyes. She felt as if she were right by Richard's side. And that's exactly where she wanted to be. If he were going to fight the wrongs of the Church, why should he alone risk his life? Their fates were intertwined now.

For the first time, she became aware of the bellows of agony from a soldier being treated with hot oil. Tess shivered, and her stomach lurched in empathy. She waited until the barber-surgeon finally turned to Bartholomew and then made her preparations. As more soldiers were carried to the castle for treatment, and as more information trickled in with them from the battlefield, it became clear to Tess and Godfrey that the fight for Marly Vale would be long and drawn out. And so she made plans to accompany the barber-surgeon to the campsite near Hawk's Mound so they could be closer to those who needed treatment. Richard would object to her presence out of concern for her safety, she was sure of it. She didn't care. She sensed he needed her. And she realized, with a sweet tug of her heart, that she would go to the ends of the earth to help him if she could.

At the end of the day, Richard made his way through the still and somber campsite toward his tent. Scattered campfires burned low. The lingering scents of scorched beef and stale, warm ale rose with the smoke of the hissing fires to the starry sky above. Richard's men hunkered around the burning embers, recalling the wins and losses of the day, gathering courage for the morrow. Few talked, too weary. They'd planned on instant victory from a surprise attack. But there had been no surprise, and they were sobered by the realization of how long the campaign might be. A long campaign with no other reward than their wages, for they would not be allowed to sack the bishop's castle after victory as they would in a foreign battle.

A minstrel with the voice of a girl strummed his lute, singing of the great battles won by King Arthur. The wind rustled through the trees overhead in subtle harmony. Envisioning a noble and fearless Arthur, Richard wanted to rouse his men with a cheering speech, but his voice was too hoarse, and his eyes burned like fire. The stench of burned sulphur from cannon shots hung in the air, a choking mist. A giant moon glowed orange in the sky. *Another omen,* Richard thought as he trudged to his tent, every muscle aching. He just prayed the omen was a good one.

When he brushed aside the tent flaps, he was surprised but not alarmed to see someone sleeping on his pallet in the glow of a single candle. It was doubtless a weary page, he told himself. The boy, dressed in breeches and a hood, clutched a hand-gunne in one arm and Baron Philmore in the other. Baron Philmore? That riveted Richard's attention. The monkey bared his teeth and let out a little laughing sound, his own peculiar greeting.

"Good day to you, too, Baron."

With that the monkey scrambled the distance to Richard's shoulder, clambering up his arm. Perching on his shoulder, the tiny brown creature chirped in his ear. The monkey wrapped his hairy little arms around Richard's neck and fondled one of Richard's ears with smooth little black-padded fingers. For the first time that day, Richard laughed.

The sleeping figure stirred at the noise and pulled back the hood, revealing a lush ocean of brown hair.

"Tess! Good God, I don't believe it. Nay, strike that. I should have known you would come."

Love wrapped its arms around him, lifting his weariness as if it were an old, tattered cloak that had been draped too long about his proud shoulders. He sank onto the cot next to his wife, and the monkey jumped away. Richard stroked Tess's cheeks, studying their lacy blush of red.

"You can't stay. You realize that, don't you? You must leave. Immediately."

"Nay, I shall not." She jutted out her chin defiantly, staring him down with love blazing in her eyes. She pulled a hand-gunne from the blanket on the bed. "I thought you might need one more weapon. 'Twas my wedding gift. I may do with it as I please, may I not? I mean to use it if I have to."

She puckered her lips and leaned close to his face. "And you can't stop me. So don't even try."

"I wouldn't dream of it." He pressed his mouth to hers and all the tension melted from his hardened body. Her lips tasted like sweet, juicy slices of pears. But when he deepened his kiss and shut his eyes, he saw the eyes of the dead staring back at him. He groaned and withdrew, pulling her into his arms protectively. He was suddenly fearful that she would be slaughtered like his men on the battlefield. He would defend her like a savage bear if anyone ever tried to harm her.

"Oh, Tess, I had forgotten how gruesome was the carnage of a full battle."

In these modern times, very few knights had engaged in pitched battles, where opposing armies fought it out openly in a field. Most conflicts were resolved by siege, in which one army attacked another that was protected behind the high walls of a castle or behind the walls of a city. Then the attackers used siege engines to chip away at the fortress walls, and sappers to mine underground. Or sometimes they just waited until those defending the castle ran out of food and water. Richard had engaged in open battles with Henry against the Welsh, but that had been years ago.

"Gods, how many dead so far? How many were taken to the castle, Tess?"

"Two passed on at the castle. Actually, one arrived already dead to the world. Five more are recovering."

"And five more have died in the field." Including one of his pages, trampled under the hooves of a rearing destrier. A boy who was but ten, a towheaded little whelp with fierce determination and bright dreams. Perkins was distraught, blaming himself for the lad's death. Richard sighed raggedly.

"Five of my men, that is. I'm sure Kirkingham's loss is greater. I had somehow hoped for a swift victory, that the loss would be . . . nonexistent. Ah, Tess, is it right of me to ask my men to sacrifice their lives so that I can reclaim a piece of land?"

"Why should you even ask?" Tess said. "If you questioned the worth of fighting over land, you could not even think of sending your men to France to help Henry, since his claim to that kingdom is dubious at best."

Richard shook his head, pacing again. "Sir John's death has me thinking. Perhaps too much. If some young soldier spills his blood on Marly Vale, will my victory be any consolation to his mother? His sister? His wife?"

She grabbed his hands, which were slick with dried blood and nicked from wayward daggers. "Listen to me, Richard Avery. There is no greater cause than to fight for land, to reclaim it from a greedy baron who stole it from you. Think how many clerics have stolen in the name of God! Think how many of your father's men died trying to retain this land for you. Would you make their sacrifice mean nothing? Richard, for the first time since my father's death I have something to live for. The defeat of one of the men who, by their association with the Church, condemned my father."

He watched her intensely. Her face was so set with determination it reminded him of a marble sculpture of a

Greek goddess—smooth, noble, impervious to the whims o
man and weather.

"Go to, my lord, and be victorious. I will fight by your side
if necessary, to see that victory won. I will die by your side
if need be. Now you are noble, not just in title but in spirit as
well. Now you are fighting for a cause, like your father. Like
mine. I see a new man before me." She touched her smooth
palms to the faint stubble of a beard shadowing his sooty
bloodstained cheeks. "The light in your eyes burns fierce and
bold, Richard. We will all one day die, my lord. The question
is will we have died fighting for a righteous cause, or will we
have slunk into the night with drooping shoulders for never
having had the courage to fight at all?"

He gripped her right wrist and pressed his mouth to her
palm, kissing her in gratitude. A pungent shard of emotion
pierced him through and through, a bittersweet rejoicing he
always felt when he embraced both his mortality and immor
tality at once. Life was an extraordinary thing. And as
vibrantly as he had tried to live it until now, it had never
seemed so rich as in the presence of this wonderful woman.

"I thank God for you, Tess." His lips touched hers like a
butterfly alighting on a flower in sunshine. It was the prayer
of nature. A wordless communion. The sealing of souls.

But their love thrived, paradoxically, in a world of war, and
soon the images of decapitated squires and gutted foot
soldiers reddened his vision again. He rubbed a hand over the
deep ruts grooved in the center of his brow.

"Now I must decide whether to march on tomorrow
pushing Kirkingham back a little more as we did today, or
wait in the hopes of finding some maneuver that might cost
fewer lives."

"Push on, Richard. You have the force of righteousness on
your side."

He cocooned her in his arms. "And so I shall. I just wanted to hear you say it, Tess, in case . . ."

"In case what, my lord?"

In case I am felled and you are left with naught but my seed in your womb. He did not want to remind her of the battle she would face if that came to pass, for childbirth was as much a battleground for women as war was for men. In both cases, the risk of death was frighteningly high.

"Nothing, Tess. Lay down, my heart."

He pulled her down onto the cot. She settled into his arms, molding to his side as perfectly as a hand into a fitted gauntlet. Richard knew he had no choice but to press on with lightning speed, to slaughter the enemy quickly and completely. Tomorrow would likely be his last chance for victory, and his last chance to be true to Tess. For if Richard knew the king as well as he thought he did, a missive from Henry would soon arrive. It would contain the bargain Richard had anticipated, the one he had secretly planned on all along. Once the offer was made, Richard would have no choice but to accept and cease his fighting. And by accepting the king's deal, Richard would betray Tess's dearest wishes. That betrayal would kill their love, and Richard in the process.

Both of them slept fitfully that night. Tess had terrible nightmares. She dreamt that Richard was struck with the shot of a cannon, his thigh crushed from the impact, his leg nearly severed. She whimpered in her sleep, crying for him, wishing there were some way to save him.

Richard dreamt that he was badly wounded. But in his dream, an angel came to comfort him. An angel with Tess's sweet face.

Richard slept in his arming doublet, and after donning his suit of armor with Perkins's help, he was back on his destrier before dawn. The battle began soon after the first rays of light shot up from the wooded horizon. The trilling songs of birds flitting through the campsite were drowned out by the distant clashing of swords, by the shrieks of frightened horses and wounded men.

Tess did not have to wait long before the first victims were carried back to the campsite for medical attention. One poor fellow had been shot in the stomach; only the barber-surgeon could help him. Tess tried to comfort the soldier during the excruciating operation, but he soon passed out from the overwhelming pain.

At noon there was a very different arrival, and one that struck more fear and anger in Tess's heart than all the wounded put together: a messenger bearing the livery of the Marquess of Dolton.

"Are you the Countess of Easterby?" the spindly herald said soberly to Tess.

"I am," she replied. Fighting a surge of foreboding, she smiled lightly and wiped her bloody hands on a rag. "What do you want with my husband?"

"He must hasten to Cadmon Castle. The Marquess of Dolton awaits him there with word from the king himself."

The Marquess of Dolton. The king's bearer of bad news. He had been the one to inform Tess of her betrothal to Richard.

"My husband is engaged in battle. 'Twill have to wait."

"My lord the marquess bade me inform your husband that it cannot wait. The king's message pertains to the earl's war with the Bishop of Kirkingham. The marquess bade me inform your husband that if he does not come to hear the king's message, the marquess will himself see that the Earl of Easterby is tried for treason."

"Treason!" Tess stared at the man as if he were mad. "Lord Richard is fighting for what is right. How can that be treasonous?"

But then it all came rushing back to her. This was Henry's world and Richard would pay for defying him. Wretched Henry. She would gladly defy the king herself and pay hell for it, but could she choose that for Richard without his knowledge? She could not even assume she knew what paths Richard would take. He had to hear the king out for himself.

As a pale-faced page dashed by, Tess snatched his arm and pulled him close. "Fetch the herald and send him to the battlefield. Tell him to bring the earl back to camp. There is a messenger from the king. And be hurried about it."

"Aye, my lady," the page said. He bowed deeply, then bolting off to find a horse.

Tess said no more to Dolton's herald. She turned away in silence, mulling over this new predicament. She felt as if someone had punched her full in the belly. There she ached, for as much as she passionately adored her new husband, her old enemy, she could not shake the sense that he loved the king more. And that, like Sir John, he would not die happy until he had salved that old wound.

TWENTY-THREE

Bolting his iron forearms against the heavy oak, Richard heaved through the mammoth doors to the great hall of Cadmon Castle. The weight slowed him not a whit, and he marched with angry strides to the center of the hall, where Tess and her visitor sat before a softly burning fire.

"What the bloody hell do you want, Dolton?" Richard bellowed. His bold entry sucked in a draft of cool air. The breeze swirled through the cavernous hall, rippling the tapestries hanging against the chilled stones. Even in spring the castle's mortar and limestone walls clung to the vestiges of winter.

"Richard," Tess said nervously, rising from her place next to the marquess. "My lord, the Marquess of Dolton has brought word from the king."

"Then you bloody well better speak fast, man," Richard snarled, coming to a looming stand over Dolton. Fury churned like whitecapped waves in the depths of his oceanic eyes. "I have soldiers dying bloody and cruel deaths in a field not far from here."

Tess offered him a tankard of ale and he drew it to his blistered lips and took a long draft. His nostrils flared above the foam.

"That battle is precisely why I've come, Lord Richard," Dolton replied. "What in the name of God were you thinking to defy the king like this?"

Dolton's square, beefy face grew mottled as he stood. Richard sneered at the dutiful nobleman's superfluous rage. *Let him play the loyal vassal,* Richard thought. *I'm past it now.*

"You could not have picked a worse time to commence this ill-conceived plot, Easterby. You know that Henry needs every soldier he can get for France. He has already commissioned every available ship in the channel for their transport. Are you goading Henry? Is that why you told him all about this attack in the letter you left with Beaufort?"

"Go to hell, Dolton, and take Henry with you. I will likely waste a man or two more before my mission is complete."

Dolton's eyes dilated. "I shan't repeat that, Easterby, so as not to give the king yet another reason to hang you for treason."

"Tell him everything, Dolton. Tell him how I defied him by reclaiming the land that was my ancestors'. Tell him how I held a bishop accountable for thievery that should have been punished long ago. Tell my liege how I waited for him to ascend the throne to right the wrongs of his father, and how patiently I have waited these two years passing while injustice lived on beneath a cloak of red and a cross of gold. Tell him how I took justice into my own hands, and after I am hanged, tell the king how I loved him still."

This last line was uttered with a savage roar that echoed against the rafters. Richard's torched eyes landed on Tess. Her face was a mirror of his own rage, her eyes blazing, her cheeks flaming. God, how he loved her.

"Here, here, now!" Dolton said after recovering from his astonishment. "That is well and good, Easterby, but it does not explain the profound stupidity of flaunting the Church when many have been burned for heresy. You know how Henry loves his men of God. He cannot turn the other cheek this time." He pivoted to glimpse Tess's reaction, then glared at her as if he had hoped to find an ally. "Please forgive me, Lady Tess, for assuring you that this match would be for your own good. It seems the courtly Lord Richard is not the man I remember. But fear not—you will not be hanged for his misdeeds."

Richard sank into the chair Tess had warmed. She cozied to his side and placed a gentle hand on his shoulder. It warmed his soul even as his heart raged, even as he said, "If Henry cannot turn the other cheek, then I have naught to lose, Dolton. If I am sure to hang, then I may as well fight to the finish. And if I'm lucky, I may have the pleasure of cutting open the bishop's grotesque belly with my own dagger."

"Oh!" Dolton exhaled with a shiver of disgust, sinking back into his chair. "You are beyond redemption. Unfortunately, our king has thought fit to give you reprieve, no doubt owing to your past days of debauchery together."

For the first time since his arrival, Richard's seething anger dissipated. Gently stroking Tess's hand draped over his shoulder, he frowned at his mud-and-blood-spattered boots. Here it came. The deal. The bargain with the devil.

"What kind of 'reprieve'?"

"A complete pardon for this egregious error if you cease your battle immediately. And if you start preparations to send your troops to Southampton in preparation for their journey to France."

Richard stared shrewdly at the richly dressed nobleman. "Nay, Dolton, methinks I'll stay my course."

"Moreover," Dolton continued with exasperation, "not only will you be forgiven for your insolence, but the king will insure that the Bishop of Kirkingham returns to you your precious Marly Vale."

Richard's eyelids narrowed to dark slits. "Marly Vale?"

"You heard correctly. You will get what you've wanted all along—Marly Vale. The king is willing to anger his Church to save the neck of an old friend."

Richard shifted uncomfortably in his chair, which suddenly felt as if it were carved in stone, not padded as it was with a soft golden cushion. "Is that all I must do to regain my land, Dolton?" he asked, knowing it was not. "Cease my battle and send my men to join Henry's?"

Dolton pursed his chafed lips and studied his neatly trimmed nails. He cleared his throat and met Richard's eyes with a blank expression. "Nay, that is not all."

"What else must I do?"

Dolton's gaze slithered from Richard to Tess, though his head did not move. "Perhaps Lady Tess could see that my companions are settled. I'd have a moment alone with you, Richard."

"I'll not send her out, Dolton." He wanted to spare her having to hear the devastating condition he knew would be laid down by Henry, but he owed her the dignity of the truth.

"Nay, Richard," Tess said. "I would like to see if any more soldiers have been brought back from the field. You can tell me all about it later." She cast one last sharp gaze at Dolton, her eyes flaring with indignation.

When the doors closed behind her, Richard turned impatiently to his peer. "Well, what is it? What does Henry want? Nay, I know what he wants. But I want to hear you say it."

"I did not want to speak in front of your wife, since her father was a Lollard and died a Lollard's death. But Henry wants you to turn over the heretics in your prison. Lady Gertrude, Sir Andrew Warton, and Sir Harold Mortimer."

"Turn them over?"

"Aye. You must hand the Lollards to the king's sheriff so that they might be executed. Burned at the stake. Well, what say you? Do we have a deal?"

TWENTY-FOUR

Their lovemaking was fierce that night. They tossed and swooned and cried out in Richard's solar for endless hours, it seemed, cloaked in the inky mantle of night. A restive and sweaty conclusion to a day of mental turmoil. And through it all, Tess had no idea what ultimatum the Marquess of Dolton had given, nor if Richard had accepted. She only knew the battle had been called off. At least temporarily.

Shortly after she had departed the meeting with Dolton, Richard abruptly ended his discussion with the marquess and sent a herald to the battlefield. The liveried messenger announced Richard's orders commanding his men to cease their warfare, but to hold their quarters pending further orders. When his commanders beat a hasty retreat to the castle, Richard met with them for more than an hour in his solar. Their heated, muffled voices could be heard by anyone who cared to eavesdrop outside the door. When they emerged, Richard looked ten years older.

"What is it, my lord?" Tess entreated, emerging from the shadows of the corridor to greet him. "What did Dolton say that has brought back your commanders so quickly?"

She had known her first moment of true fear when he turned to her with a look so blank she thought it was another man who had taken residence in her lover's body. He never did answer.

And so now, when he was making love to her with such ferociousness, she couldn't help but wonder if he heaved into her so determinedly not because he felt close to her, but because he wanted to and didn't. In any event, she felt close to him. He had that power over her. He had lit an eternal fire in her depths and fanned the flames with every kiss. She arched against his long, powerful thrusts with a hunger she could not sate. Trembling beneath him with one shudder of pleasure after another, she was content to know that he would share his thoughts when he was ready. Meantime, he would share his body. His exquisite, hard-muscled body.

For Richard, making love was a journey to a forgotten land, a distant garden from which he never wanted to return. Only inside of Tess did he feel at one with himself and with his soul. Away from her, his monster of a conscience wailed and beat against the walls of his brain. Ever since Dolton's arrival, he had known no peace save for the hours in Tess's arms. And after hours of lovemaking, he finally threw his head back, his face racked with so much pleasure it was contorted in a twist of pain. He thrust his hands into the bed and arched his back as if he'd been lashed with a mighty leather whip, his face shocked and wild. Then he collapsed on top of her, burrowing his head into the pillow.

"Hold me. Just hold me," he muttered, never wanting to move.

She wrapped her arms around him, tracing a tickling pattern with her fingers along the ribs that lined his back, and hummed softly. Her voice was sweet and comforting. It made him want to weep. But he couldn't. No one would or should ever spend tears on his account again, he vowed ruefully to himself. Oh, what a devil he had become.

When two out of three burned-down tapers sputtered out,

giving way to the sensual shadows lurking in the solar, Richard sat up in the light of the lone flame. His hair fell to the fore and he methodically tucked the wavy strands behind his ears, sinking back onto his heels, kneeling in the moistness left from their lovemaking. He smoothed a hot hand up and down her cool torso—over the perfect mound of one breast and then the other, tilting in a gentle slope along her rib cage, over the flat, silky skin of her abdomen, down to the soft fur between her thighs and back up again. Over and over he made the journey by hand.

"I do not like it when the world encroaches upon us, Tess," he mused softly. "I want to make love to you for days and stir only to eat and drink enough to sustain our lovemaking."

Her lips parted in a sultry smile as she purred and stretched like a cat. "Aye, Richard, let us not think about the world outside. There is just you and me now."

"It feels that way when we make love. I feel like I could conquer the world. You have given me back something I had lost."

"What?"

He shrugged. "A certainty of what is right and what is wrong."

"You make me sound like St. Peter sitting in judgment at the Pearly Gates."

"In a way you are. Condemn me to solitude, keep me from the comfort of your arms, and I am cast out from Heaven."

He stretched out beside her, propping his head on one hand and tucking the other around her waist. Her rose-petal skin shimmered with the scent of sex.

"Tess, I cannot put this off any longer. I was hoping to make love to you a dozen times before our peace was spoiled by Dolton's message. . . ."

"So you succeeded a half dozen times," she saucily replied, but there was a desperate, jagged edge to her voice.

"How do I begin?"

"At the beginning."

"That you've already heard. The king wants me to send my troops to France. And he is willing to give me back Marly Vale. 'Twas the condition of that return which you have not yet heard."

She frowned, not liking the regret she heard in his voice. "What is it?"

"I must give over the Lollards."

"And, of course, you told him no." Her voice was shrill, not at all casual as she had hoped it would be. "You told him no, did you not, Richard?" she added breathlessly.

When he did not confirm her assumption, Tess's eyelids shuttered with dread. She felt her very life seep out through her pores, heard it groan defiantly from her lungs. She was sinking. Sinking. "Gertrude? He wants us to send Gertrude to him?"

"Aye, Lady Gertrude. Sir Andrew Warton and Sir Harold Mortimer as well."

Gertrude had warned her. She had warned her and Tess had been too much in love to listen.

Tess's gaze narrowed, straining to better read his indelible features in the shadows. His crow's-feet were smooth, marked only by tan lines. His blue eyes were pale and empty. Impatiently, she sat up and snatched the remaining taper from a bedside table, holding it aloft before his bronzed face. The yellow flame pulsed, casting a ghastly glare, elongating his features. "Did you accept the terms?"

"Nay, I did not."

Her death grip on the waxy taper loosened.

"Nor did I refuse them."

She blew out the flickering candle with an impatient puff of air, not wishing to see his features in any light greater than that cast from the moon, not wanting him to see the terror on her face. A trail of smoke from the extinguished wick snaked up into her eyes, stinging them. She blinked hard, angrily.

"Richard. 'Twould be wrong. For you 'twould be very wrong."

"I know." He sat up, cross-legged, just like her. Naked, their bare knees touched, his thick with bone and corded muscles, hers white and delicate.

"Then you cannot do it."

"Aye. I can."

He regarded her with hard, distant eyes. He was a stranger. Nay, it could not be. He was her lover. They had just made love. They had just loved each other. She coiled her fingers through his satin chest hairs. Yes, he was still her love. Her hand still tingled to his touch. She gripped his hands.

"Oh, Richard . . . I . . . I love you. Do you know that?"

"Aye," he whispered hoarsely. "And I you."

"Do you, my darling? Do you?"

"Aye."

"Do you know then that you can't do this? Do you know that?"

"Oh, love." He ran a broad hand through his tangled hair and swung his legs over the bed, as if ready to flee.

"Oh, Richard, do not turn away—look at me. Richard, please tell me you will not do it."

His hard eyes were fixed on an unseen enemy.

"Tell me!" she shouted.

When he did not answer, she forced herself not to begin dissimulating before him. She steeled her shaking voice like a honed and ruthless sword. "What would your commanders have you do?"

"They want me to accept the king's terms, and I cannot blame them," he replied in a dead voice. "There is no need to fight if the king will give me back Marly Vale and all that I must do for it is obey the law I must eventually obey anyway.

'Twas just a matter of time before Henry demanded the Lollards. And I knew he would bargain for them if I pushed the limits. My men would rather fight for Henry in France. There is much more booty to be had sacking French villages than fighting nobly for a cause here in England."

"And so you are resolved." Her voice was hollow.

"Nay, I am not. I just tell you what my commanders would have."

The chamber air cooled on her shoulders like a frosty cloak, and she wrapped a cover around her, hunkering down in her dread. "If you give the Lollards over to Henry they will be executed."

"I know."

"Just like my father."

"I know."

"Then how can you even consider accepting the king's terms?"

"Because of Marly Vale," he whispered harshly, his head whipping around, daring her to tread on that sacred territory. "I have waited all my life to reclaim that land, and you would have me turn it away with disdain when it is presented to me on a platter."

"A platter soaked in blood. What profiteth it a man to gain the whole world if he loses his soul?"

"Not 'loses his soul.' Regains his friend."

"You mean Henry?" she scoffed. "What sort of friend is he? No man is truly the friend of a king, Richard. He will embrace you only as long as it suits him. Friendship is too steeped in politics for Henry. When you have served him well in France, he will not be so friendly, methinks. Then you will be left with your conscience. Think of your father, for God's sake. Think what he would do in this situation."

"Do not invoke his name, Tess. He is dead."

"But his spirit lives, because he was a man of conscience,

and that sort of legacy never dies," she said fervently. She was fighting for the life of their love. *Damn him, doesn't he know what is at stake?*

"Richard, I know how much I am asking of you. I do not ask it lightly."

"Why ask at all? Do you love Gertrude so much?"

"I do love Gertrude. But not as much as I love you, and . . . oh, how can I explain this? Richard, you do not want to send the Lollards away any more than I do. Not in your heart of hearts. That is what is truly at stake here. Your heart. Your conscience."

"Gods, please! Spare me."

"Take back Marly Vale on your own terms. Or if you do not have the courage to do that unequivocally, then let the Lollards go. Make up some excuse. Say that they escaped."

"Now you are speaking nonsense." He rose abruptly and started pulling his clothes back on. "Perhaps you should speak instead of the men you would have needlessly die for my cause. How many soldiers have died already, Tess?"

She angrily gritted her teeth. "Eight."

"And how many more would you like to sacrifice for land that the king would give to me peacefully? Another eight? Eighteen? Eighty?"

"I would wish no man to die." Death. Why was it always death? Was there no other outcome to life's struggles?

"Then you'd best not wish me to resume my war against the bishop. There is no war without death."

"My lord," she called, stopping him just as he reached the door. *Remember this moment. Draw a picture in your mind. This was how he looked—dashing, haunted—at the beginning of the end.* "If I thought you were resolved to abide by the king, I would leave this castle before dawn and never come back. For though I love you in a way I never thought possible, I cannot live with a man who has sold his soul. And only a sadly compromised man would give up righteous men to a wrongful death."

Dark slashes molded his cheeks like the splayed wings of a raven. Tess shivered, and then burned inside as he shut the door softly behind him.

Richard spotted Father James's frail body kneeling at the altar. His head, which protruded on a slender, wrinkled neck, was bent in prayer, his back to Richard. He always had the feeling that his confessor was waiting for him, no matter the hour, no matter the day of week.

When the doors clicked shut behind Richard and the darkened stained-glass windows rattled softly from the impact, the old man looked up at the crucifix hanging over the altar.

" 'Take this cup away from me,' Jesus once said. So would you speak tonight, methinks."

Without ever turning, Father James knew who had entered and why Richard had come. Richard smiled, eager to embrace the familiarity of an old friend. And yet he felt strangely disembodied, distant, as if he were watching the drama of his life unfold from a high precipice. He sauntered down the aisle between the pews, glancing at the comforting candles that burned before a statue of the Virgin Mary in the right corner. The light always seems so eternal and the woman illuminated by it so infinitely serene. But tonight, it meant nothing. When he reached the altar, he knelt beside the priest.

"How do you know a bitter cup has been presented to me?" Richard said, leaning heavily on the altar rail.

"I hear the confessions of others as well. Not an hour ago I listened to the concerns of one who was greatly interested in what your decision would be." The old man assessed Richard with a flick of his milky eyes. "And what will it be?"

"I do not want to sacrifice any more men. From that

position, the answer is simple. I will end the battle and send my men to Henry."

"Good. Then you've made the proper choice."

The marble bit at Richard's knees. He swallowed irritation. "But that means I must send the Lollards to their deaths, and if I do I know Tess will close her heart's door to me forever. Why, God, after all these years of craving this land does it suddenly seem that the loss of Tess's affections would be a greater loss than if every last castle and manor in my possession were taken by an unknown enemy?"

"You are beginning to see life with the perspective bestowed by age," the old man said in his slow, heady rasp of a voice. "Love is the greatest of God's gifts, more important than land or possessions. But"—and here he held up a knotted finger, stressing his point—"*but* . . . not greater than life itself."

His bony hand clutched Richard's forearm and the fervency of his message transcended his skeleton of a face. "There is no greater waste than the life of a young soldier who dies for a senseless cause. Why send your men to death when you can reclaim the vale without that sacrifice?"

"But what of the Lollards? Should people be burned to death because their piety contradicts the Church?"

"I will allow, my son, that the Lollards are earnest in their beliefs. But 'tis their very reasonableness that makes them so dangerous to the Church. They want reform. The people are clamoring for it. And 'twill come one day, undoubtedly. But there is little hope for these reformers. They sealed their fate when they converged on Eltham. Do not risk your neck trying to save heretics who already dangle over a burning fire."

He made it sound so easy. But it wasn't. "You clearly want me to accept the king's offer. 'Twas not the advice I was hoping for. I was hoping you would champion Tess's cause, and I don't know why. I suppose because I think she's right."

"A sweet girl, Tess."

"If you knew her, Father James, if you knew how noble she is, how fiercely she clings to righteousness, you would think her as virtuous as a saint. God, it burns my gut like Greek fire to think I must disappoint her."

What a preposterous understatement, he thought. It would tear his heart in two. For she had made herself utterly clear: To send the Lollards to their death would mean the death of their love.

"Richard, I was your father's confessor for thirty years. He loved your mother dearly. But he did not think with his heart when it came to matters of state. Methinks your heart would soon be weighted with burdensome emotions if you send your men to a senseless death, all to please a lady. In this case, my son, methinks your father would want you to be logical."

"'Tis more than my heart I am heeding, Father. 'Tis my conscience. I can't forget the horrible cries of agony as Tess's father and his compatriots were burned to death. 'Twas almost as horrible as the time when Henry himself burned a poor Lollard and I was forced to watch."

A rasp of strained breath hissed through Richard's teeth. He'd never forget the stench of burned and blackened flesh, peeling away to the pink underside.

"Henry had his soldiers place the wretched heretic in a barrel of faggots and light a fire. After some time he pulled the man out, burned and pained, to see if he would repent, and when he did not, Henry ordered him back in the barrel. The stench of burning flesh sickened me then and it sickens me now."

"Henry is a certain leader."

"Aye, he is a king they call heroic for all his certainty. But was that justice? Is that the fate I want to thrust on Lady Gertrude? She did not try to overthrow the king. She was simply guilty of defying the Church, which I have done myself in my attack on Kirkingham."

"Richard, you have no choice. Do it for your father. Do it for the land."

A ball of fiery frustration ignited in Richard's belly. Was he talking to the deaf?

"Have you not heard anything I've said here about my conscience?" Richard snapped. "Or is it that you simply do not care?"

Seeing the dazed look on the old man's face, he regretted his harsh words. James was apparently incapable of understanding. Without Richard's notice, Father James's relevancy had faded, had shrunk like his spine. Age had dulled his wits. Richard knew he shouldn't begrudge him that.

"I am sorry, Father. I suppose there are some questions that I alone can answer. But I thank you for your time."

Richard abruptly excused himself, feeling more shackled by solitude than ever. He strode into the starry night with pain searing through the center of his heart. He sucked in a sharp draft of air and held it in his lungs until they burned. The air exploded from his mouth with a curse. One minute he saw Tess's precious face in his mind's eye—her soft brown eyes that always glittered with compassion, her succulent lips that dripped with the honey of life, her body that quivered so poignantly beneath his when they made love, teaching him that the joining of a man and a woman was the most profound truth he would ever know. And then he pictured the vale. Marly Vale. The loping green fields, the patches of farmland crisscrossing into the distance. Brown patches of fallow fields. The lowing of oxen pulling the plow in springtime when the warm air would burst with the rich smell of earth and manure and sweet hawthorn and wild cherry blossoms. Walking with his father when he was but a boy, marching over giant clumps of tilled earth, clutching his father's enormous hand. His father marching with the wide steps of a man proud to walk his land . . .

"This is all I have to leave you when I die, Richard. It is the world to me, as it one day will be to you. This land for which your grandfather and great-grandfather fought. The earth is sown with their blood."

His father knelt. Gently gripping Richard's arms, he squinted solemnly into his son's eyes. "This land will be passed on to your children when your time has come and gone. 'Twill be your greatest gift to them. A woman can give life, Richard, but a man can give only land."

He crumbled a handful of black earth between his fingers. "Never let it go. Never."

Richard had memorized the words, even the hard, narrow set of his father's mouth as he uttered the word "never." That day the admonition had been written in Richard's soul as if it were one of the Ten Commandments etched on a stone tablet. Richard had grown up with no other mission but to keep his father's sacred trust. And when the land was stolen from him shortly after his father's death, painfully ripped from the clutches of his too-young hands, Richard's life had ceased to have meaning.

Until he met Tess. Her strength and integrity acted as an anchor for his wayward soul. In her arms he found more than reckless abandon—he found peace. A peace he hadn't known he could possess without his land.

But the sense of incompletion yawned before him like a great dark cavern. And now the king offered him a way to shut the door on the frustration that had spanned the many years since Bishop George had robbed him. Marly Vale would be his. In hand. Just like the earth his father had clutched. He could fight on against the bishop and take Marly Vale by force. But he would lose his head for it, leaving his blood to soak the parched earth, to be tilled for his children's children. Save that he had no children. Or was it possible Tess had already conceived?

His ruminations ended abruptly when he felt his fingers encase the cold latch on the door to the garrison's quarters. Without intention, he had wandered to the chamber where his wounded men were recovering under the care of the barber-surgeon.

Entering, he found a half dozen men on cots. Edith, Margaret, and Rose had apparently gone to bed for the evening. The barber-surgeon was washing his hands in a basin in the corner, looking weary.

Richard silently walked through the chamber, gazing down at the men who had risked life and, in some cases, given up limb for him. One man, who seemed to Richard a boy of no more than thirteen, had lost his right arm at the elbow. The pain-induced frown that twisted his face in sleep would likely be permanent after suffering such a blow, Richard mused sadly, for life could be cruel to a man who did not have two hands with which to fight and work.

Another soldier softly groaned in his sleep, tossing his head from side to side. The strips of white cloth wrapped around his wounded torso were stained with a scarlet flower. God willing, his bleeding would stop. *Please, God, do not let him die.* Richard wished he had the power of God to heal the man. Jesus had said it took only faith to perform such miracles. Where had Richard's faith gone?

Finally, he stopped at the foot of a cot that held a young man whose face was deathly pale. A plump woman knelt at his side, weeping inconsolably. Her heart-rending sobs riveted Richard. Guilt made his flesh creep. When his long shadow fell over the woman and her dying loved one, she turned up a sooty and scarred face.

"Oh, saints! Be ye . . . be ye the Earl of Easterby?" She ran a backhand under her runny nose and sniffled, her eyes wide with shock and wonder. When Richard nodded, she pressed her hands together in a prayerful pose, supplicating herself before him in a way that made him feel wholly inadequate.

"I beg ye, milord, save my Bartholomew. He's dying. Ye see, we 'ave two little ones at 'ome, and I do not know 'ow I'll manage alone. And Bartholomew, he's my love, my husband. I beg ye, great lord. Ye have the power of might and great cannons and the ears of kings and queens. Do something. Spare 'is life. Please, milord, I beg of ye. Can you do naught to save my Bartholomew?"

Richard shook his head slowly, uncommon moisture burning the back of his eyes. "Nay, woman, I'm not a god with the power to grant life. Merely a human with the power to take life away. Such is the way of war. Forgive me."

She looked at him in bewilderment. When his meaning registered, when she realized that even great lords had no power to stop the cycle of life and death, her lips quivered and she broke into tears again, flinging herself on her poor Bartholomew.

Filled with regret, Richard left in the silence with which he had entered. He looked up at the scattered white stars again, no longer hoping for an omen. There was Orion, the warrior, with his star-studded belt and sword. In Heaven. The only place a warrior was safe from harm.

He would go to Father James and ask him to stir the young priest to give the dying soldier his last rites. And then he would return to his solar and tell Tess that he had made a decision.

TWENTY-FIVE

He opened the solar door long past midnight. Despite the hour, she was not asleep. Hearing the door hinges groan, seeing pale yellow light creep across the foot of the bed, and smelling a waft of smoke from the torches in the corridor, she propped herself up in bed and pulled the folds of her robe closer to her naked breasts.

"Richard?" she foolishly asked. Who else would it be? She tried to swallow, but nothing would pass the enormous lump of emotion lodged in her throat. Her stomach was a twisted skein of nerves and hope.

"I did not mean to wake you."

"I was already awake."

His broad shoulders loomed a second in the doorway before he ambled with heavy steps to his desk. Retrieving a taper, he lit it in the dying embers of the fire. He shoved the taper onto a pricket candlestick, and then sat, watching the wax tear and fall. It was in the pulsing glow of that single taper that she saw his face and knew everything. How could she not know? Had his eyes ever been so hard and distant, like slivers of slate? Had his lovely, high brow ever been so rutted? Had his cheeks ever been so hollow? As if he had gone hungry too long, or had bitten rue and sucked at the stinging bitter taste like the devil suckling on a witch's teat.

And even knowing his decision, she still thought him the most beautiful man she had ever seen. His lips, a burgundy granite in the shadowed light, invited her kiss.

Licking her own lips, she felt the profound stillness that always follows the recognition of an undeniable truth.

"You have decided to call off the battle and to accept the king's offer," she whispered.

His eyes brightened like two wicks set afire, as if he had not seen her until this moment. "Aye. I have."

Her naked breasts sank with the weight of the blow. She had hoped against hope he would do right. She had been convinced of it. Now she recognized the depth of her fantasy, how blind love could be, and she felt foolish.

"I am sorry." His voice was flat.

She should see that he was allowing himself no feeling, and she hated him for it. How easily men turned their feelings on and off, like a spigot of water, she thought bitterly, while women were left to feel until their hearts bled.

"'Tis not fair!" she hissed, squeezing a sheet to her seething breasts. "'Tis not fair that I have grown to love you and can do nothing about it while you . . . you can walk away."

Scathing anger replaced his glazed look, bubbling in the midnight blue of his eyes. "I am not walking away! 'Tis you who would turn your back on love."

"Me! Me?" She twisted in bed, coming to a sitting position. "How can you lie like that! Oh, knave that you are in your heart of hearts. I have given you my very soul. I have cast off my guard and my father's disapproval, which I am sure he sends from his grave, just to love you. To love you! Not merely to bed you like a broodmare for your heirs. Not merely to hold a title in your little kingdom. Gods! How stupid I have been. I actually fell in love with you!"

Tears of regret burned their way down her cheeks as roaring anger choked in her throat.

"Was it such a mistake to love me?" he answered, smiling with bitter irony.

"'Twas the gravest mistake of my life."

"You do not mean that. You are angry because you will not get your way. I see now what a spoiled child your father made you. You lived in your father's castle without ever testing your strength in the world. You do not know what sacrifices it sometimes takes to be a lord's wife. You would cast off my love so easily? Then I doubt you loved me at all. I do begin to doubt it."

"Very well," she rasped. "Doubt it if you will. I see my love was wasted. That you would think me untested! You know nothing of my pain, nothing of my desire to live a life filled with grace."

"We do not live in a state of grace!" he shouted. He slammed his hand on the desk and lunged to the edge of his seat. His elegant frame was a mass of hardened rage. "We live in a world of war and hunger and disease and treachery. You naive little girl," he snarled derisively. "You judge me by impossible standards. You would have me play at grace and yet you would expect me to protect you from harm."

"'Tis no more than I would ask of any chivalrous knight."

"Chivalry is dead. We live by more than swords now, Tess. 'Tis a new world. A world of gunnes and Court politics."

Tess sighed, surrendering to the truth of his words, if not their righteousness. She longed for a world that no longer existed. A world, long gone, of shining knights, and honor, and faith.

"I remember the first time I saw you," she mused in a hollow voice, vacant eyes staring at the fire. "How merry you were with your dashing, vibrant smile. I wondered at the perpetual light in your eyes. How could it be, I wondered, that anyone was so keen and joyful? Now I see it was a facade."

She looked up at him and saw more than beauty. She saw *him*. His essence—good and evil, noble and base. Despite the bleak crossroads they faced, she had never felt closer to him than in this moment—perhaps because she knew she had to go, so that it was finally safe to be truly close.

"I never knew you until now, Richard. I never knew the cynic who was hiding within."

His eyes sharpened and his strong jaw clenched. His throat bobbed with a swallow. "I do not apologize for who I am."

"There is no need to. You are lord of your domain. Oh, I feel so sad, Richard. And I love you so much."

His eyes softened and she saw his woundedness as if it were flowing with blood. She crawled out of bed. Like a homing pigeon, she flew the distance between them and slid into his lap, wrapping her arms around his shoulders. When he buried his head in her breasts, his whiskers chafing against their fullness, she stroked his hair, shards of tenderness ripping through her.

"Oh, Richard, I love you so much. I especially love the cynic you've been hiding, for I know I could have healed him with my love." Putting both her hands to his cheeks, she lifted his head. Her heart ached anew at the fissures of pain that surged in his eyes. She pressed her salt-stained lips to his and kissed him with the tenderness of God Himself. Quickly, tenderness transformed into craving. Oh, how she would miss that.

For the first time she wept fully. She keened from deep inside, not with tears of anger or petulance, but with horrid regret. Sobs racked her chest, and it was his turn to console her. He pulled her thoroughly into his arms and pressed her cheek to his shoulder with a broad hand, stroking her and murmuring endearments over and over. When she finally grew still, she felt a profound relief.

"Oh, I never want to leave your arms." Nestling against the warmth of his neck, she inhaled his musky scent and felt infinite comfort. But how long could she shut the world out? How long could she deny reality?

"Nay," she muttered, "nay, I cannot do this."

She pushed her hands into his chest and forced herself to sit erect, tugging at her tangled hair, smoothing the vulnerability from her face with a sweep of her fingers. She had taken her last comfort from him. With a restless, jarring sense of urgency, she began to shutter her heart against him.

"I must go now," she whispered. When his face registered confusion, she felt an uncharitable stab of glee. "Did you not understand what was at stake when you made your decision? I will leave Cadmon Castle as soon as I can send word to Roger. Tonight I will sleep with Mellie in the women's bower. I will have the ladies-in-waiting prepare a place for me in a guest chamber. I will stay there until Roger comes for me."

She started to slide off his muscular legs, but he tightened his grip. His fingers dug into her ribs. "I will not allow you to go."

"You can force me to stay, but you will have to chain me to a prison wall, for I will find a way to escape."

"I will do it then." He bolted up from the chair and she staggered out of his lap, wincing at the fury that magnified his every feature. "I will chain you. Do you think I will let you go now? After you have made me love you?"

"You do not love me," she scoffed. "You play at love."

"Oh, gods, I could strangle you, Tess. Keep spouting your nonsense and I will!"

"You do not know the meaning of love. You speak of feelings, lust. Not love. Love is brave. Love is noble. Love does what is right."

"I *am* doing what is right!" he roared. Boiling in frustration, he flung a stack of parchments from his desk to the floor, then paced the room, running his hands through his hair as if to pull the long locks out. "Gods, just consider my reasons. Will you do that? *Can* you do that?"

"I will not consider your excuses."

"*Reasons,* curse you; they are reasons, not excuses. I cannot send my men to war needlessly, Tess. The land is mine. Henry is giving it to me. There is no need to fight for it."

"The Lollards—"

"My men do not wish to die for the Lollards. And that is what they would be doing if I turn down Henry's offer. We are talking about their lives, Tess, not some vague notion of religious freedom. We're talking about life and death."

"Precisely! The life of each of the Lollards. And the death of your integrity."

" 'Integrity'?" he roared with a belly laugh. "I do not care a blasted, cursed, bloody, goddamned whit about integrity. I want my land, Tess."

"Have your bloody land!" she shouted in return. Bursting with pent-up anger and hurt, she dashed toward him and shoved at his chest, her small hands slamming against the steel wall of his muscles. Furious that the worst of her rage could not even evoke a wince of pain, she shoved him again. "Take your land. Sleep with your land. Because that is all you will have when you die—your bloody land."

Her eyes narrowed to hard slits. Her breasts heaved over her scraping lungs. She shook her head. "You won't have me. You won't have your integrity. You'll have nothing, Richard. Nothing but a pile of dirt."

She turned and stalked toward the door.

"Tess!" he bellowed. "For God's sake, stop. Don't do this. I love you! Does that mean nothing?"

She spun on him. "It means everything. Everything, Richard. I love you. And that is why I cannot stand by and watch you sell your soul. I have lost every last shred of respect I had for you. You are doing wrong. You will send my friend to her death. And for me to stand by and do nothing would be just as wrong as lighting the fire beneath the Lollards myself."

The scene played itself out in her head over and over that night. She hardly slept at all and awoke feeling irritable and completely disoriented. What would happen to her now? Was she right in her hard stance? Would he truly imprison her? She did not think so. But what would she do with her aching heart, when the pain of lost love cleaved it in two? It hurt. Lord, how it hurt. Like a physical wound, a gunneshot wound that wouldn't heal.

The next day she pondered these questions as she strolled into the heath where they had once so tenderly and stupidly danced in heather. The heather bent and undulated in a balmy breeze.

Still replaying their awful confrontation, she wondered now about something odd she had seen in the corridor as she departed. She had barely noticed, for all her rage, but now the memory nagged at her thoughts. She had seen the form of a man slip from one chamber to another across the hall, some forty paces away. The figure, or ghost, slipped past her view as she was closing the door, and she thought it was wearing a turban.

Kicking through the heather, she wondered how long it would take to reach Lady Lucretia's estate, and she wondered with keener interest if Richard would miss her or ever see the error of his ways. He would miss her, probably. But like most other men, she felt sure, he would easily shunt that feeling aside and do what his ambition demanded. As for seeing the error of his ways? Never, she concluded as she knelt and plucked a sprig of heather blossoms. Sadly, tragically, never. That certainty sat like a leaden weight in the pit of her stomach.

"What are you thinking?"

She started and twisted around to find Richard standing not five feet away. The raw hurt immediately began to rock in her stomach. She visibly winced. "I did not hear your horse."

"I walked. I wanted to enjoy the air."

"'Tis a lovely day."

"Indeed." She stood and blinked in dismay when his nearness evoked a familiar longing. She took a step back.

He wore his coat of arms, azure silk emblazoned with a sun. Rays flamed from its yellow core. Like the brilliant sun she had once thought him to be. The reality hurt.

"When will you depart?" he said coldly, his face gray and unflinching.

"As soon as Roger arrives to escort me. And you?"

"In a fortnight. I will take at least eighty-five men-at-arms and over a hundred horsed archers to Southampton, where the king's host is gathering."

Paying for it all with my father's gold. "That is quite a contribution. But no less would be expected, I suppose, of a king's man. Roger says he will join the king as soon as he sees me safely to your sister's castle."

When their halting conversation stopped completely, Richard ran a hand through his hair, working his lips in silent frustration. "Look here, Tess, I've been thinking. King Henry is showing mercy to many of the Lollards who've been captured since the uprising. All they have to do is to repent and promise never to dabble in heresy again and their lives will be spared."

"Lady Gertrude is not 'dabbling in heresy,'" she replied acidly. "She will not repent. I am sure of it. There are some people who cling to their beliefs even in the face of death, Richard. I know that's hard for you to believe."

His troubled gaze darted from her unsympathetic eyes to the landscape beyond her. He bent and plucked a sprig of heather, twirling the purple and green cluster in his long, graceful fingers.

"I will keep this as a memento." He raised the tiny blossoms to his hawkish nose and allowed his eyes to close in a slow blink of sadness. Then his eyes hardened, cooling to chips of ice. "When I return from France, celebrating the king's victory, I will expect you to produce an heir."

The coldness in his voice was worse than a frigid dagger skinning her alive.

"I will not keep you here in the meantime. Visit my sister, if you wish. I will call you when 'tis time for you to do your duty. Until then, you may live as you please."

He turned and stalked away. She hated him for being able to do it. And she hated herself for feeling hurt.

"Go. Leave," she whispered. "I care naught, for I never really loved you, Richard Avery. I care naught."

TWENTY-SIX

A nimble hand curled around the thick wooden door to Richard's solar just as he started to push it shut. The fingers were a brownish olive color, the nails smooth and pink. Richard recognized them instantly. With a mixture of relief and wariness, he let the hand push open the door. And there he stood, with a white turban, fathomless eyes of shiny onyx, and an ironic half-smile.

"Tarjaman," Richard said gruffly.

"My lord, you look haggard."

"Very perceptive, as always." In fact, sadness was eating away at his insides. Curse the blasted Persian for seeing beyond his facade. Or perhaps Richard had simply lost the ability to hide his true emotions. Love could do that—strip a man and leave him bare, as if he'd been skinned alive. "Would you like some claret?"

"'Twould be a delight."

Richard stepped back and allowed the animal trainer to enter. Serving up two goblets, he studied the Persian's composed demeanor. It seemed as if Tarjaman had been gone for no longer than a jaunt to the animals' barn.

"I cannot decide whether I should cut you in twain or embrace you."

"A simple greeting will do, my lord. I am not one to show physical displays of any kind." Irony twinkled in Tarjaman's eyes.

"How convenient," Richard said, holding a goblet aloft for his unexpected visitor. Tarjaman accepted with a gracious bow.

"I have missed you, Lord Richard."

Richard scowled at the onset of affection, wondering if he had become a total slave to emotions since falling for his wife. "And I you, Tarjaman. Why have you returned?"

"Because my presence is needed again."

"The animals survived without you."

"Needed in other ways, my lord," he replied gently, his astute gaze focusing ever more precisely on his master, his friend, like a narrow beam of light through a plate of precious glass.

Richard stared at him jadedly, unwilling to ask him in what ways he meant. "You and your damned riddles. If you won't tell me why you've returned, then tell me why you left."

"The opposite side of the same coin. I thought I was no longer needed."

Hitching a foot on the hearth and sipping his claret, Richard frowned. "What do you mean?"

"It will all become clear soon enough, my lord." Tarjaman's inky eyes glittered with affection. "Trust me."

"For some reason I still do, though that cannot be said of Sir Randolf. I hope your reasons for leaving are revealed before Randolf personally has you drawn and quartered for treachery."

"You refer to the stolen hand-gunnes?"

"Aye. Did you sell them to the bishop after stealing them from me?"

Tarjaman shook his head. "That was not my doing. I did not steal the gunnes."

"Then why did you disappear just before it happened?"

"I told you. I was no longer needed here."

"Blast your riddles, man! If you did not do it, then who did?"

"You would not believe me if I told you."

"I might."

Tarjaman paused and pursed his lips. "'Twas Father James who betrayed you."

Richard barked out a disbelieving laugh.

"I told you you would not believe me."

"You're telling me my eighty-year-old confessor stole the shipment of hand-gunnes? A man who can barely walk?"

"Not personally. But he passed the information along to the Bishop of Kirkingham, and his men did the dastardly deed."

"How do you know?" Richard cast the Persian a suspicious gaze over the rim of his goblet as he sipped the potent, sweet liquor.

"I did not steal the weapons, but I do have my spies, as I'm sure Sir Randolf has suggested."

"But why, Tarjaman? Why would Father James do it?"

Tarjaman shrugged, and for the first time Richard saw confusion in his wise visage. "That not even I can fathom."

Father James. It was the last blow. Richard bent the stem of his chalice in iron fingers and sent the deformed metal clattering across the room. It struck a precious windowpane, and shards of glass exploded. But Richard did not care. His world was shattering around him and he had endured the last betrayal he ever would.

"My lord!" he heard Tarjaman call after him as he strode angrily out the door.

Richard burst into the chapel like a mad bull. "James!" he shouted, his voice echoing three or four times off the high-domed ceiling. "Father James! Where are you?"

"Here," a faint voice replied.

Richard marched down the aisle until he spied the old priest in an alcove, lighting candles before a statue of St. Brigit. At least fifty candles flickered in a golden haze, their burning wicks spewed a cloying scent.

As soon as he saw the old priest, all his anger vanished and was replaced by consternation. Was it possible this gentle old man, who had heard his innermost secrets for most of his adult life, had betrayed him? Tarjaman must be mad to say so. It could not be.

"What is it, my son?" James said, suffocating his burning wick in a pot of sand after the last candle had been lit. He half pivoted, casting Richard an expectant smile, his gleaming lips stretched wide over teeth that looked like yellowed ivory. "I thought you would be off to France by now."

Richard sauntered to his side. Taking a moment to admire the beauty of the statue, he then said quietly, "Did you do it?"

"Did I do what?" James frowned gently, and then, blinking in a flutter of remembrance, he said, "Ah, yes, you must mean the hand-gunnes."

"Aye, the hand-gunnes," Richard said emphatically. "So 'tis true, then? You are the one who betrayed me?"

Richard clinched his hands in rage. He had never before wanted to strangle a man that he loved so dearly. His gut burned with outrage, for he knew that there was no way to avenge himself on the old man without regretting it soon after.

Father James shuffled forward and Richard reluctantly followed. The old man inched past the tomb of Richard's mother, and then past the long sarcophagus that enclosed his father. A marble effigy of Hugh Avery stretched out on top of the casket as if he were simply resting and would rise any moment. The sculptured head was ensconced in a bascinet, the neck enclosed in a beige marble likeness of silver chain

nail. His hands were frozen in prayer. James stroked the
forehead of the sculpture, gazing fondly at the beaked nose,
the creamy stone eyes.

"I loved your father as if he were a son to me, Richard.
Dear, dear Hugh."

Richard fought off a surge of sympathy. "Cursed be your
memories, old man! Why did you do it? You above all. You
whom I trusted above all."

"I promised your father that I would look after you,
Richard."

The old man looked up with a weary expression. His milky
eyes were yellowing, his only spark of life fading. Strange,
Richard mused, how he had never thought of James as old. As
Richard had grown older himself, his concept of age had
expanded at the same time. Now, with this betrayal, he saw
James as another person. He suddenly saw foibles he'd not
seen before and recognized the priest for what he was: an
aging man who would not live much longer. And Richard
steeled his heart a little against the impending grief.

"Richard, your father wanted you to have children to carry
on his name. If I let you die in a hopeless battle against the
Church, that would never happen. I had hoped that without
your new weapons you would postpone your attack. I
miscalculated."

"Is that it? Or did you use my confession to aid a fellow
cleric? I told you about those weapons in confession. You
wanted to aid Bishop George, and so you used information I
had divulged in confession. That is the worst sort of betrayal."

"Nay, foolish boy!" James returned. Anger stiffened his
bent spine and the force of many years' wisdom roaring to life
in his sunken eyes. "You cannot know in your callow
judgment what I have known lo these many years on earth. I
have lived long enough to know that dying for land is as

unfortunate and as meaningless as falling off a horse an
cracking open your head. And if you die young for such
cause, will it make you any more righteous? What honor i
there dying in combat anymore for *any* cause? The victor
goes to the man with the most powerful magic machine tha
spews black powder and shots which strike a man so far awa
you cannot even see the courage or cowardice in his eyes.
am sick to death of wars. Just as your father had come to b
shortly before his death."

"You helped my mortal enemy, James. God damn you!"

"Aye, that I did. And I do not regret it. You are alive, an
that is all that matters to me. I promised your father, Richard.

"And so I go off to fight Henry's war in Normandy
Mayhap I will die then. There will always be another wa
James. Did you not think of that?"

"At least Henry's war can be won. You can never win
battle against the Church."

Richard laughed ruefully. "I see that even your beliefs ca
be compromised by the promise of victory." It was all to
bizarre and ironic. Richard sighed in wonder. "The Lollard
do not believe in war, did you know that? They believe tha
armorers should be forbidden to ply their trade. I envy then
Their beliefs have caused them death, but at least their belief
are uncompromised."

Richard touched the cold marble arm of his father's effig
and turned to go.

"Will you forgive me, Richard?"

The voice was small and frail, just like the man. Richar
turned to consider the query. "To forgive you I would have
feel again, and my heart has turned cold. As cold as m
sword. I am sorry, but I cannot."

The old man nodded, as if he'd expected that answer. "A
well, then . . ."

"I would let you go, James, if your actions affected onl

me. But some of my men may have died because of you. Therefore, you must leave the castle. Never to return."

The next five days were the darkest in Richard's memory. He felt as if the castle walls were burning down around him and there was nothing he could do to squelch the scorching flames. He ordered Father James to return to the Priory of St. Bartholomew in London. Then he sent for the king's sheriff to retrieve the Lollards. Instead of feeling content, as he usually did after taking decisive action, he felt a knot of uneasiness.

The day the sheriff came for the Lollards was the same day Roger arrived to escort Tess to his sister's home, Montague Castle. That unfortunate coincidence meant that Tess was waiting on top of the battlements, looking for her cousin, when the Lollards departed in chains. She saw the whole macabre drama. Her erect, unflinching figure amongst the parapets cast a long shadow of guilt on the castle yards below, darkening Richard's path.

She was like a figure in a fairy tale, or in a minstrel's romance—lovely to behold, but never again to be held. It had been foolish of him to think that their match, born of politics, would ever hold aught but rancor. After their first meeting at St. Giles's Field, he should have known she would always have some lingering resentment. It had been idiotic to think that he might receive more from a woman than Elsbeth had given him. A flame that burns too bright burns the taper down quickly, sputtering out, leaving only darkness. The darkness enshrouded his heart and mind, paining him, making him rue the day he had dared to dream of loving Tess.

TWENTY-SEVEN

Richard and his soldiers left early the next day. They were two hundred strong, including pages and squires. The day was bright. Brilliant yellow rays lit their path. *At last, a bloody good omen,* Richard thought.

"Gods, 'tis good to be on my destrier again, Perkins." Richard affectionately slapped Shadow's sleek black flanks and tossed his head into the sunshine with a contented sigh. "I love battle. 'Tis the only time I do not question the meaning of life."

"Then you should have been a mercenary soldier, my lord, and you would get paid to be in a constant state of ignorant bliss," the squire replied.

Richard threw back his head and let out a bright bark of laughter. "Oh, Perkins, you amuse me. 'Twill be good to have you behind me in Henry's battle. I hope you do not regret your decision to remain my squire. I would still be happy to dub you a knight and give you your spurs."

"Your offer is generous, my lord," Perkins answered thoughtfully. "And one day I will accept. But for now, I cannot afford it. If I am knighted, I must support my own lance. I must outfit a page or two, buy horses for each, and my own destrier, as well as a palfrey, armor, and sword. Nay, not until I have land of my own, or inherit gold, can I afford to be a knight."

"We shall see what condition Marly Vale is in. Perhaps there will be a small manor house for you still standing. Or perhaps Lady Tess will enfeoff some property to you."

Perkins eyed him dubiously. "Perhaps if I were not the squire of her husband. Methinks if given the choice now, she would choose the wooden dummy on the quintain over you, my lord, be you witty or nay. Therefore, I doubt she will bestow your squire with land."

Richard laughed ruefully, and in the days that followed he laughed until the corners of his mouth hurt. His voice boomed with tense cheer against the trees that lined the road heading to the coastal town of Southampton. He was once again his old self, fearless of impending battle, at his best as he regaled his men with tales of his dissolute youth. It was good to joke with men again. His dalliance with Tess had deprived him of that. For all the pleasures of lovemaking, he loved men's company best. Men did not toil over matters that could not be grasped with their hands. He was relieved to be free of the sticky tangles of love.

Or so he thought until he laid down to sleep on the cool ground one night before they reached the coast. Spoiled by the cushion of Tess's arms, he couldn't get comfortable, and he remembered her dire warning that he would be left with nothing more than dirt to hold. The sweet scent of grass and worm-filled earth assailed him as he stared up into the starry, starry night. He wondered if his father looked down from Heaven with pride. Everything he had done, everything that had forced Tess to leave, he had done for his father. Why did he not feel close to the old man's spirit? Why did he feel so hollow inside?

The next day they traveled onward toward Southampton at a fast clip. The sunshine of the day before gave way to a gloomy threat of rain. That night Richard did not dream at all. His sleep was void of any images and he awoke feeling ill at ease. Had he dreamt of some omen he could not remember?

And if not, why did he feel so out of sorts? He refused to think of Tess as the cause. He refused to think of her at all. It hurt too much. He felt as if half his body had been ripped away, leaving him to limp along.

The next day it began to drizzle. By the time they pitched tents at dusk, Richard was soaked to the bone. They camped in a sparsely wooded meadow filled with lady's slippers and clover. After a meal of cheese, bread, and ale, Richard retired early to his tent. He stripped off his wet garments and crawled under a light blanket, and though the night was warm, he began to shake with chills. The bread sat like a stone in his stomach. His head began to ache, and he realized that he was ill.

When he began to vomit, word spread through the camp that Lord Richard was sick. And when he succumbed to diarrhea, it was rumored that he had the bloody flux. Dysentery was a common disease among men-at-arms and often caused more fatalities than enemy soldiers. Blast it! His men would not forget this sign of weakness at the launching of Henry's campaign.

Perkins faithfully carried a bucket back and forth, pressing a cool rag to Richard's forehead, but no matter how comforting his squire's ministering, Richard felt like hell. His teeth clattered together like broken glass. His skin hurt to the touch. His intestines were doing backflips like a mad jester, and a cold spike jabbed through his belly.

"Do not ever fall in love," he growled to his squire as he dry-heaved into the stinky spittle-filled bucket. "This is what 'twill get you, Perkins. She ripped my heart out. Now she can have my guts as well."

"Shhh, my lord," Perkins whispered near his ear. "You do not mean it. You've been babbling for the last hour. Do not curse Lady Tess. She is your wife."

"Go to hell, Perkins," Richard muttered, and then heaved again, retching with a throat-ripping roar.

Shortly after midnight, Richard sent Perkins away to get some rest. Richard felt a bit better and actually dozed into a moderately peaceful slumber. He woke an hour later with a tremendous urge to purge his stomach. But there was nothing left to purge, and he retched painfully. His stomach twisted in knots as he gasped for breath, swallowing the burning taste of bile. When the heaving stilled at last, he wiped away the drool from his chin and blinked open his eyes, only to discover Tarjaman sitting cross-legged at his side.

"Tarjaman? Is it you?"

He'd left the flaps to Richard's tent open and white moonshine filtered inside, illuminating the Persian's calm expression.

"My lord, 'tis good to see you."

"Tarjaman? What are you doing here?"

"I followed your troops. At a distance. I did not want to alarm Sir Randolf with my presence."

Richard's head began to pound again, and he sank back onto his pallet. "I am glad you are here. If Sir Randolf bothers you, tell him for me that he can rot with the devil. I . . . need you now."

Richard's fingers crept along the floor of the tent, and when he touched Tarjaman's hand he squeezed it fiercely. But the pounding in his head was so excruciating he was forced to put the butt of his palms to his eyes to relieve the pressure. Red spots and white stars skidded into view. But no matter how poor he felt, he had questions that could wait no longer.

"Tarjaman, you know the answers to many riddles. Tell me why I am rewarded with the flux for my obedience to the king. S'blood! I will curse my way to hell if I die before I get to Normandy."

"You do not have the flux," Tarjaman replied in his clipped accent.

"Then what in God's name is it? I've never been this ill in my life."

"You would not believe me if I told you."

Richard creaked open one eyelid and studied his sober countenance. "God, what now?"

"You are ill, my lord, because your body is trying to purge the rancor in your spirit, the disease that eats away at your soul."

Overcoming a choking wave of nausea, Richard propped himself on one elbow. "What in bloody hell is that supposed to mean? Are you going to tell me next that this is Allah's will?"

Tarjaman blinked slowly, patiently. His black eyes shimmered with blue in the eerie moonlight.

"It means that you lived a long time with deceit and compromise. That way of life ended for you when you attacked the bishop. Your soul was freed of the lies at last. And you were happy. And you found love. But then, against your better judgment, you accepted the king's bribe."

"To save the lives of my men!"

"You have bargained with the devil again to reclaim Marly Vale and your spirit does not want to go back to the old ways. And so your body is trying to rid itself of your disease."

Richard groaned. "Tarjaman, you've been in England too long. You've lost your mind. Get back to Persia. You're making no sense."

"I speak the truth. Will you listen?"

Richard sank onto the pallet. "Go on."

"You should not have turned the Lollards over. Not because they do not deserve to die, but because you *believe* they should not be killed for their beliefs. The time has come, Richard, for you to cleave unto your beliefs, even if it means losing your head."

Richard opened his eyes and felt a sudden peace. Tarjaman was right. "Are you saying 'twould be better to lose my head and keep my dignity than to live forever knowing I did not have the courage to stand up for what is right?"

"Precisely."

Richard clutched Tarjaman's silk-cloaked forearm. The material was sleek and cool. "But I did it for the land, Tarjaman. And to save my men needless deaths. I gave up the Lollards, but I reclaimed Marly Vale. I saw justice done."

"The land means nothing."

Richard sat up with strength he didn't know remained. "There you are wrong, fool. The land is everything."

"Not if you have lost your soul, my lord. That is what Lady Tess tried to tell you. Now drink some water. You must fill up on the liquids you have lost."

He's right, Richard thought, watching with dulled eyes as Tarjaman poured water from a sweating pitcher into a cup. Richard drank greedily, soaking his swollen tongue, his parched mouth. Tess was right, too. Gods, he hated when others were right and he was wrong. He licked his parched lips. "I begin to suspect a conspiracy between you and my wife. You still have not told me why you left Cadmon Castle and then abruptly returned."

"I left because I saw that you had finally embraced the soul of another. I trusted you would listen to Lady Tess's pleas for mercy for the Lollards."

"And your return?"

"I returned when I saw you fall asunder. I wanted to speak reason to you where Lady Tess had failed."

"And why do you care about the Lollards?"

"Because I am a Lollard."

Richard began to laugh. He fell back against his pallet, surrendering to the absurdity that had consumed his world. "What next?"

"What next? You must save Lady Gertrude and the others."

"Why?" Richard snapped. "Why do I care? Because they're your friends? Not a chance, Tarjaman."

"You must do it because 'tis right. Because you are sick and you must become whole again."

Richard scowled. "Do you mean to tell me that I will remain sick as long as the Lollards are imprisoned?"

"You do not have the flux, but you are gravely ill. Act now to free them or risk dying before the sun rises."

The remains of Richard's laughter gave way to a shiver of fear. "And if I do not act tonight?"

"If you survive through the morning, then you can put your conscience behind you and live a heartless existence. You will have no trouble doing wrong and will feel no guilt, though one day you will have to meet your Maker and pay your penance. Or perhaps you will *not* survive. You could die before the sunrise."

Richard recoiled, repulsed by the power he sensed in his former servant. Tess had warned Richard he might be an Assassin. "Do you mean to kill me, Tarjaman?"

"What do you suppose?" the animal trainer replied darkly.

Richard's gaze fell to the clay water cup he'd dropped by his pallet. Had the water been poisoned? A metallic taste lingered on his tongue. Were the growing pains in his belly the first signs of poisoning?

"Nay," Richard whispered hoarsely. "I still do not believe you mean me harm."

He doubled over in pain as another wave of vomiting and diarrhea set in. Soon a fever blazed across his forehead, burning him up, and he remembered little after that.

He awoke hours later to the sound of birds singing and men packing their gear for another day's journey. Blinking open his eyes in the dusty pink light of dawn, Richard found Tarjaman sitting cross-legged, exactly as he had been late last night.

"How long have you been thus?"

"I stayed by your side the night through."

Richard looked away, unwilling to be burdened with

gratitude or guilt. He was too intent on enjoying his returned health. The sickness was gone.

"I survived," Richard said, feeling the incredible relief that comes after a severe illness.

Tarjaman nodded solemnly. "Then you can do as you wish. Ignore your conscience as you will."

"Did you really think I might die?"

"Yes. But I was referring to a spiritual death."

Richard grinned weakly. "You crafty bastard. You had me worried."

"That was not my intention, my lord." Tarjaman frowned. Sadness had painted creases around his grim-set lips. "I will go now and bother you no more."

When Tarjaman started to rise, Richard's hand flew out and grasped his forearm. "For all the betrayal in my life, Tarjaman, I have always trusted you. You have never done me wrong. You have always advised me well."

Tarjaman considered this, and nodded tersely. "I am glad to have been of service."

"You can be of service again. I would ask for your help one last time."

Tarjaman waited.

"Take Taliesin and sell it." Richard crawled to the corner of the tent and pulled the sword from amongst his belongings. The jewel-encrusted scabbard was cool in his hands. He lovingly smoothed his fingers over the hundreds of pearls that formed a snake writhing up the slender sheath. He fondled a plump ruby and a walnut-sized emerald adorning the hilt of the priceless sword.

"Sell this sword and scabbard. Take the gold you receive to the Tower of London and bribe the guards. Buy the Lollards' freedom. Send them into hiding. And then bring the remainder of the gold back to me. I want to buy my squire horses, a sword—all that's necessary for him to become a knight. He deserves it. Whatever is left you can then take to Lady Tess."

Tarjaman embraced Richard in a rare display of affection. "You please me greatly, my lord."

"Nay," Richard murmured, patting Tarjaman's back, "I am pleasing myself."

When Richard finally arrived at Southampton with his troops, he was amazed by the bustling war preparations. Some five thousand men had gathered for transport by sea vessel, and more, he soon learned, were arriving every day. In the blazing summer sunshine, dozens of sails dotted the choppy seaside port. Sailing barges and enormous cogs bobbed in the harbor, sails snapping, lines flapping against their tall masts. The ships would transport not only knights, archers, and gunners, but horses, cannons, siege engines, barber-surgeons, minstrels, cooks, and many others. Everything needed to sustain the host during what was sure to be a long campaign.

Hundreds of tents surrounded the small town, dotting the sandy coastline like puffs of white wool. The prickling, salty ocean breeze was rife not only with the smell of fish flapping on the wooden docks, but with smoke from campfires and the manure of thousands of horses awaiting transport.

When Richard had arrived, King Henry had heartily embraced him, asking him how many men he'd brought. But it seemed there was never time for them to speak in private. Richard realized that such an audience was not desired by the king, for he controlled time as well as men's fates and could have set aside a moment alone if he'd wanted to. Richard understood. He and his men were needed, but he had not been forgiven for his attack on Kirkingham.

The days stretched into weeks as more troops gathered for the imminent departure. Each day Richard practiced war games with his men, and each night he drank with his peers, among them the Duke of Clarence, Henry's younger brother, and the Earl of March, heir to the late King Richard II. The Earl of March would have been king had Henry's father not usurped the crown, and many who had held allegiance to King Richard still wanted to see the earl in what they considered his rightful place. It was that very subject which buzzed through the encampment as men grew bored waiting for the war to begin. Although only in whispers, of course, some even dared to call Henry the Usurper, just as they had referred to his father, and Richard realized that his friend's hold on the kingdom, barely two years old, was not yet firm.

His concerns for Henry's reign proved founded when, shortly before they were scheduled to set sail, the king uncovered a plot to murder him and to put the Earl of March upon the throne in his place. The Southampton Plot was a blow to Henry personally, for the men who orchestrated the fiendish plan were three of his friends—Henry, Lord Scrope of Masham; Richard, Earl of Cambridge; and Sir Thomas Grey of Northumberland. Grey was executed immediately. Cambridge and Scrope demanded a trial before their peers, which included the Earl of Easterby. The jury of peers quickly sentenced the noble plotters to death.

It was after the executions that the king sought out Richard, who was playing chess in his tent near the ocean with Perkins. A delightful breeze wafted through the stuffy tent, Seagulls cawed a distant, soothing song, and waves crashed steadily on the nearby shore, lulling the two men into a comfortable sense of contentment.

"Checkmate," Richard pronounced, maneuvering his king just as Henry loomed in the doorway. Lean and moderately tall, he wore a short black and gold houppelande with pearl buttons. His aquiline nose cast a shadow on one of his high cheeks. His unflinching gaze fell briefly upon Perkins before landing with blossoming warmth on Richard.

Perkins darted up in awe, then fell to his knees in supplication. "Your Majesty."

Richard sat a moment, rooted to his chair, not quite believing Henry had finally come, wondering why. With his eyes glued irresistibly to the fierce gaze of his old friend, Richard wondered about the Presence, the extraordinary, almost godlike magnetism of the man. He had changed since the coronation. He truly had been touched by God. But he still had a man's soul. A man's foibles.

"Your Grace," Richard managed at last, rising and bowing.

Henry said nothing. He continued to stare, hale and handsome. His hair was cut in a short bob, which accentuated his long, straight nose. His fulsome lips, which he had smacked upon Richard's own in drunken, youthful stupors—showing his affection freely—were a fine piece of work.

"I have survived what I believe will be the last revolt, Richard."

"Aye, Your Grace."

"The Southampton Plotters had planned to raise the Scots and the Lollards against me. Oldcastle was supposed to rise again. But I found them out in time."

"By the grace of God," Richard said.

"Indeed, and by the observations of those who are loyal to me. I will never forget the nobles who stood by me in this time of crisis, Richard."

"Very good, Your Grace." *Of course I would come to your aid,* Richard thought. He still loved Henry. He always would.

"Very good, indeed."

And then he was gone. *He has thanked me for my loyalty,* Richard thought, *but he has not forgiven my rebellious attack on the Church.*

TWENTY-EIGHT

Three months later, Tess swished her leather-clad feet through a bed of crisp autumn leaves. She was certain she had turned the corner, figuratively speaking. Giving herself a victorious hug in the chilly October air, she realized she could finally close her eyes and not see Richard's face.

Her long walks in the woods surrounding Montague Castle had done much to heal the painful longing for Richard. She tried not to speak his name, for the word burned on her tongue and brought back a storm of unwanted emotions. Right now it was imperative that she be at peace. She had more than herself to consider.

Lady Lucretia's estate provided the perfect haven. The simple square castle was lost in a primeval forest, neglected by enemies and time alike. The gray stone walls were at one with the surrounding nature, embraced by ivy and gnarly vines. It was an ideal retreat for Tess to heal her wounded soul, to be pampered by her dear friend Lucy.

On this particular morning Tess noticed the wonderful array of browns in the forest. There was the dark brown bark of gnarled oak trees, and paler brown dried leaves nesting with more brilliant shades of yellow, orange, and red. There was the rich brown of chestnuts and the greenish brown of acorns; tan mushrooms and reddish brown squirrels. Lord, how she loved the earth. Particularly in autumn. Fall always brought the promise of change and the threat of cold, all wrapped up in one. In autumn, she could appreciate that which others might consider dull—like the color brown— knowing that soon the snow would come and take even that.

"'Tis a lovely wood."

Tess heard a masculine voice and a second later the sound of twigs snapping behind her. She twisted around with a shocked gasp and found Tarjaman.

"Tarjaman! What are—you are the last person I expected to see."

He stood serenely, his hands clasped together at the opening of a pale black cloak. He wore a black turban and an uncharacteristically carefree smile.

"This is something that I like very much about your country," he said as if they were continuing a conversation only briefly interrupted. He flicked his hand through the air, gesturing to the disrobing trees.

"In my country, we do not see these colors. This deep orange," he said, bending to pick up a maple leaf and twirling the stem in his fingertips. "In my country there is merely sand and sun and cold nights."

"Then I pity you. For I do not know what I would do without the changing seasons."

"Like the seasons, you have changed, Lady Tess."

She hugged herself in her amber woolen cloak, judging herself harshly, feeling old pain in her heart. "I cannot assume you meant that flatteringly. Lucy tells me every day that I must eat more to regain my color."

"Everything in its time, my lady. Everything in its time."

The wind shifted and swirled around the Persian, billowing his cloak. He smiled down at his feet, as if in wonder at the magical breeze. A moment later Tess inhaled the remains of incense that clung to his clothing. She had thought he might still have some lingering hostility, though she had never proven to herself that that was what he felt toward her. Studying his even features now, however, his thin, deep blue lips, his small nose and placid eyes, she could see only kindness.

"What are you doing here, Tarjaman?"

"I have brought something for you from Lord Richard."

Even hearing Richard's name brought on a wave of vertigo. She gathered the collar of her cloak and pulled the rough wool closer to her bare neck, shrinking like a turtle into its shell. She turned away so that Tarjaman would not see her pained expression and clutched a nearby oak, digging her fingers into the rivulets of twisted bark.

"I . . . I cannot accept anything from him, Tarjaman."

"Why not, my lady?"

She would tell him. She had to tell someone. And she did not want to burden Lucy any more than she had already.

"Anything that reminds me of Richard brings only pain." His name was a molten rock in the pit of her stomach. "I foolishly thought that when I threatened to leave, Richard would back down. That he would do as I wished, and we would live happily ever after. Even you thought so, Tarjaman. When he did not, and I had no choice but to go, I realized I was losing the love of my life. I didn't know what price I would pay for insisting Richard live by my ideals. And what hurts the most is that I know now that he never loved me as I loved him, for no man who truly loved me would let me feel this savage pain."

Rage at Richard stirred, as if a witch had begun to churn a poisonous brew, green and bitter. She was deeply angry at him for the pain.

"No man who loved me would ignore my wishes so willfully.

Lord, why did I have to fall in love? I miss him. I miss him so much."

Through her tears she saw a squirrel nibbling an acorn on a branch, eyeing her suspiciously. She felt the warmth of Tarjaman's fingers cupping hers. He brought her hand to his mouth in a gentle, consoling kiss. "I am sorry, my lady. I was wrong in my assessment of Richard, and you have paid the highest price. I beg your forgiveness."

Tess smiled at him, withdrawing her hand and brushing away a teardrop from her chilled cheeks. "I do not blame you, Tarjaman. And I thank you for listening to me ramble. Walk with me. Tell me about your escapades—why you left Cadmon Castle, and what you have been doing since we last spoke."

"As you wish, my lady."

They strolled through the lush woods and Tarjaman spoke to her at greater length and more intimately than he had during all her days at Cadmon Castle. He spoke serenely and confidently, never losing his breath, not even when they ascended a steep, rocky slope to reach High Peak Grove. The trees there, mostly birch and elm, were called the Old Ones. Unprotected against the high winds that swirled over the crag, the trees had grown bent and twisted over the years, hunched over like old people. Tess thought they might be inhabited by the spirits of ancient druids, for whenever she paused to listen to the wind amongst the Old Ones, she always heard something more—a whisper, a whimper, a soft laugh.

"And so, my lady," Tarjaman concluded his report as they paused amongst the bent trees, "I left because I thought Lord Richard would heed your concern for the Lollards. I returned to Cadmon Castle when I learned that was not the case."

Tess draped her winded figure against the cold bark of an elm, waiting for its comfort. "I still condemn myself for failing the Lollards."

"Nay, Lady," Tarjaman said sympathetically. "I see now that love was not enough to persuade Lord Richard. You did not fail. He did."

She looked up sharply, seeking affirmation in his expression, and she found it. Tarjaman was utterly serious, and his words made her feel better as none had heretofore.

"I do not know if you are right," she said, "but I thank you for saying so. In any event, Lady Gertrude and her friends are very likely dead by now. And I can never forgive myself for that."

Tarjaman smiled sweetly and held out his arm. "May I?"

She laid her hand on top of his and allowed him to lead her onward.

"Lady Tess, there is one part of my journeying I have not yet mentioned. I've just come from the Tower of London. There I was able to bribe the guards into setting Lady Gertrude, Sir Andrew Warton, and Sir Harold Mortimer free."

Tess stopped in her tracks, pulling her hand from atop his and scouring his face with hopeful eyes. "What?"

"Lady Gertrude is alive and free. She has escaped into the countryside, where she will live a peaceful existence in hiding until she dies a natural death."

"Oh, thank the saints!" Tess cried out, and impulsively embraced Tarjaman. "Thank you. Thank you, Tarjaman." She squeezed him tightly and found him to be surprisingly tender.

When she withdrew, her face alight with sunshine, he smiled. " 'Tis Lord Richard you should thank. I went to the Tower upon his orders. He gave me Taliesin to trade for the gold with which I bribed the guards."

"Taliesin?" Tess whispered. "He gave you Taliesin? Are you sure it was not another sword?"

"Quite sure, my lady. I doubt there is another sword in all of Christendom to match the beauty of Taliesin. I would not mistake it."

"Nay, of course not." Tess distractedly tugged at a brown oak leaf that clung tenaciously to a low-hanging branch, studying the tiny webbed lines wending just under the surface of the crisp leaf. "I do not understand why Richard did that."

"The wonderful thing about life, Lady Tess, is that we can redeem ourselves before we reach the afterlife. And so Lord Richard has done."

She dropped the leaf, watching it flutter to the ground. Then she looked up at Tarjaman cynically. "What are you telling me? That Lord Richard has had a change of heart?"

"Precisely. He has freed the Lollards because he knew it was the right action to take, regardless of the risk."

Tess closed her eyes as a flood of gratitude and joy surged through her body. She felt the pain lift from her heart as if it were a veil lifted by an unseen angel. Her deepest wish had come true: Her beloved had at last followed his conscience. Thank God in Heaven. Just in time. It was just in time. She pressed her hands to her abdomen in a loving gesture, and then her eyes flew open.

"Tarjaman, there is something . . . something I must tell you. Something you must tell Lord Richard when next you see him."

"That will not be for some time, my lady. He is in Normandy, fully engaged in battle, I expect."

Oh, Richard, please live. Do not die!

"What is it, my lady?"

She opened her mouth to speak, but a shadow fell over Tarjaman. She looked up and saw a black raven swoop overhead, its slick feathers glinting in the sun. The sight sent a shiver coursing down her spine.

"Tarjaman, did Lord Richard, when he sent you to free the Lollards, did he speak of his love for me?"

The pause that followed was long and loud. Tarjaman

shifted weight from one foot to the other. "Nay, my lady. He did not. But 'tis not something a proud man speaks of."

"Richard is not proud," she said with a sweet smile her upturned lips could not maintain. "'Tis one of his greatest attributes. For all his beauty and grace, he is not proud."

And for all her love, he had made no mention of her. He had done right, but it was not done for her. As much as she was happy to see him follow his conscience, she feared with all her heart that she would now be forgotten. She had been a teacher of sorts, and now that the student had learned the lesson, he had no need of further tutelage.

"What do you want me to say to my lord?" Tarjaman queried gently.

"Nothing. Nothing at all."

Tess led Tarjaman back to Montague Castle, where the animal trainer was warmly welcomed by Lady Lucretia. That afternoon they supped together before a roaring fire in the castle's modest great hall. Lady Lucretia, who seldom had visitors, listened with rapt attention to Tarjaman's tales of his life in Persia. Tess listened as well, feeling affection for the man she had once feared. And she knew her liking stemmed from greater wisdom, and perhaps from the strength she had gained from her love for Richard. For all the discipline and stoicism of her previous life, she had never known what courage it took to love another human being, to intimately share her passion. She was stronger for it.

Tarjaman spent the night and saddled up his palfrey early the next morning. Tess met him at the gatehouse to bid him farewell.

"I thank you, Tarjaman, for all you have done," she said. She squinted up at him in the bright morning sun.

Adjusting himself in his saddle, he smiled down at her. "My lady, I will always be your servant. And do not fear: As soon as Lord Richard returns from France, I will tell him that you are with child. Methinks he will be happy to learn that he will soon be a father."

For a moment Tess did not breathe, did not move. She was just three months along. How had he known? She had not said a word. She had wanted to, but had held back. Still, he knew. Just as he had known she carried the misericorde on her wedding night.

"How do you divine these things? How do you know I am carrying Richard's babe? Are you a warlock?"

She meant no insult, for she no longer feared Tarjaman, but curiosity burned inside her. "How did you know?"

He drew the reins taut, steadying his prancing mount. He shrugged. "I saw the swell beneath your gown."

Her hands flew to the slight swell of her belly.

"Fare you well, my lady. I bid you adieu."

TWENTY-NINE

Tarjaman left Montague Castle on Friday, October 25, St. Crispin's Day. The same day that King Henry's army staked out a portion of a field near a French village called Agincourt.

Henry's troops were badly outnumbered: some six thousand men-at-arms and archers readying to attack a French army nearly thirty thousand strong. Impossible odds.

On the field of Agincourt, the French host waited a thousand yards away in the clear light of day, amused by the pitiful English army. The French soldiers joked upon their horses and ate breakfast by their standards. Some even wandered away, so sure were they the ragtag English army would not dare to attack such an overwhelming force.

The British were nearly starving and exhausted from their long trek from Harfleur, where they had successfully laid siege to the French port city. Though Henry had been victorious, the siege had taken far longer than anticipated, five weeks, and his men had long ago exhausted their food rations. Marching from Harfleur north along the coast, veering east and then north again to Agincourt, Henry's troops had survived on berries and nuts and rank water. They were weak, wet, and hungry, and many were stricken with the flux. Two thousand of Henry's men had died from the disease, including the Earl of Suffolk. Nearly an equal number of men, including the Duke of Clarence, had to be sent home to recuperate. Many of those who continued on with the flux marched through France with bare bottoms, shitting as they walked.

But Henry forged ahead, and seeing no noble way out of his predicament, he launched the greatest battle in British history—the Battle of Agincourt.

Whack! Whack! Whack! With pummeling force, Richard swung his sword at enemy knights over and over. He used a fine sword made of Bordeaux steel. It was three feet long and bore a heavy pommel and a simple cross-guard to protect his hands. It was not Taliesin, but it was a good sword. A damned good sword.

An hour into battle and he had already beheaded one foot soldier, severed the hand of a knight, and knocked six others to the ground, half of them mortally wounded. And that was only with his sword. He had yet to wield his vicious poleaxe, a wicked hatchet on a five-foot-long pole.

Whack! Whack! Whack! His muscles burned. He did not know how much longer he could swing his sword. His stomach was twisted into an empty, hungry knot. Sweat poured from his head, which cooked inside his heavy open-faced bascinet. The sweat dripped into his eyes, red with rust. He blinked back the sting. *Kill. I must kill. Man after man. For Harry. For England. For St. George.* God knows Richard did not fight for glory. He did not fight for himself. He didn't even care if he lived. He just wished he could see Tess one more time before he died. And he would die. How could the English, so badly outnumbered, possibly win? Henry, ambitious, bold Henry, had finally gone too far.

Henry. Richard blinked several times, not believing his eyes. There in the distance, in the sodden wheat field, sludgy

from autumn rain, stood Henry, without a sword. Richard
immediately recognized the crown of gold encircling his
bascinet. The fleurettes and crosses pricking up from the
golden crown told Richard all he needed to know. It was his
old friend, and someone had just knocked his sword from his
hand.

Just then a French man-at-arms galloped through the crush
of horses and whacking swords, reining in near the king.
Seeing what Richard had seen, the golden crown, his teeth
flashed in a greedy smile through the haze of the misty,
humid afternoon. He was doubtless thinking of the ransom he
would get for capturing a king.

"My God, Henry!" Richard roared, plunging his spurs into
Shadow's belly. The horse reared and lunged forward, but at
half-speed, it seemed to Richard. He squeezed his thighs
against the saddle, urging the horse faster. As Shadow
pummeled through the melee, Richard saw another sight that
sent a fissure of deadly cold shooting through his limbs. A
second soldier had spotted Henry, and he had the battle
madness in his too-white eyes. He raised his sword to the
side, shoulder level, preparing to behead the English monarch, too frenzied with his quest to kill to realize the ransom
Henry would bring.

"Fool!" Richard thundered. "Henry! My liege!"

Richard's horse bolted closer, and Henry looked up. As he
did, the mad soldier's sword met with his helmet, lopping off
a fleurette and denting the steel. The king fell to the
side—luckily, in Richard's direction.

"Ho, my liege. Take hold," Richard barked, and with a deft
move, he grasped Henry's outstretched arm and plucked him
from the blood-drenched field. Henry clamored up on the
horse's haunches and they dashed on to safety, not daring to
slow until they reached Henry's squire. When the shaken king

dismounted, he paused and gazed up at his old friend. "You saved my life, Richard."

"I just evened the score, sire. You saved my life once in battle against Owain. Do you remember?"

Henry nodded, his eyes warming with remembered love. "Let us end this perverse competition now, then."

"Aye, Your Grace." Richard spurred his destrier and headed back into the thick of the battle. *You saved my life, Richard.* The words soothed his mind like a balm on a savage wound. The words brought comfort, even as a new wound was inflicted.

Coming from nowhere, a bloody, gleaming steel poleaxe slammed down on Richard's thigh. The sharp blade splintered his steel leg armor, cut through flesh, sliced cleanly through muscle, and lodged with a chilling thud into bone.

"Aaaaahhhh!" Richard roared. Then a soldier whacked a mighty blow to his head, felling him from his mount. Landing facedown in mud, Richard spit gritty earth from his tongue and tried to crawl to safety.

"My lord!" Sir Perkins cried, throwing himself headlong through the throng of dancing horse hooves, scrambling to his side. "My lord! Sweet Jesus, your leg! God save you. God save you. God save you," his former squire frantically cried over and over.

Perkins had been knighted on the eve of this battle. He was no longer a squire, but the bonds of duty were not so easily broken. He hauled Richard into his arms, heedless of his own safety. "God save you, my lord."

"God save me," Richard echoed. Then all went black.

In that great darkness, which seemed to last an eternity, he dreamt of Tess. She came to him with open arms, tears streaming down her face.

"Oh, my lord. Oh, my lord," she whimpered. Her chestnut eyes were doleful; her hair was loose and tangled about her.

"Tess! Tess, I love you. I love you. I was wrong about so many things."

"Oh, my lord," she whispered, leaning down over his pallet, gentling his butchered leg with soothing fingers. She had not heard him.

"Tess, listen to me," he struggled against tremendous pain to say. "The land means nothing to me. Nothing. If I die now, Tess, yours will be the only memory I bring to Heaven. The land is not mine. 'Tis God's. But you . . . you are mine. Our love has made you mine. Just as I am yours. Do you hear, Tess? Do you hear?"

"Oh, my lord," she said again, weeping over his leg, which was nearly severed.

She could not hear him! How could he make her hear?

The dream changed then. They were on a wind-swept heath. His leg was no longer wounded. He danced as if there had never been a battle at Agincourt. They skipped amidst a field of heather, its sweet smell filling him with exquisite contentment. He held Tess in his arms, knowing that he would never again let her go. Never.

And then he noticed a child dancing at their feet. A little girl. And he knew. *He knew!* Tess was with child. She was going to have a baby. *His* baby.

The great darkness lifted. Like a drowning man being pulled up into acres of fresh air, he sucked in a breath, his eyes fluttering open, returning to consciousness. Painful, chaotic consciousness.

"Dear, merciful God, I must live!" he prayed. "Tess needs me."

THIRTY

"Perkins!" Richard roared.

He thrust himself up from the hard pallet upon which he'
found himself lying. His impatient call ended in a twisted
groan. Pain shot up his thigh and down to his toes, as if
jagged spike of glass were scraping along the bruised bone

"Shhh, my lord, easy. Do not expend yourself."

Richard obeyed. Sweat burst out on his temples as the pain
screamed in his head. When the explosions of light dissipate
behind his clinched eyelids, he blinked his eyes open and
found his devoted friend's carrot-topped head looming over
him. At close range, Perkins's freckles were enormous, little
pumpkins dotting a dry field. He touched Richard's forehead
His hand reeked of herbal balm——the same intense odor that
wafted from Richard's bare chest.

"You've been nursing me, eh, Perkins? Soaking me with
balms and poultices? You shouldn't, you know. You are no
longer my squire. You are a knight."

"I was helping the barber-surgeon. Now hush, my lord, you
need to conserve your strength."

"I'll do that, as soon as I figure out why this pallet is
heaving to and fro."

From beneath the creaking floorboards came a groan of

protest that no human could mimic. A gnashing of wood. Holding his breath, Richard listened harder and detected the lapping of water.

"Where are we? At sea?"

"On *La Trinité Royale*. The king's flagship was the first to set sail from Calais, and King Henry wanted you aboard. We're heading home."

"Agincourt . . . What happened at Agincourt?"

Perkins gripped his hand and gave such a squeeze Richard nearly winced. "We won, my lord. We won."

Richard sank back onto the pallet, overwhelmed with pride, exhaustion, and astonishment. "How? How was it possible?"

"The bloody French couldn't recover from shock after we attacked. They weren't ready. Never thought we'd do it," he said with an amazed and victorious sputter of laughter. "And our longbowmen let loose such a rain of arrows that their archers cringed away, retreating like cowards. Then came their cavalry, marching against the sun, with no archers to clear the way. They advanced against the shower of arrows with their heads bowed, horses stumbling in the muddy field. Their soldiers could barely see, let alone fight with any precision. Their commanders were battling dogs, one contradicting the other. They fell into disarray. No match for our King Henry. When all was said and done, there was a mountain of bodies. At least seven thousand French were slain."

"Gods . . ." *Seven thousand.*

"Your leg, my lord, your leg was . . . nearly severed. The barber-surgeons wanted to amputate, but the king would not let them. He said to give you a chance. He kept you close by his side all the way on the journey from Agincourt to Calais."

"Seven thousand dead. Was it worth it, Perkins? How thick

Henry's garden will grow, so rich will the earth be with ferti
blood."

"At least it wasn't your blood, Easterby."

Henry. That voice. For a moment it transported Richa
back to their youth, when they had boasted of their conques
when they'd dreamt of immortality.

At the gruff sound of the king's voice, Perkins stoc
abruptly, then fell to his knees in the cramped quarters. "Yo
Grace . . ."

Richard turned from his former squire to the short doorw
and found the Presence looming. Henry wore a simp
houppelande the color of blood, which matched the hue of h
healthy cheeks.

"My liege."

"My friend," Henry replied, his stern face softening.

Time fell away, and through squinting eyes, Richard sa
the man as he had been ten years ago—brash, brav
passionately devoted to anyone who touched his heart. O
love bubbled in Richard's veins, and he blinked hard throug
throbbing pain, through stinging, salty sweat that beaded c
his forehead, seeping into a multitude of small cuts. With h
eyes, he searched for a sign of the forgiveness Sir John ha
sought so desperately before his death.

"Richard, I told them you would survive." The king can
forward and sat on the floor by his side. Richard reached o
half blindly and gripped his massive forearm. The king
muscles were corded steel. Henry gripped his in turn, and
a moment of silence, the love was said, exchanged, pulsin
through their hands, healing the final wound. Hot tea
burned behind Richard's eyes. All was forgiven. There w
nothing standing between them now.

Tess. He thought of Tess. Wanted her here to see th
healing. She had taught him to love. Perhaps that was whe

the forgiveness came from. In the ability to truly love, without condition.

Henry cleared his throat of some slight obstruction and chuckled with contentment. "You've got your leg, man," he whispered. "How much use 'twill be the surgeons cannot say. But you've got your leg."

"Thank you, my liege."

"Harry," the king corrected. "Better yet, Hal."

"Hal," Richard repeated, the word sweet and easy on his tongue.

"Richard, I will be the monarch of two kingdoms—France as well as England. There is much to do. You must get well and help me."

Richard nodded. "Of course, Hal. Whatever you wish."

"I owe you much, old friend. Not only for the loans of money that, in part, made this campaign possible, and not only for my life, which you saved at the turning point of the battle. I owe you for reminding me that the past can never be forgotten. Even when we want to forget."

A shadow of regret flickered across the king's face, like the tiny pulse of a flame. A minuscule blue vein at his translucent temple throbbed in kind. "I thought I saw Sir John several months ago. In London. Near Eastcheap. I almost spoke to him. If 'twas him."

"Sir John is dead, Hal."

The king nodded and blinked slowly, the motion shielding sadness and relief. Then his face hardened back into his perpetual and kingly look of power. "Many men are dead. Our losses in France were great. But the victory was greater. I am glad that one from my youth can share in the joy."

The king tightened his grip and Richard felt a renewed urge of affection pouring over him, as if a vein had been cut or a bloodletting.

"I will be busy in the coming years, Richard, and may not

have the time to say it again, but I have loved you, old friend.
Boon companion."

The king bent to him then and kissed him on the mouth.
The gesture was hard, fervent and manly, but his lips were as
soft as a maid's. Henry rose and gave one final order. "Get
well. I need another loan and cannot get it if you're dead."

"Aye, Your Grace. Hal."

And then he was gone.

"Perkins."

"Aye, my lord?" The young knight stepped from the
shadows, wiping a tear from his freckled cheek.

"I must go directly to Montague Castle. I must see Tess."

"My lord, you cannot think of it! You will be lucky to leave
Southampton once we arrive. The king has ordered you to
recuperate at Porchester Castle under the care of his physicians. 'Twill be months before you are well enough to ride to
Cadmon Castle. Montague Castle is out of the question. Lady
Lucretia's estate is too far. You are too ill. You could lose your
leg yet, my lord."

"Then I'll hobble on one," Richard snarled. "But I must get
to her."

Tess. Just thinking of her filled him with savage desire and
bleak despair. His child. She was bearing his child. She could
die, leaving him alone with his love. She said she would die
if she bore a child. And Tess, he'd concluded, knew everything. He prayed she would be wrong about this. She had to
be wrong.

THIRTY-ONE

"Sweet Jesus!" Tess cried out, her composure suddenly shattered. Pain ripped through her innards, fairly tearing her apart. "Jesus, Lord, help me."

She clutched wildly at the hands flitting near her, anything to anchor her in her sea of excruciating labor. The midwife's wizened fingers flitted like starlings over Tess's face as the old woman tersely ordered about the other woman in the birthing chamber. Mellie's smooth, white fingers pulled at the covers. Lucretia's nimble hand stroked her forehead, and it was those hands Tess gripped in desperation. They were the closest. In her agony, she could see only those objects that presented themselves to her, for the pain was so gripping that all her thoughts now lay in this bed. She saw only the dark, square rafters directly above her head, where dried roses hung in bunches. Now and then she saw the looming visage of the old midwife, shriveled like an apple in the sun, bending to within inches of Tess's eyes, murmuring through dark yellow teeth, "There, there, dear, all will be well." This birthing bed was Tess's entire life now. And she was certain it would also be her death.

"Forgive me, Lucy, I do not . . . do not want to hurt you," she said, tightening her grip around her friend's lithe fingers, as if by doing so she could squeeze the pain from her belly.

"Fear not; squeeze harder if it makes you feel better."

"Oh, God!" Tess bellowed, certain she was giving birth to a calf and not a human. What else could cause so much pain?

It felt as if her innards were being cauterized, as if a red-hot poker were being jammed into a place inside her she hadn't even known existed. And it was getting worse. Worse and worse.

"Nay, I can't take it, Lucy. I won't make it."

"You will. You can, Tess. Hold on. This one will subside soon. Be patient."

"Ohhhhh," Tess replied in an incoherent gurgle of desperation.

Lucy was right. The pain reached a peak and tapered off. But Tess knew another one would soon follow. It was bloody unfair that women should pay so high a price to continue the race. And this was just the beginning. Hard labor had begun only an hour ago, having followed four days of lighter labor *Four days. Just like her mother.* No, this would be different It had to be. Lord in Heaven, she did not want to die. *God, do not take me yet. Not until I see Richard. Oh, Richard, can you hear me? I need you. You said I would live forever.*

"Richard," Tess groaned.

"Shhhh," Lucy whispered near her ear. "Richard is no here, Tess."

"Tell him . . . tell him I love him more than life itself."

Richard. She had not realized how desperately she misse him until her birthing pains had begun. That's when the terro had set in, hunting her down at long last like a rabid dog that cornered a quivering rabbit. Four days ago, when she' realized how cruel fate could be . . .

"Tess, why are you crying? Is the pain already so terrible? Lucretia had said upon being called to Tess's bedside. It wa the middle of the night. Always serene and assured, Lucy had taken the time to dress, though her long blonde hair flowed freely down her back.

She sat at the edge of the bed and brushed a finger soothingly against Tess's wet cheeks.

"Nay, the pain is not so terrible. But I am terrified nevertheless. Does that make me a coward?"

Lucy's sea-blue eyes moistened with a rising tide. "Every woman who undertakes this miracle knows that she may not survive. I'll not mince words, Tess. I am afraid for you, too."

Outside the snow fell quietly against the black night, blanketing the land with the heavy cloak of winter. Tess ran her hands over her drum-tight belly.

"And do you know what saddens me the most?" Tess asked.

"What, darling?"

"Not that I shall die. But that I won't see Richard one last time. And yet the sadness is sweet, too. At least I loved. I am so . . . grateful that I was able to love another like that."

A swirling mass of fear, joy, and sorrow opened a spigot of tears and she wept, not knowing if sadness or gratitude was the cause.

The ensuing frown that etched itself on Lucretia's porcelain features was deep and slow to develop. "Richard? You miss Richard? Why? What did he ever give you but heartache?"

"He gave me love. And he gave me a child. But more important, he gave me the chance to love in return. I love him, Lucretia. I love him with all my heart. And now I must admit the truth I have avoided thus far: He is dead. He died at Agincourt, just as Roger did."

Tess had mourned her cousin keenly. Though she'd known she could not expect all the men in her life to survive that fierce battle, she had been shocked and saddened by Roger's untimely end. And she had cursed Henry for taking yet another loved one from her. But she had refused to think that Richard was also a casualty . . . until now.

"If he were alive, Lucretia, I know he would have contacted me by now." Clutching the sheets, she pressed them to her eyes, blotting out horrifying visions of Richard lying on the battlefield. Had he called out to her in the end? Had he needed her, and she not there to help him? "He would have responded to my missives if he were alive. I know he would have."

"You never told me that you loved him," Lucretia said shrilly, thunderstruck by Tess's admission. "When you first arrived here, you told me you loathed him more than ever. Why did you not tell me this before?"

"When I first arrived at Montague Castle, I *did* hate him for not loving me as much as I loved him. But as time passed I did not care whether our love was evenly matched. All wanted was to hold him again. Just to hold him, to see that dazzling light in his azure eyes, to touch his dimples, to stroke his velvet lips, to bathe in the sunshine of his incredible smile. Oh, Richard, Richard, I loved you. I loved you."

Admitting it opened up a well of sorrow, a seething cavern of vulnerability. She began to weep uncontrollably, hugging her womb, knowing that the child inside her was the last remnant of their love. A child without a father.

As she wept, Lady Lucretia slipped from the room, returning a quarter of an hour later with a bundle of folded and sealed parchments in her hands. She dropped them onto the bed at Tess's side. A waft of stale parchment and dust billowed.

Taking in a sobbing gasp, choking on saliva, Tess rubbed her runny nose. She looked down at the cluster of missives and then up at the guilt-ridden expression of her friend. "What are these?"

Lucy's skin faded to the faintest shade of white. A sickly pallor gutted her cheeks. "Missives from Richard."

"What?"

"He's written you a dozen times since your arrival." She shrugged and shook her head, her silken blonde hair, so like Richard's, gliding over her shoulders. "I've read a few of them. It seems Richard was nearly killed at Agincourt and is recovering from a terrible leg wound. He was forced to stay at Southampton for several months, then at Westminster, under the king's watchful eye. Only recently was he well enough to return to Cadmon Castle. He said he was unable to travel, but wanted you to know he loves you. And he wanted to know if—" She stopped and swallowed a sob, stuffing a fist against her mouth. "He wants to know if you are with child. He says he had a dream . . ."

Tess could hear no more. Frustration exploded in her mind and she let out an inarticulate cry, snatching up one of the missives in trembling hands.

"My dearest Tess, I must speak with you. Are you well? Can you travel? Come to me . . ."

"Oh!" Tess cried out, sadness and rage sapping her of all breath. In a fit of fury, Tess flung the letter down. "How could you?"

Lucy's delicate face hardened with ancient anger. "Because I did not want Richard to hurt you as he hurt me. I thought reading them would only upset you. I thought he lied to manipulate you. I did not know you loved him. I did not think it possible. I thought you would be safe here. I was thinking only of your welfare."

"You *thought*!" Tess shouted incredulously. "And my letters to him?"

"I never sent them."

Tess pounded the bed with her fists. "Send for him!" she hissed. "Send for him immediately. I must see him before—"

Before I die.

That had been four days ago. How could he possibly make it in time, injured as he was? And so she said her farewells, in the quiet of her heart, for she knew she would not survive this birthing.

Richard rode harder than he had ever ridden in his life. He ached with every pounding of his horse's hooves, from his toes to his neck. His injured thigh throbbed, almost audibly, like a giant drum booming so loud he could feel the vibration. His blood pulsed with the rhythm. But he would not stop. The physician at Cadmon Castle had forbidden him to make this journey, fearing Richard would suffer permanent damage to his muscles. The wound still had not healed entirely, like the wound that would gape in his heart until he held Tess once more.

Richard could not help but think that if he could just see Tess again he would be healed once and for all, physically and mentally. That was why he was willing to risk the journey. In truth, after the winded messenger had informed Richard that his wife was in labor, nothing in the world could have kept him away, neither plague, nor sword, nor fire. He had been a fool to believe Lucretia's message informing him that Tess never wanted to see him again—not that he could have done much to reach her even if she'd been longing for him.

When Richard and Perkins rounded the crest of a hill, the young knight pulled up short. "My lord! There is an inn in the village below. We must rest. We have ridden two days straight. You cannot go on."

"Just watch me," Richard raged, blinking furiously against the snowflakes that fell with cruel persistence. His lashes were frozen with the stuff. "I'll not stop until I'm at Tess's side, damn it. If you want to rest, then do so. But I shall keep going."

"Do you want to die before you see your first child?" Perkins shouted with uncharacteristic frustration and anger.

"Nay, I will make sure I don't die until just *after* I've seen her." For some reason he suspected the child would be a girl. At least she had been in his dream. And one day he would dance with her in a field of heather, just as he had danced with her mother. Just as he would dance with her again. *Please, God, let Tess live.*

THIRTY-TWO

After three days of wrenching pain, Tess's mouth was as dry as the desert sands of Persia, and she thought of Tarjaman, wishing he were here to soothe her with his serenity. She wished Lady Gertrude could come out from hiding to be at her side. And thinking of Gertrude, Tess remembered the story of her mother's last moments alive.

If there was any feeling unique to childbirth, the one that she would remember the most, if she lived to remember, was the loss of control. She no longer controlled her body. She had given it up to the force of life. And in giving life, she knew she might well be soothed by the hands of the Reaper; the brilliant, fierce agony of giving birth might deliver her to the falsely comforting hands of death. So it had been for her mother. Her poor, dear mother.

"Mama. Mama . . ."

Tess moaned as her legs convulsed of their own accord. She ignored the wild, crazy movement, intent on remembering as much of her mother as she could before she departed this earth. She owed her mother so much. Gratitude. Life. More than life—the spirit of God. The spirit of God was transferred in a woman's womb. That sacred vessel. What greater purpose could she ever have? Did it matter if Tess died giving birth? Was it not worth the sacrifice? She was ready. Oh, yes, she was ready. She would die to give Richard's child life. Their child.

After four days of light pain and three days of excruciating labor, she was ready to die. All she wanted was to expel the child clambering at the door to her womanhood. *Let the next generation have its chance,* she thought. *I've lived fully. I've loved. And I'm weary. So weary. God, I would gladly die if I could just stop hurting.*

"Richard, my darling Richard," she moaned. "Mama . . . Mama . . ."

Through closed eyes, Tess sensed a shadow creeping over her. A benevolent shadow. A ghost, perhaps? The ghost of her mother? Whatever it was, it was a warm, soothing force. Using what was surely her last bit of strength, she forced her eyes open and saw a woman wearing a pale green hooded cloak.

"Mother?" Tess croaked. She blinked hard against the shadows. "Is it you, Mother?"

"Nay, child, 'tis I."

Gertrude. Tess would have recognized the deep, wise voice anywhere. Gertie slipped from the clutches of the room's shadows and sat at Tess's bedside. Her smooth and aged fingers stroked Tess's heated brow. Cool. Comforting. It felt so good. Tears of gratitude sprang into Tess's eyes.

"Oh, Gertie, I had hoped you would come."

"I cannot stay long. A few moments. Then I must slip back into hiding."

"I am dying, Gertie. Just like Mother."

"Nay, the battle is not even half fought. You are not your mother, Tess. You have your own unique fate. And you have such determination. Fight! You must fight for your life."

"I can't fight anymore. I am so tired. Too tired. Oh, but what will I have lived for? What will remain of me? Nothing."

Excruciating fear, desire, and weariness tangled together in a complicated and bittersweet dance.

"A child," Gertrude said. "A child will remain. With your blood, your eyes, your heart. And the legacy of your love."

Tess no longer felt the bottom half of her body. It was numb and dead. She wasn't even sure she still had legs. But she did feel the agony of her heart. Searing, white heat burned in her chest, the festering child of mischance and foolish pride.

"What love? What love did I give? I left Richard. Perhaps when he needed me most."

"You left him just long enough for him to put his castle in order, Tess. He set us free, we Lollards. He followed his conscience, at last. If you die now, you will leave him a whole man. What greater gift could you have given?"

"The gift of my arms, my kisses, my comfort!" Tess returned angrily. In a flash, her anger dissipated. She studied the hundreds of lines mapping a lifetime on Gertrude's noble face. "But again, I am thinking only of myself. You must leave. Someone will report you to the sheriff."

Gertrude nodded. "I will always be with you. Just as your mother is with you."

"Is she?" The room seemed to darken suddenly. Tess's temperature plunged. A chill of prescience and knowledge crept up her limbs. "Is my mother here with me? Here? Now?"

"Aye, child. She always has been. But now you are woman enough to feel her undying love."

Tess nodded.

"Fare you well, Tess. I will never wander far from you."

Gertrude kissed her forehead and slipped back into the shadows, leaving Tess with her thoughts.

"Mother, be with me," she muttered.

She began to feel the pain again. It sent Tess into a new delirium, and time passed in its own warped way.

"Richard," she uttered incoherently. "Richard . . ."

"Aye, Tess, I am here," he replied, gripping her hand. It was cold, clammy. Little half-moons of blood had encrusted in the palms of her hands where her nails had bitten into flesh. Dark blue circles were smudged below her eyes, like bruises. Her breath came in short rasps. A death rattle.

Kneeling beside her, he ignored the shooting pain in his leg. It wasn't fair. God damn it, but it wasn't fair! Why did she have to suffer so to give him a child? Why did having an heir mean risking the life of the person he loved most?

I can't live without you, Tess. I can't. I don't want to. You are the only real thing in my life. You taught me what true love is. I didn't even know myself until you came into my life.

"God!" he roared in agonized frustration. He was so helpless. There was nothing he could do.

Her eyelids fluttered, but did not open. Her cheeks were sallow, as if life were already leaving her. *God, am I too late? Are you luring her away to Heaven so soon? Before I've shown her love's rewards? She's paid love's price—can't she enjoy the rewards? Can't we enjoy them and grow old together? Toothless, wrinkled, holding hands in an endless sunset?*

"Oh, Tess, I love you."

He bent his feverish forehead into one of her upturned palms. Her icy fingers soothed his hot brow.

"I cannot live without you. God had best take me as well if He takes you. Do not leave me. Please."

He pressed his lips to her drenched forehead and stroked her damp, tangled hair. "My darling, I lived only so I could be here for this moment," he whispered, willing his words through her forehead. "Now do not disappoint me. I wanted to die, to end the pain, but I could not leave you to this all by yourself . . ."

He paused and waited for an answer, but none came. She had not heard him. She was in another world, a world where she could not feel the unbearable pain splitting open her vagina.

He pressed his moist lips to her parched ones in a kiss, but she did not feel it. Or if she did, she did not respond. She was beyond him now, in the grip of a miracle that rendered men inconsequential. He had given her the seed that had brought her to this destiny, but once the seed had taken, he realized now, he could do little to lighten Tess's burden.

He remained kneeling at her side until he lost all feeling in his leg. He wanted to suffer, to pay for what he had done to her. He wanted to snatch her back from the jaws of death. He prayed, wildly, desperately, willing her to come back. To live. He had promised her she would not die. By God, this was one promise he could not break. He prayed, still dressed in his riding clothes and mud-spattered boots, his hair wet with melted snow.

He did not know how much time passed; he was in another world himself, a world where hope just might congeal into a miracle, where prayerful thoughts just might be more real than reality. He was lost in that limbo when the midwife returned, greeting him with a loud harrumph.

"Now look what you've done," the old woman snarled at him as she placed a pan of fresh water at the bedside table. "She's passed out. She can't push now, can she?"

"Nay," Richard said, wiping the tears from his cheeks, darting a guilty look up at the gray-haired crone. The midwife had forbidden him to enter the lying-in room, but Richard had insisted. The old woman had walked out in an angry huff and returned now only to gloat, to blame Richard for the difficult birth.

"She's not going to make it," the woman thoughtlessly muttered.

"Can you do nothing?" Richard spat each word from tightly clenched teeth. "What good are you if you cannot save her?"

"I'm not God, now am I?" the old woman snapped back. "If I were you, my lord, I'd pray and keep my harsh words to myself. I've been here long enough. Not much more I can do at this point. Unless you want me to fetch a barber-surgeon to cut the babe from her womb. At least you'll save your child that way."

The image filled his mind with horrifying detail: Tess's belly being cut open like that of a slaughtered pig. No! He wouldn't let that happen.

"Nay, it cannot be. There must be another way."

"The babe is breeched. It won't come until it straightens out," the old woman announced authoritatively.

"Then turn it," Richard demanded.

"Can't," the midwife replied smugly. "Do you think I wouldn't have already if I could have? She's still tight as a knot in a tree. She must open before the child can be turned."

Richard's face reddened with rage, but there was nothing to deliver him from his anger. He wanted to fix the problem, to take the problem into his own hands and fix it. But childbirth was not as simple as building a castle or tearing one down. And so he prayed. He prayed that God would save the baby. Even more fervently, he prayed that God would save the mother. And he prayed the midwife would not make him choose between the two. He prayed the old woman would not call the barber-surgeon, with his dirty, thick knives, to cut the babe free, leaving the mother to die.

"Richard," Lucretia whispered from the door.

Looking up from Tess's still form, Richard saw a woman

who looked familiar. He blinked away his exhaustion and focused on blue eyes that mirrored his own. The same mouth. His heart turned over in his broiling chest. *Lucy.*

She was fully a woman now. No longer the child he remembered. He blinked in the dim chamber light, too weary to feel anything toward the sister he hadn't seen in so long—neither anger, nor wonder, nor joy.

"Richard, come away for a moment. Tess is resting now. The midwife will call us if she stirs. You must change and eat something. You look like death."

"I feel like death," he said. He looked into the corner, where the midwife was resting in a chair. She nodded to him reassuringly, her sour disposition now somewhat mollified. "Very well. A rest would do me good."

He wondered if his leg would allow him to stand. When he tried and staggered, Lucy rushed to his side. The arms she wrapped around him were strong, and he sank into them, thinking how much he had missed having the love of family in his life.

"Come, I have a bath prepared for you in my solar."

Richard did not argue. He bathed and dressed with the help of a page as Perkins looked on approvingly. His former squire fussed over his weeping thigh wound, wrapping it with a fresh poultice. When Richard was fully dressed and had eaten before the fire, Lucretia entered the chamber, studying every nuance of his grim-set face. Perkins bowed discreetly, leaving them to their long-awaited reconciliation.

"You look a sight better."

Richard nodded, taking her in at last. "And you look even more beautiful than I'd imagined you would be."

She was slender and willowy, her complexion pale, her eyes containing a world of wisdom bitterly wrought. A stab of pain pricked him when he recalled all she had endured. How could he judge her for anything, knowing what her life had been like? How could he judge her, even for misleading him about Tess's intentions? He knew Lucretia had only been trying to protect Tess from perceived danger.

Lucy crossed her arms and riddled her lips betwixt her teeth. "I have much to apologize for, Richard."

"Nay, sister, 'tis I who must beg forgiveness. If only I'd done more to try to protect you."

She lowered her arms, letting down her guard, apparently surprised by his understanding. "Nay, you were a child, Richard. Tess explained everything to me. 'Twas not your fault. 'Twas foolish of me to think otherwise."

Richard blinked several times as a memory returned unbidden. He remembered a time when Lucy had been knocked down in the woods by a herd of pigs scavenging for acorns. She couldn't have been more than four years old, and he seven. He had run with all his might, flinging himself through the snorting throng of animals, searching for her yellow hair. Then he had scooped her up in his arms, though she had been nearly as big as he, and carried her to safety. And remembering that, he acknowledged to himself that he had always done his best to protect Lucretia.

"Sister, sometimes even our best is not enough."

She swept across the room. He rose with a wince to meet her, and they embraced. He had no more shields to raise, no more pretense with which to distance himself from his feelings, and tears gushed to the fore. Brother and sister wept, venting regrets coddled too long. She smelled like a rose. And how strong she felt in his arms, despite her delicate appearance. He had always admired her mettle. When his heart felt healed and his aching leg cried out for respite, he withdrew and kissed her forehead.

"You are my family, Lucy. You always have been and always will be. I will never let you go again."

She helped him back into the chair and knelt by his side,

then laid her head in his lap and let him stroke her hair, the same flaxen texture of his own.

"I have missed you, brother."

"And I you."

But it did not matter. Nothing mattered except for Tess.

He did not know how long they sat thus, for he quickly fell asleep, his chin resting on his chest. The next thing he heard was a shriek from Tess, like the lowing of a cow in deadly labor. The sound sent shivers of ice shooting through his veins. And Richard knew that the bellow had either signified the birth of his child or the death of his wife. Or both.

THIRTY-THREE

The first thing Tess noticed was the sweet, rustic scent of heather. The odor swirled around in her head, infusing her lungs with goodness. She tried to blink her eyes open, but it seemed they were weighted, encrusted shut. So she could not rely on sight to determine just where she was. Perhaps in Heaven. Perhaps she had died and Heaven smelled of heather. Her body was nestled in fresh, dry sheets. Were there warm, cozy beds in Heaven? The piercing pain between her legs had turned into merely a dull throb. She heard muffled voices, the nasal drone of an old woman and the rich boasting of a deliriously happy man. And from a distant room she heard the cry of a baby. High and furious. Tears filled Tess's sightless eyes, for she knew it was her baby. She had given birth. And she was alive!

With herculean effort, she creaked open her grit-filled eyes and found Richard's blue ones staring back, full of love and hope.

"Richard?"

His strong, warm hand grasped one of her smaller ones and she squeezed fervently. The comfort was so profound every muscle in her body turned to liquid.

"Aye, my love. 'Tis Richard, your husband. You survived.

God granted my prayers this time, but I owe Him an eternity of good deeds in return."

He bent and kissed her. His mouth was warm and soothing on her splitting lips.

"I love you, Richard," she whispered against his mouth, inhaling his soothing, musky essence. "I love you. I love you." She wrapped her arms around his neck, embracing warmth so brilliant it was as if she held the sun in her arms.

"I love you," he murmured. "I love you. I love you. I love you." He said it over and over, and felt the words heal the wounds of the past.

Tess sighed and breathed in another overwhelming breath of heather. "That scent . . ."

"Oh, that," he said, withdrawing from her embrace. He reached to her side and plucked a sprig of heather, then dangled it before her eyes. "'Twas too snowy to carry you to a moor filled with heather. So I brought the moor to you."

She managed to lift her head, straining the tendons in her neck, and saw that her bed was full of blossoming winter heather, pink clusters of flowers bedded against dark green leaves. The sight of it brought back memories of their dance when he had treated her so gently, so lovingly, despite her awkwardness. Her head sank back onto the pillow and she laughed as tears bubbled over her temples, for laughter and crying are as one when in the grips of a love so dear. She had reached Heaven after all. Somehow she had managed to live and still reach the Pearly Gates.

"As soon as you recover from your courageous battle," Richard whispered in her ear, his hot breath sweeping intimately into her skin, "and when my leg has healed, we will dance in heather. You and I. My lady. My love."

Lucretia appeared in the doorway carrying a swaddled bundle. The baby was no longer crying, but cooed contentedly.

"Your daughter would like to see you, Tess," Lucy said, beaming proudly at her niece.

"A girl," Tess said, her voice catching. "A girl."

Again she thought of her own mother and wished the dear lady could have felt the same pride she now felt having given birth to a girl. A girl who one day, Tess had no doubt, would risk all to give love and life.

But as Tess took the tiny bundle into her arms and saw the puffy little slits that were her daughter's eyes, and her button of a nose, she felt the infinite love of motherhood and realized that her mother was with her, looking down on them, just as Lady Gertrude had said. Her mother had been here all along, all through her labor. At last Tess had touched her, if only her soul.

Richard puffed up her pillows and helped Tess into a sitting position. It was painful, but Tess barely noticed. All she was aware of was the cuddly little infant cradled in her arms, and her love for Richard.

"My beautiful baby," she murmured, stroking the child's pink face. Two little rosebud lips worked silently, rooting for one of Tess's nipples. She offered one of her milk-swollen breasts, and the babe latched on, suckling with surprising force. Tess had never seen so precious a sight, so wondrous a miracle. This tiny creature had come from her! She had wanted power? This was power. The power of life. Life that would link the chain from one brief generation to the next.

"I've been trying to think of a name all morning," Richard said. "And I cannot think of anything that seems to fit her. She has a lot of spirit, if her ear-piercing cries are any indication. And yet she's a sweet little girl. Just like her mother."

Tess tenderly stroked the baby's forehead. Her fingertips were conduits of pure, potent love. She drew back and quirked her brows with a sudden thought. "I have the perfect name."

"What?"

"Heather."

Richard smiled. "Heather. Of course!" He kissed Tess's cheek and gazed adoringly at their infant. "Leave it to your brilliant mother, Heather."

EPILOGUE

Four Years Later

"Here, my darling, wipe your face."

Tess handed a hand-coverchief to Heather. The angelic four-year-old dutifully wiped crumbs of sugar from her mouth with her perfect little fingers. The sugar cake was the last course of their noon picnic meal, and the one Heather had been eagerly anticipating all morning.

Richard inhaled the rich summer breeze sailing over the heath. Waves of purple heather undulated in the baking sun. He was sprawled leisurely on the picnic blanket, doing what he loved best—enjoying the company of his wife and daughter.

He studied Heather's every move with unbridled adoration. He loved how her little hands delicately maneuvered the cloth, how she folded it and patted it upon her lap when she was finished, as if the world depended upon the precision of each crease.

"There, Mummy, I am all fixed again."

"Thank you, darling."

The wind on the moor picked up and blew the child's sandy-blonde hair hither and thither. It was frizzy and free-flowing, a texture unlike that of either parent—just another reason Richard was convinced that Heather was part angel.

"Well, Tess," he said, rising from the picnic blanket. "The time has come. . . ."

Tess's hazel eyes locked with his, speaking a love that no words could have adequately expressed. A love that was like an exquisite rainbow, a miracle after the storm—elusive, but real to those with the eyes and the faith to see it.

When Richard held out his hand, she took it and they rose together. She was with child again, but only a few months along, and her belly was not too terribly swollen. Richard led her to a clearing in the heather, limping slightly, as he had ever since the Battle of Agincourt.

"Are you going to dance like you said you would?" Heather asked, tagging along behind them, the light of wonder burning brightly in her soft green eyes.

"Aye, my darling," Richard replied. "'Tis your birthday. And every year on your birthday, your mother and I celebrate with a dance in heather."

"A dance in heather?" the little girl echoed. "Can I dance in heather, too, Papa?"

"Aye, my darling. As long as there is love in your heart."

MEDIEVAL GLOSSARY

Aketon: A stuffed jacket or jerkin worn under chain mail.

Bailey: A courtyard surrounded by a castle (curtain) wall.

Barber-surgeon: Someone who performs the functions of a barber, a surgeon, and a dentist. Physicians were university trained and, as scholars, considered bloodletting and surgery tasks beneath their lofty status.

Bascinet: An open-faced helmet with a movable visor.

Battlement: A parapet with notches, or crenels, bordering the wall-walk.

Braies: The medieval equivalent of male underwear. In the early 1400s braies looked like snug boxer shorts with a drawstring tie.

Canon: A clergyman belonging to the staff of a cathedral.

Castellan: Commander of the castle, who governs in the lord's absence.

Chain mail: Flexible armor made of thousands of tiny interlinking metal rings.

Chaperon: A hood or cap. Styles varied from a squashed top-hat look to a modified turban.

Chaplet: A wreath for the head, usually a garland of flowers or precious stones.

Chatelaine: The mistress of the castle, governing as th
castellan.

Cog: A medieval ship.

Crenelation: A battlement with square notches, or crenels.

Curtain: The thick stone wall surrounding a castle, mounte
with a wall-walk and parapet, patrolled by sentries.

Danse à deux: A dance for two.

Destrier: A warhorse used by a knight in battle.

Donjon: The main stronghold or great tower of a castle.

Doublet: A short, close-fitting garment worn by men. Th
hem of the doublet met the top of the thighs. Leggings,
hose, were worn below.

Emblem: A symbol used as a heraldic device to identify
knight or lord, used decoratively on a banner, shield, an
coat of arms—among other items.

Enfeoff: To endow someone with land for the duration of th
landowner's life.

Foot-mantle: A blanket-like garment that protects the lowe
portion of a woman's gown during horseback riding.

Frumenty: Hulled wheat boiled in milk, spiced with cinn
mon and sugar.

Garderobe: Latrine or privy.

Greek fire: An incendiary substance used in warfare.

Herald: An official messenger who transports letters, a
nounces the lord's proclamations, and organizes comba
ants in tournaments.

Hill-fort: A simple prehistoric fort built on a hilltop.

Houppelande: A voluminous gown, sometimes with a lor
train and immense funnel-shaped sleeves, worn by me
and women.

Host: The medieval term for army.

Hundredweight: A measurement equal to one hundred twelv
pounds.

Jape: A story or gibe designed to evoke laughter.

Kirtle: A floor-length gown or dress.

Lance: A unit composed of a man-at-arms and his staff, including squires and pages. Also a term for a spear used to charge opponents in tournaments and in battle.

Mangonel: A form of catapult used to hurl stones.

Matins: A late hour of devotion.

Mummers: Performers who wear costumes and use pantomime to enact stories for festivals and special occasions.

Oubliette: A small section of the dungeon where a prisoner could be locked away and forgotten.

Palfrey: A saddle horse with a light and easy gait.

Parapet: A low wall or rampart on the outer side of the wall-walk on top of the curtain.

Quintain: A vertical pole with a horizontal cross-beam. A mock soldier hung on one end of the beam and a sack of sand hung on the other. The knight would charge the dummy with his lance, then speed past the quintain, hopefully before the beam swung around and knocked him from his saddle.

Rood: The cross on which Christ was crucified.

Rushes: Grass-like stalks strewn on the floor, sometimes mixed with flowers and other sweet-smelling plants.

Tankard: A drinking vessel with one handle, often made of silver or pewter.

Sapper: A soldier who digs under the foundation of a wall.

Sennight: One week.

Servitor: A personal or domestic male servant.

Steward: Manager of the lord's estate and household affairs.

Stone: A unit of measure equal to fourteen pounds.

Swive: To engage in sexual intercourse.

Tabard: A short sleeveless coat or tunic.

Templer: A headpiece that covers the hair knotted at each temple.